BEWITCHING THE ALPHA'S SON

THE VAMPIRE KING'S FEEDER
BOOK FOUR

BELLA MOONDRAGON

CONTENTS

1

THE PRINCE

BLOOD-RED WALLS CLOUD MY VISION. I FOCUS ON THE SPIRALING, floral velvet details of the wallpaper instead of the tall, dark-haired man pacing vigorously across the room, leaving tracks in the carpet.

Roses. Mom has always loved roses, and this room is a testament to her love of daylight, sunshine, and those late summer flowers that bloom in such a rich, dark red it reminds everyone of blood.

Fitting for a family of vampires, I surmise. Well, mostly vampires.

I check my wristwatch and sigh as Cole continues to mumble curses under his breath and twist his fingers through his black, slightly wavy hair.

"Shouldn't it have started by now?" Cole's ocean blue eyes meet mine. His normally handsome, chiseled features are blurred by stress as he pulls his hand over his face, pinching the bridge of his stately, regal nose.

We don't look alike, not at all. As cousins, we share the height passed down through our male line. Tall, with broad shoulders and muscular frames, we're a physical match for each other, but where his

1

skin is bright and fair, reminiscent of a polished opal, and his hair is raven black and glossy, I'm...

Different.

I run my fingers through my dark brown, curly hair and shake my head at him. "Your incessant pacing is stressing me out."

"I'm stressed out," he echoes, throwing his hands up in emphasis. He moves with phantom grace in my direction—a vampire trait. As an adult who has known this man since we were born, essentially, I'm used to his ability to walk so quietly no one can tell he's there until he opens his fat mouth, but to anyone else, this would be completely, utterly menacing. I'm used to vampires and their ways. Probably because I am one, in a strange, distorted way.

"Don't posture at me, Cole. It's not my fault your betrothed is late to her own wedding."

"She's more than late," he growls. "She's not even here yet."

"So... she's running late. Are you telling me now that you're suddenly excited for this? You've been moping around for weeks, acting like your world is collapsing." In truth, Cole's world is, in fact, imploding. Cole grew up spoiled rotten by his father, my uncle Lex, and the kind-hearted, sweet-tempered Ivy, who I believed for years to be his actual mother.

At twenty-six, I've learned the family lore, however, and now understand Cole's inability to act rationally in most situations, seeing as his birth mother was the deranged Opal, who died when he was young.

Still, Cole grew up loved, spoiled by his parents, and has an infinity for women and feeders that can make even the most hardened commanders of my dad's army blush. Being forced into a political marriage is Cole's worst nightmare.

But I wouldn't mind, honestly, if I were in his shoes.

With another long, drawn-out sigh, I turn toward the antique desk I've been leaning against for the last hour and pour myself a second dram of scotch, sans the blood. Cole scoffs, rolling his eyes to the ceiling as I turn to him, taking a sip.

"Enjoying your apéritif?"

"Jealous?" I grin around the rim.

"I'm starving," he growls, starting his pacing again. "It's been ages."

"Didn't you just come up from the feeders?"

He throws me a hard look and turns to pace to the other side of the room, his black tux fitted perfectly to his frame and his black shoes polished so effectively they shine like obsidian. Cole mumbles something under his breath that sounds a lot like, "Stupid hybrid motherfucker," but I ignore him and check my watch again.

"Have you considered that maybe she's not coming at all?" I ask.

"It's not up to her. This is an alliance between my kingdom and her father's."

"But in the event King Mattias… changed his mind… you'd be off the hook."

"I'm not getting my hopes up." Cole snarls, his fangs elongating.

"Put those away," I smirk, setting my glass down on the desk just as the door to the Rose Room opens and a male servant steps inside looking weary as he scans the room. "Prince Michael, your mother needs your assistance."

"Thank the gods," I mutter as Cole gapes at the servant.

"What about me?"

"We're still trying to locate the bride," the servant replies nervously, his face going pale as Cole simmers with rage.

"So I'm supposed to stay here by myself?"

I cross the threshold into the hallway, murmuring to the servant in passing, "Will you please have a decanter of wine spiced with blood sent up for him, for all of our sakes? I really don't want to deal with him biting maids again."

The servant swallows hard as he nods and quickly shuts the door behind me, guiding me to the ballroom.

Mom is standing in the center of an elegantly decorated room. Candles that have been burning are now down to the wick, given that the ceremony was supposed to take place three hours ago. It's nearly morning, and I watch as she and my dad dismiss the last of the guests who'd gathered to watch what was supposed to be a show of faith and unity between two precariously friendly kingdoms.

"It's off, then?" I ask, coming to a step beside them and bending to give Mom a quick kiss on her cheek.

Dad narrows his eyes at the empty archways where the last guests have disappeared. "I knew this was going to happen."

Mom signs and grimaces. "No, you didn't. There's a good chance the poor girl is held up in one of the rural villages between our kingdoms in this storm, Kane."

Dad shakes his head, his blue eyes shining with displeasure. He's so much taller than Mom, whose head barely brushes the top of his shoulder as she turns into him, laying a hand on his chest. "Kane, go find Lex and talk to Cole. I doubt he'll be disappointed by the *delay*."

Dad shakes his head, his eyes sliding over mine on his way to Mom's face. "King Mattias has been mum on every detail about the wedding he demanded of us–decades ago. He had no plans to actually send his daughter to my kingdom, despite months of back and forth and his insistence the wedding happen here, in our home, regardless of the fact Cole is the heir to Scarlett Thunder. You have to see that, Em. This is not a delay." His voice dips to something soft and warm as he says her name, her nickname, something he's only allowed to call her. It warms my chest as I watch them, in love after almost three decades together–a vampire and a wolf shifter.

But Dad isn't looking too happy right now as he continues. "He did this to try to embarrass us, to put us through the show of unity and togetherness with no plans to make good on his end of the bargain, that fucking bastard."

"Kane!" Mom hisses, her eyes sliding in my direction apologetically, as if I'm still a curious three-year-old who just learned a new word that I'll repeat consistently and out of context, possibly naming my imaginary friend "Bastard" and insisting he joins us for dinner. That did happen once, in her defense.

I clear my throat, coming to my father's aid. "Dad's right. King Mattias ignored several attempts to introduce Cole to his daughter before the wedding and hasn't even sent us a picture of the girl."

"We don't even know her name," Dad adds, giving me a ghost of a smile in thanks for having his back on this.

Mom, ever the optimist, tilts her chin in defiance. "Send a few guards out on the road, anyway, just in case her car is in a ditch, and she's stranded in the rain." With that, Mom turns, her crimson gown and cloak trailing behind her.

Dad and I watch her go in the glare of dozens of candles and red velvet.

"Have you given any thought to what we talked about recently?" I ask into the silence. I glance at Dad, noticing his jaw tightening as he tucks his hands in the pockets of his pants.

"You know how your mom feels about it, Michael."

I take a breath. "The odds of me finding a mate are slim; you know that. I'm more vampire than wolf."

"I know, but she's holding onto hope that you can marry for love."

"And what do you think is more likely?"

He swallows, shaking his head. "I agree with you. We need to find you a wife, a vampire, for the good of the kingdom. It'll break her heart, though."

I nod, hating the sinking feeling tightening my chest, but turn for the exit. "I'm going to make sure Cole stays away from the feeders. He's a bit of a mess. I think he was secretly looking forward to this."

2

THE GIRL

Michael

It's early morning when I finally leave the castle for home, shifting into my wolf form and splitting the fog as I race across the castle grounds. I made sure my cousin was tucked into bed before making the rounds a final time, talking to my uncle Lex and Aunt Ivy, who were remarkably upset about the failed wedding.

Lex, I don't think he could have cared less about the idea of Cole marrying, but Ivy was excited about the prospect of bringing what she called, "the daughter I always needed" into the family, given that she and Lex only have Cole, the eldest, and James, their nineteen-year-old son. Ivy had been so excited for the wedding and Mom had turned my family's home into a testament to all three vampire kingdoms in anticipation for the nuptials.

I can't imagine what they're all thinking right now.

I skirt along the boundary of the castle grounds in the fog. The first glimpses of sunlight dust my dark-brown fur. I'm not going to get my hopes up for a sunny day. Those never happen here. But the vampire half of me loves the thick fog and late summer rain that are already moving back in after the storm last night washed out several roads and flooded a few creeks, based on the sheer amount of guests who decided to stay at the castle today to get some rest before moving on.

I leap over an old stone wall and rush through the forest between the castle and the sleepy vampire village of Ravenfell Hollow. It's very, very old, and it was something passed down to me when I came of age and got my first titles. Royal Prince Michael of Crimson Peak, Duke of Ravenfell Hollow, General of the Crimson Peak Army, so on, and so forth.

To some, I'm His Highness, Your Grace, Prince. To others, I'm Michael. Mike. Cole calls me Mikey to grind my gears.

To most, even my own people, I'm the halfling prince. The hybrid. The monstrosity.

My manor rests on a hilltop overlooking the fogged-soaked village. Its pitched black roof casts a shadow over the village, where the slate rooftops are just visible through the silver mist. Dark storm clouds back over the abnormally blue sky, casting the village in gray. It's another beautiful day in Crimson Peak.

I run along the outskirts of the village toward the manor, avoiding the inner circle of stone buildings and homes. When I reach the house, the front door swings open for me before I even reach the front step, and a robe is thrust through the crack in the door before I've ever shifted back to my… hybrid form.

"Thanks." I watch the pale, thin arm slide back behind the door as I take the robe and shrug it on, tying it loosely over my waist. "May I enter my own house now, Emelda?"

The door swings open, and my housekeeper, a pretty vampire who might be thirty, or two-hundred, fades into view. Her black hair is twisted in a bun at the nape of her neck as she folds her thin arms around over her chest and follows me with ocean blue eyes as I step into the foyer and slide my bare feet into the house slippers she leaves out for me.

I might be the heir to my father's kingdom, and the owner of this house, but she is the boss.

"So, how did it go?" she croons, following me on silent feet as I walk toward the kitchen, which is newer than the rest of the ancient, heavily haunted and bloodstained manor because *I can eat.*

But I pull a carafe of blood out of the fridge and pour myself a glass.

Sure, I could eat breakfast like a wolf, but I do need blood to survive. Don't ask me why, or how, this works because none of us are sure.

"It went horribly," I say after a swallow and a sigh, feeling my strength returning. Shifting really takes it out of me, and blood is the only thing I want after being in my wolf form, even for a short period of time.

"Cole was that misbehaved? Shocking." Emelda smirks as she flutters around the spotless, seldom used kitchen.

"Cole was actually very well behaved because he was cloistered away in a sitting room all night. The wedding didn't happen."

Emelda raises her perfectly shaped dark brows. "How come?"

"The bride never showed up. My parents had to dismiss all the guests. Dad believes this was King Mattias's plan all along–string us along, force our hand when it came to holding the wedding in Crimson Peak instead of Cole's own territory in Scarlett Thunder, hold this massive, ornate party and look like complete idiots when the bride didn't show up." I lean against the counter and pour a second glass of blood. I hate it cold. I like it from the source, but I've learned my wolf side makes biting people...tricky. Tricky emotionally. Wolves have strange traditions and beliefs around the act of sinking teeth into someone's flesh that goes beyond survival. For them, it's an act of love.

"Do you want me to warm that up for you?" Emelda asks, noticing my wince as I sip again.

I shake my head. "No, it's fine. I'm going to try to sleep for a while. I just needed… something."

"Well, you missed quite an evening here in Ravenfell." She takes a second glass from one of the cabinets along the wall and proceeds to pour herself some blood. She likes it cold. She's a strange woman but runs my house and staff like a general.

"What happened?"

"There was a small skirmish a town over, in Hidesmith. Some wolf marauders attacked a vampire inn. A few villagers here went to aid in breaking it up. I was at my sister's house when it happened. It was quite a commotion."

I stand up a little straighter. She arches a brow, smiling like this news is the most entertaining thing that's happened in Ravenfell lately, which it definitely is. Just because there's a wolf Queen of Crimson Peak doesn't mean the two kinds are at peace. If anything, wolf versus vampire violence, and vice versa, has been on the uptick in recent years.

"Some poor young woman staying at the inn showed up here, in the village, last night. She's injured pretty badly, honestly."

"Do I need to squeeze the rest of the story out of you, or are you going to tell me the details?"

She rolls her eyes at the edge in my voice. "She's a young thing, a vampire. Likely twenty years old at the very most. An infant, by all accounts. She was apparently traveling alone, if you can believe it. I can't." She smooths a rogue lock of hair away from her face, tucking it behind her ear. "She's at the infirmary in town. Healing, I assume."

"How long ago was this?"

"A villager found her face down in a ditch about a mile outside the village roughly four hours ago. I was on my way to my sister's house when I heard the news, and shortly thereafter, the news of the attack at the inn in Hidesmith. I figure they must be connected, but the girl isn't talking."

I leave my glass behind and go upstairs to change, draping my body in a white shirt and matching trousers. It's pouring rain when I leave my manor and walk steadily down to the village. The infirmary is rarely used, so coming upon it to find people hovering just outside the entrance is a strange sight. They dip their heads and move out of my way as I approach, throwing the doors open and letting them slam shut behind me.

In a room along the far wall, light spills from a cracked door where several voices are lifted in an argument.

But a flash of pale gold catches my attention.

"Your Highness," the vampire healer croaks in surprise, jumping out of the way of the door as I push it open, but my eyes land on the young, beautiful mouse of a woman in the bed in the center of the room, the sheets pulled up to her chest.

Her eyes are the palest blue I've ever seen, edging on gray, a strange color given that most vampires have pure, crystal blue eyes, like the ocean. Her fair skin pales as she takes me in. She sinks against the flimsy pillow at her back, pale fingers gripping the sheets.

Is she the princess who failed to show up at her own wedding last night?

My heart thuds once, then twice, as I hold her gaze.

3

THE STRANGER

Faye

HE'S TALL AND HANDSOME, WITH EYES THE COLOR OF POLISHED JADE. His eyes sparkle as he steps into the overhead light, but his expression is dire–serious with a hint of concern, maybe even skepticism, as he keeps his gaze honed to my face.

I'm trembling from pain and also the feeling like this man is very important in some way and I should be weary. The healer, whose rough hands have been doing nothing to help ease the pain in my body, bows his head and steps back to allow the stranger a better view of what's left of me, and I feel myself trying to shrink away, to disappear completely into the homespun sheets and goose down pillow that smells like whoever used it last.

"Who are you?" he asks.

My lips part and quiver. Who am I? Why can't I remember? My head hurts so bad. I close my eyes and reach up to cup the left side of my face, hoping my cold hands will ease the pain.

"She hasn't said a word. I believe she might have been hit over the head with something. No gaping wounds, but bruises, for sure. Whoever did this to her wanted it to hurt, wanted to kill her."

"It's impossibly hard to kill a vampire," the stranger says under his breath. I keep my eyes closed as his heavy footsteps edge closer until I can sense him standing at the foot of the bed. The bed squeaks as he presses his hands to the mattress on either side of my feet.

"Do you speak?" he asks roughly.

I open one eye. My stomach is hollow and tight. I need blood. I need to lie down. I need…

I lick my dry lips, opening my eyes to slits. He sighs heavily and rises, giving me his back as he faces the healer. "What happened to her?"

"We don't know exactly. The reports from Hidesmith make it sound like she might have been caught up in the attack there early last night, but her injuries seem… personal. She was found in a ditch between Ravenfell and Hidesmith" The healer's voice tapers off. I watch with blurred vision as the healer leans in to whisper, "The head injury is alarming, Your Grace. But her chest—she was beaten so badly several ribs are broken, and I believe… I believe someone might have tried to…." He hisses, whispering something under his breath before continuing, "Someone might have been trying to drive a stake, or a knife, through her heart, based on the pattern of bruising."

The stranger is quiet for what feels like an entirety. "Any claw marks?"

"No." The healer is suddenly at my side. I squeeze my eyes shut as he gently takes the sheets and pushes them down to reveal what's left of the cream-colored shift I'm still wearing.

The silence is deafening.

Fingers brush over my chest above the bodice of my shift, landing on the twin bite marks on my neck, and crook of my shoulder. The fingers disappear, and the sheets are righted, but I feel a sense of being watched.

"A vampire did this to her." The stranger isn't asking a question. He's deciding. He knows what happened to me even though I can't really remember. "Was she... assaulted otherwise?" he asks in a low growl.

"I think she may have been fighting off something like that, yes. Her fingernails are broken, but there was no sign of–"

"I'm taking her up to the Ravenfell Manor for her recovery. This is a matter I must take to the king."

"I understand. I can spare a nurse to stay with her."

"Don't bother; I have plenty of staff to help care for her."

More heavy footsteps and then I'm being lifted and I... panic. Pure, unfiltered fear grips me. I scream, sinking my cracked nails into the neck of the stranger. He groans, hissing through gritted teeth as he cradles me like an infant, carrying me out of the room like I weigh no more than a feather.

"If you bite me," he growls, low in his throat, "I won't hesitate to drop you on the ground. Do you understand? I will not hurt you if you don't hurt me."

He pins my arms against my chest with one strong, calloused hand. My head swims with pain. I blink up at him, my vision going black around the edges, but I can... smell him. I can smell his blood, and I am so, so hungry, and he doesn't smell like a vampire. My fangs elongate as he stands in the entrance of the building I'd been carried into hours ago. It's still raining. Maybe it never stopped. I don't remember.

He's looking down at me as others rush around, looking for a blanket to shield me from the rain. He turns his head as the healer reappears. "When did she last feed?"

"Not since she was brought here, so I'm not sure. She'll need a feeder, though. Cold blood will be hard on her stomach in her condition."

The stranger grinds his teeth. "I'll call on you tomorrow, Thomas. Thank you."

"Your Grace." The healer bows his head, and it's the last thing I see clearly before the stranger carries me out into the rain, into the blanket of thick fog.

The next few minutes are cold and damp. He adjusts me several times, mumbling and cursing under his breath. "You're heavier than you look," he says without the growl or gravel in his voice like before.

I'm losing consciousness and trembling wildly when warmth bursts toward me, making my skin tingle, followed by a feminine shriek.

"Get a fire going in the guest room and extra blankets, now," the stranger shouts at the female standing near my head. She scurries away, and I open my eyes to warm, dimmed lights and the smell of the man everywhere. Overwhelming and delicious in a way that makes me want to… sink… my… teeth…

"Do not bite me," he reminds me.

I look up at him through hooded eyes, unable to break fully out of the hungry haze gripping my body. He's looking down at me in awe, confusion lining those strange, jade eyes.

"Who are you?" I croak, my voice raspy from lack of use.

"I'm Prince Michael. Who are you?"

"I don't remember."

4

—————

THE FEEDER

Michael

I carry her upstairs, my manor passing by in a blur of stone and dark finishes. Emelda hurries behind me, followed by a handful of maids who peek their heads out of the various rooms off the main second-floor hallway. It's such a large house for one person, but right now, it feels crowded and suffocating as several pitched female voices call after me in alarm.

Emelda does her best to calm the fray as I slip into a bedroom–the blue room, I like to call it–and quickly lay the trembling little vampire woman on the bed. She looks like death itself. Her skin is so pale, she's nearly silver in the gray daylight pouring through a break in the navy blue curtains.

Emelda rushes out a breath as she slides into the room, shutting the door with a snap. "You brought her here? Why?"

"She was attacked."

"Well, I told you that already–"

"I don't think it had anything to do with whatever happened at the inn." I glance over my shoulder at Emelda, who has her back pinned to the door and her upper lip twisted in confusion. "I believe this might be Cole's fiancée. The missing princess."

Emelda arches her brows and steps forward. "I'll call for someone from the castle to fetch her–"

"Yes, of course, but she's practically withering away. She needs to feed–now."

"I have blood downstairs–"

"A feeder," I rasp as the girl starts to moan in pain. Vampires can go a while without feeding, but this… this seems like it's been more than a while. Longer than a day. Maybe a few days. My mind races as I throw a quilt over her body and stand back, running my fingers through my hair.

"Oh," Emelda hums, her hands planted firmly on her hips. "My sister's companion, the shifter, we could use him."

I shake my head. I'm not sure why, but something about this entire situation doesn't sit well with me. Vampires are impossibly hard to kill and rarely ever get sick. Tainted blood can cause stupors like this. Ash wood, hawthorn, silver… all things that could cause an otherwise healthy, young, and likely blood-born, vampire to go into such a state as this.

"She's very ill," Emelda notes. "So pale. What exactly happened to her?"

"I don't think we have time to debate that. Go call at the castle."

"But–"

"I'll handle this."

"You should have left her in the village at the infirmary," Emelda says as she steps toward me, a hand outstretched.

"Her attacker is still out there for all we know. If she is, in fact, the princess like I believe, it's my duty to make sure she's protected. So please, call at the castle. She'll need to be moved there immediately."

Emelda hesitates before leaving the room, her tone growing sharp as she hisses at the maids eavesdropping in the hallway. My eyes drop back to the girl, taking her in. Her hair is pale gold but lackluster, and her skin is a soft gray as her eyelids flutter open, pale blue-gray eyes holding mine.

"Prince," she mouths.

"Yes?"

"Where am I?"

"Ravenfell. It's a small village in Crimson Peak, a few miles from Castle Graystone." My voice is thick and gravelly as I look down at her. Her dress is a mangled mess of silken fabric that does nothing to cover the slope of her breasts and the twin bite marks marring her skin. To think one vampire could do this to another, especially one so young, is hard to fathom. "Where are you from?"

"My head hurts," she admits, her tongue pressing against her lower lip. Her fangs are sharp and elongated, glinting in the dim light. "The curtains–please–"

I move to the window and draw the curtains closed. She sighs, but a pinched sob escapes her throat as I turn back to her.

"Were you poisoned?"

"I don't know. I don't feel well–" She starts to shake again, arching her back like she's in terrible pain, and I... fold.

I sit on the side of the bed, rolling up the sleeve covering my left wrist. She blinks into the darkness as I reach for her and haul her into a seated position, clutching the back of her neck and guiding her mouth to my wrist.

She acts on instinct, letting out a soft moan as her teeth graze my skin. I'm warm, like a wolf. She'll know what to do. Her mouth trembles as she slowly, carefully, bites down.

I close my eyes at the tingling sensation of my blood rushing toward the wound she just inflicted and the way those tingles settle in my lower spine. No one has ever bitten me before. Why would they? Vampires don't feed on other vampires, but I'm not really one of them, am I? Not totally.

Hopefully this doesn't make matters worse, but without a feeder here, in my own home, and only cold blood downstairs in the kitchen, this is all I have to offer.

I keep my free hand closed around the back of her neck, guiding her through each shallow swallow. It doesn't hurt, but it doesn't feel like I thought it would. A rush makes my heartbeat quicken. It feels nice, actually. No wonder some feeders like it.

She starts to pull away. I hadn't even realized I'd kept my eyes closed until I open them to look at her, guiding her back to the fang mark she left. "Take more."

"You're–you're not a vampire."

"Take what you need. I'll answer your questions later."

Her eyes hold mine as she bites down again, and it's… overwhelming, especially as she curls her hands around my forearm and holds me there, her brow relaxing, her eyes growing hazy, her cheeks flushed pink with pleasure.

She's beautiful–like a yellow rose. Her soft, plump lips brush over my skin, sending tingles of sensation traveling up my arm. I watch her in awe as she swallows deeply, her eyes fluttering closed again as she sighs against my skin, slumping with relief.

When she pulls away this time, I don't stop her. I feel dizzy, and I'm not sure if it's from the amount of blood she drank, which didn't seem like that much, or something else. Her head lulls, her hair falling over her face like she's dipping into unconsciousness once more, so I carefully lay her down against the pillows and cover her up with a thick quilt.

I've barely rolled my sleeve down when Emelda walks through the door without knocking. She pales as she looks from the girl, to me, and the blood soaking my white shirt sleeve.

"I called the castle and they're… unable to tend to this right now."

I blink at her. "What? Did you tell them I have the missing princess?"

"I did, and I was told that it's impossible."

"What do you mean?"

"The princess is no longer… missing."

5

———

THE FIANCÉE

Michael

There's a hum of excitement in the castle as I pass through the main entrance, rain sliding off my black leather jacket and onto the dark stone floor. The bridge behind me is socked-in by fog as the doors close, and a couple of guards step back in place, standing stoically at attention while I walk with determination toward the throne room.

The entire court is here right now. Vampires of varying rank and importance roam the hallways, sending a hushed murmur of conversation through the arching corridors that overlap my footsteps as I round another corner and walk into the throne room, shrugging out of my jacket at the same moment my mom turns and spots me.

Her smile shifts from rehearsed to genuine as she excuses herself from whatever conversation she'd been having with three tall, female vampires and hurries in my direction. "Michael, I didn't think we'd see you today. Your dad mentioned there'd been an incident in Ravenfell–"

"The princess is here?" I ask, cutting her off. "She showed up?"

Mom tries to look pleased, but her expressive shifter eyes give away her nerves and downright confusion as she nods, glancing around to make sure we're not overheard. She ropes an arm in mine and guides the throne room, leaning in to whisper, "She arrived this morning with a small entourage of nobles from Red River. Apparently, they got caught in the storm and had to seek shelter overnight and were unable to send word to us about the *delay*." Her eyes, a match to mine, hold my gaze as she draws out the word *delay* like she doesn't believe it for a second.

But my head is spinning, my thoughts drifting back to the mystery woman recovering in my home, her fang marks burning back to life on my wrist. I run my tongue along my lower teeth as Mom guides me through the teeming castle. Some wedding guests from faraway villages and towns chose to stay overnight rather than risk a drive through the hellish late summer thunderstorm. The more I think about it, the more King Mattias' demand that the wedding be held here, in Crimson Peak, makes sense. So many kingdoms in one place. So many kings. So many nobles. What exactly was he planning to do in their absence?

"Were there any other attacks last night, other than the small skirmish near my village?"

"Not that we're aware of. Why?" she asks.

I grind my teeth as she turns us into my dad's office, which is a sprawling space with several rooms branching off the main drawing room where a group of familiar vampires are currently standing in a circle that parts as we enter.

My Uncle Lex slowly nods to me in acknowledgment. Ivy stands beside him with her hand gripping his upper arm a little too tightly to look comfortable.

And Cole is standing beside his bride.

I meet the young vampire's eyes. She's… lovely, in a vampire way. Tall and lithe, with pin-straight dark blonde hair that brushes her hips as she turns ever so slightly to face us, her ocean-blue eyes searching my mom's face with curiosity and a hint of disgust she can't quite keep hidden. I recognize the disgust temporarily blurring her vampirically pretty features. Those vampires who know my mother love her. Those who don't know her tend to think of her as nothing more than a wolf wearing a crown that doesn't belong to her.

One would think times would change. I'm reminded every day that that's not necessarily true.

This vampire, however, looks like she's making the decision not to even breathe in the presence of a shifter in the event she'd pick up her scent, which makes my fingers twitch with the need to curl my hands into fists. I hold my position at Mom's side, folding my hand over hers in the crook of my elbow, and stare the princess down.

She has a long, dainty neck. A straight spine. A practiced, regal posture. The only thing we knew about the princess from Red River is that she is beautiful, but we didn't know exactly what she looks like. Her fair skin is flushed a soft pink like she's recently been fed and fed well. I'm sure if I touched her, she'd be warm.

Uncle Lex is the first to speak. "This is Princess Matilda of Red River."

"I assumed so," I grind out, giving her a smile as fake as the smiles she's likely been giving my mother, and her own betrothed's mother, who is not a vampire, but a full-blooded witch. "How nice of you to finally join us. You've missed your wedding, I'm afraid."

The vampiress frowns at me.

"Michael," Mom growls under her breath.

I catch Cole's eyes, however, and they glimmer with amusement.

"We were held up," Matilda replies in a low, sensuous drawl that betrays her looks. I would have assumed her voice would be pitched and sharp. She's very thin and hard–all bone and muscle. Most vampire females are like that, I suppose, with some exceptions. One being the woman curled up in a guest room in my manor, who was soft and supple in my arms while she fed from me.

That tingling sensation prickles to life in my lower spine again, jolting me back to awareness. I turn to Mom, ignoring Matilda's cold, questioning eyes. "Where's Dad? I need to speak with him immediately."

"He's meeting with Princess Matilda's escorts. Highburton, one of the emissaries to Red River, brought her here himself." Mom motions to the only closed door nearby.

My gaze flicks back to Matilda. Why hadn't her own father escorted her here? Her mother? Any family at all? Did no one care that she was getting married? Questions dance in my mind as I meet Cole's gaze again. Through telepathy, he says into my mind, and my mind only, *"She's not that bad, huh? Could be worse. I think I would have preferred someone with bigger tits, though."*

I grit my teeth, feigning a smile around the room, at the faces turned in my direction. I'm just about to say I'll return later to speak with my father and kiss my mom goodbye when Lex says, "It's been decided that Matilda will stay here for a few weeks while we negotiate new wedding plans, preferably in Scarlett Thunder." There's an obvious edge to his voice he doesn't bother hiding. "Matilda will be able to assimilate to court life here, under the direction of Queen Emory, until a decision about the nuptials is made."

I turn my attention to Matilda, who's smiling kindly at Lex, nodding in agreement. "Why?" I ask sharply.

"Michael, what's gotten into you?" Mom asks quietly.

I ignore her for the moment. "I just find it odd that the wedding had to be held here in the first place. Why stay when she wouldn't be ruling Crimson Peak? She should be in Scarlett Thunder, assimilating to that court, not ours."

Lex holds my gaze, but it's Cole who clears his throat like he's going to speak. Matilda beats him to it. "I missed my own wedding, and you're giving me grief for wanting a few moments of peace to recuperate?"

I look back at her, not liking the teasing, slightly malicious glint in her voice, especially as she laughs, "Do you not think it's inappropriate that I shack up with my fiancé before new wedding plans are made? I'm a princess, not a lowly feeder brought here for his entertainment."

Silence grips the room. An uncomfortable beat of tension passes between the group, and all eyes are on me.

"Excuse me," I say by way of an apology, and give her a short bob of my head. "I'm needed in my territory at the moment. Mom, I'll call on Dad later."

"I'll walk you out," she says, eyeing the group before following me out of the room. Then, she pinches my arm. "What the hell is the matter with you? I didn't raise you to be so rude."

"Something's off, Mom. I know you feel it too."

"These are vampires. This is vampire business. Your father is handling it in the way he knows best."

"You're still the queen. You have a say in who gets admittance to your court, and that woman made it pretty damn obvious how she felt about standing so near to a shifter." I halt and turn to her, taking her by the shoulders. "I don't trust this situation at all."

"Trust your father, then. And me. I wouldn't let anything happen to any of us. Matilda is just… different. Red River is a cold, hard place, from what I understand."

My nostrils flare with impatience, but Mom smiles up at me and continues, "Plus, you sound like you have your hands full. Emelda sent word to the castle and said you have an injured vampire staying in your home. What's the story there?"

I sigh, unsure where to begin. "I'm not sure what the story is yet, but I should go home and check on things."

I leave her standing in the corridor and find my way out of the castle, back into the dreary late afternoon rainstorm. I pause halfway across the bridge, realizing I probably should have asked to bring a feeder back to my manor with me, but flex my hand instead, feeling the slowly healing bite mark burn back to life.

It wasn't so bad. I could do it again. I think I will do it again.

6

———

HOSPITALITY

Faye

It's raining. I watch a raindrop roll down the window, absorbing its companions. The rest of the world is a dark blur as I press my fingertips to the window, finding the glass cold. Someone touches my thigh in the darkness, murmuring something under their breath. Soon, the world comes into view again, a dark forest expanding on either side of the... the car. "Why are we stopping?" I ask into the dark interior. Headlights flash ahead.

"Good evening," an unfamiliar voice echoes, pulling me out of a dream. "Wake up. Come on, you've been asleep for an entire day. You're probably starving."

I try to sit up, waving a hand wildly as a figure comes into view just a few feet away. I grasp thin air as fear prickles over my skin.

"Okay, never mind. Lie back down–just like that. Good." The woman gently presses me back to the... bed. I'm in a bed. The walls are painted a rich blue that matches the curtains and bedspread. I remember where I am. That strange man's house. The *prince's* house.

I blink several times to clear my vision, and the woman comes into full view, her clear blue eyes creased as she smiles kindly down at me. I jerk away from her, crushing myself against the pillows.

"You're a fretful little thing, aren't you?" She sits on the side of the bed, ignoring the fact that I'm actively scooching away from her.

"Who are you? Where am I?"

"Ravenfell, remember? You're in Prince Michael's house." She waves a hand around the room but keeps her eyes locked on mine. She has a kind, pretty face. Her skin is fair and flawless, and she's dressed in a thick robe over what looks like a satin nightdress.

Memories come rushing back to me. Prince Michael erupts in the forefront of my mind. His dark brown hair, damp from the rain, just starting to curl again. His sparkling pale green eyes. The way his wide, full lips parted as he sighed around the sensation of me drinking from his wrist....

This must be his wife. Obviously.

My skin flushes as I lower my eyes from her face, dipping my chin to my chest in a show of submission.

She clicks her tongue. "What's wrong now?"

I steal a glance at her through my lashes. "I'm–I'm grateful for your–your hospitality, Your Highness."

She gasps then erupts in a cackling laugh that sends a shock dancing down my spine. "Your Highness! Oh, that's hilarious." Her laugh turns to a muted giggle. "No, girl. My name is Emelda. I'm the head housekeeper. Although, I don't mind being called *Highness*. It has a nice ring to it, doesn't it?" Her eyes sparkle with amusement. "What's your name, love?"

"I–I–" I stammer, trying to form a word. Any word. My name, preferably.

She pinches her lips together in what I can only describe as sympathy. "No bother. Someone hit you over the head, you know. Probably knocked your brain around a bit. You'll be good as new in a few days, I'm sure." She rises and motions to my chest before turning toward a dresser resting along the wall beneath the windows. "I'd like to get you cleaned up, if you don't mind. That shift is lovely, but it's filthy and torn-up. Can you stand?"

"W-why?" I clutch the bedspread like it's my only lifeline in this storm, but Emelda gives me an odd look.

"Because you're going to take a nice, long, hot bath. While you do that, I'm going to change your sheets, make your bed, and lay out some new clothes. Come on. Let's test out those legs."

I reluctantly let her help me out of bed. My legs ache, but they work, and she holds my arm as I pad across plush, warm carpet the color of fresh cream. She opens a door and ushers me into an ensuite bathroom where a clawfoot tub made of black marble is the center-piece of the room. I stand, shivering, as Emelda runs a bath, pouring jars of rose scented oil and vanilla soap into the steaming water.

She wordlessly motions for me to strip out of what's left of my dress, but I hesitate for a moment before pulling the straps over my shoulders and letting it fall to the floor. She keeps her eyes on the wall as she helps me into the tub, but just as my body breaches the water, I hear her take a sharp breath. Her eyes are on my back, then my ribs, which are so brutally bruised it startles me as much as it must have just startled her.

I whimper in shock, my eyes watering as I try to wrap my arms around my chest, but she shushes me like a mother would calm an infant and gently guides me into the water.

"Don't worry about it now," she says, but her voice is heavy. She swallows hard, keeping her eyes on my hair as she pours water over my head and works vanilla scented shampoo through my tresses. I shiver despite the warmth of the water, a few tears sliding free from my lashes. "What happened to me?"

She sighs. "We don't really know yet."

"We?"

"The prince is investigating the situation as we speak. He's been gone all day. I'll speak to him when he returns. You must be hungry again." She rinses my hair and softly pushes me down so I'm soaked to the neck. "He's going to bring you a feeder, but I do have blood here. It's pretty good. I spice it up myself. I prefer it sweet."

I nod because it's all I can do. My mind is in as bad a state as my body. I stare at my reflection in the facet, seeing the bruises on my cheekbones and the gray flush to my skin. My eyes are round and bright but full of tears.

"If you remember anything at all, please let me know," she says in just above a whisper. "We'd love to reunite you with your–" she pauses and sighs, then rises from the bathroom floor. "I'm going to go lay out some clothes. There are warm towels and a robe for you right here." She motions to a stack of fabric on the bathroom vanity. "I'll come check on you in a little while."

She leaves the room. I sink underwater to hide my tears.

7

———

THE GUEST

Michael

It's the middle of the night when I walk up to my doorstep. Thunder rumbles in the distance, but Ravenfell is foggy, cool, and only slightly damp tonight. I open the door to quiet darkness. A light switches on upstairs, illuminating the second floor landing as I step into the foyer, holding the door open for the figure stepping inside behind me.

Deacon removes his hood and runs his fingers through his short black hair, sniffling from the cold as he removes his jacket. "Fuck, man. It's freezing."

I nod as Emelda walks into view in her usual robe and house slippers, glaring down at me from the top step. "Well, well, well, it's so nice of you to finally come home. It's only the middle of the night."

"Emelda," I say by way of greeting, smirking at her.

"I thought I took out the trash tonight. I guess I missed some." She glares at Deacon, who postures and bats his eyelashes at her.

"Always a pleasure to see the most beautiful vampiress in all the land," he croons, wiggling his eyebrows as she taps her foot impatiently on the top step.

"Why is he here?" she pointedly asks me.

I glance at Deacon, who's grinning from ear to ear up at the love of his life, even if the feelings aren't reciprocated. This dynamic has been going on for years. Deacon is like me—blood-born and from a royal line. He's a fellow general in my father's army and barely a month older than me. We grew up together, and he's always looked past the differences between us, although he occasionally makes jokes about my wolfish nature, like the one time I went over to his house, and he served me blood in what he called a dog bowl. Emelda is… Emelda.

One day, the two of them will fuck and get over this, but for now, Deacon takes great pleasure in pushing all of Emelda's buttons.

"He was helping me with some stuff in the village," I say as I shrug out of my jacket and hang it on the coat rack. "I invited him over for a drink."

"You should join us, darling," Deacon says as he steps past me and walks through the dark toward my formal drawing room.

"I'm not your darling, you stupid ingrate."

"Here we go," I murmur under my breath as the swishing of her robe alerts us both to her impending arrival at our side. I follow Deacon, running a hand over my face as Emelda rushes up behind me.

"Emelda, you should make those blood cocktails again. I've been thinking about them for weeks." Deacon turns on a light, glancing around at the empty, cold room. "Why are all the fires out?"

"I excused the staff for the next few days," Emelda says with annoyance lacing every word. She throws me a frustrated look as Deacon makes himself right at home, plopping down on an antique couch while crossing his ankles over an ottoman.

"Oh, because of your *guest?*"

"Yes, and she's been running hot all evening. I wanted to keep the house cool for a while, for her comfort." Emelda begins, her lips parted to continue, but I grab her arm as she makes a move for the built-in bookshelf housing my bottles of liquor.

"How is she?" I whisper under my breath.

"She's fine, sleeping." She yanks her arm out of my grasp and fetches a bottle of whiskey. "I'll make cocktails but only if you bring in some firewood, Deacon."

Deacon groans dramatically and rises from the couch. "Fine. I wouldn't want your pretty little fingers getting splinters."

She glares at him as he walks out of the room and disappears into the dark recesses of the house, then turns her glare on me.

"What?" I ask, pinching the bridge of my nose as I crouch by the dormant fireplace and start stacking kindling into its basin.

"You know how I feel about him being around," she hisses, baring her fangs at me in emphasis.

"I think you secretly find him entertaining." I motion to the bottle of whiskey, which she quickly stows behind her back, and frowns. "I needed his help today. He has connections in Hidesmith."

"He has connections at the bars and inns," she corrects.

"You were a witch once," I remind her. "Put a spell on him. Turn him into a toad."

"I'd turn him into roadkill if I still had those abilities." She watches me build a fire, hovering behind me like a shadow.

Most noble vampires would balk at the idea of having a conversation like this with a member of their staff, but Emelda isn't just my head housekeeper. She's one of my best friends, a member of the little "pack" I've created for myself. I've known her for years now, ever since I came to live in Ravenfell seven years ago. She literally showed up on my doorstep one day and told me rather bluntly that I didn't know what the hell I was doing in terms of taking care of this ancient manor and moved in an hour later, hired a dozen maids, and has been running my life ever since.

We're bonded. She's the older sister I never had.

"I know you let her feed from you."

I close my eyes against the glow of the fire. "She needed it."

"Don't do it again."

"It's not like she's feeding on a vamp–"

She clutches my shoulder, squeezing. "You're half wolf, Michael. Biting is not the same for you as it is for us."

I shrug her off. "I did what I had to do." I rise, dusting my hands off on my thighs.

"But you're going to do it again. That's why you didn't bring home a feeder for her."

"It helped, didn't it? You said she's sleeping–"

"I wouldn't call it sleep." She crosses her arms under her chest as she looks up at me.

"Then what would you call it?"

"Have you seen her–her body? She looks like she went through a meat grinder. She's fucking exhausted."

"That's why I brought Deacon into the mix, Emelda. We're going to find out who did this to her. He knows everyone, and someone has to know something."

"I think she was either poisoned or recently turned."

I turn back to the fire, closing my eyes.

She continues when I don't reply, "I served her some blood tonight. I warmed it up, spiced it with vanilla and sugar, thinking she might have been turned against her will... like I was. You know how new vampires struggle with adjusting to the taste of blood... but she barely took a sip and then passed out cold again."

I tuck my hands in my pockets, mulling over her words.

She continues, "The bruising, the bite marks... It's horrific. It reminds me a lot of what happened to me and my sister, but the fact that she fed from... you... being what you are, so easily... it makes me believe she's blood-born. She's been a vampire for a long time. Her whole life."

"And if she's blood-born, she's likely a noble. Someone of high rank."

She nods, passing the bottle of whiskey between her hands. "Yeah."

I thought she might have been the missing princess at first, but now that Matilda is here....

"Where the hell did she come from?" I say, mostly to myself.

"And who the hell is going to come looking for her?" Emelda adds.

8

———

MEMORIES

Faye

"Wait," I beg, scooching across wet grass, my palms broken and bruised from the gravel on the road. "Why? Why are you doing this?"

Another blow to my chest has me curling into the fetal position. Rain pelts my face—sharp, and cold. The dress my mother spent weeks perfecting is torn from my body, leaving me in only my shift. I whimper as I roll onto my belly and crawl toward the woods, but a blow to my back flattens me to the ground. I scream, my desperate cries for help falling on deaf ears as the group standing on the road watches in silent observation.

Hands grip my ankles and drag me backward. I claw and scramble for anything to grab onto, screaming their name over, and over. "Stop, please! Please!"

I open my eyes to darkness. A muffled curse comes from the door as a shadow steps inside and fumbles with the doorknob before pushing the door almost all the way closed. Light from the hallway spills across the floor as familiar footsteps cautiously edge toward the bed. I'm lying on my side, my arm tucked under the pillow, when Prince Michael leans down to peer at me.

"Oh, shit–" he rasps, straightening up with a jolt. "Did I wake you up?"

He backs away from the bed and grips the doorknob, half turning toward the door and hanging his head.

I sit up with some effort, stifling a groan as dull pain ebbs through my body. The bath worked wonders. I slept like the dead. I can't remember the last time I slept like this. I still can't remember much at all.

"You might have," I answer, swallowing past the dryness in my throat. I rub my eyes, feeling weak and unsteady.

"I was just checking on you." He has his head turned toward the door.

"It's all right." Is it? I haven't felt unsafe around him yet. Should I feel unsafe? I think of my dream, but the memories of it are already fading.

He sighs, running his fingers through his unruly curls. "Can we talk for a moment, or do you want to rest more?"

I don't know what I want. I feel like I'm standing outside of my own body, watching as I nod to the prince, and he reaches for a lamp resting on a delicate side table next to the door. Soft amber light spills across the room, illuminating little details I hadn't noticed before. The intricate, swirling design of the wallpaper. The old books stacked haphazardly on tables and the dresser. The dormant marble fireplace.

Thunder rumbles outside, causing me to nearly jump out of my skin. The prince notices and says, "The storm's far away; I doubt it'll pass over us." He pushes the door closed.

"That's good."

"Do you not like thunder?"

I'm not sure how to answer that question. A blurry, fragmented memory of sitting in a warm, soft lap floods my mind. Gentle hands hold mine as I'm rocked back and forth, a sweet, gentle lullaby lulling me back to sleep.

"Sometimes I like it."

"Ah," he says, clicking his tongue. "Sometimes I like it, too." I follow him with my eyes as he paces to the center of the room, his back to me. He looks around, picks up a book and puts it down. "I have larger rooms if you'd like a change of scenery, more space to recuperate in. Different views."

I lick my lips, finding them dry and cracked. "I'm fine here."

His jaw flexes, but he doesn't turn to face me. Only his profile is visible as he asks, "Do you remember anything that happened to you?"

"Maybe. I'm not sure if it was real or just a dream."

"Can you tell me?"

Words fail me. I look down at my lap in defeat. When I look up again, he's closer, resting a hand on the footboard of the bed, but his eyes are on the window as lightning flashes in the distance.

Seeing him this close--I don't think I really got to look at him last time, this morning–I see he's remarkably handsome in a way that feels both foreign and familiar. He's tall, like most vampires. Tall and broad, with a narrow waist and a muscled build that's evident through his tailored shirt and trousers. But he's rugged and wild, not polished and flawless like most vampire men. "What are you?" I ask without meaning to open my stupid mouth.

He looks at me, amused. "Not a vampire."

I tilt my head. "But you... are."

"Somewhat," he says casually, looking back at the window with a sigh.

"What were you before you were turned?"

"I was born this way," he admits with a small, boyish smile. "Why, did I not taste good?"

Heat flares across my cheekbones. I drop my eyes to my lap, running my tongue along my lower lip at the memory of the taste of him. No, he didn't taste good. He tasted *great*. But he's a vampire... possibly. I shouldn't have been able to feed from him. He shouldn't have even offered, but he did.

"My mother is a shifter," he says. "Queen Emory. She's a wolf."

I lift my gaze to meet his. "That's impossible."

"A lot of people think so, but here I am."

I wrack my brain for any memories of Crimson Peak, but everything in my head is a jumbled mess of hazy, mismatched memories. "And your father is a vampire?"

"Yes. King Kane."

It doesn't ring a bell, but I feel like it should. I can feel him watching me again, so I meet his eyes, holding there.

"Did someone turn you recently?" he asks softly, his magnificent eyes searching mine for understanding.

"No. I'm blood-born." How I know, I'm not sure, but the knowledge is there, lodged in my soul and just within reach when nothing else is.

"Who did this to you?"

"I don't remember."

He nods, obviously not willing to pry any further, but his eyes soften as they sweep over my face. "You're welcome to stay here as long as you need. I'd prefer it, actually, over you returning to the infirmary. But I may have to move you to the castle if you don't make any progress in your recovery. You need a feeder." He bites down on his lip as his gaze drops to my chest, to the fang marks that haven't healed much, and still burn.

Again, my mouth moves on its own accord. "Your blood helped."

"I…" he trails off, lifting his gaze to mine again. "Do you want more?" he rushes out, borderline excited, like this is the entire reason he came to this room.

I do. I do want more. My fangs spring to life at the thought. I've barely had a chance to nod and catch my breath before he's rounding the bed and rolling up his sleeve.

9

—————

MELTING

Faye

PRINCE MICHAEL SITS ON THE SIDE OF THE BED. I EDGE CLOSER, holding his gaze like I'm in a trance. I can hear his heart thumping even from this distance. I can hear his blood rushing in his veins. His scent is warm and overwhelmingly comforting, adding to the dizzy feeling cascading over my body.

I'm hungry and weak. It hurts to move like this, to try to keep my back straight in a seated position and curl my legs beneath me to essentially kneel beside him.

He's a large man. Large—and strong. Our size difference is almost as overwhelming as his scent, which wraps around my senses and tugs tight, making my head spin.

"Wait," he rushes out, catching me as I pitch forward, my vision blurring at the edges. He lays me back against the pillows with a tender touch. I puff out a sigh as fatigue creeps back into my bones, threatening to pull me back into sleep. But then he's beside me, pushing his arm under my shoulder and pulling me against his chest.

39

He raises his wrist to my mouth. "Here," he whispers breathlessly. "Don't pass out now."

I bite him without realizing I'm doing it, letting my instincts take over, and inhale deeply as the scent of his blood mingles with his skin. He's everything warm and bright. He tastes like the sun. Golden and rich.

I melt into his touch, closing my eyes as his blood fuels my tired, aching body. I needed this so much.

He makes a low, tight noise in his throat. I let go with a pop. "Am I hurting you?" I ask, risking a glance up at him, my head nestled in the crook of his shoulder.

"No," he breathes, his eyes closed and face washed in lamplight. He looks... relaxed. Impossibly so. "Take more."

I do. The pull of his blood is a rush. The feeling of his muscles flexing against my teeth has tingling licking down my spine, settling low in my belly. I moan against his skin, whimpering as he tugs me closer so we're settled chest to chest. "Good," he murmurs into my hair, breathing deeply. "Don't stop. Take more."

I'm afraid I'm taking too much, but I obey, sighing dreamily against his skin. I writhe against him with each swallow, my breasts feeling suddenly heavy and sensitive. This is... should it feel like this? Like I'm losing myself in him?

I let go, warmth rushing through my body, but he tugs me back against him.

"I shouldn't," I whisper, my breath hitching.

"You need it," he whispers, looking down at me through heavy, hooded eyes. His cheeks flush a ruddy rose color as he takes a shallow breath, lips parted. He looks undone–wholly and utterly, undone. "Take more. I'm fine." His jade eyes shimmer with pleasure as he raises his wrist to my mouth again. I obey, but we lock eyes as I take another long pull. It's all I need. It's all I have the energy for, and then I'm feeling that dark, endless sleep settling heavy again. I run my tongue over the marks I left on his skin, reveling in his taste one last time. Why does he taste like this?

His body pressed against mine is exotic, a touch I've never experienced before. I'm vaguely aware of my hand gripping the fabric of his shirt and the way his free hand is resting on my hip, his thumb making slow, lazy circles along my hip bone over the black satin nightdress Emelda laid out for me.

"Thank you," I whisper, expecting him to immediately move away, but he stays, his eyes searching mine.

"You need a name," he whispers.

"I don't remember it."

"You will." His voice is weighted by the same kind of exhaustion coiling through my own muscles. His thumb continues its lazy dance over my hip bone as I curl into his warmth. He is *warm*—almost fevered with heat. I wonder if he's always like this or if his vampire side ever makes an appearance, turning his skin as cold and hard as marble.

I absently pick at the buttons of his shirt, ignoring the fact that I'm nestled against a man I don't really know, but he opened his home to me. He offered me his blood. He's caring for me, and he doesn't even know who I am.

Neither do I.

Maybe there's a reason that goes beyond my injuries.

I don't need to look up at him to know he's asleep. His chest rises and falls rhythmically, his heart thumping slowly, at rest.

I close my eyes, letting the fatigue coasting through my body dull the aches and pains, and slip into sleep curled against the prince.

I wake several hours later to dreary, rainy daylight peeking through the navy curtains. Prince Michael is gone, replaced by a cold hand resting over my forehead. Emelda's sleek figure comes into view as she faces the window with a sigh, pulling the curtains closed, and quietly leaves the room.

I feel trapped in my own body as my eyes flutter closed again. The weakness is back despite Prince Michael's gift of blood. It's a never ending presence I can't shake.

I lie there in the dark, praying my mind stays on his memory and doesn't dip back into the hazy dream, those fractured memories.

"Stop! Stop!" I shout, raking my nails against my assailant's skin. My

nails tear and shatter. He has my arms pinned at my sides now, straddling me as another set of hands hold a damp cloth over my mouth. I struggle against the fabric, sucking in droplets of something damp and acidic that makes me dizzy.

"Do it," someone nearby says, their voice distorted. "Kill her, now. Get it over with. My clothes are getting wet."

A low, cackling laugh echoes through my head before I feel the sharp sting of fangs. I scream my name, over and over.

"It's me! It's me! It's Faye! Please! Why are you doing this?! What have I done?!"

10

NO FAVORS

Michael

Emelda silently returns to the kitchen with her tray of tonics and potions and sets them on the counter, wordlessly scribbling doses in the black leather notebook she's been carrying around in her pocket since the night I met the witch-turned-vampire seven years ago.

I lean against the counter, flexing my left hand and curling it into a fist over and over, wearing a thick bandage around my wrist.

Emelda glances at me with a sigh before dropping her gaze back to her notebook. "You're wasting your time and energy, Michael."

I tuck my hand behind my back on impulse. It's not like this is some big secret. Emelda found me in the girl's room this morning anyway, shaking me awake and hissing curses at me all the way down the hallway when I'd retreated to my own rooms.

"She needed it. She was cold as ice and withering."

"She's a vampire," she sighs with frustration lacing each word. "That's what we're supposed to feel like. It's what you're supposed to feel like, and letting her feed off you is… going to have repercussions."

"You seem to know everything," I mutter, crossing my arms over my chest. "Tell me, Emelda, what exactly am I risking by letting her drink from me? I'm a shifter as well as a vampire. My blood is compatible with what she needs right now."

"Not totally," she retorts, closing her notebook with a snap. "It's enough to keep her alive, but her healing has stopped completely. Her bruises are getting worse, not better. Spreading, in fact, based on my examination of her this morning. She needs more blood. Better blood. The blood of a feeder, preferably someone strong and hearty who has a protein and fat-rich diet, not someone who spent most of the night drinking blood cocktails!"

My fangs lengthen as I snarl at her.

"You know I'm right," she says with a bitter edge to her tone. "You're not doing her any favors by keeping her here. You need to bring her to Graystone as soon as possible or have a feeder sent here." She rounds the kitchen island, standing within a few feet of me, tilting her head from side to side as she takes in my rigid stance and bared teeth. "You're bonding to her, aren't you?"

"I don't know what you're talking about."

"Haven't you learned anything from your mother?" she snaps, resting her hands on her narrow hips. "You can't just go around biting people, Michael. You're a wolf, too. They bite for love, pleasure, and to kill, not sustenance. This is over. You're not going near her again."

"I am the Duke of Ravenfell, the prince, and the owner of this house. You don't get to decide that for me."

"I am your friend, and I'm warning you, as someone who loves you, that this girl is going to die in this house if she doesn't get help from other vampires. There's nothing else I can do for her. She's weak, Michael. You have to see that."

I'm currently seeing red at the idea of the girl's fangs sinking into anyone else's skin but mine.

"Snap out of it, you big, furry, stupid fool!" Emelda shoves me hard. Hard enough to jolt me back into awareness. "You're going to kill her if you keep letting her feed from you. Vampires don't feed off other vampires. Your shifter blood isn't pure enough, Michael. It's not what she needs."

A scream echoes through the house. Emelda and I take off in a sprint toward the sound, shoving against each other to access the girl's room. Emelda has the upper hand. She slides under my arm as I throw open the door and slips inside, using her unearthly vampire strength to hold the door open long enough to say, "She's having another nightmare. That's all. Make a decision, Michael, because this is only going to get worse. She was poisoned with something and needs to be tended to." She slams the door in my face, locking it from the inside.

I whirl and sink against the door, fuming, holding my face in my hands while I listen to Emelda's voice drop to something soft and gentle while the nameless girl moans as if she's in pain. The girl starts sobbing, begging Emelda for help, and it's my undoing.

Emelda is right. Whatever this tugging feeling is in my chest, it's clouding my senses. The desire to keep the girl here is misplaced. She's not mine. I barely know her. I don't even know her name. She needs help I can't provide.

An hour late, I'm passing through one of the servants' entrances to Castle Graystone. Mist funnels in behind me as a trio of maids rushes me inside, the girl draped in my arms. Emelda hurries in behind us, speaking rapidly to the maids, who scurry away to ready a room upstairs for the new, and very sick, royal guest.

It takes less than twenty minutes for word to spread about my arrival in the castle. I'm just backing away from the four-poster bed where I laid the girl in its center, pained by how small she looks comparatively. Small, weak, and turning gray once again.

"She needs a feeder immediately. She's too weak to go down to them herself. One will need to be brought here. Someone strong and healthy, preferably young and male." Emelda's voice is distorted by the thrumming of my heartbeat in my ears as I watch a group of maids tuck the girl in, fussing over her.

"We have someone who will be perfect. He's a nice man. Gentle. He won't frighten her."

"That doesn't matter at this point," Emelda says hurriedly. "Where's the lead physician? I need to speak to her." I stand in the center of the room as Emelda drops into conversation with one of my mother's head housekeepers. They leave the room, which spins with activity around the girl, but her eyes open to slits, and her gaze holds on mine.

"I'm sorry," I say as best I can, but the words barely leave my lips.

She takes a shallow breath, shaking her head as she mouths a word I don't recognize, but then more people are rushing into the room, and a familiar, gentle touch rests on my tense back. "Michael?" Mom murmurs. "What's going on?"

I turn to the door and walk out. Mom's huff of frustration follows me out, but she doesn't chase after me. I walk with determination to my father's office, rounding a corner, and run into Emelda talking to Adriatta, the head physician for the castle, and a tall, sturdy looking shifter who's nodding along with whatever the women are discussing.

I clench my fists, ignoring the way my fangs sharpen and elongate. I want nothing more than to storm back into the girl's room and offer her my wrist–hell, my neck.

But the group walks away, toward her room, and it takes all the strength I have to keep walking, putting distance between myself and the young vampire woman who has suddenly put some kind of spell on me.

"What's all the commotion about?" a deep, seductive female voice says, and I stop in my tracks. Matilda steps out of the shadows wearing a crimson strapless gown that drapes over her narrow features. She reminds me of a candlestick–waxy and acrid. Her blue eyes shine with curiosity as she folds her narrow arms beneath her breasts, fixing me with a sharp look. "Hello? Prince Michael?"

"Nothing that concerns you," I remark, trying to step past her, but she blocks my progress with a hand on my chest.

Her fingers toy with the buttons on my shirt as she looks up at me with a flirtatious smile. "Concern yourself with me for a moment, then."

11

BOXED IN

MICHAEL

I carefully pluck Matilda's cold fingers from my shirt. "Where's your fiancé?"

"Hell if I know," she replies smoothly, her full lips curving at the edges. "Not around, obviously. He's keeping his distance."

I want to say that I don't blame him. Something about her makes me want to crawl out of my skin. I'm used to vampires touching me. Their coldness doesn't bother me. If it's been a while since I've had blood, even as a hybrid, my body temperature drops as well, but she's cold as ice as her fingers catch mine. "Why don't you give me a tour?"

"I don't have time," I say with more force than I mean. I yank my fingers out of her grasp, tucking my hands in my pockets and taking a calculated step away from her. She smirks, rolling her eyes to the ceiling.

"This court is so boring. There's nothing to do. No one to eat."

"I'm sure you've been told where the feeders are kept. You could ring for a glass of blood at any time."

"It's not nearly as fun as finding your own source." She licks her lips, smiling–with fangs on display. "I hope Scarlett Thunder is more... entertaining than this."

"Maybe this is a conversation for your father, given that he demanded you get married here instead of the kingdom you're meant to rule one day, alongside Cole."

"Maybe so," she drawls, feigning a delicate yawn. Her eyes slide to mine again, narrowed to cat-like slits. "You smell so strange, Prince Michael. It's not a bad thing. Don't worry. You just smell... warm. Delicious, honestly. Are you a feeder as well as a vampire prince?"

I don't like this at all, but I'm not in the habit of letting myself be intimidated by other vampires.

"No, I am not," I growl.

"Pity. You and I could have had a lot of fun together." She whirls, walking off, swaying her hips.

I curse under my breath and turn away from her, begging whatever gods are listening to get rid of this woman. The gods don't care, of course. But my father might.

I waltz into his office and find him talking to an unfamiliar vampire man, who stands and bows when I enter the room, which is a nice change of pace from being fondled in a darkened hallway.

"Michael, this is Aamon Acheron, emissary to the King of Red River." Dad waves a hand toward the tall, finely dressed man with light blond hair and... red eyes.

"Prince Michael," he says smoothly, politely, giving me another practiced bob of his head. "It's a pleasure to finally meet you."

I nod back. "Yes, thank you. Father, I need a moment."

"We'll finish this conversation at another time," he says in dismissal to Aamon who leaves the office without another word, closing the door behind him.

My gaze holds on the door for several seconds before I turn to my dad and say, "What exactly is happening here?"

Kane exhales deeply, leaning back in his desk chair. "With Red River?"

"Yes, obviously." I sink into a chair across from him.

"You've never liked new vampires," he murmurs, flipping his ledger closed.

"I don't like Princess Matilda."

"It's a good thing you're not the one marrying her, then." He straightens, smoothing the fabric of his suit. "I understand your feelings, trust me. I don't like being boxed into a corner by another king, but we have his child in our possession right now, and I'm doing what I must to make sure this alliance only strengthens."

"Princess Matilda isn't a child."

"What, exactly, is your problem with her?"

I flex my jaw. I could snitch—tell him she came onto me on my way here—but I bite my tongue instead. "This isn't our business. It never was. This is between Red River and Scarlett Thunder."

"Be it as it may, Lex is my brother. Our kingdoms are forged by family alliances. This is our business, plain and simple. One day, you'll be king, and your relationship with Cole and Matilda will matter. It's better you stay on her good side, possibly become her friend, Michael. She will be Queen of Scarlett Thunder one day, and you will want them as an ally."

He's not wrong. I just don't like it. Especially knowing how the princess feels about shifters.

"So, the girl," he says, barreling into the next topic, the most important one. "She's here?"

"She needs access to blood. My housekeeper, Emelda, insisted I bring her here, and I agreed. But this is Ravenfell business. The attack took place between our boundary with Hidesmith."

I explain what I know, which is very little. But just as I thought, Dad is uneasy about the idea of vampire on vampire violence.

"I want you to investigate this further."

"I plan to."

"And she doesn't remember anything?"

"Not even her name."

"But you believe she's blood-born?"

"Yes," I confirm, nodding. "Blood-born and possibly born of high rank. I don't think she belongs to our court, though. I'd recognize her."

Dad watches my face as I try to hide the memory of falling asleep with her tucked against my chest the other night. Emelda might have been right. I shouldn't let her feed from me again. It's complicating things. I should be wanting to find out who did this to her to ensure my own village–my people–are safe, not because I want to track this monster down and enact unspeakable violence on them for daring to touch her.

"Your mother is holding a ball in two weeks. I want things to go smoothly, with no threats of violence. I want this criminal caught by then."

"I'll make it happen."

He rises. So do I, realizing I'm being dismissed. But he says, "Michael, this ball… it's to celebrate the engagement of Cole and his bride… a compromise, I suppose, something to appease the King of Red River since the wedding will now be held in Scarlett Thunder against his original wishes. It will be an opportunity for you to find someone for yourself. We've invited all the vampire nobles we know– and their daughters."

I'm suddenly not as enthusiastic about the idea of an arranged marriage as I used to be. "Wonderful."

"If that's still your prerogative, of course."

"It's my only option," I counter.

"Well, I need to get back to discussing business with the emissary of Red River. Stay for dinner tonight, if you can. Your mother's been worried about you."

I see myself out, passing Aamon in the sitting room outside the office. He stands as I pass, bowing again. I resist the urge to roll my eyes as I step out into the hallway and try to gather my thoughts.

But then Emelda rushes toward me, smiling like mad. "She remembers her name! Michael, she remembers!"

12

WHO I AM

Faye

I'M SITTING AGAINST PLUSH PILLOWS FEELING LIKE MYSELF AGAIN, whoever that is. My memories are still hazy, but I'm starting to remember key things. My name is Faye. I'm twenty. I like to read, draw, and play the piano. I'm actually very good at playing piano. I like the color pink, even though it does nothing for my complexion.

I like to keep my hair braided. I like ribbons and other pretty, girly things. I like animals. I like going on long walks on foggy, rainy days.

I smooth my hands over the warm sheets and watch the rain pattering against the window, itching to throw on a coat and walk for miles, and miles, just to feel the slight burn in my legs.

I want Michael to come with me. He's the only thing taking up space in my head right now. Emelda said she was going to go get him, but it's been a while since she left me here, in this room, in Castle Graystone.

I'm happy I finally remember pieces of who I am, but the reason I'm here is still hazy. I know this isn't my home. I'm from somewhere else. Why am I here, though? There has to be a reason. People are looking for me, perhaps. Maybe I have a mother worrying over my whereabouts.

I press my knees to my chest and keep my eyes on the window. The door opens, Emelda slipping inside. She gives me an apologetic smile. "Faye," she says, smiling around my name. "Prince Michael had to return to Ravenfell, but he'll be back tomorrow."

"Oh." I try to hide my disappointment. "That's all right."

She edges into the room. "I'm going to stay with you tonight. I've already cleared it with the queen. Adam, the feeder from earlier, is going to send up more of his blood for you. If you need more, just ask. There's plenty. He's a very big, strong man, isn't he? I rather like him."

I purse my lips at the memory of the shifter I'd met roughly an hour ago. I'd refused to feed from him, but I drank his blood from a cup instead. All the while, he chatted with the maids fluttering around the room, laughing and carrying on easy conversation. Shifters are strange. Not in a bad way, but just... different. They're so warm, both in personality and the aura they radiate. They smell spiced and woodsy, like the outside world is laced in their very blood.

Emelda looks out the window with a frown before pulling the curtains closed, much to my disappointment. "Do you want something to do? A book, maybe?"

"Yeah, that'd be great."

"They have an amazing library here. What will it be? Romance? Adventure? Something boring and logical?" She wiggles her eyebrows at me.

"Romance, I think."

"I'll make it happen, but first, how are you feeling? What do you remember?"

"Nothing really," I admit. "It's coming back to me slowly."

"It's great you've remembered your name. I spoke to the physician, and she assured me you'd make a full recovery, and your memories will come flooding back. Michael wants to reunite you with your family as soon as possible."

I nod. "What will happen if–if you can't find them? I can't remember them."

"Then you'll stay… in Ravenfell, I'm sure. Michael doesn't like that you're here, honestly."

"Why not?"

"He can be rather territorial." She smiles, sitting on the edge of the bed. "It's a wolf thing, I think. What's his is his, and I think letting you feed from him might have triggered that feeling. He's not a very talkative man, truthfully, so I don't know if what I'm saying is remotely close to the truth."

"But you know him well?"

"I've known him for a long time." She nods as she looks down at her hands, flexing them, the narrow golden rings stacked on her fingers shimmering in the light of the crystal chandelier.

I rest my chin on my knees. "How did you meet?"

"I came to work for him at his manor when his father made him Duke of Ravenfell and gave him the village. No one had lived in the manor for a very long time. It needed a lot of work, and Michael was young, practically an infant by vampire standards. He was nineteen at the time, and that was… seven years ago. We became friends after a while. It was hard for him during those years. He was just coming into his wolf traits–shifting, especially. When he turns into a wolf, you know."

"I can't even picture it in my head."

"It's a trip, for sure, seeing it for the first time. I'm sure he'd show you if you ask."

I smile at the thought. "How is it possible that he's both a wolf and a vampire?" What I really want to ask is if he has fangs in his wolf form, but I digress.

"Well, that's a very good question and requires a long answer. The only thing that matters, that I feel I should make clear, is that…." She readjusts her position, tucking her legs beneath her. "Michael is a kind man, but he's a bit stern and coarse and often has a hard time erasing certain expressions from his face, so if you see him tomorrow, and he seems cross with you, it's only because he's worried. He's been stressing over you since you dropped into our lives."

"I'm sorry–"

"It's nothing to be sorry about," she amends, shaking her head. "Michael has a lot on his plate right now and seems determined to get you back to where you're supposed to be. For now, that's here at Graystone, until we can find your family. Then he'll have to find something else to distract him from–oh, never mind…"

"District himself from what?"

"Finding a wife, for one," she breathes, shaking her head. She clicks her tongue, obviously mulling the idea over in her head.

I can't help but feel a slight ache at the news. "A wife?"

"He needs a queen to rule beside him, eventually. His cousin, the Prince of Scarlett Thunder, was supposed to get married the same night you were found, actually. The bride was missing and then showed up the next morning acting like it wasn't that big of a deal that she missed her own wedding. Michael's been a bit of a mess the past couple of weeks, though. All the talk about Cole and his bride has put Michael under pressure to do the same–marry. Try to have a child, an heir."

The mention of a wedding spurs faint, fractured pieces of memory to come back together in the recesses of my mind. I sit up a little straighter and frown, rubbing my eyes as if that will clear my head.

"Are you all right?"

"I think–I think I was supposed to get married," I murmur, shock echoing through my system. "I think that's why I was… in a car."

"You were in a car?" she echoes, her brow pinching with suspicion.

"Yes. I remember watching the rain. I remember… the car stopping."

She rises from the bed. "I'll be back shortly… with that book, all right?" She hurries away, her back straight and shoulders rigid.

13

—————

TRUST

Michael

"Michael! MICHAEL!" Emelda's voice rips through the gloom just as I'm about to reach my front door. I'm in my wolf form, my dark brown, nearly black, coat dusted with beads of mist as I turn on the top step to look down at the vampire rushing in my direction. She's soaking wet and moving at the speed of light as she runs up the steps, coming to an abrupt stop.

She huffs several breaths before running a hand over her wet face and opening the door.

I stride in, shift back to my usual form, and cover myself with a robe before she's even closed the door behind her. "Michael, why did you leave the castle like that? After I told you she remembered her name?"

"Because that means she's getting better, and my services are better suited to finding out who did this to her rather than tending to her at her bedside." I breathe, adjusting the fit of the robe. "Why are you here? I thought you were staying with her?"

She shakes her head, sucking in a breath. "She remembers more things. I was just talking to her, and she said—she said she thinks… she thinks she might have traveled here in a car and that she was supposed to be getting married."

"Getting married?" I echo, not liking the sinking feeling in my chest.

"But I think she's confused, and that's why it was imperative I chased you down. I think she might have been traveling to Graystone, to the wedding, as a guest."

She follows me as I head upstairs to change into real clothes.

"This is great news, right? I wanted to make sure you knew," she continues, following me into my room.

"Do you want to watch me change? Is that why you're here?"

She glares, clearing her throat as she steps into the hallway, shutting the door behind her.

I quickly pull on pants and a long-sleeved shirt, something casual, since I don't think I'll be returning to the castle today. It's probably a good idea to put distance between myself and… Faye.

I whisper her name out loud, smiling around it. Faye suits her. It's a beautiful name—simple but elegant.

Emelda knocks on the door. "Are you dressed yet?"

"Come in," I sigh, sitting on the edge of the bed to pull on shoes as she strides inside, her hands on her hips.

"Anyway, I was thinking you could show her the guest list and see if any names ring a bell. She's probably on it, you know."

"We don't know her last name yet, do we?"

She shakes her head.

"I think it's more likely she's a daughter of a noble who attended the wedding," I say, but Emelda shakes her head again.

"No, because your parents would have heard about it by now if someone's child was missing, right? So, she must have been invited alone."

"My parents would have known who she was if that's the case."

Emelda frowns, tapping her foot. "So… she's not a wedding guest?"

Now, I'm shaking my head. "I don't think so. It seems too unlikely."

"Then she's engaged and her fiancé hasn't come looking for her yet? That seems unlikely to me, too."

"She's probably just confused. I'm sure she's been hearing lots of talk about the wedding in the castle." I rise and start walking to the door.

She follows. "Michael, she asked about you. She looked disappointed that you didn't come to see her again."

I pause in the doorframe.

"I think it'd be good for her to get out, maybe go for a walk."

"So, take her on a walk."

"I think you should do it. She trusts you. Maybe take her to the place where she was found, see if it rings any bells. Jogs new memories."

"You were telling me to stay away from her."

"I told you to stop letting her feed from you," she corrects.

I consider her words, bracing my hands on the doorframe and hanging my head for a moment. "Fine. I'll fetch her tomorrow. She can stay the night here tomorrow night. It'll probably be a long day."

"Great, I'll go back to the castle and let her know–"

"I would prefer you stay there with her for the time being," I interject, nodding to myself.

"I plan on it. I like her. She's a sweet little thing."

Yeah, she is, unfortunately for me. I can't stop thinking about her. It's a problem. I change the subject entirely, asking, "What's the name of the man who lives with your sister?"

"Lowe? Why?"

"He's a shifter?"

"Yeah, of course."

I scan Emelda's face. I've known her for years, but I've only spoken to her twin sister a few times. I don't even know for certain they are twins, but I know they've been vampires for decades now, and recently, her sister, Alma, started cohabitating with a man in the village. I don't know him, but I've noticed another wolf around. I've caught his scent in the fog when I go for my daily runs in my wolf form.

He's a full shifter, which means I could use his help when it comes to picking up scents, which is one shifter attribute I lack.

"Can you arrange for him to meet me here tomorrow morning?"

"Sure…why? Alma's pretty territorial about him."

I arch a brow. "I'm not going to bite him. I need his help with this investigation."

Her eyes brighten. "Of course. I'll go to her house before I go back to the castle."

She hurries past me, dipping under my arm.

I let out a sigh, feeling worn out and a bit overwhelmed. I pass Faye's old room and catch her scent—sweet and mellow. Soft and warm, like clean linen.

I can stay away from her. I can keep her at arm's length.

Even if I don't really want to.

But tomorrow, I plan on finding out exactly what happened to her and if she really is someone's fiancé.

Because I *hate* that idea.

14

A LONG WALK

Faye

EMELDA TUCKS MY HAND IN THE CROOK OF HER ELBOW AS WE WALK through the fog. It's drizzling, and the sky's a deep gray in the faint early morning sunlight peeking through the mist.

"Does it always rain like this here?" I ask, turning to Emelda. She smiles down at me, her face shielded by the hood of her crimson cloak.

"It does, honestly. There's a thunderstorm almost every night. I actually really enjoy it."

"Does it ever snow?"

"Sometimes." She smiles with a shrug. "Usually around the Winter Solstice. Queen Emory celebrates it–she goes all out. It's something both vampires and shifters honor. The longest night of the year," she smiles wistfully as we cut through the expansive royal gardens, edging around a row of rose bushes.

She shoves open a rusty, old wrought-iron gate and leads me through the woods, following a narrow, overgrown trail. I look behind us as the castle fades from view, sucked into the fog.

"What are these trails for?" I ask, clutching her arm as we pick our way over tree roots.

"These are wolf trails. Michael uses them all the time. His mother, too, I assume."

"I'd love to see him in his wolf form," I admit, blushing.

Emelda smirks at me, rolling her eyes to the canopy of trees overhead. "Of course, you would. He's not a cute little puppy, if that's what you're imagining."

"I honestly don't know what to expect. I can't remember ever seeing a shifter, especially in their wolf form."

"Well, you can't remember much of anything," she teases, and I smile. I can't help it. I like Emelda. She's easy company, and honestly, a riot. I only spent a few short days in Michael's house, but I know she runs it well, going as far as bossing the prince himself around. Still, her soft laughter fills the air as we reach the end of what must be a greenbelt, which fades to fields of... fog.

"Ravenfell is only a mile that way," she says, pointing through the fog like we can even remotely see through it.

"Where was I found exactly?" That's where we're going today. She came back to the castle in the early hours of the morning. I'd been awake, unable to sleep, and had been passing the night reading books some of the maids brought me from the expansive royal library. When she asked if I felt well enough for a walk into Ravenfell, I nearly jumped out of bed.

Now, my legs ache from lack of use, but the cool fog brushing over my skin is exhilarating. I needed this, even if it jogs memories that maybe are better off left forgotten.

"Pretty much smack dab in between Ravenfell and our closest neighboring village of Hidesmith." She clicks her tongue, steering us to the left. "Hidesmith is a bit of a madhouse, honestly. I don't like going there."

"How come?"

"Well, Ravenfell is a vampire village. There're a few shifters that live there with their vampire companions, and Prince Michael is the duke, of course, but Hidesmith is... well, it's a bit of both. Hidesmith has an Alpha in charge, a shifter, and the vampires that live there are a bit rough around the edges. It seems like the two groups that live within the village are constantly at odds. There was a skirmish between shifters and vampires at the inn in Hidesmith on the night of the wedding. We assumed you'd been a part of it when you were found."

"Was I?"

"I'm starting to think your situation was isolated." She frowns, her brows pinching together in thought.

It feels silly having to ask another person about the attack. I should remember. I should be able to see the face of whoever did this to me, but it's so hazy. I should remember why I feel like I belong to someone–a partner or a husband. At least, a fiancé. My mind is still a tangled nest of broken, hazy memories, but at least I'm well enough to be outside.

We walk for another twenty minutes before the sense that we're no longer alone jolts me back into awareness. Emelda smiles from ear to ear when a young vampire who looks strikingly like her waltzes up to us through the receding fog.

"Emmie," the woman grins.

"Alma. Thanks for coming." Emelda matches her grin.

I look between the two women, coming to the conclusion that they must be twins. Emelda is just a bit taller than her sister, but that's pretty much it.

A very tall man… a shifter, breaks through the fog. His hair is light red–a soft, coppery color that shines in the gray daylight as the fog rolls back, revealing the sweeping country and sleepy village directly below us at the bottom of a hill. Ravenfell is beautiful from up here.

"She told me I wasn't allowed to shift, that'd I'd scare your guest," he rasps, leaning down to kiss Emelda on each cheek.

I find that a little odd. He's a wolf, so he must be a feeder, right? So why is he knitting his fingers with Alma's and smiling down at her like she's the most beautiful thing he's ever seen?

But all three sets of eyes are on me now. My cheeks burn, but I smile nonetheless. "Hello," I squeak.

Emelda gives me her characteristic cat-like smirk and turns to her sister and her sister's… *companion*. That's what she meant by that word. This man is more than a feeder. He's her *lover*.

"Faye, this is Lowen."

"Lowe's fine." He smiles at me–his skin a warm gold, with pink, rosy cheeks. He looks warm, both in temperature and temperance. "I heard you really went through it recently."

"Uh, yeah. I suppose I did."

"Are you well now?" he asks.

The twins share a glance.

"I am," I reply, resisting the sudden urge to lick my lips. I'm not hungry, but I haven't had a drop of blood since early last night, and I don't want Alma to think I want to bite her boyfriend, so I smile at him, giving him a brief nod–a curtsy, like it's a tic of mine.

Emelda raises her brows. "That was a beautiful curtsy. See, this is why I think she's high-born."

"And blood-born, by the look of her," Alma adds, giving me a thorough once over.

"How–how can you tell?" I ask, and the sisters glance at each other again, sharing some private, internal conversation.

"These broads are very, very old," Lowe teases. "Don't let them make you nervous, all right?"

"We're not doing that, Lowe," Alma cuts in, playfully swatting his arm. Her eyes meet mine, soft and radiant. "Blood-born vampires are always very beautiful, that's all."

I open my mouth to ask how old the twins are, but another figure comes through the fog, and my slowly beating heart stops for just a glimmer of a second.

"Good morning," Michael says, his dark hair damp with mist. I watch him run his fingers through it, and suddenly I'm starving again.

For him.

"Are we ready to do this?" he asks, his eyes sweeping the group and holding on mine.

15

ANOTHER SHIFTER

Faye

"Lowe," Michael says, nodding in the shifter's direction in greeting. "I'm glad you were able to join us."

Lowe stretches his arms over his head, smiling into the pockets of bright sunlight poking through the clouds. "Miss a few minutes of sunlight? Absolutely not. When Alma told me I needed to help her and be a wolf for a day, I wasn't going to miss it for the world."

I rock on my heels while standing beside Emelda, watching the two men interact. Compared to a full-blooded shifter, I can finally see the similarities, and differences, Michael shares with their kind. Vampire men are tall. Michael is tall. His hair is a deep auburn that turns a radiant chestnut in the sunlight, which is exactly like the wolf queen, his mother.

But where Lowe's skin is a rich gold and radiates warmth, Michael is on the paler side. The sun casts his skin in shades of opal instead of pure, raw gold like Lowe.

He breathes–like Lowe. He gives off heat–like Lowe. I can hear his steady heartbeat as he steps beside me, still engrossed in conversation with the other shifter as he extends his arm to me.

He's warm—like a shifter would be.

My brain has a hard time differentiating what traits are vampire compared to shifter as he steps to my side, tucking my hand in the crook of his arm, and deftly raises the hood of my cloak to shield my face from the suddenly blinding morning sunlight.

"How long of a walk is it going to be?" Alma complains, frowning as she adjusts her hood. "It's so bright!"

"We have about ten minutes of this absolutely stunning weather," Lowe grins, winking at her. "Enjoy it while it lasts, sweetheart."

"I hate it." She grumbles but allows him to take her hand again, nonetheless.

"We didn't use to," Emelda remarks, pinching her sister on the ribs before skipping ahead of the group through the dewy grass, her footsteps creating a damp trail of silver through the bent green sprigs.

"It's a mile," Michael says after a moment, answering Alma's question.

Alma turns to us and frowns. "Why not shift then? And we'll catch up? We're so much faster than the two of you when we run, and you're still in your usual forms!"

Lowe turns to look at Michael, his brows raised in challenge. "Are you going to let her talk to you like that, Prince Michael?"

"Hey!" Alma laughs, swatting Lowe. "You're supposed to have my back!"

"Always, darling, but you're talking to two wolves right now."

I glance up at Michael and find him smiling as he watches Lowe and Alma lovingly bicker back and forth. I notice Emelda, Alma, and Lowe are walking a lot faster than we are, and within a few minutes, they're several yards ahead and nearly out of earshot as we reach the bottom of the hill and cross the road leading into Ravenfell.

We start walking up the next hill, watching the clouds roll back in, before Michael says anything to me at all. We reach the top of the hill, and I gasp in shock when Lowe takes off his shirt, turning back to look up at Michael as he raises a hand.

"What's he doing?" I ask, my cheeks burning red.

"He's, uh, he's getting ready to shift."

"But he's taking off his clothes?"

"I'm sure he wouldn't have if Alma hadn't said something about not doing his mending tonight," Michael chuckles.

I peer up at him. "You can hear their conversation from this far away?"

"Shifters have incredible hearing. I did inherit that trait."

I turn to face the opposite direction as Emelda's shouts of ridicule reach us as Lowe strips out of his pants.

Michael looks down at me with an innocent smile. "You've never seen a shifter, have you?"

"Just… just you, I think. And Lowe… twenty minutes ago."

He laughs again—a deep, gentle sound that sends a shiver of want licking up my spine. I love his voice. He's so soft and patient with me, but I imagine he can turn the deep tenor of his voice into something menacing when he needs to.

"He's about to shift, if you want to watch."

I turn even more pink, and he purses his lips, hiding a smile. "He's as naked as the day he was born, isn't he?"

"Yeah, but he'll be covered in fur in a few seconds."

"Are you going to shift?"

He looks ahead as a guttural howl breaks through the air, followed by Alma and Emelda yelling at Lowe for showing off.

"Yeah, I am. My senses are heightened in my wolf form."

"What kinds of senses do you need to use today?" I ask, trying not to look at his fingers as he begins untucking his shirt and undoing the buttons of his pants.

"Scent, mostly. Emelda told me you thought you might have been traveling in a car?"

I nod, but my attention is locked on him as he shrugs out of his shirt, his exquisitely muscled frame on full, delicious display. He's built like art. Like someone sculpted him from marble. His muscles gleam in the gray daylight as he crumples his shirt in his hand for a moment before extending it to me. "Can you hold on to my clothes for me?"

"Uh, sure," I croak, my voice breaking out of sheer nerves.

Michael's eyes search mine for a moment before he smiles to himself, shaking his head. "It's going to be fast."

"What will?"

"Shifting. You'll blink, and I'll be a wolf." He hesitates before sliding his pants down enough I can see his boxers and the sharp V of muscles leading too... I swallow hard. "Faye?"

"Hmm?" I murmur, meeting his eyes. I'm sure my face is as red as blood right now.

"I said not to be scared. It's still me but a wolf. I'm totally in control, and I won't hurt you."

"I trust you," I blurt, the words falling from my tongue.

He holds my gaze for several seconds as a warm smile spreads across his mouth. "All right. Ready?"

I close my eyes and brace myself like he's going to explode. He chuckles low in his throat, and I feel him place his pants in the pile of fabric I'm already balancing in my arms, then a soft rush of air ghosts over me, making my skin tingle.

I open one eye to a slit, then two, then look at him in all his glory.

16

NOTHING TO SEE HERE

Faye

A HUGE BROWN WOLF WITH JADE EYES PEERS DOWN AT ME. THE TOP OF
my head would brush against the underside of his shoulder. He's
just… massive, and I hadn't expected that.

I swallow hard, trembling, as I tilt my chin to meet his eyes.

"Oh." It's the only sound that could possibly leave my lips other
than a muffled scream. He tilts his head toward the receding fog in…
invitation, I think, to rejoin our group. "Can you–can you talk?"

He holds my gaze for a moment before giving me a wolfish shake
of his head. I accept this as a no and shrug, trying to gather my wits. I
tuck my shaking hands in the fabric of his clothing and walk beside
him until Emelda and Alma come into view, chattering and giggling
about the other impossibly large creature darting through the fog.
The second wolf–Lowe--slides to a stop on the wet grass before
lowering his head in Michael's direction, his ears perked up straight.
Michael goes still as Lowe kneels in a… playful position? I have no
idea what they're doing right now, but it's a whole lot of posturing.

"You better move out of the way!" Alma calls out with a laugh.

"Why?" I shout, then squeal, leaping out of the way as Lowe barrels toward Michael.

I scramble over the wet grass toward my... friends. Yeah, my friends, who welcome me with open arms as Michael and Lowe sparrolling through the wet grass and out of sight through the fog.

"Why are they doing that?" I gulp back my nerves, clutching Michael's clothes for dear life. I nearly jump out of my skin when the wolves appear again a few feet away, chasing each other. "Are they fighting for real?"

"No," Emelda chuckles.

Alma sighs, tucking Lowe's clothing under her arm. "Wolves are simple creatures–male wolves, especially so. They're playing."

"Playing?" I gape at the massive creatures as they dart back into view again, splitting the fog, then disappear into a tangle of fur and mist as they chase each other down another hill and out of sight.

"Michael needed this." Emelda sighs, a bit wistfully.

"So did Lowe. We should get our dogs together more often."

They laugh together, and I find my mouth twitching into a smile, but as we stand in the fog and watch the shifters... play... I find my mouth moving on its own accord, speaking without my permission, "Does Lowe work for you?" I ask Alma. I'm already under the impression they're a lot more than vampire and feeder... or vampire and house staff.

But for whatever reason, I want to hear the truth from Alma. I ignore the real reason why. The idea that a vampire and a shifter could be in love... could be partners in life....

My eyes set on Michael as he darts into view, tackling Lowe to the ground.

"Oh, no." Alma laughs as we start walking again. "I mean, it started that way. He used to come to my house to fix things, chop wood–"

"He chased away that vampire lord who had his sights set on you," Emelda reminds her with a nudge.

Alma frowns, giving her sister a cutting look. "I had that situation handled myself."

"Sure." Emelda snorts, giving her a second, harder nudge.

"Anyway," Alma huffs, turning to me with a smile, walking backward to face me. "Lowe and I have been together for a few years now."

"They're mates," Emelda croons, obviously teasing her sister.

But Alma blushes. "Vampires and shifters can't be mates, but Lowe calls me that, and I love it, thank you very much. I love him, and he marked me."

"Marked you?"

Emelda purses her lips, shooting her sister a warning glance, but Alma barrels forward, replying, "It's a thing shifters do to their mates. They bite us really hard, leaving a scar. It means we belong to them and them to us." She grins with pride, tugging the collar of her jacket down to show me the half-moon scar at the base of her neck.

Questions dance through my skull, but suddenly, Michael is beside me, panting, and Lowe trots into view beside Alma, licking her on the side of the face. She scoffs and shoves him away, saying, "You beast!"

He simply rests his chin on the top of her head for a few seconds before darting off again.

Michael gives me a nudge on the back of my neck before sprinting after Lowe.

Alma's eyes go hazy for a moment before she says, "They picked up a few scents they're going to check out. We're going to meet them on the road."

Emelda nods, but I'm confused. "How do you know?"

"Lowe told me," she shrugs, skipping ahead of us.

Emelda falls in step with me, saying in a low tone, "Vampires have telepathy. Shifters have something similar called the mind-link. Alma and Lowe communicate through the mind-link."

"But how? She's a vampire."

"Like she said, they're mates. He marked her, giving her that ability."

My mind swims, but Emelda gives me a little nudge. "Michael can explain everything to you, if you want to know. I'm sure he'd be happy to tell you all about his wolf side."

I nod, swallowing hard as I try to gather myself enough to think clearly.

We walk in silence the rest of the way, eventually meeting a fog covered road. It starts to rain–a haze, first, then heavy droplets that sting my cheeks. I tuck Michael's clothes in my cloak and raise my hood to try to keep my hair dry.

We eventually find the wolves, and Alma, about a quarter of a mile down the road.

Alma sighs as we reach her side, saying, "The rain is making it difficult for them to pick up the scents. They're going to call it a day."

"Already?" Emelda says, her voice dripping with disappointment as she glances at me. "Tell Lowe that Faye and Michael should stay for a while and explore. It might jog her memory."

I open my mouth to argue, but Alma conveys the message to Lowe. Within a few minutes, I'm standing beside Michael in the rain watching the vampire twins and the wolf walk back toward Ravenfell. Rain pelts us in cold sheets, but I look up at Michael.

"Well, I guess it's just the two of us." I'm not sure why my voice wobbles, or why I'm suddenly excited for this time alone, but Michael looks down at me, and I can see the relieved smile shining behind his eyes.

He tilts his head toward the rain-glazed road, toward the familiar trees hugging either side.

Time to remember what happened to me… I hope.

17

—————

A LITTLE ROOM

Michael

We stay in the rain for an hour. I walk ahead of Faye but turn to keep an eye on her as she picks her way off the road into an overgrown easement. I've lost the scent I was following with Lowe earlier. It was a vampire, for sure. A group, we believe. At least two females and a trio of males had been on this road at one point, outside of a vehicle, in a gathering.

But Faye's scent is long gone, making this trip pointless.

We reach the place she was found, and she stops, realizing it without me having to show her.

A few feet of brush have been beaten down, grass turned to mud. She stares down at the spot, her eyes wide and full of confusion. I can tell she's trying to remember, but can't, and it's killing her that she knows this spot and not the events that led her to being left here, nearly dead, and alone.

I shouldn't have brought her here. I hate the lost look in her eyes as she slowly looks up at me in defeat.

"I can't remember."

'*It's okay*,' I say in my head, to myself. She can't hear me. In my wolf form, I'm just a silent, looming beast beside her.

She jumps when lightning turns the sky an eerie blue. Thunder booms, and wind shakes the trees. I give her a nudge, and we're moving again, her hand gripping my fur as she tucks her chin to her chest to avoid her face being pelted by rain.

We're several miles from the castle and far enough away from my house in Ravenfell that I have to make a decision about finding shelter until the storm passes.

Thankfully, the inn is nearby, and I still need to investigate the area in the event her problems began there. Two birds, one stone.

She hesitates when we reach the inn, and I guide us to an outbuilding. She's soaking wet and nervous when I slip behind a stall meant for the few people who have horses and carriages instead of cars. I shift back to my human form and instantly regret it. It's freezing, and the sun is going down, causing the already chilly temperature to drop.

"Are you all right?" I ask, biting back the tremble in my voice from the cold as I extend my hand for my clothes. She passes them to me, turning away to give me privacy the stall already provides.

"I'm fine. Just cold."

"We're going to stay here until the storm passes," I assure her, making quick work of getting back into my clothes.

I hurry her inside the inn, which is busy and full of travelers stopping through to seek shelter from what's becoming an epic storm. The bar is full, and all the tables at the meager restaurant are taken. Just our luck.

"I need a room," I tell a young shifter woman behind the bar.

"We might have one left. I'll check," she assures me, scurrying off to inquire about it. I glare down the bar at a group of shifter men eyeing Faye with more interest than I think is appropriate, but she's standing owl-eyed, glancing around. It strikes me that she's the only vampire here right now, and everyone can tell.

I need to get her into a room as soon as possible. Then, I'll start interviewing the staff here about the fight that happened last week.

Finally, the shifter woman returns with a single key and an apology about the size of the room, but I'm beyond caring. I hurry Faye upstairs, down a narrow hallway, and into the very last room at the very end of the hallway.

I bustle her inside, closing and locking the door behind me. "You need to stay here–" I turn, and sigh with disappointment.

There's a full sized bed and a fireplace–that's it. There's barely room to pass her without brushing against her to reach the fire, which is burning to embers. She steps out of my way, her back hitting the door.

"I'm sorry, Faye," I breathe, crouching to stoke the fire enough to warm the room and hopefully dry her clothes. "I have some business to attend to here. I don't want you downstairs at all while I'm gone. We'll get out of here as soon as the storm passes."

"I'll be fine."

I rise and turn to her, noticing the soft smile touching her beautiful mouth. Our proximity is suddenly overwhelming, especially when the faint glow of the fire catches on her fangs. My skin prickles with a sudden need to have those fangs piercing my body.

"You should... take off your clothes," I say, then pale, quickly correcting myself, "so they can dry. I can–I can lay them out in front of the fire."

"Of course," she whispers, slipping out of her cloak and handing it to me. I look away as she slips out of her dress, fighting the urge to just watch her undress like I have any claim to her–her body. I allow myself a single glimpse of her as she sits on the bed and wraps a blanket around her shoulders, wearing nothing but her shift.

I stoke the fire a little more to distract myself before turning and heading for the door.

"Michael," she whispers.

I whirl toward her, feeling totally and completely unsteady. "Yeah? Are you hungry?"

She smiles slightly but shakes her head, much to my disappointment. "Not yet, but... thank you."

"For what?"

"Caring this much."

That breaks my heart. It shatters, honestly, as I hold her gaze and notice the lines of grief and stress around her eyes and mouth. "I'm going to find out who did this to you. I promise."

It takes all of my strength to slip out of the room.

Whatever this feeling is… this hold she has on me, it's becoming too much to bear. I need to keep my distance from her, especially if we're stuck in that little room together tonight.

18

WANT

Faye

I'M NOT SURE WHAT TO DO TO PASS THE TIME. DESPITE THE HEAT coming from the fireplace, I'm chilled. Rain pelts the window so furiously it sends a rapid pinging sound throughout the room, mingling with the crackling fire.

It's rather cozy when I sit in the single wooden chair near the fire, wrapped in my blanket, listening to the rain. Somewhere in my fractured memories, I remember liking the rain. Liking when storms rolled through… wherever I'm from.

Because she would be there to comfort me. The woman with soft hands and a gentle, beautiful voice. Instead of remembering her face, or her scent, I remember an ache that spreads through my chest.

I lost her at some point, I think. Whoever she is. She's not here anymore.

Tears sting my eyes on instinct. I blink them away, scooching closer to the fire, the chair squealing over the floorboards.

I nearly jump out of my skin when the door opens, and Michael returns with a dry robe and a… glass of blood.

His eyes catch the light of the fire–sparkling like polished jade. "I, uh, figured you might need something to tide you over until tomorrow, when I return you to the castle. The storm isn't going to let up soon, so we're going to have to stay the night."

I nod but make no move for the blood. I can already tell it's cold–probably stale and lifeless. Michael moves closer, draping the robe over the edge of the bed before crouching to stoke the fire again.

"Are you cold?" he asks.

"A little," I say through chattering teeth. He smiles softly in return, tossing another log on the fire. "Did you eat anything downstairs?"

"No, the food is terrible here, and I'm not really in the mood."

"Do you need blood like I do to survive?"

He nods, but then tilts his head to the side as he rises, dusting off his knees. "Yes, I do. But I also need to eat real food. Not often. Not often when it comes to blood, either. It's mostly just after I shift."

He is looking a little pale, actually. His skin has lost that warm, lively peach color in his cheeks. I turn my head toward the glass of blood on the table by the door–motioning toward it. "You should drink that."

"You need something, too. It's all they had."

"I'd rather have…fresh blood." Why is my body suddenly thrumming to life with warmth and excitement when our eyes meet?

His eyes grow wide for a moment before he blinks, clearing his throat. "I could… help with that."

I want to say that I'll be fine until morning–that what I'm asking of him is too much. But he's… addictive. His blood is like nothing I've ever tasted, and I burn for more, every second of every day.

It has nothing to do with hunger.

He holds my gaze as he starts unbuttoning his shirt, saying, "You weren't here the night of the fight. I asked around when I was downstairs." He pulls his shirt off, his heavily muscled frame glinting in the firelight. He's all warmth and… life. He smells divine–like the rain-soaked forest, like the air as a fresh storm rolls in. I stand, turning to face him, my blanket falling from my body.

I can hear his heartbeat as I close the distance between us, laying a trembling hand on his chest.

I feel... strange. My skin tingles where my fingers meet his skin. I can feel his steady heartbeat under my hand, but it skips beats, thumping erratically as I slowly look into his eyes.

His scent overpowers my senses. Alarm bells whirl through my skull, telling me to tread lightly, to ignore the feeling of desperation and blind lust causing my knees to weaken and my core to turn molten.

I want more than his blood. I want his body. I want his heart.

My lips part in a strangled gasp as those tingles work up my arm and erupt through my chest. I pull my hand away, but he grabs my wrist, a wild, dark look flaring behind his eyes as his pupils expand, stealing the jade-green I've come to love.

"What was that?" I ask with a weak voice. "That feeling?"

I think Michael might be beyond words. He leans down. I close my eyes as his lips gently–tenderly–brush against mine.

My world spins on its axis... but he pulls away, breathlessly taking my hand and guiding me to the bed. He sits, offering me his wrist, but I'm... lost in a haze I can't find my way out of. My vampiric instincts take over, blinding me to action. I straddle him, lifting up on my knees to look down at him, caressing his face as I lower my mouth to his.

His hands hold my waist, nothing but my thin shift separating his heated touch from my skin. I kiss him, and it feels like we've been doing this forever–that my body knows him in a way that's now ingrained in my soul. He kisses me back, his hands rising up my sides, toward my breasts, my nipples hardening under his warmth.

He lets out a muted groan when I grind my hips against his. "Faye–what are we doing?"

"I don't care," I murmur, and then his mouth is on mine–hot, wet, and starving for *me*.

He flips me onto my back, covering me with his body, his knee resting between my legs while one hand kneads my breast and the other cups the back of my head.

His heat radiates between us, warming me to the bone, but I can feel that ache in my fangs–that need for his blood.

Only his blood. It's the only blood I want. I crave it. I crave him.

He lowers himself onto the bed beside me, pulling me against his chest, and tilts his neck to the side.

"Drink," he rasps, his eyes heavy and dark with need.

19

A HUNGER

Faye

I KNOW WE SHOULDN'T BE DOING THIS… OUR BODIES FLUSH AND MY LIPS grazing his fevered neck. His hybrid heart thunders against my breasts and I'm… trying desperately not to writhe against him, chasing friction I shouldn't want–shouldn't *need*.

I almost wish he were still wearing a shirt so my fingers had something to grab instead of lying flat against his bare skin. I grip his shoulder, my other hand resting on the back of his neck as I lift my head to press a kiss to his neck, tender and… sweet.

Now is my chance to back out–to tell him I don't need this–need him to fulfill this desire for blood but *I am hungry*.

Hungry for his touch, the little groan that leaves his lips when I bite down on the crook of his neck, the sound that haunts my dreams.

He's on top of me, gathering his arms around me so I can't move. One of his knees splits my legs apart, his thigh sliding toward my center and putting delicious pressure on a part of my anatomy that makes my entire body sizzle to life.

Michael makes that sound I love. I fill my mouth with his blood and swallow, moaning around the heat of his blood as it slides down my throat and sends my slow, tender heart beating erratically. I'm being greedy. I want more. So, so much more. I arch my hips, chasing the pressure his thigh has pressed to my clit, grinding against him as I take another drink, another swallow.

One of his hands slides down my back when my fingers tangle in his hair and tug to give me better, deeper access to the delicious vein in his neck. His hand leaves my back, roving over my hip and then begins to bunch the fabric of my shift up over my legs.

The chilly bite in the air, not quite staunched by the roaring fireplace, tickles over my thin tights and my… nakedness beneath.

Michael blows out his breath—a hungry, entirely male sound of satisfaction ghosting over my skin as his hand grips my thigh and moves… upward.

I release his neck, my eyes glazed as my head rolls back. His finger brushes over my drenched folds, sending a thrum of white-hot desire ripping through my core, my lower belly. I'm all heat. All overwhelming, greedy, mouth-watering heat.

"You're so wet for me," he rasps, his pupils still the size of tea-saucers, like his wolf has taken over completely, and it wants *me*. "Feeding from me… it turns you on, doesn't it?"

I can't do more than whimper with longing as a single finger splits my folds, drawing a lazy line from base to clit.

I'm not sure if I've been with a man before. I would remember that, wouldn't I? All I know is that my body is begging for this, especially when he flattens his hand over my sex and drags his thumb through the pooling desire soaking my inner thighs. He draws circles over my clit, his eyes scanning my face as I let go of a needy moan, arching into his touch.

"You're beautiful when you feed," he breathes, holding my gaze as my body throbs for him.

His lips part as he slides two fingers inside me, his eyes darkening with desire.

I gasp as he splits his fingers, stretching me. The feeling is overwhelming and unreal. "M-Michael!"

He jerks his fingers, his thumb still circling my clit and I'm... undone.

He pressed a wet kiss to my lips, his tongue sliding over mine in time with the motion of his thumb. I lift into his touch, grinding and writhing while my body practically bursts into flames. Tension coils in my thighs, begging for a release I'm not sure exists, but whatever's happening to me right now feels so incredibly, impossibly, divine.

He roughly kisses along my jaw, then my neck, dragging his teeth over my skin until he reaches my breasts. He gives them animalistic attention, drawing my nipples into his mouth one at a time, sucking hard, nibbling... leaving a trail in his wake.

His hot, hungry mouth travels down my belly, his tongue stroking and tasting all the way down to my core, where it suddenly replaces his fingers.

"Michael!" I cry out, arching my neck and gasping toward the ceiling as his mouth covers my sex and *feasts*.

He pushes my legs apart, groaning and growling against my skin, his tongue lapping exquisite circles that have my breath coming in shallow gasps.

He hooks his arms under my legs, dragging me down the bed, arching me off the mattress so I'm totally, completely, at the will of his tongue.

"You taste–" he growls, looking into my eyes as his tongue sweeps through my folds, "Amazing."

My entire body gives in. A bright shimmer of unreal, unending pleasure soars through my center, fanning through my tense muscles and sending my body into a spasm.

I lock my thighs on either side of his head, screaming toward the ceiling as the pleasure edges on too much. I can barely breathe through it. I whimper, shaking as he keeps sucking, licking, and nibbling my clit.

I thought I was hungry for his blood. I thought I needed it, that I'd die without it. But this... I'd die without this, without *him*.

He presses wet, hot kisses to my inner thigh before pulling out, lost for breath.

He wipes his hand on the back of his mouth, but his eyes never leave my face. My hooded gaze leaves his, however, to greedily sweep over his body, landing on the hard, thick cock straining against his pants.

I'm still hungry.

He starts to slide off the bed, but I sit up, grabbing him by the back of the neck. I lay a trembling hand on his chest, sliding it down until I'm cupping him, feeling the heat and desperate need coming from him.

His eyes meet mine, curious and… waiting. He won't do this, I realize, unless I tell him I want him.

In answer to his silent question, I glide the heel of my hand up his length. His lips part in a silent groan.

"Come back to me," I order, my voice low and sultry, barely above a rasp.

I release the button, then his zipper.

20

COME UNDONE

Faye

PRINCE MICHAEL WATCHES AS I HOOK MY THUMBS IN THE WAIST OF HIS pants and try to pull them down. He gently presses his hand against my chest and pushes me back onto the bed, kneeling over my legs. He makes quick work of taking off his pants and his boxers until he's... fully naked and... in his full glory.

A tremor of doubt courses through my veins as my gaze sweeps over his body. He's pure art. He makes my mouth water, but when my gaze travels down to his cock...

He's enormous. Beautiful, lengthy, and wide, and I'm....

Any lingering doubt turns molten when he grips my shift between his fists and rips it open. I gasp, my chest rising and falling in a sharp exhale that rattles through my soul as his hands grope my breasts, his eyes heavy and dark as they sweep over my fully naked skin.

His wolf takes over again. I can sense the shift in his body, his mind. That animalistic hunger replaces the heat in his eyes as he roughly nudges my legs apart with his knee, gripping the underside of my left thigh to spread my legs even further apart, and I'm... desperate. Aching, almost painful desire floods my body again, my breath coming in quick, shallow rasps that fill the room.

He grips his cock, sliding the head through my folds, his eyes locked on mine the entire time he teases me.

My skin flushes with heat. His blood echoes through my system, filling me with a bright warmth that makes my desire for him flare to unreal heights.

"Does it–" I breathe, my eyes fluttering as he presses his cock through my folds, testing, "does it feel like this with everyone? Every time?"

He must understand what I'm trying to say. That we fit together. Not just our bodies… but this desire? This feeling like his body is made for mine?

"No," he whispers, his face contorted in pleasure as his cock splits through my folds and presses inside me, stretching to the point of near pain. "No, it doesn't. You're… fucking perfect." He groans loudly, not even considering holding back, and presses his cock further, deeper.

I arch into the sensation of his dick stretching me. The pain gives way to a fullness that has a pitched, hungry moan leaving my lips.

"You're so tight," he groans, rolling his neck and shuddering as he grips my hips and pulls me toward him.

He lowers himself on top of me, gathering me in his arms and kissing me hard, his tongue chasing mine as he continues to ease into me, taking his time.

"You've never been with anyone before," he says against my lips in a low growl. Something like pride shines behind his words.

I haven't. I know that with sudden startling clarity. Relief skitters through me, which surprises me. I want him to be my first–my *only*. My mind, body, and heart are at odds as his hand slides down my body to grip my thigh again, moving my legs apart even wider and giving him the access he needs to thrust deep.

The pain is brief and delicious. I suck in a breath, letting it out in a shattering moan that bounces around the room, cutting through the rain and crackling embers.

The feeling of him inside of me is overwhelming. My fingers tangle in his hair, his nose pressed to mine as he grinds into me, moving his hips in a mix of rolling thrusts and circles that have stars lighting behind my eyes. I'm whimpering. The noises leaving my lips are pleading and whiny, begging him for more.

He slams a hand against the pillow behind my head and squeezes hard, grimacing as he growls with pure, male satisfaction.

"You feel incredible," he rasps, kissing me again, and again, "you're squeezing me so tight—*fuck*!" The groan that leaves his mouth sends glimmers of pleasure coasting through my entire body. My heart beats erratically as my pleasure begins to peak.

We move like water—natural and easy, like we've done this together a thousand times. I arch into his hips, meeting him thrust for thrust, my brain focusing less on his voice, his showered praise, and more on the way he's making me feel.

"You're going to come," he rasps against my ear, smiling around the words. "I can feel it. Don't hold back. I love the little sounds you make, Faye. I'll dream about them later."

"Oh—" I squeeze my eyes shut as pleasure that shouldn't be real tightens and erupts through my core and lower belly, fanning through my thighs. I tremble, moaning and whimpering as I clutch his shoulder and wrap my legs around his waist.

"Good girl," he pants, his movements suddenly erratic. He slams into me so hard the headboard knocks against the wall. He kisses me again, long and hungry, and jerks into me twice more before pinning me against the bed, gripping my hips as he comes completely, utterly unglued.

Warmth spreads through my lower belly as he spills himself inside me.

He slowly pulls out, then presses back in, his body glazed in sweat. I'm breathless as I cup his cheek, then trail my fingers over his jaw, up to his ear, tucking his wild dark curls behind it.

Echoes of pleasure leave me totally boneless. He looks down at me, his eyes still dark with desire and another emotion I feel like I should remember… something tender and deep. Something I want to remember forever.

Love?

I couldn't be that lucky, could I?

He kisses gently, but he's trembling as much as I am when he finally pulls out and lies beside me. I watch the firelight dance over the ceiling, taking deep breath, after deep breath.

My brain returns, unthawing. Reality crashes down on me the same moment it happens for Michael, who briefly stills beside me.

We've complicated everything, haven't we? He's a prince and I have… no idea who I am.

Where could this possibly go?

"Faye," he whispers.

I slowly turn my head, blinking, thankful he's still there when I open my eyes.

"I want you to come live in my house again. I want you to stay. Maybe that's… reckless, but… I feel like…"

I grab his hand, pressing a trembling kiss to his knuckles. "I want to stay with you."

He nods, his eyes heavy and dreamlike as his wolf lets him go and the vampire side of him returns. The calculated side. The side that makes his skin grow cold and his eyes brighten with thoughts I'm sure are full of contradictions.

We say nothing further because of what there is to say, the questions plaguing us both… I doubt either of us wants to voice them. Instead, he pulls me close, curling his body around mine in the warm haze of the firelight and calming patter of rain… where I fall asleep, feeling safe and guarded…

For the first time in my life. At least, the first time I remember.

21

I KNOW THAT SMILE

Faye

THE NEXT MORNING, I WAKE UP ALONE IN THE LITTLE INN ROOM. SOFT gray daylight filters through the curtains, illuminating the rumpled sheets on the bed and my clothing from yesterday still hanging near the fireplace.

I blink into the shadows, rubbing my eyes as a figure appears to my left, pulling on a jacket.

"We need to get back to the castle," Michael says under his breath, his eyes locked on his fingers as he adjusts his coat. They raise to meet mine–the softest shade of jade. "I'm going to–figure some things out before you return to Ravenfell."

I nod because that's all I can do for the moment. The memories of last night are still fresh, still real and all-consuming, as I watch him walk around the room, gathering my now dry clothes. The pinch of soreness between my legs is a stark reminder of what we've done, and the fact we can't go back to the way things were before, but the tension between us is thick in air that's scented like us. I slide out of bed, letting my torn shift fall back over my thighs.

Michael's eyes darken as they sweep my body. He clutches my coat until his knuckles turn white, but slowly turns away, giving me a minute of privacy to dress.

Wordlessly, we turn for the door, but we both hesitate, neither of us ready to cross the threshold into reality... not yet.

"I'll take care of everything," he assures me... or himself.

"I know," I whisper, reaching out to touch him, to lace my fingers around his forearm. Touching him again... it sends a jolt whizzing over my skin. That same overwhelming desire that plagued me all night returns in full force, making my clothes suddenly too tight, too hot.

I look into his eyes and see the same desire–something deep. Something unnatural. Or, just maybe, this is the most natural thing of all, and we've both been denying ourselves of it.

One moment, his hand is gripping the door handle, and the next, his mouth is on mine.

I stifle a moan as he leans into the kiss, caging me in against the door. His mouth awakens my whole body, and I melt into him, my knees going slack and my heart begging me to let him lead me to the bed.

But he pulls away, breathless, and opens the door. He grips my fingers, his eyes holding mine, and leads me into the hallway–into real life.

The journey back to the castle is mostly silent. I carry his clothes like the day before while he lumbers in his wolf form, his ears ticking toward every sound in the unforgiving mist. Hidesmith falls away, and so does the road where I was found–left for dead. As we cross the hilly pastures between Ravenfell and the castle's territory, I let my mind wander, reeling over the memories I haven't found continue to shatter, and piece together what I can.

The feelings of despair and rejection I'd felt when my memories started returning have faded to something bright and warm–acceptance. The idea that I wasn't left for dead, not totally. I was left and given a chance at a better life, a life full of love and friendship... of the warmth and safety of this shifter–vampire hybrid man stalking at my side, my fingers warmed to the bone and tangled in his dark fur.

We near the castle and go about a routine I'm sure I'll take part in often. Michael shifts. I hold out his clothes. But instead of covering himself or stepping into the shelter of one of the many outbuildings scattered around the exterior wall of the castle, he holds my gaze and smirks, stark naked in the gray fog.

I ignore the blush creeping across my cheeks, rolling my eyes to the sky, but his smirk grows wider, and deeper.

"You're enjoying this too much," I gripe.

He arches a brow. "I think you're the one enjoying it."

"Aren't you getting cold?"

"We can warm up later," he says, pulling on his pants and donning his shirt. He slips his feet into socks and his boots and then we're off again, his fingers sliding into mine during the short walk around the towering, slightly overwhelming and impossibly grand main entrance.

But once we reach a smaller, shadowed servants' entrance, he lets go of my fingers and rests my hand in the crook of his elbow instead.

The warmth of the castle radiates around us. Maids scurry, busy with their daily chores. Male servants rush around with messages, and a few warriors linger in a common space used for their meals.

A faint memory of my past life trickles into my mind. A dark castle. Fearful, silent maids. Words spoken barely above a whisper.

But here, the air is full of chatter and laughter that fades to nothing but our footsteps as Michael guides us into the castle proper and to my room.

But another sense sprints to the surface, making me stop in my tracks. Unease ripples over my skin as a tall, lithe woman with platinum blonde hair appears around a corner, her glossy crimson gown rippling like liquid blood as she spots us and turns.

Her hair falls straight down her back, glimmering in the amber-hued lighting spilling down the corridor we're all standing in...

"Prince Michael?" she says with a glimmer of shock in her pitched voice.

"Fuck," Michael murmurs under his breath as she walks toward us, slowing her pace as if in caution.

Her icy, ocean blue eyes sweep over Michael's profile with cat-like affection before she notices me. Her eyes narrow sharply. Her chest rises and falls. I notice the way she tucks her hands behind her back, balling them into fists. "What's the meaning of this? The maids are supposed to be preparing for my engagement party this weekend!" She glares at me, snapping her fingers. "Get back to work!"

"First of all, Matilda," Michael cuts in, his voice dripping with malice, "you have no authority over the staff in this court. Secondly, she is not a maid. She is my guest."

"Your guest?" Matilda glances between us, her cheeks losing what little color they held. Something about the look in her eyes gives me pause. She's... familiar. Familiar in a way I'm desperately trying to place. She opens her thin mouth again in what can only be described as the beginnings of a snarl when a very tall, lean vampire waltzes around a corner and immediately tries to retreat when he sees her.

"Cole," Michael says loudly.

"Shit," Cole says audibly, licking his lips and grimacing as Matilda whirls toward him. "Darling, I didn't see you there."

She rolls her eyes at his sarcastic tone and spins back to me and Michael. "The queen didn't mention that you were bringing a guest to my party."

"Our party," Cole corrects grimly but gives me a half-cocked smile. "Any friend of Michael is a friend of ours. Isn't that right, sweetheart?"

Matilda glares furiously before scoffing and stalking off, but I notice her stop a good distance away, giving me a look that has ice skittering through my veins. The slight lift of her lips–her smirk–works its way through my body, sending alarm bells blaring through my skull.

Why do I know her? Why did her proximity immediately make me feel on edge?

22

AN ALLY?

Faye

"WHAT ARE YOU DOING HERE? I THOUGHT YOU RETURNED TO SCARLETT Thunder?" Michael gives Cole a skeptical look, but Cole rolls his eyes, crossing his arms over his broad chest.

His dark hair catches the light and gleams as he replies, "My mother thought it would be best to return a few days before the big party to get to know my fiancée," Cole grumbles, tapping his fingers on his elbow as he stares down at me.

I feel a sudden urge to shrink against Michael under his gaze.

"You're looking well."

I'm not sure what to say, so I say nothing, leaning further against Michael instead. Cole smirks, rolling his eyes back to Michael with an arch of his brow.

Michael narrows his eyes, having some internal conversation with Cole, then nudges me forward.

Over his shoulder, he says, "Keep a tight leash on your bride, okay?"

"Better yet," Cole drawls with a laugh, "I'll keep her muzzled."

Cole's footsteps recede in the opposite direction as Michael hurries me toward my room. I bite back the urge to ask him what all that was about, deciding it's probably best if I don't get involved. Still, my body locks up at the memory of Matilda, especially as Michael opens my bedroom door and says, "Emelda is on her way from Ravenfell to fetch you. You'll be staying there from now on while I sort all of this out."

"All of what, exactly?" The air in the room shifts, and whatever warmth and comfort we've been sharing recently goes stale.

I regret the question immediately because I can tell Michael doesn't have an answer. Emelda told me he was in the market for a wife.

Is that… going to be me?

Or am I what he just told Matilda I am? His guest?

Before my mind can settle on the worst possibilities–like I'm nothing more than a pretty plaything to warm his bed–Michael strides toward me, clutching my arms and kissing me tenderly on the forehead. His warmth floods my body, chipping away at the ice. "I'll see you tonight, at home, and we'll talk."

"Okay."

I watch him walk away before sinking to the edge of the finely crafted bed in this beautiful castle.

Only a few minutes after Michael takes his leave, however, the door opens again. Instead of Emelda casting her light and friendship through the room, Matilda appears, gripping the doorframe before entering and shutting it firmly behind her.

I stiffen, paralyzed, as she skirts the edge of the room, running her fingertips over the fine furnishings. "So, you're Prince Michael's *guest*. Is that right?"

"Is there something I can help you with?" I ask, my voice wobbling. The door opens again, revealing a trio of maids I don't recognize. Two of them stand by the door while the other carries a tray with a carafe of fresh blood, still steaming, and two empty wine glasses.

"I'm just making a point to introduce myself to everyone in this court," Matilda says, motioning for the maid to set the tray down on a nearby table. "Guests included." She smirks around the word guest. "It must be so… degrading, doing what you do."

"What?"

Matilda motions for the maid to leave, and she does, taking her comrades with her. Closed in alone again with the icy vampire woman, I maintain my position at the end of the bed, praying Emelda gets here soon.

"Well, warming Prince Michael's bed, of course. You smell like him. My guess is that he was between those pretty little legs last night, wasn't he? Sore are you, guest? Surely a professional would be better at hiding that instead of limping around with him on your arm." She chuckles as she pours two glasses of blood. "Seeing as you have your own room here, you must be rather good at what you do. Tell me, does Cole come for your services, as well? I'm terribly curious about how well-endowed my soon-to-be husband is–"

"You have no idea what you're talking about."

"What's your name?" she asks, thrusting the glass at me.

"Faye."

"Lovely. Drink this. You look exceedingly pale."

My hand curls around the glass just to stop it from dropping. The blood smells rich and sweet, and the scent of it curls through my body, igniting the hunger I hadn't realized was coasting through my veins. I take a small sip, watching as she pours herself a glass but doesn't bring it to her lips.

"I'm not–I'm not here to service Prince Michael."

"Then why are you here?" she asks pointedly, that odd look shining behind her eyes again.

"I–I don't know."

"Ah," Matilda says, pacing the room with her blood. "So, you're the sickly little thing the royal family has been all in an uproar about lately. You really can't remember a thing?"

I shake my head, noticing the slight smile touching her lips.

"How terrible," she sighs dramatically, setting her glass back on the tray, untouched. "I apologize for my earlier assumptions. I'm rather…

out of sorts myself. Torn from my homeland to marry a devilish prince who wants to fuck anything that moves... except for me, of course."

I take another sip of blood. She watches the movement, smiling to herself.

"Us girls need to stick together here, don't we?" she continues, walking toward me. "We're safer that way. You never know who you can trust, especially in a place that's not our home." She tilts the glass back, forcing me to take an even larger drink than I needed, but her eyes... I can't stop looking into her eyes.

"I know you," I whisper, feeling suddenly... hazy.

"You don't," she whispers back, clicking her tongue. "Goodnight, little one. For real, this time."

2 3

***

FATED MATES

Michael

I find my mom out in the garden. I had a feeling she'd be here, surrounded by petals and green plants–things that keep her grounded to the nature shifters crave. She's kneeling, deftly pulling up weeds–or something. She straightens and lifts her head as I approach, reveling in her smile.

"When did you get here?" she asks, wiping her hands on her apron.

I don't ask why she's kneeling in the dirt, surrounded by fog. I also don't mention that she could easily have the maids tend to her garden–which is full of flowers and herbs.

This has become her hobby, especially during the rare moments of warm sunlight that break through the fog.

"A few minutes ago," I answer, watching as she takes off her apron and hangs it over her arm. I squint at the sky, noticing the rain clouds moving in.

She follows my gaze and sighs, clicking her tongue. "Another rainy day, I'm afraid. Soon, it'll be snow. I was just gathering the last of my herbs. I thought you were out investigating in Hidesmith?"

95

"I came back with Faye. I didn't find anything of substance, and she doesn't really remember what happened before she was found, so we called it a loss."

I walk side by side with Mom through her tidy garden as the first droplets of rain fall from the sky. "She's a nice girl, isn't she? I've been going through the guest list for Cole's wedding and haven't been able to place her at all."

"I didn't think you would," I reply, opening the door to the greenhouse for her. She steps inside, and we're immediately doused in warm, humid air. She's been in here most of the day, I assume, judging by the stacks of herb bundles gathered on her worktable and the last of her summer flowers sitting in vases.

"Do you think anyone's looking for her?" she asks lightly, hanging up her apron.

"I… I want to think so, but it's been quite some time now, and no one has come forward to claim her." Which is why I'm here now, toying with my hands and trying to gather my thoughts enough to tell my mother I'm the one claiming Faye. "Is it hard being bound to a vampire?" The words fall out of me before I can stop them.

She sighs, moving toward her workbench where she keeps her hands busy by winding twine around the herbs. "Your father is my mate, Michael."

"I understand that." I sit on a nearby stool. "But he can't feel for you what you feel for him."

"That's because what we're able to feel is biological," she explains, not meeting my eye. "It's something we're born with that ignites when the Goddess sees fit to give us that gift. Your father is my mate, whether he can feel it or not. I accepted long ago that, while he loves me, I will always love him… a little more." She turns to me, giving me a weak smile. "Because I'm a wolf, and we mate for life. He's a vampire, and his life is… too long for that."

The pain in her eyes makes my stomach curl with sudden sadness. I grew up surrounded by love. I was raised by parents who not only loved me, but loved each other in a way that now, as an adult, seems impossibly rare.

"Dad doesn't like to talk about this," I murmur, looking down at my hands as I curl them into fists.

"Because your father has... a few decades with me left, if we're blessed by the Goddess in that way." She leans her hip against the workbench. "That's the folly in being a vampire and loving a shifter. Their time with us is short–a blink of an eye, honestly. He knew our time was limited from the beginning."

"Yet he still chose to be with you," I say, more to myself than to her.

I can feel her gaze boring holes in my profile but refuse to look at her when she asks, "What is this about, Michael?"

"Faye," I whisper, running my tongue along the edge of my upper teeth. "I think I might–might feel something for her that goes beyond attraction." I slowly look at my mom, hating the excitement and relief sweeping across her features.

"Your mate?"

I haven't allowed myself to accept the fact that yes, I'm almost sure that's what I feel, but it's tricky, isn't it, being mated to a vampire?

If she were a wolf, this would be far less complicated. We would have simply looked at each other and known, but this....

"I'm going to bring her back to Ravenfell with me today. You likely won't see me until your ball this weekend. I need some time to figure this out."

She nods, but her mouth is a tight line as I rise from the stool. "Michael–"

"I'll keep you updated on my decision, but don't tell Dad yet. Seeing as this is... I need to marry someone who can be queen–"

"You don't think she can feel the same way you feel?"

I stop in my tracks as my mom voices the feeling that's been plaguing me from the moment I woke up this morning with Faye in my arms. The moment I felt my mortality for the first time.

"You're a vampire as much as you're a shifter," Mom says slowly. "What your father and I went through... it'll be different for you."

"You don't know that yet."

"You're only just past the age of maturity for vampires," she presses. "You could stop aging, and then we'd know. You and your mate could have a very long life together—"

"Your Highness!" A maid comes screeching into the greenhouse, nearly missing the glass entrance and flattening herself against the door. Her face washes of color as she storms inside, panting and motioning to the castle.

"My Goddess, what's the matter, Hildy?" Mom gasps, rushing to the maid's side. "Are you all right?"

Hildy, one of the senior maids, grips my mom's arms. "The vampire girl—Miss Faye—she's terribly sick. She's—she's—"

I push past both women and sprint into the castle.

24

PASSED OVER

Six Weeks Ago

Faye

My slippers pad across the pale marble tiles. I hike up my dress—pink, just like the slippers I spent hours upon hours embroidering with little stars and white flowers. My hair fans out around my shoulders and down my back in my haste to reach my father's office. Cara, my lady's maid, scurries behind me, puffing her breath as she tries to keep up with my rapid footsteps.

I come to a stop, swipe the wrinkles from my dress, and gently knock on his office door.

Several seconds pass before my father's voice echoes toward me, saying, "Come in."

Father rises from behind his desk as I enter, leaving Cara in the hallway.

"You wanted to see me?" I ask, edging toward his desk.

Father's gaze sweeps over me from head to toe before he says, "The time has come that you marry."

I hang my head, knitting my fingers behind my back. I know better than to speak right now. It's useless to ask who I'm going to be marrying. Father has had this planned out since before I was born.

"Long ago, I made a deal with the King of Scarlet Thunder," he begins, pacing away from his desk. "That his son, Prince Cole, would marry one of my daughters. That daughter is you."

I furrow my brows and look up at him. "But–Matilda–she's older."

"Matilda is out of control, and you're higher born, anyway," he says with a wave of his hand. "It's done. You'll leave for Crimson Peak in two days."

I startle, unsure I heard him correctly. "Crimson Peak? But–"

"The wedding will be held there, under the direction of King Kane. It's done." He gives me his back, motioning with his hand to dismiss me.

I'm used to his coldness, but it weighs on me as I leave his office, unsure what's going to happen next. Cara waits for me dutifully, her eyes wide as they search my face. "Miss, are you all right?"

I sniff back my tears and give her a soft smile, praying the pain doesn't show on my face. "I'm going to take a walk… alone."

Cara nods as I whirl away, walking briskly down the corridor. I keep my mind totally blank until I reach a side door leading outside, to the sweeping, rolling hills and dilapidated outbuildings surrounding the castle.

Once, there were gardens here. Father let them wither to nothing in the wake of my mother's death fifteen years ago. What was once a field of tulips and poppies is now nothing but fog and upturned earth, the memories of the gardens fading just like the memory of my mother's face.

I've been told I look like her. That she had the same golden hair, the same sweet voice and quiet disposition. I often wonder if I inherited anything from my father. I have none of his coldness. I have none of his bloodlust or desire to kill, and expand, and kill some more.

Maybe this marriage isn't a bad thing. It's the start of a new life somewhere else, where I might be surrounded by... by love.

I push through a rusted wrought-iron gate and stumble into the cemetery.

There're very few headstones. I follow a stone path overgrown with dead grass leading to the royal tomb where my ancestors are buried—a huge, gray building covered in moss—neglected.

I step inside, sniffling, and walk the narrow corridor to the very end before stopping in front of the tomb of my mother.

She was twenty-five when she died. That's so incredibly young for a blood-born vampire. Her life had been a speck in comparison to my father's life.

I smooth my hand over her coffin—white marble marred by age. I'm the only one who comes here; I know that much. I'm the only one who sweeps the floors and cleans the dust from her resting place.

"I'm getting married," I say into the silence. "I think it'll be good. I can leave this place, just like you said I would—one day."

I'm met with... nothing. Her voice doesn't ring out through my thoughts. Her soft, comforting touch doesn't fall on my shoulder.

"I'll be happy," I tell her. "I promise I'll be happy."

Because that's all she ever wanted for me.

I leave the tomb and walk slowly back to the castle, picking my way through the fog. Night's falling, and when I reach the castle, the hallways are busy and noisy with the sounds of my father's court.

A few distant screams from the feeders blur the noise. I still haven't been able to drown them out. Maybe this new court—this new family—will be kinder to their feeders. Maybe their castle will be warm and welcoming, and I won't feel so alone.

I reach my room without any issues from my father's courtesans for once and slip inside, leaning on the door to close it with a sigh.

But I'm not alone.

"I heard the news. Were you not going to tell me?"

I turn toward my sister's voice and wince, seeing the look of disgust and rage turning her dainty features to something sharp enough to slice through glass. Matilda stalks toward me, sizing me up.

She's taller than me, leaner than me… meaner than me. Older by ten years, she should have been married by now. But while Matilda is blood born, like me, her mother wasn't high ranking.

Her mother is a maid. One of the mistresses of our shared father.

"I should be the one going to Scarlett Thunder," Matilda sneers, scoffing as she turns from me to face the full-length mirror across the room.

"You know it wasn't up to me," I bite out, hanging my head.

"Of course, it wasn't." She slips her fingers through her long, straight platinum blonde hair and frowns at her reflection. "You should have told me the second you found out. You went to her grave again, didn't you?"

My lips part to reply that Matilda can't stop me from holding vigil with my dead mother, but I choose to say nothing at all. There's no fighting Matilda. She might only be a princess because Father decided she might forge him some lower alliance one day, but she's cold and steely–the perfect vampire female. She could rule in his stead, honestly, and everyone knows it.

Which is why, I surmise, he's keeping her close. Not because he needs her, but because he's intimidated by her.

"I'll escort you to Crescent Peak," she says under her breath. "It's already arranged."

"You don't have to do that," I counter, my stomach curling.

"Of course, I do. We're sisters. I'm not letting you out of my sight."

Again, I can't argue. Matilda has her mind made up. She probably has some plan, some scheme she's going to enact just to piss our father off, knowing her.

"Don't ruin this for me," she murmurs, passing me in a blur of white hair.

2 5

CAN'T LOSE HER

FAYE'S ROOM IS CHAOTIC. NURSES AND THE PHYSICIAN CROWD HER BED to the point I can't see her through the fray. I push through them, seeing her pale and writhing, arching off the bed in pain.

"What's wrong with her?!" I shout.

Faye murmurs, white foam tinted with blood bubbling from her lips. Her unseeing eyes are glassy with pain as she bucks off the bed before going completely still.

"A seizure," the physician begins.

I don't believe it. I scoop her into my arms and run like my life depends on it–because her life depends on it.

Shouts of confusion and alarm follow me out of the room. My mom rushes around a corner so abruptly I nearly run her over, but she leaps out of the way. "Michael!"

"Lock down the castle!" I shout over my shoulder. "She's been poisoned!"

"Where are you going?!"

"Home," I say, more to myself than any of the worried onlookers stepping out of doors to see what the big commotion is.

I race out of the castle with Faye in my arms, locking into my vampiric abilities. I'm even faster than I am in my wolf form as I sprint across the rolling fields separating the castle grounds from Ravenfell, but every minute that passes is a minute less I have to save Faye's life.

She's as cold as ice—colder than a vampire should be. She's limp, blood streaming from her lips and ears, and I'm... I'm...

"Michael? Michael!" Lowe's voice cuts through the fog. Surprised, I miscalculate my next step, almost dropping Faye.

"Lowe? Lowe—Get Alma and come to my house."

"What happened? Is she—"

"She needs help," I manage to say before my voice breaks with emotion.

He disappears back into the fog heading in the direction of Ravenfell. I follow, cutting toward the edge of the village where my manor rises out of the mist. I count each step I take until I burst through the back garden and race into the house just as Emelda, dressed in a cloak, prepares to take her leave to the castle with the intention of fetching Faye, just like I told her to do.

Emelda screams in surprise, but her voice is broken by the crashing of glass and books as I sweep my arm over the kitchen island and lay Faye down flat on its surface.

"Michael—" Emelda cuts herself off when Faye starts shaking uncontrollably again. The witch-turned vampire bursts into her action, her cloak falling in a heap on the floor at her feet. "Keep her steady," she commands. She starts opening and shutting cabinets, gathering jars of herbs and snatching her mortar and pestle.

The front door opens in the depths of the house, and several voices approach—Lowe, Alma, and surprisingly, Deacon.

Alma rushes into the kitchen to her sister's side without so much as looking at me and Faye.

"I need dandelions," Emelda says, slightly panicked. "I can't find them—"

"I have some," Alma says, fishing in the giant bag hanging over her shoulder. "I have cloves and black peppercorns, too, already ground."

"I need–I need a carrying oil–"

"Use blood."

The women turn as Deacon and Lowe enter the kitchen. Lowe steps out of the vampire's way to allow him to step further into the crowded space. Deacon's eyes slide to mine, nodding gravely. He was likely at the castle when this happened and heard about it, seeing as he's a guard for my father if he's not out in the field enacting justice, or whatever the hell he does. "Use blood. She's a vampire. It'll take quicker."

Emelda shoots me a desperate look while I continue to hold Faye down, trying to stop her from banging her head against the surface of the counter. "Someone get me a knife."

Lowe pulls open drawers, but I'm holding Deacon's gaze when Lowe hands me a knife, and I slice through my hand, making a fist over the pestle Alma holds out. My blood sizzles into the herbs, foaming.

Time stands still for what feels like eternity while Alma and Emelda work, and all the while, I hold Deacon's gaze, my heart beating rapidly.

'Your parents locked the castle down. Your mom sent me here to make sure you were okay,' Deacon says into my mind.

'Thank you for coming.'

He nods. Emelda moves swiftly toward Faye, directing me to hold her still, and begins pouring the blood tonic into her mouth. Faye bucks, choking. I keep my weight pressed against her arms, pressing her into the counter. My eyes water with emotion I can't rightfully name. Fear? Yes, I feel that. Fear of losing her when I've just found her.

'She's yours, isn't she?' Deacon's eyes search mine. *'The wolf found his mate?'*

"It's not working, Emelda," Alma whispers beside me, panicked.

"Give it a few seconds," Emelda says, her voice pinched with worry. "I can try–I have something else I can try–I—" Her eyes spill over with tears.

Faye goes completely still.

26

A CONCERNED VISITOR

MICHAEL

ALMA AND LOWE SPEAK IN QUIET TONES IN THE FOYER WHILE HE HELPS her into her thick coat. The usual, ceaseless sprinkle of rain has finally turned to sleet–a vicious mix of freezing rain and the first hints of snow that's going to make the village an icy mess when day turns to night.

Lowe pushes a hat over Alma's thick hair, and she smiles lovingly up at him, her cheeks burning a pale pink. Real love shines behind the vampire's eyes as she takes his hand, and he leads her through the front door into the storm.

Lowe is lucky. Alma's love for him radiates from her like it's her aura, her reason for living. He found his mate in the form of a vampire and is… okay with it. Accepting of it, and everything that comes with it… like his own mortality.

I tear my attention back to the fireplace, a glass of whiskey untouched in my right hand.

Deacon's familiar footsteps echo in my direction. He leans against the doorframe into the front sitting room, sighing heavily–waiting for me to acknowledge him, I assume.

"She's stable," he says, edging into the room, his gaze boring holes in my profile. "Emelda's going to stay up tonight to tend to her."

"There's no reason for that. I'll be with Faye."

"When's the last time you slept?" His tone slices through the air between us like a knife.

"I sleep," I counter, sniffing indignity before tilting my glass back and swallowing every drop in one go.

"No, you fucking don't, I can tell–"

The front door opens with a snap and a swift inrush of bitter cold air. Deacon straightens as Cole storms inside, looking around the foyer before spotting us. I don't even bother to rise or take my eyes off the fire.

"What the fuck is going on, Michael?" Cole rushes into the foyer with a murderous look on his chiseled face. "Your mom said someone was poisoned at the castle." He notices Deacon and glares, stepping past the warrior with a holier-than-thou air about him that grates on my nerves immediately. "You should be at the castle." He sneers at Deacon, who simply curls his upper lip and flashes his fangs at Cole.

Great.

They snarl at each other, and I finally leave my chair. "Deacon is here with me, for support."

"Ah, you're collecting little pets now, are you, cousin?"

Deacon curls his hands into fists. He's a good man–a man with serious control over his body and emotions–but Cole is the opposite. One smartass remark from Deacon's mouth will cause a full-on fight between them, and I don't have the energy to separate them right now.

"Why are you here?" I say to Cole in a bored tone as I walk to the shelf on the far side of the room to pour myself another dram of whiskey when what I could really use is blood.

"I came to check on you–"

"Because my vampire pet got poisoned?" I sneer.

Cole's face flushes. "What happened to her?" He glances between me and Deacon for an answer, but neither of us speak. "Hello? My betrothed is at the castle right now locked in her room and panicking thinking she's going to be the next victim in whatever murderous plot is taking place–"

"I don't give a fuck about Matilda," I snap, turning on my heel. "If you're only here for gossip to spread through the court and to appease your bride, get out of my house."

Cole narrows his eyes. "Ah… I see what this is."

Deacon crosses his arms over his chest and takes a calculated step in my direction that Cole misses entirely.

"What?" I taunt, swirling the contents of my glass before letting the liquid scorch my throat and numb my veins.

"You fucked her. That little vampire… you're laying claim, huh? Someone must not be very happy about that if she was poisoned in your own home–the very castle she'll rule if you marry her."

"She has a name," I grind out. "Faye. And yes, she's *mine*, and whoever did this to her is going to pay in blood."

"Will you keep it down?" Emelda's voice echoes down to us. She grips the banister, her body shielded by a muted red robe and silken nightgown beneath, but her hair is uncommonly loose and flowing over her shoulders and back in the thickest black waves.

I often forget that Emelda is beautiful. I know how that sounds, but she's one of my oldest friends, and I've never seen her as anything but that…. Cole and Deacon, however, stare at her like they're seeing a living, breathing, star fallen from the heavens.

Cole whips his head toward me, his eyes full of rage and panic. "Why is she here?"

"Emelda?"

Emelda scoffs, swishing her robe as she descends the stairs. "I live here, you fucking idiot."

"I am a prince, and you will not speak to me that way, witch–"

"You are not *my* prince, and right now, you're an unwanted quest in my house where we have a very sick vampire hanging on by a fucking thread, and you're making too much noise!"

Cole winces at her tone, but I'm smiling around the rim of my glass.

"I only came here to check on you," Cole says to me. "When I heard what happened–I was worried."

"Maybe say that instead of jumping down his throat next time," Emelda snarls.

"I wasn't speaking to you," Cole retorts, but his eyes betray the way he's flashing his fangs at Emelda. I've never seen him look at anything like this before–like he's… in awe, and suddenly off-balance.

"Go back to your bride," she hisses, planting her hands on her hips. "We don't need your help."

Cole glares at the three of us before turning on his heel and storming out of the house.

Deacon blows out his breath, saying, "I'm going to stick around tonight in the event whoever did this to Faye comes back to finish the job."

"I think that's wise," I tell him, nodding, then turn my attention to Emelda, asking, "How is she?"

2 7

———

TWO HUNDRED YEARS

Michael

Three hours later, in the dead middle of the night, I stand in the doorway leading into the cozy guest room I brought Faye into what must have been weeks ago. I guess that much time has passed since then. It feels like seconds, honestly. I feel like I haven't had a chance to catch my breath since the moment she barreled into my life.

Now, she's lying still and prone in the bed covered in at least six quilts—all thick and stuffed with goose down. A normal, warm-blooded person would be sweating profusely, but she's ice cold.

I grip the doorframe, steadying myself as rage burns through my system. I've always leaned more toward my shifter side, but right now, the only thing I want to do is bite someone. I want to sink my fangs deep into someone's, anyone's, neck and rip out their throat.

I'm not sure how I manage to tear myself away from Faye's room, but I do, leaving the door open in the event she miraculously wakes up.

I stumble down the darkened staircase. The entire house is dark

111

and empty, save for the kitchen, where the sound of Emelda's mortar and pestle grinds through the lower level of the house. I follow the noise, finding her standing in her favorite part of the kitchen–the crook where the cabinets converge. Her back's to me as she dumps her herbs into a pot of simmering water that fans the scent of lilac and rosemary throughout the kitchen but says nothing as she reaches for another unlabeled jar and pops the cork.

I sink onto a bar stool and belly up to the kitchen island where a decanter of fresh blood–half full–and three glasses rest. Emelda's glass is barely touched. Deacon obviously had a few before he went outside to do his rounds, guarding the house and keeping tabs on the village below.

I pour myself a glass and drink deeply, then wince. "Lowe?"

"How could you tell?" Emelda says with a hint of a smile in her tone.

"It's fresh," I choke, picturing Lowe in his wolf form that day we went running while the women walked nearby. "And tastes like... shifter."

"I'm sure that's what you taste like." She chuckles then sighs as she turns to pull a bundle of thyme from the herb drying rack that hangs over the kitchen island. "It's what all the feeders taste like."

"I guess I've never noticed." I watch her work, fascinated. I've seen her do this before–grinding herbs. Brewing tonics. Making ointments and salves. But never to this degree and never using the little jars of unlabeled, horrific smelling herbs or... whatever they are.

I watch her inspect a jar full of completely white... ash. "What is that?"

"Bone," she murmurs, her eyes on the jar before she deftly measures a teaspoon of the substance and turns to the pot on the stove–which she normally uses to make food for me or reheat blood.

"Bone of what?"

She leans down and sniffs the concoction. "Hopefully newt, but it's been a while since I've used it. Two hundred years, in fact."

The air is immediately sucked from the room. I set my empty glass down and watch her stir her potion counter-clockwise exactly three times.

"Are you ever going to tell me how it happened?"

She taps her spoon on the side of the pot and goes back to her herbs, but her shoulders are rigid.

I fist my hands, running them down the length of my thighs like I'm trying to subconsciously relieve the tension in my body. "Emelda, I just–I'm trying to wrap my mind around how a vampire could do something like this to another vampire–"

"Vampires are violent," she says calmly, but I shake my head.

"I grew up–"

"Sheltered?" She looks at me over her shoulder but doesn't give me that cocky smile I'm so used to. Her face is pale and washed of emotion, but her eyes... her eyes are full of pain.

"What did they do to you?" I press. I wave my hand at the mess of jars, herbs, and healing... potions, not just tonics. Actual potions. Potions made by a *witch*.

"What didn't they do is a better question," she murmurs, turning away.

"Emelda–"

"I was a girl," she whispers over the simmering water and crackling herbs. "That's the truth of it. I was young, naïve, and brave. Brave and stupid, Michael." I watch her shoulders contract, her entire body going so tense she nearly splits the pestle in half.

But she takes a breath and relaxes, resigned. "They came to our village in the night. A horde of vampires... and we were just mortals. I was studying apothecary... potions and herbs. I had parents. I had Alma and Ewan–" She shudders, gripping the counter.

My stomach hollows out. I can sense her pain. She tucks her chin to her chest, but silent sobs rip through her back.

"Who's Ewan?" I ask, knowing the answer is going to gut me like it's gutting her.

"I was supposed to wear flowers in my hair," she whispers. "I was supposed to walk to him under the lantern light on the first morning of spring, to have our hands bound by fabric stitched by his mother and my mother. We were supposed to marry. Instead, that morning, they made me watch him die. All because I wouldn't–I couldn't–"

I close my eyes, bowing my head.

"They wanted me as a feeder. They kept me alone and made me watch as they tore through our entire village, but their leader... he wanted me willing. He wanted me to bow to him, to let him use me in–in ways–" She sucks in a breath. "They killed Ewan. Then my parents. My father begged me not to give in on his last breath, but then Alma–Alma–"

I regret asking her. I shouldn't have asked her.

"I broke. I told them I'd do whatever they wanted. They thought my sudden surrender meant Alma was something special, so they kept her, too, and once they burned our village to the ground, they... fed from us. Drained us. Drained us when they only killed the others, dancing in their blood."

"Emelda–"

"I woke up in the dirt," she whispers. "I wasn't that innocent girl anymore. The flowers in my hair were withered, and my white dress was stained with blood–everyone's blood. They made me into–into this–this body I can't escape. Gave me a life I never wanted." She turns to me, heartbroken. "I wanted love, Michael. I wanted warmth. I wanted children—more than anything—and that was stolen from me–from Alma. She was the only reason I carried on. Two hundred years of purgatory led us here, to you, to your family–the first vampires who ever showed me they can be kind–that they're more than just their bloodlust. And now–" she points a shaky finger toward the ceiling. "Faye? She was born *good*. Whatever she went through before this–I don't want her to remember, to steal that goodness from her. I want whoever did this to pay, too, Michael. So, that's why I'm making potions for the first time in two centuries. Potions meant to kill vampires, but if I tweak the recipe just enough, could bring her back from eternal death... because she's dying. You need to know that. She could die in a matter of hours, so–so let me get back to work."

She turns from me before her first tears fall.

"What was his name?"

"Who?"

"The vampire who did this to you?"

She chuckles low and dark. "You don't have to worry about him." She picks up a jar that's nothing but black and ink-like. It catches the light, shimmering like onyx. "He's not with us anymore. I made sure of it."

She pours half the jar into the pot and stirs, just once.

2 8

TWO LIVES

Michael

I pace the foyer, running my fingers through my hair over and over again as I listen to the voices of Emelda and Alma drifting down the staircase.

Lowe walks in from the kitchen with an armful of firewood, his face drawn with fatigue. I nod at him in greeting as he walks past me toward the sitting room where he kneels, adding more wood to the fire.

It's a freezing cold morning. Fall has officially bled into winter, and winter came quick. Frost covers the windows as the embers begin to crackle, and the first logs catch fire, but my mind is on the vampire still lying dormant in her bed.

"Alma told me," Lowe begins, his voice just above a whisper, "that the fact Faye survived the night is telling–it's a great thing. She has a better chance of recovering."

My mouth is totally dry as I edge into the sitting room, leaning on the archway. "I'm not getting my hopes up."

"Yeah, I know. I wouldn't be, either." He rises, dusting his hands on

117

his thighs. "I'm going out on patrol with Deacon, but we'll be back in an hour, two hours, tops. Do you… want to go? Maybe shift for a bit?"

I shake my head. I couldn't shift even if I wanted to. Right now, my vampire traits are in control, and my wolf is just… terrified. Terrified of losing its mate.

I haven't been able to acknowledge that fact yet. I want to. I want to scream it from the rooftops, but Faye can't hear me, and she's the only person who matters.

Lowe takes his leave. I lean my head against the wall and close my eyes until I hear Alma's footsteps on the staircase.

"She's stable," Alma says with a sigh as she approaches. She picks her coat off the rack by the door and shrugs it on, her eyes lined with dark circles. "Did Lowe leave already?"

"He just left." I notice the red and purple stains on her fingers and the grime on her apron. She was up gathering, grinding, and preparing herbs just like her sister.

She sighs as she stuffs her hands into gloves. "We need silver bark. There's a grove nearby, so I'm going to go harvest some."

"I'll go with you. It's not safe for you to go out alone."

"Don't worry about it, Prince Michael. I'll catch up to Lowe. You should go stay with Faye for a while. It might make her feel better."

I try to swallow past the lump in my throat, but it's impossible. Alma slides through the door, disappearing into the billowing snow that sucks away the daylight. I stand dumbly in the foyer for another few minutes before making my way upstairs to where Emelda is cleaning up her potion bottles and tidying Faye's room.

"Did you see Alma?" Emelda asks in a rush.

"Yeah, she just left."

"All right, I have some more potions to make–"

I hold out my hand. "You're exhausted. You should sleep."

"I have to keep dosing her, and we're nearly out."

Something… something breaks within me as I turn my head to look at Faye. She's so weak, barely alive. Her skin is gray and sunken, and her hair has lost its golden luster.

"Is she in pain?" I ask, my already shattered heart dissolving to ash.

"I assume so, yes," Emelda answers with heartbreaking honesty. "We're doing our best to keep her comfortable."

Her tone tells me everything I need to know. Faye is going to die, regardless of the potions. We're just lengthening her suffering.

I've been focused on the impossible when I should have been focused on finding her murderer.

"I want to be alone with her," I say, my voice like gravel. "Please, go rest."

"Michael–"

"You've done enough." I look at my friend. She sees the resignation in my eyes.

"I can… I can make something that would… ease her gently into death, if you want." I close my eyes. Emelda continues, "It would be painless. She wouldn't feel a thing."

"Please," I tell her, and that's enough to get Emelda moving. Maybe she was thinking the same thing I was all morning when Faye's condition didn't change, when she'd exhausted all efforts to save her.

It's time to let her go.

I sink to the edge of the bed and smooth my hand over Faye's arm, wincing at her icy temperature. Emelda's been using Lowe's blood as a carrier for the herbs in her potions to try to sustain Faye during her recovery. She should be warm. Warm to the touch.

"I'm so sorry," I whisper. "I am so sorry, Faye. We're mates. I should have told you. I know it wouldn't have mattered, that you wouldn't have been able to feel it like I can, but… you were mine. I was made for you, and you for me, and I wasted so much time trying to ignore that feeling. I should have been the one protecting you. I'm sorry. Forgive me."

I lie down beside her, dragging her toward me and covering us with the blankets. I can't even cry. My body and soul are in shambles as I rest my cheek against the top of her head and close my eyes against the anguish.

Somewhere in the haze, I fall asleep. My body drifts on a wave of pure exhaustion I can't fight, and when I wake up again, I'm not in

Faye's room. I'm in my room, and the sun is warming the sheets, and summer is in full bloom.

Rapid footsteps race down the hallway, followed by sharp childish giggles. The door opens as I sit up, surprised, as a blonde little boy no older than three barrels toward me, half dressed, his hair half brushed and face stained with berry juice.

"Get back here!" It's Faye's voice lifted in a laugh that spirits down the hallway after the boy who's now climbing on the bed and crawling toward me, choking on his own laughs.

"Daddy!" he gushes, grabbing my arms and crawling into my lap just as…just as Faye walks into the room, holding a hairbrush and his pants.

She's glowing. Her hair falls in strands of golden silk over her shoulders, and beneath her pale pink dress, her belly is round and swollen with the late stages of pregnancy.

"He's too fast for me now," she pants, wiping sweat from her brow with the back of her hand. "He wants you, Michael. He needs you."

I wake up with a start back in the snowy, dreary darkness, curled around my dying mate. My hand moves to her stomach, clutching her tight.

"No," I whisper, choking on the words at the very moment Emelda walks through the door in tears, clutching a bright red potion in her hand so tight her knuckles are white.

"It will take only a few minutes for the effects to take in–"

"No, Emelda, we can't," I growl, sitting up and pulling Faye into my arms. "We can't."

"What happened?"

"She's pregnant."

29

EVERYONE HAS SECRETS

Emelda

MICHAEL HAS OFFICIALLY LOST HIS MIND. I EDGE CLOSER TO THE BED, the vial I hold trembling as I raise a shaking hand. "You can't possibly know that for sure. It's too early. Far too early."

He looks down at the nearly dead vampire in the bed, his eyes wide and glossy with shock and the last glimmers of a very deep kind of sleep. "Is there anything you can do to check–"

"Not for several more weeks," I cut in, gripping the vial like it's a lifeline. In all actuality, I have Faye's life in my hands right now. A few drops of this will kill her within a single minute.

Just a few hours ago, when I left my closest, dearest friend in this room with what I firmly believe is the love of his life–his mate, as the shifters call it–I'd been ready to let Faye slip away. He'd been ready as well; that was more than clear. While Alma, Lowe, and Deacon had more positive affirmations to shower throughout the house this morning when Faye survived the night, I saw it for what it was... we are elongating her suffering. Even if she had woken up, there's a chance she wouldn't be the same, stuck in a body that will always work against her.

But now Michael's running his fingers through his hair and squeezing his eyes shut like he's in pain.

He changed his mind.

Thank the gods.

I slip the vial into my pocket with plans to throw it in the fireplace at some point this morning. "You need to sleep more."

He shakes his head.

I exhale sharply through my nose. "What makes you think she's pregnant?"

"We slept together."

"Well, yes, that could produce a pregnancy."

He opens one eye in a glare.

"How long ago?"

"Maybe a week ago. I'm not certain how much time has passed given the circumstances." The circumstances being that we've been holed up in this house for close to three days with little contact with the outside world.

Deacon's been visiting the castle, of course, given that he's a soldier, and that's where he's stationed. He brings what news he can, which is more of the same. The castle is locked down while they investigate, but so far, it's considered an isolated incident.

I haven't found it imperative to relay these messages to Michael, seeing as he's holding onto his sanity by a single, fraying thread.

"Then we can't test to be sure. In a few weeks from now, I could easily confirm a pregnancy." I risk a single step in his direction, holding a hand out in surrender. "But I can assure you, Michael, that the chances of her surviving this poison were minimal, but the chances that an early pregnancy survived..." I hope he hears the pain in my voice and knows I have his back when I continue, "It's impossible."

"We'll give her a few more days," he whispers, looking so incredibly broken I can't stand it anymore.

I lick my lips. "Are you just hoping she's pregnant to give yourself an excuse to try to keep her alive?"

"I don't need you to question my moral high ground," he bites out, and I take his tone as a firm dismissal.

I hear the door shut behind me with a crack, the lock clicking into place. I sigh heavily, toying with the outline of the vial in my pocket. On second thought, destroying it would be a waste of the precious, rare herbs I used to create it. I need to be more conservative going forward. Poor Alma's out in the cold and wet, peeling bark from trees over six miles away just to make more of the potion we're using to keep Faye alive. I can't afford the money and time it would take to brew this potion again, especially not when half of the ingredients are technically illegal to possess.

I go about my usual duties for the rest of the morning. I stoke the fire. I beat the ever living fuck out of the rug in the foyer with my broom and vacuum up the ash, dirt, and muck left behind by snowy boots. I go to the kitchen to organize and take stock of my herbs, making a list of what I'm low on, what I might need to reach out to the castle for to restock.

A swift knock on the door to the back garden catches my attention as I start making a potent sleeping draft I plan to give to Michael.

I turn to the shadow passing into the room and freeze. "Can I help you?"

Cole closes the door against the freezing rain–so close to being snow I can also smell the cold, earthy scent carried in on his wool coat. His blue eyes scan the room before settling on me, but he drops his icy exterior and runs his tongue along his lower lip before whispering, sounding like a wounded puppy, "Any change?"

"No."

"How is he?"

"The same, as well." I eye Cole skeptically before adding, "He's considering ending her treatment and allowing me to help her along."

"To die?"

"Yes."

Cole grits his teeth. "You shouldn't have to, Emelda. She could be brought to the castle, to the physicians, they can–"

"Drain her? Leave her empty to die a miserable, broken death? No."

"I don't want her death on your conscience."

"Why would you even care?" I ask sharply, but the look behind his eyes…

"How can you even ask me that?"

Cole grips the edge of the counter, his expression softening to the point I recognize him again. I've known Cole longer than I've known Michael. It's the only secret I've ever kept from my friend… and I plan to continue keeping it.

Cole takes a step toward me, reaching for me, my name a whisper on his lips, but then Michael steps into the kitchen looking forlorn and exhausted.

Cole tucks his hand to his side, curling his fingers into a fist.

"What are you doing here?" Michael grinds out, dragging a hand down his face.

"I have news from the castle," he says, scanning my face before turning to his cousin. "The ball this weekend will continue as planned, and your parents want to know if you're still planning on showing up. After this weekend, I'll be taking my bride back to my kingdom," he says, but his tone tightens on the word bride as his eyes meet mine again–only briefly. "Matilda will no longer be your problem."

Michael rolls his eyes to the ceiling. "I have no answer about my attendance at the ball at this moment."

"I'll let them know."

Voices in the foyer steal Michael's attention. He turns to the sound of Deacon, Lowe, and Alma returning from their gathering trip, and he steps their way without another word.

Cole exhales, adjusting his coat before turning toward the back door.

"Wait," I say before I can stop myself, my hand somehow wrapping around his forearm.

He slowly turns back in my direction, looking stony and expressionless as I hand him the list of herbs. Our fingers brush. I ignore what his touch ignites.

He looks down at the list and nods. "I'll do what I can."

"Thank you," I whisper, but the words are lost in the whoosh of air that ripples through the kitchen as he disappears through the door into the horrible weather.

3 0

INSIDER INFORMATION

Michael

Lowe spins his pint of beer in a circle, his eyes scanning the run-down dive bar and its grizzly patrons. He wrinkles his nose when a duo of rough looking vampires walk by, baring their fangs at our table.

"It stinks here," he says under his breath before sipping from his glass. "The beer's not bad, though."

The tavern, tucked on the far edge of my parents' kingdom, isn't somewhere I'd normally hang out, but Deacon insisted we meet him here.

Two days have passed since my vision of what my life could be if Faye pulls through. Two days of torment in the manor, watching her continue to waste away before my eyes while I try and try to tell myself I'm doing the right thing by keeping her alive.

"You didn't have to come," I tell Lowe, who shrugs, draining his pint.

"My hands needed a break from grinding herbs. If I'd stayed behind, that's exactly what Alma and Emelda would have me doing."

I can feel his gaze scanning my profile but refuse to meet his eyes. We drink in silence for a moment, watching the patrons gathered around high tops or in booths.

But then he says, "Have you considered marking her?"

"No, of course not."

"What's stopping you?"

"Uh, probably the fact she's dying and can't consent." A prickle of unease ripples through my senses as Lowe leans back and eyes me curiously. I choose to ignore him, but I can already tell he knows something he shouldn't.

"When did you figure it out?" he asks as a waitress stomps over to refill our pints. Beer splashes over the table's worn surface, but he gives her a kind smile, showing off his not-so-sharp-teeth, and she scowls, her fangs on full display.

"Figure what out?"

"Don't tell me you don't know," he drawls, his chin perched on his fist. "The mate bond. With Faye."

My jaw tightens as I bite out, "I don't know what you're talking about."

"You smell like her. You carry her scent–it's a mate thing."

"Stop."

He leans over the table. "Mark her."

"Why would that even matter now? Plus, she's a vampire. It wouldn't feel like anything to her–"

"Then you understand what I'm trying to say?" he searches my eyes, looking more serious than I've ever seen. "Give her your mark. Carry some of her burden. I can't say for sure if it'll wake her up, but if she's stuck in there, fighting… give her that gift. Your strength, your acceptance of your bond with her."

My muscles tighten as we stare at each other. "I can't. She's incapable of understanding the gravity of the act–"

"Fuck it," he grinds out. "Do it. She's running out of time."

He straightens as Deacon finally arrives, his head and shoulders dusted with snow. He shakes his shoulders as he side-steps through the crowd to our table where he immediately lifts two fingers in the air and silently motions for the waitress to bring him a drink.

Lowe's eyes hold mine for another second before I turn to Deacon and ask, "Why the hell are we here?"

"I wanted to meet with you somewhere we wouldn't be immediately recognized," he rushes out, shrugging out of his coat. It's army issued and worn, and he looks like he might have just come from patrol based on his thick boots and uniform. He scans the room before settling on a stool, nodding his thanks as the waitress sets a glass of blood mixed with some kind of liquor on the table in front of him. When she leaves, he says, "I've news from the castle. Gossip, actually."

"You brought me out here for gossip?"

"The physicians have determined that Faye was likely accidentally poisoned by whatever feeder gave her blood last. Nightbane was found in the kitchen. It looks like parsley to the naked eye. It's likely the gardeners or a maid out for a walk found it growing wild and brought it back to the castle, and it was fed to the feeders."

"Faye wouldn't have been the only vampire exposed if that were the case," Lowe argues.

"Yes, I agree, and it seems Queen Emory and King Kane weren't too keen on the consensus of the physicians, but they have no clues as to how this could have happened."

"So that's why they're going forward with the ball," I say to myself, closing my eyes. "Because what happened to her was deemed an accident."

"Yep. Sounds like it."

I open my eyes to find both men looking at me. They're wearing similar expressions of doubt.

"This wasn't an accident," Lowe says before I can even open my mouth.

"I think whoever's responsible wanted it to look like an accident. Nightbane might look like wild parsley, but it doesn't grow around these parts, especially not this late in the year," Deacon adds with a nod.

"What do you suggest we do from here?" I ask Deacon, toying with the frost on the outside of my pint glass.

"Whoever did this, in my opinion, is high ranking," Deacon says after a moment of thought. "Your parents have impeccable security, so something like this shouldn't have been able to happen. Only someone with access to the private rooms of the castle accessible by the royal family and their guests would have been able to get close enough to Faye to poison her."

"Maids, servants," Lowe cuts in, but Deacon shakes his head.

"There'd be no reason for that. Faye isn't a threat to them by any means; it wouldn't make sense."

Deacon turns his gaze to me.

I stare at him while my mind reels. "Whoever did this to her is the same person that tried to kill her the first time. They came back to finish the job."

"And whoever it is… they're a royal guest at the castle."

ACTING ON INSTINCT

MICHAEL

EMELDA MOVES LIKE AN AGITATED FLEDGLING AS SHE DUSTS LINT FROM my shoulders. She swats my hand when I reach for my hair, shaking her head and scowling before adjusting a single rogue curl trying to fight against the hold of the hair gel she slathered through my tresses.

"Don't move. Don't touch anything. Don't bump into anything," she instructs, stepping back to examine her work—me, in a royal uniform, all of my medals of rank displayed across my chest—and purses her lips.

"It barely fits," I grumble, shrugging with discomfort as the stuffy, thick fabric of the suit scrapes across my skin.

"Take that up with the seamstresses at the castle," she says through gritted teeth as she fights another pin through the sash.

The ticking of the clock on the far wall fills the silence for several minutes as she puts her final touches on my outfit, finally stepping back to take me in for the hundredth time. She wipes her brow, sniffing tiredly as she glances at the watch and curses under her breath. "You're nearly an hour late."

"That's not late enough," I say under my breath. "It's a ball. It's fashionable to show up late."

"You're the prince, and from what I heard, an honored guest."

Because my father has someone for me to meet. A princess from some far-flung vampire kingdom, I assume.

He wouldn't have arranged this if I'd told him the truth about the guest taking up residence in my manor. He assumes Faye is my charge because of the investigation into her attack. If Mom said anything about our relationship… it likely didn't involve the mate bond. That's something Dad can't truly understand.

I wasn't going to go to this ball, but I've been plotting all week with Deacon. Whoever did this to Faye is going to be at the ball, I'd bet my life on it.

Emelda gathers her sewing basket and everything else she tortured me with tonight and rushes out of the room, murmuring something about a potion simmering on the stove. I step into the hallway and watch her shadow retreat, adjusting my sleeves and pulling on my collar before walking toward the stairs.

I pass Faye's room and stop, hesitating. My hand hovers around the knob as Lowe's words from days ago dance through my head.

I told Emelda I'd give Faye a few more days to recover. It's been a few days. It's been almost a week since the day I said that, and she hasn't changed. She rides the line between life and death like she's unsure if she even wants to survive, and Emelda needs to give her more and more of the hard to source potion now that her body's used to it.

Emelda hasn't complained even though her fingers are raw and blistered from grinding herbs day in and day out. She's waiting for me to call an end to Faye's suffering, and I can't find the strength to do it.

I open the door. It creaks painfully, but Faye doesn't so much as stir.

I've been doing my best to keep my vampire side dominant. I need to be logical and unaffected, both vampire traits. I can't allow myself to lean into the emotionally driven, somewhat primal drive my wolf traits bring out in me. I tell myself I want her to live because she deserves it, not because the idea of losing her is so painful I can't eat or sleep knowing it's coming.

I sit at her bedside at all hours because I owe her justice. I won't let her slip into death without punishing who hurt her.

Not because my wolf is screaming for me to stay near her.

I run my hand over her hair, her cheek, cupping her jaw. She's cold and pale, but her expression is sleepy–childish, almost. She looks… peaceful for the first time in days.

I bury the hope trying to rush to life and kneel, taking her freezing cold hand in mine. "I'll be back later," I tell her, pressing a kiss to her knuckles. "I promise. Hold on for me until then."

She says nothing, does nothing, and doesn't move. Pain like I've never felt before sprints through my body, settling in my chest, throbbing like it's carried by my heartbeat. I wince, leaning over the bed and burying my face against her shoulder.

Guilt, shame, and immense regret blur my senses. I need to go. I had a plan for the night. I was supposed to pinpoint her assailant and put an end to this, once and for all. I was supposed to give her justice before letting her go, but I….

I gather her in my arms before I can think about what I'm doing. Her head drops back, her hair falling in a cascade of pure gold.

I fight against the feral urge taking over my senses. My teeth lengthen. My fingers threaten to turn to claws as I press her to my chest.

My mate. My mate.

Her skin is soft, cold, and smells like lavender as I press my mouth to the crook of her neck, breathing her in.

"Don't," I say out loud, gritting my teeth.

I've never felt like this before–so completely out of control. I have no choice but to give in, to let my wolf side take over.

I open my mouth against her skin, my teeth grazing her sweet-scented neck, and then I'm biting down so hard I bend into the motion, clutching her hard enough to leave bruises. I want to fuck her. I want to breed her. I want to keep her close, locked away in my house. I want to be with her forever–however long that is for something like me. A hybrid. A mutant. A thing that can't control himself around her.

I break her skin. Her vampire blood is dark and doesn't run like a feeder's would. A sensation I can't put into words explodes through my chest. It's like tasting color, like the world has slipped on its axis and suddenly everything I've ever questioned makes sense.

But then I remember where I am–and what I've just done.

I break the bite, letting her go. Her body slumps over my arm like a corpse as I gape, fighting for breath.

What have I done?

I lay her down quickly, stepping back so rapidly my back slams into the wall, sending a mirror and several frames cascading to the ground.

Emelda rushes into the room, her eyes wide when she sees me against the wall and Faye in a heap on the bed, one of her legs hanging off the mattress. Emelda looks in horror at Faye's neck before meeting my eyes. "Michael? What are you doing?"

I wipe my mouth, suddenly unable to breathe. "I have–I have to go."

"Michael!" she shrieks, but I rush past her, several pins coming loose from my sash.

32

SHE'S AWAKE

Emelda

I'M SHAKING. I QUICKLY DAB SPOTS OF DARK, VAMPIRIC BLOOD FROM Faye's neck, my fingers trembling with rage and confusion as I watch her take several shallow breaths in a row.

There's been absolutely no change in her condition. She's been still. Cold. Dead, in all honesty. Dying a slow, drawn out death we've been staving off like she has a chance of ever recovering.

But now, I watch the skin around the half-moon shaped mark Michael left on her neck turn... a soft pink.

I lean back with the bloody rag clutched between my fingers as her chest rises sharply, holds, and then falls in a whoosh before she settles, a soft moan leaving her pale lips as her body slumps against the tangled sheets.

The front door off the foyer opens and shuts with a slam against the cold wind. Alma's voice echoes upstairs, calling out my name, but I'm watching... color creep into Faye's features again.

Alma rushes upstairs and slides to a halt in the doorway, panting, her face washed in pink from the chill outside. "How is she? Any change? Lowe found feverfew and fairywand at the market a few villages over." She holds up two bags of dried herbs. "I was thinking about making a compound tonight–something warming. I have some of Lowe's blood, too. It's fresh. We can make a warming compound tonight–"

Faye gasps, her body stretching and arching off the bed. Alma screeches before clapping her hand over her mouth, her eyes wide in shock.

I leap into action, jumping on Faye and wrapping my arms around her. She shakes violently, gasping for breath, her teeth chattering as her eyelids flutter open.

"Emelda!" Alma rushes out, coming to my aid.

"Go downstairs into the kitchen and fetch the ginseng root powder. Mix it with Lowe's blood and bring it to me. Hurry!"

Alma sweeps out of the room so fast her body's a blur against the shadows creeping in from the hallway. Faye gasps and groans, her limbs jerking against her will.

"You're okay. You're okay," I repeat over and over, holding her against my chest.

"Emelda?" she croaks, her voice hoarse from lack of use.

"Yes. I'm here. It's me." I close my eyes, whispering a rapid prayer to whatever higher powers are listening, watching this right now.

"I–I remember–"

"Hush now," I whisper into her hair, listening to Alma's thundering footsteps on the stairs as she races upstairs.

"I know who did this to me," she rasps, her eyes fluttering closed again as she takes a painful, shuddering breath. "I can't–I'm cold–"

"Here," Alma rushes out, running around the side of the bed and thrusting a bowl of steaming blood in my hand. She remains close as I try to press the bowl to Faye's lips, but she shakes so hard blood spills over the rim instead. Alma clutches Faye's head while I guide the bowl back to her mouth, whispering encouragement as Faye chokes, then swallows.

We don't give up on her until the bowl is empty. Faye calms, her body slumping into rest again. Alma throws me a look as we tuck her into bed, covering her with several thick quilts.

I stoke the fire until it roars while Alma braids Faye's hair away from her face, and when we finally turn from the door, my sister grabs my hand.

She leans in, whispering, "Is this it? She's waking up?"

"No," I rasp, unable to give myself a shred of hope. "I don't know. I want to think so, but she's been on the verge of death for over a week."

I glance over my shoulder at Faye, who's totally still but turning a pale peach under the glow of the nearby fire.

"Where's Lowe?" I ask, turning back to my sister.

"At home, I assume," she says as we step into the hallway.

I close the door halfway, my mind racing a hundred miles a second as I try to form some kind of plan. "She'll need blood. A lot of blood."

"I'll send him up," she says, touching my arm. "That's fine, Emelda."

"I need him to go to the castle first and tell Michael. The ball–he's at the ball." My mouth continues to move without sound as I grapple with the idea of telling Alma what he did to Faye.

But my eyes glaze over the scar peeking out from the collar of Alma's sweater–the same half-moon shape, inlaid with teeth marks.

I meet her eyes. "Have Lowe give Michael the message that Faye woke up briefly but is resting now, then have him come back here. I can drain him a bit, just so we have enough for her."

"I will," she says, squeezing my upper arm. She whirls toward the staircase in a flash of black wool and disappears into the shadows of the quiet house.

I back into Faye's room, leaving the door open so I can hear if anyone arrives, and sit in the armchair by the fireplace.

An hour passes. I nod in and out of sleep. It's been days without sleep, I surmise. My body feels beaten to a pulp. I can't remember the last time I had any blood, either.

Faye stirs from the bed behind me, so I rise and walk over to her, sitting on the edge of the bed and smoothing my fingers over her hand.

She blinks a few times, trying to clear her vision. Her brow furrows with confusion before she looks up at me.

"Don't try to talk," I whisper, forcing my lips into a smile. "You're probably wondering what happened."

"I know what happened," she rasps, and an expression I've never seen from her crosses her face, turning her eyes to something sharp and cunning. She tries to rise up on an elbow but is still weak.

"Don't rush, Faye. I sent Alma to fetch Lowe–"

"I need to talk to Michael," she says, her voice cracking. "Right now."

"He's not here."

"Where is he?" Her eyes search mine, desperate and pleading.

"He's at the castle. The ball for Princess Matilda and–and Prince Cole's engagement is tonight, happening right now."

She shoves the sheets down, her face twisting in sudden fear.

"Faye? Faye, please, lie back down–"

"She did it," she cries out. "She's trying to get to Michael."

She swings her legs out of bed before I can catch her and immediately falls to the ground with a yelp of pain. I try to pull her upright, but she starts fighting me, her nails raking over my skin.

I bare my fangs at her in warning. "Faye! Get back in bed! You've been deathly ill for a week!"

"Matilda is my sister!" she cries out, clutching my arms. "Matilda wasn't the one meant to marry Cole."

I freeze, my lips popping open as Faye searches my eyes for understanding.

"You're the missing princess," I say, and she nods.

"She tried to kill me. She failed. She tried to kill me again–"

"Why?"

"I don't know. She wants Michael for something. I have to warn him."

"Get back in bed."

"I need to–"

"I will go." I hold her gaze, but tingles of warning skitter over my skin. "He's probably already on his way here. Lowe was supposed to tell him that you woke up–"

A slow creaking sound echoes from downstairs–the sound of the front door slowly swinging open.

"That's him now," I assure her, pressing her down on the bed before wringing my hands and edging toward the door. I can't see the lower level from here, but someone is definitely walking up the stairs.

But the footsteps aren't familiar. I notice that a second too late.

"What are you doing here?" I ask, praying my voice doesn't shake.

33

THE TELL

Michael

The ballroom is a hellscape of color and noise. It feels like every high-ranking vampire is here right now, everyone commingling and walking around the room with flutes of sparkling blood. I snatch a glass for myself off a tray being touted by a waiter and drain it quickly, letting the blood work into my system without so much as tasting it.

I can still taste Faye, though, and it's killing me. My entire body is screaming to get back to her, to be with her, to claim her in other ways, and I can't take it.

I'm out of control. This needs to end.

I spot my parents toward the back of the ballroom standing with my aunt and uncle, all four of them looking somewhat subdued, those fake, royal smiles plastered on their faces.

But someone blocks my progress toward them—toward my mother, who I desperately need to talk to about what I just did.

"What the hell is wrong with you?" Cole rasps, catching my arm and practically dragging me through a set of thick, velvet curtains covering one of the archways off the ballroom. A small sitting room expands around us, quiet and empty. He scans my face, his eyes narrowed. "Are you sick?"

"No."

"You're so–so pale."

"I'm a vampire, Cole. We're all pale."

"No, you've never been this color," he argues, reaching up to touch my face, but I swat him away.

"Get off. I have business to attend to, and you're supposed to be with your betrothed."

He grinds his teeth, his fangs on full, gleaming display. "I'd like to talk to you for a moment if you'd give me a fucking minute."

"What do you need to say to me?" I snarl.

"What the fuck has gotten into you lately? You're a mess."

"What do you think?" I step into him. "Really, Cole? Is it not obvious?"

"Holy shit," he whispers, taking a step away from me. His serious expression shatters, replaced by something I've rarely ever seen from him. Joy.

His blue eyes sparkle as he says, "You found your mate, didn't you?"

"I did." It hurts. The words tumble out of me and sting more than being bitten.

Cole notices the edge in my voice as his gaze sweeps over my face. His joyous expression falters. "It's her, isn't it? The vampire–"

"I did something I shouldn't have. I couldn't control it–"

"What did you–"

"I marked her, and if you'll move, I need to talk to my mother–"

"You marked her?" he hisses. "What the fuck is wrong with you? She's practically dead!"

"You can't understand because you're not a wolf, okay? It's imperative–"

Deacon slides through the curtain, looking relieved to see me but annoyed I'm with Cole. "I saw you come in. We need to talk. I have the guest list–"

"Why would you need the guest list?" Cole hisses.

But Matilda's grating, sing-song voice calls out to Cole before she bursts through the curtains. She eyes the group like a cat preying on a mouse, her mouth ticking into a smile when she spots me. "I'm so glad you could make it, Prince Michael. I've heard you've been so busy–"

I step past them, Deacon right behind me, and try to exit the sitting room, but Matilda steps in my way.

"Are you always so rude?" she asks, giggling. "It almost seems like you don't like me."

"I do not," I say sternly, and Cole rolls his eyes to the ceiling not to laugh.

Matilda scoffs, turning to Cole with her lip curled up, fangs bared. "Are you going to let him talk to me like that?" She looks at me over her shoulder, smirking. "It's not very nice to bully someone, Prince Michael."

"Come on," I tell Deacon, but Matilda has no interest in letting me leave.

"Prince Michael, I've heard so much about your tender heart in the last few days. Your mother said you took in that poor dying vampire girl. It must have been so hard to have her pass in your own home."

I pause. Something in her tone... it's off. I swallow, playing a mental game of chess as I slowly turn to the horrible vampire woman. She tucks her icy blonde hair behind her ears, smiling with teeth as she waits for my next words.

I make her wait for a few seconds, scanning her face, looking for cracks in her armor. "It was difficult, yes, but my housekeeper used to be a witch before she was turned. She's been caring for the girl, and we're still hopeful she'll make a full recovery."

There it is. A flash of panic. A single crack in the mask of indifference and boredom.

"How lucky," she says sweetly, then looks down at her shoes. I don't miss the way her long, slender fingers curl into fists so tight I wonder if her nails are leaving indents in her palms. "Excuse me, dear," she says to Cole. "I need to continue making introductions to the guests who came to celebrate our engagement."

She disappears in a flash of blonde and crimson fabric.

My heart hammers in my chest. "Deacon, keep an eye on her."

"Why?" Cole asks firmly.

I turn to Cole, my jaw flexing. "Do you not notice how odd she is?"

"She's a bitch, I get it. I don't like her either. I don't have a choice here–"

"She is up to something."

Deacon leaves, and I follow, making my way toward my parents, but they've moved on and are now talking to a group of older vampire royals I'd rather not converse with.

Instead, I grab another flute of blood and pick my way through the ballroom, looking for any signs of Matilda or Deacon, but after ten minutes, I realize neither of them are in the room.

34

FAYE IS DEAD

Michael

Something like dread creeps through my body as I scan the ball room. I can hear my heartbeat in my ears–a heavy *thump, thump, thump* that increases in speed as I search for Matilda. Deacon appears looking just as stressed as I feel, and we lock gazes. He gives a single head shake before disappearing back into the crowd.

Matilda is not here, that's clear enough. The closeted shock in her eyes had been confirmation that she didn't like the news that Faye was somehow surviving. That's enough for me to believe she might have done this to her, but why?

A tickle in the recesses of my mind momentarily steals my attention. but I brush it away as I move in on my parents. Dad looks relieved to see me, his lips parting to introduce me to two wealthy-looking vampire men, but I cut him off, asking, "Where is Princess Matilda?"

"Oh," Mom says, turning from the group and taking my arm. "She went up to her rooms to change. Apparently, she has multiple outfits for tonight. I–I can't imagine what she'll wear to her wedding." Titters of laughter split around the group, but Mom catches the uncertainty behind my eyes. "Michael, what's the matter?"

"I need to-"

"Prince Michael," a slightly familiar voice says somewhere behind me. I turn, locking eyes with a man I met only briefly in my father's office weeks again-Aamon Archeron. He's the emissary to Red River-one of them, at least. He's part of Matilda's posse who stayed here the past month in her company.

He gives me a slight bob of the head I don't return. I glare instead.

"You and I haven't gotten a moment to properly introduce ourselves. I'm afraid that when things went awry on our arrival to your kingdom, I was swept up in diplomacy. I'm sure you can understand."

Mom glances between us before turning back to her group, but I'm staring at the man in front of me. His eyes are slightly on the red side, which I don't see very often anymore, not since moving to Ravenfell. Most of the vampires I know have blue eyes, so I'm immediately on edge.

He's tall and vampirically handsome but rather plain otherwise. A face I'd forget-and have forgotten.

"I believe apologies are in order," he continues, looking down at his feet in submission before meeting my gaze again. "Princess Matilda can be rather abrasive. She's not as bad as she tries to be, however. I can attest to that."

"I don't care. I'm not the one marrying her."

The corner of his mouth ticks into a knowing smile as he takes another step, shortening the distance between us. "I understand you completely. In fact, I'm sure her father is happy to be rid of her, whatever the circumstances may be. I was lucky enough to fall into King Mattias's good graces when I married Matilda's sister."

I narrow my eyes. "She has a sister?"

"Yes, my wife. She's the younger of the two. She was a... beautiful thing."

Something isn't sitting right. Out of the corner of my eye, I see Deacon moving through the crowd, talking to another warrior as they head in my direction at a rate of speed that immediately has me on edge.

"Congratulations," I tell Aamon in a bored tone. "If you'll excuse me–"

"I'm curious about your territory," he cuts in, stepping close enough to touch me if he wanted to. His hand hovers over my upper arm. "Ravenfell, is it? I've heard it's lovely. Matilda talks about it often."

"And why are you here with her and not back in Red River with your wife?" I ask sharply.

"Oh, I should have clarified," he says, clearing his throat. "My darling Faye passed away last year–"

Faye. Her name works through my body, ringing like a death knell. I grab Aamon by the arms and shove him to the ground against the chorus of shocked cries from startled onlookers.

Someone shouts my name. My father, most likely, but my heartbeat is hammering through my ears, and I can't hear anything else. "What did you just say?"

I'm pulled off Aamon by Deacon, who whispers rapidly in my ear, "Matilda was seen leaving the castle."

"Michael!" Dad roars, but I'm already moving through the crowd, pushing and shoving against the guests hurrying to catch a glimpse of the commotion I caused.

I'm nearly at the main entrance when Cole shouts my name, his rapid footsteps echoing through the corridor and over the hum of noise spilling from the ballroom.

"What did you do? What's going on?"

"Go to the house, now," I rasp to Deacon, who breaks into a sprint and races through the door before I whirl on Cole, grab him by his shirt, and slam him into a stone pillar. "Matilda isn't who she says she is."

"What are you talking about?"

"The woman I've been caring for–my mate–is her sister. I don't think–" I suck in a breath as the pieces of the puzzle finally fall into place. "You were supposed to marry Faye. She was the princess that was sent here for you. Matilda is her sister, and she tried to kill her to take her place."

Cole shoves against me. "How do you know?"

"I just do."

Cole relaxes, his eyes searching mine. "Where is she now? Where is Matilda now?"

"She left." I let him go, stepping away.

Cole looks at the door, at the sheets of freezing rain pouring over the dreary landscape. "Where is Emelda?"

Emelda? "She's with Faye."

Cole looks at me, and his expression is so utterly broken I can almost taste his fear. He's gone in a flash, his vampiric speed splitting the rain like a knife.

I shift, tearing through my clothes, and race after him, but my heart begins to sink. I feel... intense fear. A sudden, overwhelming sense of urgency and adrenaline that has nothing to do with my own feelings.

It's the mate bond. Faye is awake, and she has no idea what's coming her way.

35

HOW DO YOU KILL A WITCH?

Faye

MY ENTIRE BODY REVOLTS AGAINST EVERY MOVE I'M TRYING TO MAKE AS
Emelda stands in the doorway, her body casting a long shadow across
the floorboards. My skin feels numb. My mouth is bone dry, and my
eyes sting against the firelight, but I can see the outline of a tall, darkened figure moving in Emelda's direction.

Anger ignites, waking my body from what *she* meant to be an
eternal slumber. A final rest.

"What are you doing here?" Emelda asks sharply into the darkness
as Matilda's face appears, glowing with amber light cast from the fire
in the hearth.

Her blue search Emelda's face as she takes another step closer to
the door Emelda's guarding. Matilda braces herself on the doorframe
and smiles... with fangs dripping with blood. She clicks her tongue,
rolling her eyes to the ceiling before laughing bitterly. "You fucking
fool. You should have just let her die. I thought she was dead, actually
for days. Imagine my surprise when I found out that bitch was still
living, holed up here in Prince Michael's shitty little house."

"Get out," Emelda snarls, her feet firmly planted. Her voice and posture drip with aggression as she looks up at Matilda. "Get out, right now. You are not welcome."

"I am going to be your queen soon. You shouldn't speak to me that way," Matilda drawls in a sing-song voice that sounds like nails being raked over stone. "Once my darling sister is out of the way, that is. Move."

"No," Emelda growls, fangs lengthening.

Matilda arches her perfectly manicured brows and laughs, "What a silly thing you are, witch. I can still smell it on you, you know. That undercurrent of feral, untamed magic. My family annihilated the witches in his kingdom. Extinguished them like blowing out a match. Oh, how they wailed when they were drained. I do miss the taste—"

Emelda slaps Matilda so hard her teeth clack together, and her head snaps to the side. "Get out of my house. This is your last warning."

Matilda turns murderous eyes toward Emelda as I struggle to stand. "You will regret that."

"Prove it."

Matilda lunges, snarling like a beast as she scrapes and claws at Emelda, dragging her to the ground. I leap onto my feet, hurrying across the mattress, but my legs are weak from lack of use. I'm like a newborn doe—unsteady, and unsure. But I grab a lamp off the opposite bedside table, ripping its cord free of the wall, and wield it over my head before slamming it onto Matilda's back. She screams as shards of porcelain bite through her crimson red gown, black blood pooling through the fabric.

"FAYE! GO!" Emelda grunts with frustration, trying to push Matilda off her, but Matilda is so strong.

Matilda… held me down like that once.

I didn't even fight.

But now… now I'm going to do what I should have done before.

I yank the remnants of the lamp back and slam it against the top of her head. Her cry of pain echoes through the silent house, but she's still fighting, wrapping a hand around Emelda's throat and squeezing so tight her nails pierce Emelda's skin.

I beat Matilda with the lamp until it's broken into pieces, nothing left but the cord. The bed is covered in glass and porcelain, but I don't feel the shards as they slice through my feet. I jump onto my sister's back and roll with her toward the fire.

Emelda goes suddenly quiet–too quiet. But I can't even look back at her because Matilda's hands are flying at me, and it's taking all of my strength to keep a hold on her. We roll back toward the bed, then toward the fire again, her hair catching in the flames.

"Why are you doing this?" I cry out, shaking her as the flames sizzle through her tresses. I'm straddling her, pressing all of my weight into her solid stomach, but it's no use. I meet her gaze–seeing my sister. The one woman I had in my circle that always listened to me, that knew me... and hated me.

But I never hated her. I loved her. She was all I had–

She throws me off. I hit the side of the dresser, my back splitting and lungs squeezing tight as all of the oxygen races from them. I gasp, pain echoing through my body, rendering me useless for several precious seconds–seconds Matilda uses to stand, her burnt hair falling off in ugly, crispy clumps that hit the ground and turn to ash. She smirks at me, wiping blood from her mouth, like she's recently fed. No wonder she's so strong. "You'll enjoy this," she says slyly, turning back to Emelda, who's struggling to swallow past the swollen bruises on her neck.

"No!" I cry, leaning forward and bracing my hands on the floor, trying to crawl to Emelda as Matilda kneels, gently brushing the witch's thick, dark hair away from her face and neck. "STOP!"

Matilda lifts the fabric of her dress, her pale, muscular thigh on display. She pulls a knife from a secret thigh holster and raises the blade to the light of the flames, smiling deliriously at her own reflection.

Smoke begins to fill the room. I glance at the fireplace, doing a double take as the rug catches on the embers that spilled out of the hearth during my tussle with Matilda, burning into the fabric and sending licks of flames skittering toward me–and Emelda.

My eyes dart back to Matilda, who catches me staring at her in disbelief through the reflection in her blade. "Funny, isn't it?" she says, licking her bloody lips. "Father always overlooked me because you were the pureblood, the royal. I'm just a slut's daughter, but look at me now. I'll be queen of it all. And when I take that throne from King Kane and dance on his shifter filth of a wife's bones, I'll be father's favorite, and he'll forget about you, and your disgustingly weak mother."

"S-Stop," I pant. Smoke funnels around us. An armchair next to the fireplace catches, flames licking up the fabric legs to the cushions. "You have to stop–"

"Your little shifter pet was delicious, by the way. I always wondered what he'd taste like." She giggles, licking her lips again while my life flashes before my eyes.

"No," I rasp, the word wobbling off my tongue. "Not–not Michael–"

A crash downstairs rattles the entire house at the very moment the curtains catch fire, flames licking to the ceiling, scorching the trim. Matilda screams with madness as she raises her blade. "Do you know how to kill a vampire, sister? You have to slice off our heads after being drained of all blood, and we wither…. But I'm curious… how do you kill a witch turned vampire? Because back in the good days, when we used them as food? We'd cut out their hearts and feast–"

The blade races downward. My scream is… earth shattering. A shadow cuts through the smoke at the very moment I close my stinging eyes.

36

THE AFTERMATH

Faye

THE SOUND OF SHATTERING GLASS BURSTS THROUGH MY EARS. THE ROAR of the fire overwhelms my senses, heat licking my face. I can't open my eyes against the smoke, and my voice is nothing but a strangled, choking gargle as I try to scream Emelda's name.

I'm grabbed from behind and dragged across the burning rug on the floor. Someone hauls me upright, throwing me over their shoulder like I'm nothing but a rag doll, a sack of potatoes.

I thrash and scream until my voice gives out entirely, and the smoke overwhelms my body, forcing me back into the haze of the deep, endless dreams I'd been living through against my will.

I sink my nails into the back of whoever's sprinting down the stairs as the house groans against the fire. A great, heavy sigh echoes through the hallways leading to the foyer before a thundering crack from above signals the fire has reached the roof.

I don't recognize the person holding me. Their smell is distinctly male, however. Leather and coarse fabric. Homespun, perhaps. Real cotton that carries the scent of the outside world. Still, I bite the stranger on the shoulder blade, sinking my fangs into his leather jacket until I meet skin, and he curses loudly but doesn't stop running.

"Who's still inside?" he rasps, but his voice is distorted by the blood rushing in my ears.

He tastes strange–wrong, in many ways. I gag and let him go, hissing and snarling while trying to fight out of his iron grip.

"Where the fuck is Michael?!" Someone else shouts from behind us–another male voice. Cole? It has to be Cole, but he sounds so broken, that cocky, lazy drawl pitched with worry. "MICHAEL!"

The fire absorbs his voice, and I'm dumped on the ground in the wet grass.

"Don't bite me again," the stranger hisses before shoving my hair out of my face. His hand swipes over my cheeks, my eyes. He blows hard, and it takes me a minute to understand what he's doing. I'm coated in ash, soot, and smoke. I blink rapidly to try to clear my gritty vision and see the face of either my captor or rescuer.

"I'm Deacon," he says, his blue eyes scanning my face. "I work for Michael. Where is he?"

"I–I don't know."

"Fuck! Cole! COLE!"

"I'm here–"

Another body is laid beside mine, but Cole puts her down gently, carefully, his face ravaged by concern. I reach over and grip Emelda's hand.

"Come on, Em," Cole rasps. "Please, just hold on–"

Another scream echoes through the night, but I can't tell what direction it's coming from. New faces blurred by shadows appear above Deacon's head as he kneels in front of me and covers me with his jacket–a uniform of some kind.

"The rain isn't doing anything to staunch the flames," someone says.

"The manor is a total loss. Was there anyone else inside?"

"Where is Prince Michael?"

I close my eyes against the unfamiliar voices of the villagers gathering to find out what happened. Many footsteps echo around us, squelching in the grass and slipping over cobblestone as they race toward the manor to help, but when I open my eyes again, I see nothing but the dark cloud of smoke rising through the rain, which pings off my face like little balls of pure ice.

"NO! NO!!!"

I freeze, my body going absolutely rigid at the anguish in the voice of the woman screaming somewhere in the distance. Emelda jolts to awareness while Cole fights her to stay down.

"My sister–" Emelda chokes. "That's Alma–"

"Listen to me," Cole says hoarsely, his tone full of pain. "Emelda, I'm sorry–"

"What happened? Where is Alma? She's screaming–"

Lowe's name is carried through the rain by a gentle breeze fueled by Alma's despair. I imagine Matilda's bloody mouth and teeth and feel my heart begin to race.

She'd killed someone tonight–a shifter. Fed from them until her ravenous appetite was satisfied. She'd made it sound like it was Michael–my Michael.

"Oh, no," I whisper, tears welling along my lower lashes. "Oh, no, not Lowe–"

"Someone help her!" Cole screams into the night while he fights to keep Emelda on her back.

I try to sit up, still fighting weakness from my long slumber and fighting my sister. I'm so frail. I can't be like this anymore. I can't let Matilda hurt the people I love any longer.

The next twenty minutes are a blur of activity. Guards from the nearby castle arrive to investigate. Deacon gathers me up and takes me into the same building in the depths of the village where I'd laid eyes on Michael for the first time–the physician's house.

Through the window in a small, empty room with nothing more than a worn couch and a rickety table, I watch the manor burn to the ground, steam and smoke rising into the rain, which has now turned to wet, thick snow.

Emelda and Alma are huddled beside me on the couch, all of us covered in blankets against the cold. A fire roars in the hearth at the far end of the room, but it does nothing to warm me. I keep watching the door. I keep waiting for it to open, for Michael to come back.

Cole stands beside the couch talking to Deacon in low tones. I have to strain to listen as Cole says, "I told him to just get her out of the house. That's all he needed to do. I was going to handle the rest."

"Where could they have gone?"

"I have no fucking idea," Cole grinds out, running a hand over his soot-smudged face. He glances down at Emelda, his hand fixed on her shoulder as she tries to comfort her sister, who's silently sobbing into her hands.

"Some of the villagers stopped the fire from spreading to the outbuildings, but there's nothing left of the manor. Are we–are we at the point where we need to look for their bodies, or is Michael still alive?"

I stare at the men. They glance at me, carrying on like I'm not sitting right here, listening to every word they say.

"If Michael killed her, he'd be here right now. He's not going to stop until he finds her. You won't find his body in the ashes, I can guarantee it–"

The door bursts open. I turn, my heart fluttering with hope that quickly dims as Queen Emory surveys the group of us on the couch and nearby. She holds my gaze for several seconds before looking at Cole and Deacon. "What the hell is happening?"

"Aunt Emory," Cole begins, taking a step away from Emelda.

"The young shifter found near the castle," she rasps, her body covered by a thick cloak and nothing else. Her hair is loose and wet, and she's panting like she ran here... in her wolf form. "Who's his mate?"

Alma sniffles and rises on unsteady legs. "He's mine," she answers so softly and painfully it kills the tension in the room. "He's mine. Can I–can I see him? To say goodbye?"

I wait for the queen to tell her there's nothing left, but she says,

"Come, you must go to the castle immediately. He is in very bad shape."

"He's alive?" Emelda rises but stumbles. Cole grabs her arm to steady her.

"Barely. Who did this? Cole? Who did this?" The queen is furious as she stares down her nephew. "And where is Michael?"

37

THIS MEANS WAR

Michael

I pull my battered body off the snowy ground, shaking out my coat. In my wolf form, my vision is much better than normal, but against the storm raging this far up in the mountains, I'm barely able to see more than ten feet in front of me.

Matilda's footprints have faded, carried away by the wind, and the trail of vampire blood I'd been following is long gone.

But I've been chasing her for miles... to the outskirts of my family's kingdom–high in the mountains, where even a shifter would struggle to survive against a storm like this.

If she's out here, she won't be alive for long. If she ever steps foot in my kingdom again, I'll make an example out of her and string her body on the front gates of the castle for everyone to see and know what I'd do to protect what's mine.

The storm batters my back as I make the decision to turn and go home, to where my mate's awake and waiting for me.

Memories of the last few hours clog my mind, tearing my focus from the snowy hellscape all around me. Finding Lowe in bloody

159

pieces. Watching flames burst through the upper windows of my house. Having to choose between going to Faye and pulling her off the ground where she was kneeling, screaming, and killing the vampire who did this to her in the first place.

I chose to tackle Matilda through a window in my wolf form, falling down two stories in a tangle of fur, blood, and smoke, while I trusted my mate with Deacon, knowing he'd save her.

I think of Cole, and the memories flood away, replaced by his increasingly odd behavior at any mention of Emelda.

He'd run to here like I'd run to Faye—with every ounce of focus dedicated to getting back to the woman that meant more to me than the air I breathe.

I've never seen him move so quickly toward anything before, and now I'm wondering what the hell is going on between my cousin and my best friend. I don't like it, knowing Cole. I love him because he's family, but he's not the kind of guy I'd want for Emelda, and she... she hates him, doesn't she?

I race down the mountain back into the endless rolling hills and open plains, through sparse woods that bleed into villages and small towns while my mind wanders. I have to get home, but my body is begging to turn around and continue hunting the vampire who hurt my mate and my family, but I can't. Morning light is already starting to creep through the clouds, and I want to be home, with Faye, who's awake, finally.

But as I near the outskirts of Ravenfell, I slow, my mind dragging my tired body to a dead stop. Down here, off the mountains, the snow has turned to another day of heavy, freezing rain... and remnants of smoke and steam rise over the village.

I edge closer along one of the hilltops that gives me a view of the village below as the first light of morning casts shadows through the alleys. There's a black, empty spot where my house once stood. It burned to the ground completely, leaving ruin and embers in its wake.

But I'm close enough to my family that I can hear them calling out to me through their minds every few minutes or so, their voices dripping with desperation.

I go to the castle on impulse–tired, beaten, somewhat scorched and freezing cold–and I'm let in immediately by guards who usher me into a private sitting room where fresh clothes are waiting for me.

My heart pounds against my ribs as I button my shirt, my hands raw and bruised along with the rest of my body from a two-story fall and dozens of miles spent chasing a rabid vampire through the mountains.

When the door to the sitting room opens, my dad appears, looking gravely concerned despite the icy royal mask of indifference shielding his expression.

He opens his mouth to no doubt ask what the hell happened, but I beat him to it.

"Matilda of Red River," I say, pulling my belt through the loops and securing it on my waist. "The princess… she did this to Faye, her own sister. The attack, the poisoning, it was all her."

He's silent as I sit and pull on a pair of socks and shoes.

"I believe Faye was the princess that was meant to marry Cole, and for whatever reason, Matilda tried to kill her to take her place."

"Michael–"

"Cole will not be marrying Faye. I plan to, if it's what she wants. Matilda is still out there, but I chased her deep into the mountains–she won't survive the day."

"Michael–"

"If King Mattias wants to march on our kingdom, so be it. I want a war for what he allowed to happen. His daughter is a deranged lunatic, and I will not stand for it."

Dad purses his lips. "Her companions have also left the castle. We have no idea where they are."

"Hopefully they know what's good for them, because if I see them, they're dead. There's nothing else to say about it."

He steps further into the room. "King Mattias is not someone to be fucked with, Michael. This treaty of peace is precarious and dependent on Cole's marrying one of his daughters."

"I don't give a fuck," I say, meeting his eyes. "Let him bring his soldiers. I'll meet him on the battlefield. Faye will not be going home to Red River, and that's final."

"You love her," he says, and it's not a question.

"She is my mate, like you're mom's mate. You can't understand–"

"I understand more about that than you're aware, Michael, but what you're doing… there will be a war, you have to understand that. You haven't experienced war, and for that, I'm grateful, but you have romantic notions about what this will look like. Our kingdom has been at peace for over twenty-five years. Lex's kingdom, as well. That's unheard of in our history. Even the shifters have had decades of quiet–"

"I will not be quiet about what happened to my mate. If they try to come for her, there will be war."

"And if she chooses to go home to her father?" he asks loudly, his voice echoing around the room, "Because she can't feel the same way you do, Michael. What will your answer be then?"

I suck in a breath, searching his gaze for understanding, for a glimpse of what he feels as a full-blooded, blood-born vampire in love with a shifter–a mortal.

"And what do you feel for Mom? Would you start a war in her name, even if you couldn't love her as deeply as she loved you?"

"You already know my answer."

"Then we'll stand as a kingdom beside Uncle Lex," I tell him with a sharp nod. "When Mattias comes calling for retribution from Lex for failing to meet the terms of their treaty, we'll answer."

He exhales deeply, and after what feels like an eternity, nods. "We will go to war if it comes to that."

If it comes to that…. Ridiculous. It's already coming to that. I can feel the shift in the air as I rise and leave the room, walking on steady feet full of determination.

I can feel her here. The bond between us tugged tight. I marked my mate, and now she's bound to me, and I have no plans on letting her go unless… it's what she desires.

I throw open the door to a bedroom in the upper levels of the castle–the personal rooms used by my family and my family only.

She's pacing the room by the window, her golden hair loose and falling in gentle waves around her waist. She's alone, and lifts her head, not daring to open her eyes.

"Faye," I whisper, closing the door behind me, and her eyes flutter before opening, her chest heaving with relief before she lets out a strangled cry and runs to me.

38

______

IT'S OBVIOUS

Faye

I DON'T KNOW WHY I THROW MYSELF AGAINST MICHAEL LIKE MY LIFE depends on feeling him firm and whole in my arms. Maybe this feeling inside my chest is a rushed, fleeting echo of something deeper, something I've only known to be true in fairy tales. Maybe he doesn't feel the same—maybe he sees me as a burden, a nuisance.

After what I've put his friends and family through, I wouldn't be thoroughly shocked to be shoved away and scolded—then banished.

But his arms wrap around me, lifting me into the air as his warm breath tickles my neck. He breathes my name against my skin, and it awakes those overwhelming feelings of possession and utter, all-consuming lust in my bones. I am his. Whatever high powers decide whose names are written together in the stars? They chose me for him, didn't they?

That's the only explanation....

He sets me down so gently I momentarily feel like I'm floating until my slippered toes brush the carpet. His eyes hold on mine as he brushes back my hair, scanning my face. He looks exhausted—worried

165

and tired. The sharp crease between his brows deepens when I pull away, my hands pressed to his chest, and stammer, "Lowe–he's–he's very hurt–"

Michael nods. "I heard."

"He's with the physician. They're trying to put him back together again, but it's looking impossible. Alma–" I choke on her name, fresh, hot tears stinging my eyes and blurring my vision to the point I can't see past them. "I'm so sorry. Michael, I am so–so sorry. This was my fault."

"It was not," he reassures me, reaching to swipe tears from my cheeks, but I turn away from him to face the window again where bright, fluffy snow is falling in the thickest of sheets. "Faye–"

"I understand if you need to send me away, to give me back to my father. I do. I will go," I rasp, looking at him over my shoulder. "I was sent for Cole. I will–I will go with him, and be his wife, if it's asked of me."

"No."

I shake my head. I've been gnawing on my lower lip so hard it feels puffy and bruised. "It's not up to you. It's not our decision–it's your kingdom at stake."

"Do you want to go back to Red River?"

Silence drags through the room, falling between us like a wet blanket. I find it hard to breathe as memories of home come rushing back–most of them good. The maids and servants who cared for me and treated me like a friend, like family. The governesses and tutors who spent their days, their weeks, their years in my company treated me like I was more than a pretty little doll being prepared to be some-one's new toy.

But I had no friends of my same rank. I was ostracized for being what they called weak hearted and sensitive, unable to behave like a high-ranking female vampire should. I wasn't like Matilda, and I paid dearly for that, didn't I?

I think of my mother–her soft hands and sweet voice, like honey. Her scent like lilac on a warm, sunny summer breeze. She never spoke of dancing in the blood of the lesser species. She never took pleasure in telling me stories of the "filthy" shifters and the curses of the witches.

She didn't belong in Red River. She was sent there to give the king the girls he needed to barter like chattel. She was given to him against her family's will because she was beautiful, and that's all it takes.

I was beautiful. My soft heart was mistaken for submission. I was chosen because my father thought he could use me like a puppet from miles and miles away—to turn this family into putty in his weathered hands.

I am not my mother. I will not die on my back. I will not be laid to rest in a forgotten, neglected tomb. I will not let those vampires in Red River hurt me anymore, or anyone I love.

"No," I answer, meeting his eyes.

"You will not be marrying Cole," he says softly, risking another step in my direction like I'm a frightened deer ready to sprint away at any moment. "You will be marrying me."

Shock echoes through my body. "Is that what you want?"

His gaze slides from my eyes to my neck and holds before he meets my eyes again. "You were dying. I thought..." He grits his teeth, his jaw clenched tight. "I thought I was losing you—every second of every day you slipped further away, and I felt like I was letting you suffer because of my own selfish desire to keep you. Whatever you've done to me, Faye, I couldn't... I couldn't accept that you were ready to go."

He steps toward me, hanging his head, and continues, "Emelda kept you alive for my sake. It was wrong to let you suffer like that, and I... I did something to you that can't be undone. Not unless you reject me."

"Reject you?"

His eyes tilt upward, meeting mine. "I marked you. I claimed you as my mate. I did so without your consent or knowledge, knowing you'd never feel the same way I feel. The way shifters feel when they find that one, singular person that defines their life—their path."

My world ceases to exist as his mouth moves, the words flowing through me like water through a stream. "What does it feel like?" I ask, wondering if I'm even awake or still dying in a poison induced coma. "Finding your mate?"

Another step in my direction, closing the distance between us again, his knuckles gently dragging down my arm over the silken fabric of a nightgown his mother loaned me. "Like seeing your own heart walking outside your body," he says, his touch lingering on my wrist. "Like tasting color, like hearing music in each word that comes from your mouth. Like everything I was before you was just an illusion, and I am forever changed."

I close my eyes as his touch works back up my arms. I press my cheek against the palm of his hand, feeling his radiant warmth–the closest I'll ever get to feeling the sun on my skin.

"But you can't feel the same way," he says softly, painfully. "And I understand if you… I'm a shifter."

"That doesn't matter–"

"You're a vampire, Faye. I might be half, but I don't know what that means for the longevity of my life yet."

I'd never thought of that before. A sudden sharp ache spreads through my chest at the thought of losing him… this man I've known for mere weeks but feel as though I've been searching for my entire life.

It's crazy, isn't it? Mourning someone you haven't lost yet?

"Do you want me?" I ask, my voice trembling. "Do you want me to stay?"

He searches my eyes for understanding, looking slightly confused.

"Do you love me, Michael?" I ask, and this time, my voice doesn't tremble.

His answer is the softest brush of his lips against mine. "Hasn't it been obvious from the beginning, Faye?"

3 9

—————

WHAT HAPPENS NOW?

Faye

I PACE OUTSIDE A SET OF GILDED DOORS THAT STRETCH NEARLY TO THE domed ceiling somewhere in the depths of the castle. Dressed in a nightgown with a thick, dark purple robe resting over my shoulders, my feet leave imprints in the rug as I walk back and forth, wringing my hands.

I try to tune out the male voices talking over each other, but it's impossible. Michael cuts in aggressively, but with the door in the way, his voice is a distorted muffle. Someone else, King Lex, I believe, replies, and Cole's heated answer sends warning bells skittering through my brain.

The door suddenly opens and shuts with a slam that rattles the impressive paintings on the red walls as Cole stalks toward me.

I step out of his way but reach out to him at the very last second, grabbing his wrist. He flinches, giving me a shocked, somewhat furious scowl like he's not used to being touched.

"Emelda was moved to a room upstairs. She's resting in the south hall, the fourth door on the left."

His expression softens. I watch the column of his throat bob as he swallows, nodding to himself. I let go of his wrist, watching him whirl toward the massive stone archway leading into the network of darkened corridors and stairwells–a spider web of history, leading to rooms I can't name or number.

I turn back to the door and watch it open a second time. Queen Emory slips out looking drawn and weary but whole. She closes the door softly against the argument still taking place inside but gives me a tight, although warm, smile.

"You don't need to be here for this," she says softly, her green eyes shining with emotion I can't read. "I'm afraid it's only going to get worse."

"They're talking about me. I should be in there, facing it head on."

She gives me a small, knowing smirk. "No, darling. In this family, we let the men handle these things while we… plot the real course of action."

I raise my brows as she gracefully walks in my direction, extending her hand.

"Come, you must be famished. I know I am."

I allow her to lead me away from the door and into the corridors, our footsteps sending echoes through the quiet castle.

I glance in the direction of the numerous guest rooms, wondering if Cole went to see Emelda. She follows my gaze at one point and says, "Emelda is a very brave woman. I've always liked her. She's good for Michael. She's been… a rock for him, so to speak."

"She's wonderful," I echo, feeling choked up all of the sudden. The image of Matilda beating Emelda shears through my mind, making my eyes water. I tighten my grip on Queen Emory's forearm unintentionally, but she lays her hand over my fingers and pats my hand. "Emelda is going to be okay."

"And Lowe?" I rasp, barely able to meet her eyes.

She looks away, her eyes going distant and hazy as she chews her lower lip. "I hope so."

She leads me up a flight of stairs and into a surprisingly sunny sitting room full of plants. Even the wallpaper is multicolored and floral, and the scent of sugar hangs in the air as she walks to the windows and pulls the curtains closed against the light. Snow is still falling as she closes another curtain, leaving just one window uncovered, and turns toward a young vampire maid who dutifully nods her head as the queen orders fresh blood for me and a pot of tea for herself.

"Actually," she says to the maid, her cheeks going a little pink. "Something stronger than tea would be better, I think."

The maid nods and hurries away, the door closing us together, sending a vibration through the room.

Queen Emory paces for a few minutes while I stand near the uncovered window, squinting into the daylight reflecting off the snow before it starts to hurt my eyes. Neither of us says anything until the maid returns with tea, blood, and a bottle of clear liquid that smells like juniper berries and leaves again.

I pour myself a glass of blood and sit on a lounge chair, unsure what to say or do besides take a few sips. I am hungry. I can feel that gnawing ache starting to ignite, and I know it's been far too long since I've had a good, long feed, but... I take another drink, then another, until I've finished the glass.

The queen herself pours me a second helping.

"Faye," she says, glancing at me before popping the cork on the bottle of alcohol and mixing a heavy serving into her teacup, "has Michael told you about..." She eyes me, and I realize she's not trying to give anything away... Like the fact Michael believes I'm his mate.

I rub the mark on my neck without realizing what I'm doing, and her cheeks flush as she sits, crossing her legs.

"Yes," I tell her, my own cheeks burning. "He did tell me, yes."

"I see," she whispers, sipping from her teacup. Her eyes are on her knees, however.

I wait for her to tell me there's no way in hell she's allowing me to marry her son, to say I'm scum like my murderous sister and our horrible father, but she... smiles, then chuckles, shaking her head.

"Michael has always worried me in the romance department. He's so like his father. Just–" She waves a hand over her face. "It took me years to tell what Kane was feeling. You can never tell in his expression or his eyes. Michael is the same–worse, I think. But when you arrived, he seemed so... on edge."

"That doesn't sound like a good thing."

"Any emotion from a vampire is a good thing. He cared about you, worried about you. You meant something to him–still do, of course." She waves a hand in dismissal, blushing a bit. "He told me you were his mate, and we had a long talk about it. I think he was nervous to even broach the subject with you."

"Because he thought I wouldn't feel the same?"

"Because you're a vampire, darling."

I feel something like... frustration bubbling through my veins. I take another swallow of the blood–which is very nice, honestly. Mellow, and sweet–then cross my legs and my arms, and frown against my better judgement. "Just because I'm a vampire, that doesn't mean I'm incapable of feeling things like–like love, and possession, and pride."

"Oh, you vampires do feel pride, I know that for a fact," she teases, but I'm still simmering.

"I love him. I feel–I feel connected to him in an odd way, like even if I wanted to, even if he pisses me off and drives me insane, I won't be able to give him up, or get rid of him. Like he's stuck, right here." I press a finger against my chest, over my heart. "I can't get him out of there. I won't be able to, will I? Ever?"

"Do you want to?"

"No, I'd like to be with him," I mumble, unsure why I'm spilling my heart to Michael's *mother* of all people, but here I am, wiping a drop of blood from my lips with the back of my hand and saying, "I love him. I hate that I'm the reason all of this has happened–that my sister has done so much wrong to your family. I never–I didn't have a choice to come here. I remember that now. I was supposed to marry Cole–"

"Did Michael tell you that won't be happening?"

"Yes," I grind out, feeling on the verge of tears again, but I am so incredibly tired of crying. "But I would, if it would make things better for you."

She furrows her brow. "We wouldn't do that to you, Faye. We wouldn't force you and Michael apart."

"But that's what they're fighting about, isn't it? My father going to war because King Lex broke the treaty between them that was dependent on my marriage into this family–"

"Don't worry about that now," she says softly, motherly, a tone that makes me feel a kind of warmth I haven't known since my own mother died. "You're safe now. Matilda is dead."

"She's dead." I meet the queen's eyes. "You're sure? Her body has been found?"

4 0

IT'S ALL SETTLED

Faye

"No, her body hasn't been found. Not exactly," Queen Emory says, shifting her weight in the chair opposite mine. "That's what they were fighting about, actually. Michael wants to send some warriors into the mountains to hunt her down, or find her body, whichever comes first, just to be sure."

"And what about Cole?"

She sighs, rolling her eyes to the ceiling before closing them. "I'm not sure what his problem is, but Cole is often just mad at the world in general."

"He's upset because Emelda got hurt," I whisper, remembering his choked concern in the aftermath of the fire.

Queen Emory looks at me, confused. "I didn't realize they were friends. He's never had a nice thing to say about her, which always shocked me because everyone loves Emelda."

I suddenly realize they are not friends. Definitely not friends. More than friends, maybe. I clear my throat, deciding that's none of my business, for now.

A few moments pass in silence, both of us lost in our thoughts and conspiracies, apparently, when the door opens wide, and a pair of heavy footsteps echo in our direction. Two vampires darken the doorway–father and son.

Michael glances at his mother, looking relieved to find us together instead of me being missing again, or worse.

King Kane walks over to his wife, resting a hand on her shoulder while she brings her teacup to her lips. "Drinking already?" he teases in a tone that seems too soft for a man with a reputation like his. "It's not even noon. Are you having a rough day?"

"Don't tease me, Kane," she snaps back, but she smiles around the words, and I feel as though I'm intruding on a private moment.

But Kane looks at me, then Michael, who's just come to stop behind my chair.

"So?" Queen Emory asks, setting her cup down on the table between us. "What's the plan?"

"I've dispatched a group of men into the mountains for the next week or two to find any signs that the vampire lived," Kane says, refusing to say her name like it's a curse. "Lex and Ivy are returning to their home tomorrow morning."

"And Cole?"

"He's returning to his kingdom with his parents."

Michael rests his elbow on the top of the chair, drumming his fingers.

Kane purses his lips, staring down at his wife. "That's it. Life moves on as normal."

But Michael says, "King Mattias will be notified of the whereabouts of both of his daughters shortly, whenever our messenger arrives in Red River."

I stiffen.

He continues, "We'll deal with whatever fallout comes."

"I want warriors stationed in the shifter territories between our kingdom and his," the queen says, nodding. "Just until we know there won't be unrest."

Kane and Michael look at each other, and I realize quite suddenly they're leaving an important piece of information out of this narrative.

Before I can open my mouth and ask, which I'd likely regret, Michael says, "Faye needs to rest."

"So do you," Queen Emory replies with a ghost of a smirk touching her beautiful mouth.

I feel the tension in the room shift and decide I should leave. I rise, thank the queen for her time, and let Michael lead me out of the room, down more corridors and darkened hallways.

Neither of us speak until we reach an unfamiliar area in the castle. He pulls a set of keys out of his pocket, picking through them until he finds the one he's looking for and slips it into the lock.

His scent reaches me before my eyes adjust to the darkness. I step into a foyer with archways branching off it in all directions.

A small kitchen and dining room, tastefully furnished. A sitting room with a library attached. An office, a sunroom, and a hallway leading far back, where a large bedroom and ensuite stretch toward the far corner of the castle.

Everything is painted in dark blues and emerald greens. The dark wood furniture and floors make the space feel cozy and slightly moody–which reminds me of his manor... which is now gone.

"These are your rooms, aren't they?"

"Yes," he replies, closing the door behind us and locking it. "It's my section of the castle. One day, when I'm king, I'll likely live in the royal suites my parents use now, but this was home until I moved to the manor."

I turn to him, balling my fists to stop from touching him. "I'm sorry about the manor."

"Don't be."

"It was your home," I press, looking up into his eyes. He steps forward and leans down, his forehead resting on mine as his lips brush over my cheek.

"It doesn't matter. This is all I need to be whole again."

I close my eyes as my stomach flutters with anticipation, and he kisses me–slow and tender. I shudder as feeling thrums through my body, waking me up again, making me feel like I didn't just spend a week flat on my back on the edge of death.

But he pulls away. I briefly chase him, desperate for more, but his thumb swipes over my lower lip, his eyes dark and heavy with the same need turning my insides out. "Are you hungry?"

"Yes," I breathe, clutching his shirt.

He takes a rattling breath, his eyes slightly glazed, then picks me up and carries me to *our* room.

4 1

REBORN

Faye

Michael has satin sheets in the same dark blue as the walls of his enormous bedroom. A fire crackles in the hearth, spraying warmth that mingles with the heat beneath my skin as he slowly, achingly, devastatingly slowly lays me on the bed and slides the robe free of my shoulders. The loose straps of my nightgown go next, gliding over my skin in a featherlight touch that has gooseflesh erupting all over my body.

I'm on fire. I'm chilled. I'm everything in between as his mouth brushes mine, my name a whisper as it leaves his lips.

There's nothing rushed about this compared to the first time. I don't feel a single ounce of desperation, of burning, unquenchable lust. This feels... easy. Natural. I know his taste. I know his smell and recognize the way it feels to be touched by his warm, calloused hands. My body has already memorized the way it feels to have those hands ghosting down my sides, dragging my nightgown down until the cool night air shimmers over my naked breasts.

I suck in a breath and close my eyes when his lips brush over my neck–over the scar he left on my skin. His scar. His mark–the brand I'll wear for all eternity that binds me to him, even when he's... gone.

I grip his upper arms at the thought of losing him and quickly banish it, reminding myself neither of us know that for certain. This is just the beginning. We have an entire mortal lifetime together. That's still a long time.

"Come back to me," he orders, smiling against the crook of my neck. He presses a heated kiss there, the kind that makes me hiss at the fleeting jolt of warmth replaced and cooled by his tongue. He laps at my skin–licking and sucking until I'm effectively pulled from my terrible intrusive thoughts and back to the present, where I'm totally bare and splayed beneath him on silken sheets.

His skin glows like polished gold in the firelight against the deep blue of the wallpaper. I reach to run my fingers through his hair, sighing and mewling as his mouth travels down to my breasts.

"Take off my shirt," he says before dragging his tongue over my left nipple.

My lips part in a silent moan, but my fingers don't tremble as I fumble with the buttons until losing my patience and ripping his shirt clean off. A sharp pinging sound echoes around the room as the buttons fly in all directions. One hits me in the shoulder, making me yelp in pain.

"You're in a hurry," he croons, obviously enjoying himself as he sucks my nipple into his eager mouth and caresses my other breast–kneading it to the rhythm of his tongue on the other side.

I bring my knees up, and he settles between them on impulse, rocking against my core, but he's still wearing his damn trousers, and I'm growing suddenly, inexplicably, needy.

"Michael, please!" I gasp, arching my hips to chase any friction I can find.

He hums a laugh as his mouth travels further down, wet and unhurried, until he reaches my hip bone.

It tickles.

I inhale sharply, trying not to squeal at the sensation of his tongue dragging over that surprisingly sensitive spot, but he only grins against my skin.

"You're tormenting me and enjoying it." I growl but bend my head back as his mouth reaches the apex of my thighs. His tongue darts out–tasting, teasing–just an inch from my clit. I moan against my wishes, and it's a needy, impatient sound that only adds to the amount of fun he's having.

"I love seeing you like this," he admits, looking up at me with his hair wild and jade eyes heavy with desire.

"Like what? Whiny?"

"Bossy."

I gape at him. "I'm not bossy."

"Only here, and I don't mind. I don't mind it all. I like it." His eyes go as dark as polished obsidian. "So tell me what to do, Faye. Where do you want me?" He keeps his eyes locked on mine as he dips lower, dragging his tongue through my folds.

Every rational thought leaves my body, my mind going blissfully blank.

But he clicks his tongue. "Do you want me here, like this?" Another lick has my toes curling and my eyes rolling back in my head. If he does it again, I'm a goner. As quickly as that, he asks, "Or inside of you?"

How can I possibly choose?

My body acts before my mind has a single second to process his question. My hand flies out, my fingers tangling in his hair and pushing his head down between my legs. He wraps his arms around my thighs and pulls me closer, his tongue dragging and dancing over my clit, through my throbbing folds until I'm crying out his name.

But just as I'm on the precipice of losing all sense of time and place, he roughly rolls us over to the very center of the bed, and suddenly I'm on top of him.

I grab the headboard to steady myself, panting, and look down at him.

His eyes shine with heat and mischief as he looks up at me, just as breathless, smiling like a cat with cream, and I... I feel a fire ignite deep in my soul. Something new and all-consuming. Like everything I was is dead, and I've been reborn, given a second chance.

My nails sink into the hardwood—likely antique—headboard as I rock my hips against his tongue, his lips.

"Very good," he praises, his hands gripping my thighs. "Don't stop, Faye. You taste amazing."

4 2

———

IT'S NOT A QUESTION

Faye

I'M SHAKING. MY ARMS TREMBLE AS I GRIP THE HEADBOARD, FIGHTING for purchase. My hair falls loose down my back, tickling my skin as I give myself over body and soul to the man beneath me.

Michael comes up for air with a satisfied sigh as pleasure shimmers through my body. He kisses up my thighs, then my stomach, until he reaches my breasts as he sits up and slips out of his pants.

I'm still above him. I'm still throbbing with heat when his hands drift up my back, his knuckles dragging back down the length of my spine. I arch into his touch, rolling my neck and closing my eyes as his touch reaches my hips again, and he guides me down onto his hard cock.

The tip breaches my folds. He groans, sliding his cock through the wetness pooled there while he presses me down until I'm fully seated on top of him.

My hands leave the headboard to grip his shoulders, gasping as he stretches me wide, the slight pain of it fading to the feeling of fullness

183

that makes me inhale sharply and close my eyes. I move my hips on instinct. My body knows what to do as I lean forward, resting my cheek against the side of his face.

Michael guides my movements, determining the tempo with a firm, but gentle, touch, his hands gripping my hips and moving them up and down, then side to side.

"Look at me," he rasps.

I shake with building pleasure as I slowly turn my head to look at him. I'm sure I look insane–blushing and sweaty with my hair falling around my face in unruly waves–but he looks into my eyes as he kisses me, gently nibbling my lower lip until I open for him and melt against him.

I'm straddling him in a way that makes it possible for him to have access to every part of my body. I'm on full display, and he takes advantage of my breasts, my hips, his hands eventually cradling the globes of my ass as he lifts and lowers me on his cock.

His breathing becomes more erratic, his movements still honed to my pleasure, but I can feel him holding back. He's riding the same edge I am but determined to take his time, to not rush this, to savor every minute.

My inner muscles tighten, and he smiles darkly. "You're so close, aren't you?"

"I can't help it," I whimper, closing my eyes to slits as I pick up the pace, bouncing on his cock. The pressure on my clit is unreal–too much yet not enough. My whining, needy moans echo through the room as his grip on my body tightens.

He presses a kiss to my neck, murmuring praise against my slick skin.

But it's not enough. I want something… else. Something I'm not sure I should want.

I lean back, looking down at him, panting. "Michael?"

His gaze meets mine, heavy and hooded with need.

"Bite me again," I whisper, unsure if the words even left my mouth.

But his brows raise just a touch, and his… pupils expand to the point I can no longer see the sparkling jade.

A glimmer of hesitation spirits through my body. I freeze as his grip tightens, realizing I've just awakened the one thing that sets the two of us apart.

I yelp in surprise when he flips me onto my back, my body bouncing on the mattress. A second later I'm on my belly and he's dragging my hips upward.

I grip the sheets as a flicker of fear creeps through my system. His hands are steady on my hips. I feel him leaning down over me, and then he presses a kiss to my spine. "I'm not going to hurt you," he whispers tenderly. "You don't need to be afraid."

"I'm not–not afraid," I stammer hotly, but he chuckles, nudges my legs apart with his knee.

"I can feel it, Faye. You felt a little unsure just then."

"You can't possibly know what I'm feeling–"

"It's a mate thing," he says under his breath, his voice dropping an octave.

Something I can't understand.

I have a single second to process his words before he drags his cock through my folds, letting out a breath. He presses inside of me in a single rough, full thrust. I tilt my hips higher, arching into the feeling of him filling me so fully I have to bury my face in the pillow to stop from screaming. The easy, rhythmic love-making when I'd been riding him is over. Now, I'm at his mercy–at a shifter's mercy.

No wonder Alma left all ideas of taking a vampire lover behind and went to the dark side.

I scream his name to the ceiling when he covers me with his body and bites down hard on my shoulder. The sound of our bodies meeting over, and over, mingles with his low, throaty growls of ecstasy and my strangled moans. My body is on fire. The tension in my lower belly peaks as he buries himself so deep my toes curl, and I almost arch out of it, but he holds me there, refusing to let me move.

"Come for me," he orders. "I want to feel you coming undone." He bites my shoulder again, groaning as he grinds into me. He's not worried about being rough. He knows I can handle it–that I want it, need it, and love it. He knows that I'm on the edge of losing myself to him completely and smiles against my neck, chuckling low in his throat as I whimper and moan, begging for more.

He licks and sucks my neck as he thrusts hard, burying himself to the hilt.

It's all I need to be rocked over the edge. The tension in my lower belly and spine explodes, sending shimmers of unreal pleasure rocketing through my muscles. I cry out his name, tears of ecstasy sliding free from my lashes as he pumps into me once more, groaning as my inner walls clench his cock and pulse.

He holds me close, panting, as he spills himself deep within me, filling me with a heavy, full warmth.

"Marry me," he whispers into the darkness, still buried deep.

"I thought–I thought you said I was–"

"I never asked if it was what you want," he pants. He hisses out a breath while pulling out. I almost expect him to pull away completely, to walk across the room and turn on the lights to have this suddenly serious conversation, but he flips me over onto my back and covers my body with his.

Nose to nose, I blink up at him, still coming down from the high of my life. "Why would you want to marry me anyway, Michael?"

"It's convenient. I need a wife."

I scoff, but his sleepy, satiated smile tells me he's just being an ass.

"Why would I want to marry you?" I tease.

"I could make you a queen."

"What if I don't want to be a queen?"

"Then I'll put you up in a cottage somewhere where you can read and paint and play piano all day. I'll come to you at night," he says, pressing a slow kiss to my lips.

"And what if I do want to be your queen?" I ask in all seriousness, my chest growing suddenly tight. "What if… we can't? What if we're stopped from–"

"I'd go to war for you," he replies with another kiss.

"I'd go with you," I tell him, running my fingers through his hair. He leans into the touch, closing his eyes, exhausted.

"Marry me," he repeats, and I smile.
"I will. Yes, I will."

43

SHE BROKE ME

Emelda

SNOWY DARKNESS STRETCHES AHEAD OF ME. WHATEVER LIGHT FROM the moon is blocked by thick clouds that spread snow across the hills leading from the castle to Ravenfell. I pull my cloak tight to fight the bitter chill in the air and breathe in the fresh, crisp night. It smells clean. I love that smell. I love when it snows. I always have.

But tonight, I'm not tucked in bed with the fire roaring while I read a book. I'm not in my kitchen mixing herbs or baking for Michael's insatiable shifter appetite. I'm not settled near the window mending a seam in his favorite jacket while watching the snow fall in dizzy circles.

Now, I'm walking to what remains of my old life.

I stop at the edge of the manor's property line. A few outbuildings remain, but that's it. What was once a great house with a rich history is now nothing more than a pile of rubble and snow-soaked embers, some still flickering like stars against the blackest of night skies.

Part of me thought there'd be something left. A single room. A set of curtains. A portrait, a picture, an empty frame.

It's all gone.

I swallow a sob. My eyes remain dry, but I wipe them anyway, then turn, facing the village. Night is when the normally sleepy town comes alive, but now it's… solemn. Shadows pass between alleys and across snow-packed streets. I scan the village, my gaze lingering on the singular shifter establishment in town where a group has gathered at its entrance.

It's a bar with a small restaurant inside that sells both food and blood.

Lowe owns it.

My heart sinks as I move toward the village, taking the stone steps I used to climb day in and day out that lead to the manor. I can feel the stares as I cross into the village–the people who stop to look and whisper as I move like a ghost toward the gathered crowd in front of the bar.

There's only a handful of shifters who live in Ravenfell full time, and they're all standing outside the bar talking in low tones to the vampires who take up the majority of our meager population, but not a single person is snarling or on the verge of shifting.

Heartache is ripe. I can taste it on my tongue.

Finn, a shifter who works as the bartender, and his mate, Cassidy, who runs the kitchen, spot me and go silent.

The crowd of vampires turn and parts to let me pass between them, and all eyes are on me.

Finn, tall with dark hair and bright hazel eyes, scans my face for answers about his friend. My heart lurches, my mouth going painfully dry.

"Emelda," Cassidy croaks, her blue eyes glassy with unshed tears. She reaches for me, taking my cold hand in hers, sharing her warmth without flinching. She pulls me close, wrapping me in an embrace, and I… hang my head against her shoulder.

The vampires behind us don't cackle or make comments about aligning with the shifters. The shifters don't click their tongues and growl.

We're unified under a blanket of grief and confusion.

Cassidy releases me but cups my cheeks, shaking her head. "How's Alma?"

"She's at the castle. She won't leave him."

Cassidy nods, sniffling as she looks over her shoulder at her mate. They're older–likely in their sixties. They have children and grandchildren who live deeper in the shifter territories–a large, beautiful family–something I dreamed of for myself.

Finn turns from us to the crowd, quietly saying, "Everyone come inside. Warm up. I'll get out the blood–the good stuff."

Murmurs of thanks drift between the bodies now shuffling toward the door. Cassidy wraps her arm around my waist and guides me inside where, within minutes, I'm tucked in an armchair by the fire with several other forlorn vampires, a mug of warm, sweetly spiced blood in my hands.

Finn leans against the fireplace while Cassidy stokes the fire, but everyone is waiting for me to talk. That's why I came here, after all. To share news from the castle about our duke and our friends.

"Lowe is likely going to survive," I say to the group, ignoring the shuffle of feet as people turn to look at me. "He's hanging on as hard as he can, but he was… nearly drained."

A few of the vampires look down at their hands in shame. Finn adjusts his position, crossing his arms over his chest and looking down at the ground.

"Prince Michael chased her–Matilda–the one who did this, into the northern mountains. It's unlikely she survived," I continue. I look up, scanning the familiar faces of both vampires and shifters alike. "But we need to be on guard. If any vampires we don't recognize come to Ravenfell, we need to assume they're not friends of ours."

"And Prince Michael's… vampire friend?" someone asks. "The girl–"

"She's alive and well," I choke out, relief I haven't given myself a chance to feel after spending over a week trying to keep Faye alive spreads through my body. "She's alive. She'll be fine."

Murmured conversation whispers through the group. People are asking what they can do to help. My mouth moves, but I can't find the answers they need.

Cassidy's hand on my shoulder breaks me out of another spiral of grief. "I'll be cleaning and taking care of Alma's and Lowe's house while they're away. I could use some help."

A few of the vampires jump at the opportunity. Finn, as well, starts naming things he needs done around the bar.

While the voices in the bar overlap, I sip the blood but barely taste it. My mind is split between my duties here in Ravenfell, my duties to Michael, and the turmoil of knowing Matilda might be alive.

I reach up without realizing it, wrapping my hand around my neck. There's a bruise there still–black and angry. It throbs with pain anytime I swallow.

Cassidy lays a hand on my shoulder. "It's nearly morning. Do you want to stay here? We have an extra bed upstairs."

"I should get back," I rasp, rising.

"Emelda, it's really all right if you want to stay. You look like you haven't had a second of rest in two days, and you're hurt–"

"I'm fine!"

I instantly regret the edge in my voice as faces turn in our direction. Cassidy doesn't shy away, however. She just nods, saying, "Don't worry about Ravenfell. We have it handled here."

"Michael will be back to check on things," I murmur, turning away from the group and walking steadily toward the door. I try to swallow again past the pain, but it's impossible.

I hurry out of the village as the sky turns from a deep black to a dark, stormy gray. The snow piles around my ankles as I hike out of the village, closing my eyes and breathing deeply, preparing myself for whatever kind of day awaits me at the castle.

But I sense I'm not alone.

I open my eyes to a shadow breaching the darkness.

Cole walks toward me when my feet refuse to continue moving forward. I've been holding myself together for days now, burying my feelings of dread, pain, and grief as deep as I possibly can, but... Matilda hurt me. She hurt my friends. Her violence brought back memories of how I became a vampire, and I just...

"Em," Cole says softly, closing the distance between us.

I close my eyes, take a breath, and lean my head against his chest.

44

I CAN'T GIVE YOU WHAT YOU NEED

Emelda

"Why are you out here?" Cole asks, his hand moving up my back as he presses me closer. "You're freezing."

"I wanted to check on Ravenfell–"

"I was on my way–"

"It's not your responsibility–"

"I was on my way to find you," he cuts in, taking a breath.

I open my eyes, breaking out of the haze of his scent, and pull away. "Why?"

He searches my eyes like the answer to my question is already in my mind. Maybe it is because we've already had this conversation before, haven't we? A few years ago when…

I turn from him, but he catches my arm. "I'm leaving for Scarlett Thunder in a few hours."

"I know. I'm aware of that." I try to yank my arm out of his grasp, but he tightens his grip until it stings. "Let me go, Cole."

"Can we talk? Please?"

I scoff, ripping my arm free from his hold. "That's the first time I've ever heard you say please. I didn't realize you had manners!"

"Why are *you*," he growls, his ocean blue eyes going black as midnight, "upset with *me*? If anything, I'm the one who gets to be angry in your presence, Emelda!"

"I'm not having this conversation right now," I huff, swirling away from him, my cloak billowing in the snowy breeze.

"Em!"

I whirl back in his direction, pointing a trembling finger directly at his chest. "No. I can't–I can't talk to you right now–"

"I need to understand," he breathes, his mask of pure, unaffected boredom slipping enough for me to see the rare raw emotion behind his eyes.

I throw my hands up in surrender, shaking with feelings I've tamped down for far too long. "There's nothing to say, Cole. I have no idea what you want from me. I never have."

"That's not true," he scolds, his voice heavy and laced with sudden rage. "I made my position very clear. From the beginning, I might add."

"Oh, is that how you saw it? You thought–you thought you could just return here, and I'd be ready and willing in your bed, at your will, at your fucking service?"

"Shut–" he shouts, his fangs on full display, "--the fuck up with that fucking nonsense, Emelda!"

His voice carries through the vacuum of snowy silence, echoing a great distance. I can feel my undead heart beating out of rhythm as he takes a cautious step in my direction but stops, his hands tightening into fists at his sides. "I wanted you as my wife," he says, the rage blurring to a kind of grief I know completely. That all-consuming, soul-crushing grief one only feels when they lose something that made them whole, leaving them broken beyond repair.

I hate that my feet act of their own accord as I take a step away from him.

He tracks the movement, shaking his head. "I asked you–"

"I'm a maid," I grind out.

"I've never given a fuck–"

"Cole!" I cut him off with a wave of my hand, tears blurring my vision. "I can't have this conversation again."

But now, he's gaining on me, closing the distance between us in four easy strides of his long legs. I've mapped every inch of this man. I know every scar, every curve and hard line of muscle.

Memories from four years ago threaten to push me over the edge. I can't banish them, not this time.

There was a time when I loved him with a kind of passion I hadn't known existed. The shifters call that the mate bond. Vampires don't have a word for it, and that's a shame… because it's as beautiful as it is heartbreaking.

I shake my head as he grips my upper arms, leaning down to shelter me with his body as I start pulling apart at the seams.

"Come to Scarlett Thunder with me."

"No."

"Why not? There's nothing holding us back now. I'm not betrothed–"

"It was never about that," I say as I look up at him. I make the mistake of running my fingertips over his cheekbone. He closes his eyes and leans into the touch. I squeeze my eyes shut as I try to pull away, but he stops me by taking my wrist, pressing my hand to his skin. "We *can't.*"

"We can."

"Cole–" It takes all of my strength to push him away. He staggers backward, his eyes shifting back to that deep blue where his emotions flare to life. Hurt. Confusion. Rage at my rejection.

"What is it with you?" he growls, shaking his head. He chuckles darkly, running his fingers over the spot where I've just touched him. "What is it about me that made you hate me this much?"

"I don't–I've never hated you–"

"You have, and you do," he retorts, his fangs glistening in the hazy, gray morning light beginning to creep over the hills. "Because I wanted to keep you as a mistress? Is that it? That was our only choice, and you knew it as well as I did."

I shake my head, sniffling, trying to pull my tears back into my eyes but fail miserably. They trickle down my cheeks, freezing to my face. "We would have been caught."

"I wouldn't have cared. I still don't!"

"You were getting married–"

"I've been betrothed since I was a child," he says hotly, gritting his teeth. "It was never my decision."

"We can't do this. You're a prince. I'm–I'm nothing–"

"You are the love of my fucking life," he says, exhausted, and the world around us goes so silent I can hear his heart racing from feet away. "And I never wanted to leave you. I considered telling Michael–"

"You promised you wouldn't–"

"And I haven't," he amends, holding out a hand in surrender but then points toward Ravenfell. "But then you almost died, and I'm highly considering telling everyone and forcing you to come back to Scarlett Thunder with me, where I know you'll be safe."

"I'm safe here," I shout, but he smirks, laughing cruelly as he shakes his head again.

"You're Michael's employee, Emelda. His priorities have shifted. He's going to have a wife soon. You're no longer the lady of his fucking house–"

"Do not tell him–"

"What do I need to say to you to make you understand," he shouts, pleading, "that I have been sick over you for four fucking years? That on my wedding day, you were all I could think about. That I prayed to gods I'm not sure exist that something would happen to stop the wedding, that I'd be freed from these chains, and I'd be able to go back to you–"

"No–"

"Why?!"

"Because I–because–" I suck in a breath, my heart shattering as I look at him. At him. The man I've loved for four years, the man I've forced myself to hate, the man I've tried to keep just out of reach.

"Because why?" he says, his tone softening to heartbreaking confusion. "Please, Emelda–"

"You're a prince. You'll be king one day–"

"I already told you your rank means nothing–"

"You're blood born, Cole," I whimper, shaking my head. I press my hands to my stomach, curling them into fists. "I'm not. I can't–I can't give you what you need. I can't give you an heir."

He stares at me in disbelief.

"You knew–you knew I was turned," I stammer, swallowing past my internal turmoil. "You knew my story from the beginning–"

He cuts me off with a wave of his hand, "I've never cared about that. That's not something I need–"

"Maybe not now," I cut in, swallowing hard. "But years from now, when you're the king, and you're heirless with a useless, barren–"

"You are not useless–"

"I am," I rasp. "You know–that is the one thing I wanted in my life. To be a mother. To be loved by the man who gave me our children, and I can't–that was taken from me, and I won't take that from you in turn."

"Emelda, I don't give a shit–"

"I do. I won't do it. I can't be with you and watch you grow to resent me and regret us."

"I wouldn't–"

"You would. We're different. I was made; you were born. You have to be with someone who can give you what you need to keep your kingdom strong."

"I would let Scarlett Thunder burn to ash before I let myself lose you."

"There's nothing between us to lose," I whisper.

His eyes go dark with hurt and rage, but I turn from him, walking in the direction of the castle as light begins to creep over the hills, morning coming in shades of gray and white.

I hope he hates me. I hope he never wants to see me again. Because this is what will kill me one day, I'm sure. The true, empty kind of death.

When I return to the castle, cold and empty, the maids are tittering in the kitchen as they arrange breakfast trays. Apparently, King Lex and his family won't be leaving until tomorrow now. They're staying an extra night because of the snowstorm.

I slip through the kitchen, holding back tears, and only let them fall when I reach a downstairs room normally dedicated to the servants and maids who live in the castle.

This is where I belong, where I deserve to be.

"Princess Faye is asking about you," a maid says as she passes the room where I'm still standing, shellshocked, my hand braced on the door.

"I'll be there in a minute," I croak, drying my tears with the back of my hand.

45

HE'S ALIVE—FOR NOW

MICHAEL

I WATCH FAYE RUN A COMB THROUGH HER HAIR, OVER AND OVER. THE yellow strands shine like golden silk in the pockets of sunlight shimmering through the curtains. Beyond the glass, knee-deep snow covers the castle grounds in a blanket of pure, untouched white.

Deep inside, I feel a flicker of my wolf rumbling to life.

Faye turns to look up at me as I pull the curtains back just enough to see but carefully avoiding spraying her with bright sunlight.

"You want to shift and go play in the snow, don't you?" she smiles, setting down her comb.

"How can you tell?" I let the curtains fall again and lean on the wall beside the vanity.

"Your scent changes, actually," she shrugs, rising and swishing toward the closet, her silken robe hanging off her slender shoulders as she moves with vampiric grace across the room. She's wearing nothing but a thin nightgown beneath, and as the sun plays over her back, I can see the outline of her figure fully.

I watch her pick through the closet. My mother had clothing

brought up for her—just something to get her by while new items are made in her exact size.

She pulls a thick sweater from the rack and folds a pair of wool trousers over her arm before turning back to me.

I take in her small details. The cool ocean blue of her wide eyes. The golden eyelashes that brush her pale blonde eyebrows. The button nose, the fair skin. She's beautiful, and she's mine.

"Are you all right?" she asks, breaking me from my stupor.

"I am. I'm going to go see Lowe today."

She nods but looks down at the clothing in her arms. While she can't feel anything between us on a level deeper than knowing I love her... I feel everything when it comes to her. The mate bond aches with her worry and guilt. I should tell her that this isn't her fault, but we both know it's more complicated than that.

She passes me by again, setting the clothes down on the edge of the bed. I watch for a second longer, imagining it's my fingers brushing the soft skin of her upper arms instead of the fabric of her robe as it drops to her feet, but tear my gaze away and stalk toward the dresser. "It's going to be cold today. The storm is over, from what I understand, but here—" I toss her a pair of wool socks to complete her outfit.

She catches them with a smile. "Do you get cold as a shifter?"

"Of course. But I'm warm-blooded, so I have a bit of an advantage," I tease, walking up to her and pressing a kiss on her naked shoulder. "I'll see you later today."

It takes all of my strength to leave the room. I'd rather lie in bed with her until nightfall, tangled in our sheets, than walk the unusually quiet halls of the castle where I was raised.

It doesn't need to be said that this is our home now, at least for the time being. I will rebuild in Ravenfell, eventually. But the ground is now frozen solid, and the snow is only going to get deeper as the winter progresses.

We're stuck. Maybe it's for the best. My parents have the opportunity to get to know their future daughter-in-law, and I have the chance to ensure Faye understands what our future as king and queen will be like.

And… King Mattias will act. I'm not sure how, or when, but he will. I need to be ready to face him when the time comes.

The air in the castle thins as I walk down a narrow, spiraling stairwell made of stone. This area of the castle is ancient–once where the feeders were kept–but now houses rooms and apartments for the servants and maids who live here full time.

Of course, the castle does have feeders still, but their living quarters are similar to that of the help; cozy apartments with amenities villagers could only dream of.

"Are you looking for a feeder, Prince Michael?" a maid says as she comes to a stop with a basket of laundry in her arms.

"No," I reply. "I'm here to visit Lowe."

"He's just down the hall." I watch the color drain from her already pale face as she bows her head and quickly scurries away. My chest tightens, and I grind my teeth as I start walking again, my footsteps echoing up and down the corridor.

Alma's soft voice reaches me at the very end of the hallway where a door is standing just ajar. I push inside, knocking lightly.

Alma looks up from her lap with wide, dark eyes on alert but relaxes when she sees that it's me. "Michael–"

"How is he today?"

I scan the room for others but find myself alone with Alma and Lowe, who's lying in a large bed near the fall wall, closest to the fireplace, which is roaring and spraying dry heat. The room is hot, actually. Hot enough to be uncomfortable, but one look at Lowe tells me that's exactly what he needs.

A massive, thick bandage wraps around his entire neck. He's shirtless, and bandages cover his chest, some blotched with fresh blood.

But his skin is still gray and sallow, and his eyes are closed. I watch his chest move as he takes a shallow breath like it takes an enormous amount of effort.

"He's alive," Alma says weakly, sniffling.

"That's good."

"Is it? The physician said he may never fully recover from this."

"What do you mean?" I lean against the door to close it.

Alma flexes her hands before tightening her fingers into fists. "He was nearly drained completely. The only reason he's alive is that it was so cold that night his blood was… moving slowly. He'd been in wolf form when she attacked him, Michael." She closes her eyes. "He shifted back, they think, to his human form, which tore the… tore the bite marks in his neck wide open."

"You don't need to explain," I say, resting a hand on her shoulder.

"I want to take him home," she whispers. "If he's going to die, I know he'd be more comfortable dying there, in our bed, surrounded by our things–"

"He's going to make it. He just needs a few more days of care. We have the best physician in our kingdom in this castle. My parents are insisting he stays."

Alma looks relieved, like she'd been internally battling the idea of being a burden on the king and his court. I squeeze her shoulder, and she sighs, reaching up to wipe her eyes. "Prince Cole mentioned Lowe going to Scarlett Thunder for treatment. They have a healer there who specializes in shifter medicine–"

"Cole came to speak to you?" I ask, taken aback.

"He was just here a few minutes ago. Apparently, he's not leaving until tomorrow morning now."

I find it odd that Cole would take an interest in this at all, honestly. "I'll leave you," I say, turning for the door.

"He mentioned needing to talk to Emelda about something," she says. "But I–I told him it was best to leave it alone."

"Leave what alone?" I ask, turning back to her.

Her eyes go wide. "They–you didn't know?"

"Didn't know what?"

46

***

COUSIN CONFRONTATION

Michael

Midday sunlight breaches the frost-covered windows when I finally find Cole in the library. He's on the second level, sipping a cup of blood while staring aimlessly out toward the horizon. He doesn't look down at me as I storm into the room, the wide double doors slamming shut so hard the sound rattles the thousands of books tucked on their shelves.

I keep my eyes locked on him as I start up the staircase. "You motherfucker."

"Hello to you, too," he sighs, setting down his cup—crystal, now stained crimson.

"I just found out some very interesting news," I rasp, seeing red.

"Is that bastard Mattias on his way here with the full strength of his army behind him?" he smirks.

I stop short of where he's lounging in an armchair next to a row of stained glass windows. Dressed casually, his shirt is mostly unbuttoned, and he smells like... whiskey. In fact, I can see the amber sheen in his cup, poorly mixed with the blood, like he was just drinking it to chase down the alcohol.

"How could you?" I ask in all seriousness.

"How could I what? Not see past Matilda's beauty and recognize the beast within?" He drinks again, deeply, finishing off the concoction as his words slur. "All vampire women are the same deep down. Monsters."

"Is that the way you feel about Emelda?"

He pauses, pressing the rim of his glass against his lower lip. Slowly, his gaze turns up to meet mine, but he makes no move to stand.

"You thought I wouldn't find out eventually?" I press.

"Did she tell you?"

"Alma did."

He runs his tongue along his lower lip and cautiously sets his cup down on the table beside him to run his fingers through his unkempt hair. He's a mess. Dark circles line his eyes, which are red and puffy. He exhales deeply, leaning his head back and closing his eyes against the light in the room. "What does it matter? It was four years ago."

"In *my* house," I growl.

"I didn't realize she's not only your housekeeper but your fucking property."

"Whatever happened between the two of you cannot, and will not, happen again or continue."

He laughs bitterly, shaking his head. "Oh, Michael."

"What the fuck is so funny?"

"Why do you think I'm sitting up here, drunk off my ass? I haven't slept in days, you know that? Do you know what I thought that night when my bride didn't show up?" He leans forward, resting his elbows on his knees, slouching. "I was finally free. I could do whatever I wanted. I wouldn't have been tied down by a marriage I was forced into. I could have whoever I desire. Finally."

"You already do that," I snap.

"I haven't touched a woman since *her*." His eyes shine as he looks up at me. "I've found it easier to spin a narrative that makes me look like a fucking monster–a player–a killer than simp over a love I lost."

"You're drunk. You don't make any sense."

He waves a hand in dismissal, reaching for an unlabeled bottle coated in dark green glass. He pours another dram of whiskey, straight this time.

"That'll kill you," I warn, but he drinks it down anyway in a single swallow.

"It's been so easy," he slurs, "to make myself look worse, to keep people away. All I've had to do is flirt, look like the worst kind of man. The kind people think take women to bed without a care in the world and discard them, just like that." He snaps his fingers, then pours another dram. I move to stop him, but he twists away from me. "People leave me alone because they're scared of me or have heard the rumors. I thought it'd get me out of my betrothal, you know. King Mattias would hear what I'd become and think his pretty, evil little princess was worth more than I could offer–"

"Don't drink that, Cole–"

"I loved Emelda," he grinds out. "So much. More than anything." He takes a heavy drink. "But I was young and stupid. I was… overconfident in my belief that she loved me as much as I loved her and would be happy to come live in Scarlett Thunder as my mistress. You can guess how that conversation went."

I grind my teeth as he raises the glass to his lips but decides against it at the last moment, saying, "I made a mistake back then. I lost the only thing I ever truly wanted, and I fucked it up again, didn't I, Michael?" He finishes the glass.

I telepathically call for the physician while saying, "You went to my house that night to look for Emelda. You lashed out at me when Faye was attacked by Matilda because Emelda was involved–"

"Emelda is the only person I care about," he says, his eyes blurry with a kind of grief I recognize completely. That empty, awful grief that comes with knowing there's nothing left to hope for, like I felt when Faye was in her coma. "Seeing her nearly dead with fire all around her… if you hadn't killed Matilda by chasing her into those mountains, I would have taken her apart piece by piece, keeping her alive while doing it just to savor her suffering."

"Goddess," I whisper under my breath.

"You came here to scold me for being with your housekeeper under your nose, so do it. Tell me I'm a fucking pig, Michael. Rub it in my face. Prance around with your princess and tell me how good it feels to be with the person you love more than life itself."

"I'm not going to do that–"

He rolls his eyes, chuckling darkly. "Then go away."

I take a step toward him. "You should have told me."

"Why would I have? There's nothing to say."

"I could have helped you get out of the betrothal."

He chuckles again. "We both knew that wasn't going to happen. My fate was sealed two decades ago, Michael."

"And now, you're right. You're free."

"It doesn't matter."

"If you love her still–"

"She won't," he says, meeting my eyes again. "I made my feelings clear, and she can't–she can't do it. She argued she's just a maid–"

"Neither your parents nor your people would care–"

"But they would," he says under his breath, turning his cup in a circle on his knee, "knowing that our union would not produce an heir."

"Fuck." I pinch the bridge of my nose, closing my eyes. "Because she's not blood born."

"She's right," he says with a shrug, the words slurring together. "The problem is, I don't care. But I should, you know."

Footsteps below alert me to the arrival of the physician, but Cole is already pouring himself another drink. When he sees the physician coming up the stairs to the loft, he glares at me, clicking his tongue. "Fuck off now, Michael. If you're not going to chew me out for sleeping with your housekeeper, I'm going to go somewhere with better company."

He rises, but sways, then brushes past me. I whirl in his direction. "Where are you going?"

"Doesn't matter. See you–see you whenever, I guess. Possibly at your wedding? Congratulations, by the way."

"He's severely intoxicated," I say to the physician as Cole staggers past her and grips the railing of the stairs. He picks his way down, and the second his feet meet the floor again, he disappears in a sprint. I growl, running my hand down my face.

The physician just shrugs at me, unable or unwilling to help a man that's obviously battling some serious internal demons.

But I check my watch. I have a meeting with my parents in a few minutes that will determine the next... decades of my life. I can't be late.

47

I DON'T CARE WHAT THE KINGS SAY

Faye

KING KANE IS A SLIGHTLY TERRIFYING MAN. HIS PRESENCE IS ALL consuming–like he sucks the light out of the room. He doesn't look his age, like all vampires. The only indication that he's a senior vampire compared to his son is the faint gray glow around his temples where his dark hair is starting to turn.

He has decades–no, centuries–of life left, of that I'm certain.

But not his queen.

Emory moves with sunlight grace around the room, dressed casually in navy slacks and a warm cream sweater. Her thick, dark brown hair is piled neatly on the top of her head, and her cheeks are pink with excitement, matching the shimmer in the polished-jade eyes, a color she shares with her son.

"You're sure?" she asks me, unable to hide her excitement. "You're sure this is what you want?"

I feel my grip on Michael's forearm tighten in a reassuring squeeze. "I've never been more sure of anything in my life."

Emory beams, her smile wide and radiant as she looks up at her husband–her mate, her king–but Kane isn't smiling.

His expression is impossible to read, but I'm a vampire, too. I've always been trained in keeping my emotions buried behind a mask of neutrality that edges on boredom.

He looks down at his spotless desk, tapping his knuckles on the worn, but polished, surface. "Congratulations are in order," he says flatly.

Michael exhales deeply beside me, going suddenly rigid.

"But," Kane continues, glancing between us before looking at his wife, "nothing can move forward until we hear back from Red River."

"I don't care about what King Mattias thinks about the marriage between me and his daughter. He should feel fortunate–"

Kane holds up a hand, cutting Michael off. "We're playing a delicate game with him now, Michael. I won't stop this union, but we need to prepare for Faye's father to say no, or worse, corner us with terms."

I watch Emory's face fall, her full lips tilting into a frown. "Oh, for Goddess' sake," she huffs, smoothing her hands down her thighs. "We don't need to worry about that now. Their wedding will be the wedding of the century, Kane. Our kingdom could use some good news. I'm going to announce their engagement and… hold a ball, of course. For both shifters and vampires."

Kane eyes Emory. She stares at him with her brows lifted in challenge.

Finally, he folds, shaking his head as he looks down at his desk. "Fine."

Emory smiles broadly and rolls her eyes back to us. Michael relaxes just a touch as his mother walks toward us, clasping his face between her hands and rising on her toes to press a kiss to each of his cheeks. "This was my dream for you–to find your mate. We are so proud of you, Michael, no matter how grumpy your father is right now."

Kane grunts under his breath nearby.

Emory releases Michael and moves on to me, taking my hands

and smoothing her thumbs over my palms. "And you," she whispers, her eyes brimming with tears. "You are a precious gift to this kingdom. You are exactly the kind of queen we need and Michael needs by his side. The two of you will do great things together; of that I'm certain."

She leans in to press a kiss to my cheek, and I... I feel like crying. Happy tears, of course, but still. It's been so long since I've received any kind of motherly affection.

Emory pulls away, resting her hands on her hips as she turns to Kane with a look shining with expectation.

He sighs, running a hand down his face as he leans back in his desk chair. "Do what you must, Emory. The family coffers are all yours."

She snorts a laugh and smiles at us, rolling her eyes.

Michael apparently takes that as a dismissal and leads me out of the room. It's late afternoon now–nearly nightfall. The sunset beams through the windows as Michael silently walks me through the castle.

But we don't go toward the private rooms and apartments upstairs.

"Where are we going?" I ask as he knits his fingers in mine.

"I want to show you something."

Several flights of stairs later, he opens a door into a shockingly dark room. The air here is chilled–so cold I can see my breath as he lets go of my hand and walks along the wall.

A grinding, mechanical sound blares, and then the last inklings of sunset erupt overhead as a dome of glass comes into view.

"Wow," I breathe as deep violet light sprays throughout the room. Shadows dance across the floorboards, illuminating a shiny telescope in the very center of the room. Several simple wooden tables line the circular wall stacked with books and loose paper.

I blink up into the sky through the frosted glass and see the first stars twinkling like they're waving hello.

"This is one of my favorite places in the castle," Michael says, tucking his hands into his pockets as he looks up, squinting toward the sky. "I used to spend a lot of time here before moving to Ravenfell."

"I can see why," I whisper, smiling as he closes the distance between us. We stand in silence for a moment, looking up at the sky together, sharing a moment of much needed quiet.

"Faye," he says, turning toward me, "this happened quickly, I know. I want to–to give you another chance to say this isn't what you want because this marriage isn't just to me. It's to this kingdom. My people would be your people, my territory, your home, and I… if it's too much–"

"I want to be your wife," I tell him, looking up into his eyes. "Michael, there's no doubt in my mind that this is what I want."

I rise on my tiptoes to kiss him, but he takes a step back and drops down on one knee.

Something reminiscent of shock flutters through my body. "What are you doing?"

He takes a small, black velvet box out of his pocket and opens it.

I gasp.

A dainty gold ring sits on a cushion of cream silk. A brilliant sapphire glints at its center, spraying fractals of light across my belly and his hands as he turns it to the last strips of light falling from the sky. Diamonds rest on the top and bottom of the sapphire, glittering against the rich shade of deep, flawless blue.

"I–" I can't form words. "What's this for?"

He blinks. "It's customary to propose and offer a ring–"

"I never thought–" I suck in a breath as emotion swells, tightening my chest. "I never thought I'd have this. I thought I'd be sold off to the highest bidder. I never thought I'd be given the choice."

"I love you," he says, and I look him in the eyes. "Will you marry me?"

My knees give out. I find myself kneeling with him, trembling. "Of course, I'll marry you. I love–"

His mouth meets mine, the ring totally forgotten between us.

48

WHAT IF I'M RIGHT?

Faye

"It really is gorgeous," Emelda says the next morning while walking with me to the library. She runs her thumb over the massive sapphire ring and smiles faintly, raising her brows. "I think it's a family heirloom, too. You should expect a load of fine jewelry to follow."

"You know I don't care about all of that." I laugh as we turn into the library. It's snowing again. The sky is deep gray, and fluffs of white race to the ground beyond the windows. My voice echoes through the cavernous space as I say, "I'm just... I'm not sure how to feel. I'm excited, so incredibly happy but also... worried."

I follow a few steps behind Emelda as she guides me to a section in the recesses of the library where Kane's family history books are kept. She starts scanning the shelf. "Why are you worried? You're a princess marrying a prince."

"My father," I whisper, and she sighs, pulling a thick book from the shelf.

"Will he say no?"

"I doubt it, but my betrothal to Cole was destined before my birth. They have a treaty because of it, and now I wonder if he'll make moves on Scarlet Thunder against King Lex even though I'm marrying King Lex's nephew."

"Well, if that happens, Michael and Kane will see an end to it. It won't affect you at all."

"Be realistic, Emelda."

"I am." She turns, placing a stack of heavy books in my waiting arms and tapping the top one, leaving smudges in the thick dust. "For now, you study and prepare to not only join this family but help run this kingdom."

"But—"

Emelda moves on, disappearing behind another rack of books. I huff a breath and follow, leaving the stack on a nearby table. "Emelda, Matilda had a scheme to kill me and take my place. I can't help but think maybe she is part of a plan cooked up by our own father."

"What do you mean?" she murmurs, scanning another shelf.

"What if it was my father's plan all along to kill me and cause turmoil here? To possibly pit the kings against each other, one blaming the other for the drama Matilda would have inevitably caused?"

"What do you think she would have done had she succeeded in marrying Cole?"

"I think that part was a… a later part of her scheme. I think she meant to get close to Michael first to try to cause a rift between him and Cole, which would have caused a problem between their kingdoms, dismantling the peace between them."

"I think you're giving that bitch far more credit than she deserves."

"But what if I'm right? And—what if Matilda isn't dead?"

"She's dead. Michael wouldn't have returned had he not thought so." She pulls three more books from a shelf and hands them to me.

"Emelda—"

"Listen," she says, turning to face me with her hands braced on my shoulders. "You're safe now. You should enjoy this time of happiness, okay? Everything will be fine, and if it's not, Michael will make sure you're safe and taken care of."

"But it's my fault–"

"Enough of that," she whispers, giving me a sad smile. Her eyes shine with words unsaid, some deeper feeling I can't place nor understand. "Be grateful for this, Faye. You're marrying the person you love. You have a future with him. And, you're both blood born, which means a baby could very well be on the way…. Speaking of that, hopefully Emory has plans to have this wedding sooner rather than later."

"Is that why you and Cole aren't together?"

It feels like the air has just been sucked from the room. Emelda freezes solid, so still she looks like a finely made statue of herself. "What?"

I shouldn't have said anything, but the signs–the little details I've noticed–all lead to some kind of history between them. Something that hurt when it ended.

"Cole's in love with you."

"Don't say things like that where others could overhear–"

"We're alone."

She moves to step around me, but I block her against the shelf. "Do you love him, too?"

"Faye–"

"He saved you from the house. He went right past me and picked you up, cradling you and carrying you out of that fire!"

She heaves a breath, her dark eyes shining the faint light filtering through the shelves, but her face is cast in heavy shadows, highlighting what I can only describe as pain.

I step back as the truth hits me. "What happened?"

"Faye," she whispers, her eyes going suddenly glassy.

But then the library door opens, and footsteps ring out, followed by Michael's voice calling out, "Faye? Emelda? Are you in here?"

I scan Emelda's teary face before whirling and hurrying toward Michael's voice, popping out of the stacks just in time to stop him from finding Emelda hanging on by a thread. "Michael." I take him in, noticing his heavy jacket and winter boots. "What are you doing?"

"Deacon and I are going out for a few hours to track down Cole. He's supposed to be leaving this afternoon, but no one has seen him."

My stomach flips. "Is he all right?"

"I'm sure he's fine. Deacon got word that a vampire is suffering from alcohol poisoning at an inn twenty miles from here. I know it's Cole, so we're going to go get him and bring him back. Hopefully, the cold journey will shock him back to his senses. I just wanted to let you know." He leans down and brushes a kiss across my cheek. "I'll see you tonight, all right?"

"All right. Be careful, please."

He smiles and squeezes my hand before sauntering off, closing the library door behind him.

I whirl back to Emelda, waiting several breaths to ensure we're alone before stalking back in her direction. She's pressing herself into the shelf like she's trying to disappear.

I take her hands. "Emelda, please. Just tell me what happened."

"It's that simple, Faye," she whispers. "I can't give him an heir, but he can't accept that as a reason to… to leave me alone."

"Do you want him to leave you alone?"

My heart shatters as she shakes her head and takes a shallow breath. "I didn't expect it."

"Expect what?"

"To fall in love with the same kind of beast who made me what I am today."

49

A TRAGIC LOVE STORY

Faye

Still in the library, I listen intently as Emelda discloses far more than I expected her to.

There was a point in Emelda's life as a vampire that she'd accepted she'd always be alone. Her bed would always be cold, her skin unblemished by a loving touch. She'd never know love again, and for decades, she was all right with it. She'd lost Ewan, after all. The man she was sure the old gods and goddesses wrote for her in the stars she used to worship as a witch.

But five years ago, when she had finally settled into life in Ravenfell and was busy running Michael's house and staff at the manor, everything changed.

Alma had been drooling over a shifter who'd recently moved into town. He was a bartender for the ancient vampire who owned the only tavern in the village. So, most nights she spent alone instead of in her sister's company and grew closer to Michael in the process.

And one night, as she was preparing for another evening talking to Michael about books and gossip at the castle, *he* appeared.

Cole was everything a vampire male should be. Fierce, terrifyingly handsome, cold and stoic. But he wasn't standoffish and rude like the other vampire men she knew. He was lively and hilarious, the life of every party Michael threw at the manor that fateful spring.

And Emelda was the object of his teasing from the beginning. At first, his attention had been a thorn in her side. He'd come up behind her in the kitchen, quiet as a ghost, and bug her about her cooking or mending, or whatever she'd been trying to do at the time. If she ignored him, he'd flirt openly with the maids who worked at the manor until she had to intervene, much to his delight. For an entire month, Cole put himself in her way until she couldn't take it anymore.

"It was raining that night," she explains, looking down at her hands. "He'd been staying with Michael for a week straight instead of at the castle. Michael was at the castle that night for a meeting with his father and some other high-ranking vampires who own territory nearby, but Cole came to the manor anyway. It had been a month of this—of his flirting and... I was so sure he was just fucking with me for his own entertainment, but that night changed everything."

Emelda had enough of his teasing remarks and constant hovering. She told him off, telling him to go bug a maid or feeder at the castle, but there was something in his eyes that night that made her feel... a flicker of something new, something that made her alive for the first time in over two-hundred years.

"He was so young for a vampire, you know. I had centuries of experience on him, even though I'd been turned, and he'd been born this way. Maybe that's why it didn't matter, that he still had this effect on me, like he could make my world slow to a crawl just by being around. But I told him to leave me alone, and normally he'd laugh, saying something teasing in response before obeying... but that night..."

That night, he asked if that was really what she wanted. Did she really want him to go, to be alone in that big house?

"I burned myself on the stovetop," she tells me, looking down at her flawless vampire hands. "It hurt like a bitch, and I yelped, moving to suck my finger to stop it from sizzling."

But he'd caught her hand and inspected her wound. His touch had been so gentle and shockingly warm. It was the first time in two hundred years that she'd been touched by someone other than a hug from her sister.

"I looked into his eyes. He told me it would be okay, that the burn wasn't that bad, but then… pressed his lips against it, keeping his eyes locked on mine."

Emelda didn't sleep well that night. She tossed and turned, imagining that moment over and over again until she couldn't take it anymore and tried to make herself busy. Cole stayed away from her until later that next night, when Michael left to go into the village with Deacon. Emelda had been in the library, trying to find a book to keep her busy through the night, to keep her thoughts from wandering back to Cole.

But he'd come up behind her, telling her he couldn't stand it, that he wanted her more than he'd ever wanted anything in his life, and Emelda gave in.

"At first it was a strictly physical affair," she says, choking on the words. "I was two hundred years old, and yet, he was my first–the first man I'd ever lain with. It was customary in my culture as a witch to wait until marriage, but my marriage never happened, and I gave that part of me to Cole willingly."

I listen intently, watching a myriad of emotions play over her face as she knits her fingers together.

"We spent an entire summer sneaking around," she says softly, closing her eyes. "He'd find me in the garden, in the library, sometimes going as far as to sneak into my room at night. We couldn't stop. We couldn't get enough, and after a few weeks it became clear that it was more than just a fling–more than the physical."

Cole told her he loved her. She told him the same, and meant it with every part of her being. But they were blinded by the easiness of summer, peace in the kingdom, and the secrets they kept from each other.

Cole didn't know that she used to be a witch.

She didn't know that Cole was betrothed.

It didn't matter, anyway.

Until it did.

"Summer came to an end, and he had to return to Scarlet Thunder," she says painfully. "I'd started preparing myself for what that meant. We'd done all of this in secret, not even telling Michael about it. But Cole came to me a few days before he was supposed to leave and told me I was coming back with him. He proposed to me, Faye."

I lean forward, enraptured.

"He wanted me as his wife, and I wanted that more than anything, but we were blinded by this beautiful, secret affair where we were the only people in the world, and nothing else mattered but us, and reality came crashing down the very next day."

Emelda told Cole she had to think about it, that she had a life and a sister here in Ravenfell she didn't want to leave behind. She didn't mention she wasn't blood born because she hadn't thought it mattered, honestly. They were both vampires. They could have a long, happy life together.

But the next morning, Michael had her come to the castle with him to help him with something, and she overheard a conversation that changed everything.

"I can't even remember why I was there, in Kane's office. I was holding some books Michael wanted to take back to the manor that he'd found in the castle's library, waiting for him to be done talking to his father and uncle, but they brought up Cole's... engagement to a princess in Red River. Lex mentioned how the girl was blood born, and how King Mattias had sworn she was... fertile. Able to have children with Cole...." She winces, shaking her head and squeezing her eyes closed. "I realized how... how stupid I'd been to believe I had even a sliver of a future with Cole at that moment."

Cole hadn't been in the room. She returned to the manor, and like clockwork, he came to her that night. He asked why she wasn't packed for their journey back to Red River. She told him she couldn't marry him, and everything fell apart.

"I told him I wasn't blood born, but he didn't care. He said it didn't matter. I couldn't bring myself to tell him why it did, in fact, matter, and I got angry. I threw his betrothal in his face, and I swear, Faye, I've never seen a man break like he did. Cole begged me to come with him, telling me we could run away together, that we could have a happy life together, even if we lived in a shack in the mountains because we were in a desperate, all-consuming kind of love."

All I can do is slowly shake my head in disbelief.

"But I could never give him what he needed," she continues. "What he didn't know he'd need–an heir. A child. A son." Her eyes meet mine. "That was four years ago."

"Do you still love him?"

"Yes."

"He's not getting married anymore, Emelda–"

"Nothing has changed," she rushes out, drying her eyes. "Nothing will change. I've made myself very clear."

"Have you talked to him—"

"Yesterday," she breathes, rising. "And he went off and got drunk enough to forget about me again, hopefully. Come on, Faye. You have some studying to do."

I watch her walk away and feel my stomach twist with grief. I gather my books, wincing at the weight, and carry them all back to the rooms I share with Michael. Day bleeds into evening, then to night, and when Michael returns, his face is drawn and eyes heavy with an emotion I can't read.

"Did you find him?" I ask.

"Cole? Yeah. He's fine," he murmurs, then his eyes meet mine. "Faye, your father sent an emissary with his answer about our union."

5 0

MATTIAS'S CONDITIONS

THE EMISSARY TO RED RIVER—THE REAL ONE—ISN'T ANYONE I recognize. He's tall and pale blond, his red eyes gleaming in the brightly lit ballroom where he and his posse of royal Red River guards have gathered.

He scans the group before him—myself, my father, and my uncle, and smiles faintly, his lips parting just enough to see his fangs.

My dad paces, his footsteps echoing through the cavernous ballroom, and Uncle Lex looks murderous as he stands with his arms crossed and feet firmly braced apart.

"King Mattias sends his warm regards and gratitude for caring for his beloved daughter, Princess Faye, in his absence."

"His absence is noted," Lex sneers. "In every sense of the word."

The emissary—Lothario Donnex, from what we've been told—flattens his smile to a tight line. "Being a king yourself, you can imagine how busy His Majesty might be at any given moment."

"And yet," Lex growls, "I wouldn't send my children to another kingdom with little more than a guard as an escort."

"Be that as it may," Lothario says calmly, tilting his head in Dad's direction, "what happened here wasn't known to my king. The vampire Matilda wasn't supposed to travel with the princess."

"Was Matilda not a princess herself?" Dad asks coldly, pacing back in the opposite direction.

"In name only. Her mother's line was not royal. She was a byproduct of a breeding situation that ended up not being needed after King Mattias found a suitable match in his late queen. Princess Faye's mother, may her soul rest in peace."

I grind my teeth. My fangs are on full display, I don't bother keeping them hidden.

"How does your king mean to pay for the chaos his... daughter has caused?" Lex asks, tapping his fingers on his upper arm. "For the many balls held in her honor, and the destruction of the Duke of Ravenfell's home?"

Lothario purses his lips and glances in my direction before reaching into his coat, pulling a file from the inner pocket. "News reached Red River of Prince Michael's intention to marry Princess Faye. King Mattias has agreed, but new terms for the union have been drawn–"

"We will not be accepting new terms," Dad says, cutting the man off. "The old contract stands. Peace between Red River and Scarlet Thunder will remain intact."

"This contract covers your kingdom, King Kane. Scarlet Thunder has been freed of the treaty they were... forced to sign, years ago, putting their own prince on the chopping block."

"Do you dare come here and insult me?" Lex chuckles darkly, taking a step in the man's direction.

Lothario only smiles–a bright, practiced grin. "I think you both will find the terms of the contract to your liking. This union between Prince Michael and Princess Faye will unify all three kingdoms. A new era of peace will dawn on the vampires, and for that, King Mattias is grateful. But as for his daughter, Matilda...." He thumbs the file, shaking his head.

"What of her?" Dad asks, glancing at me before looking back at the emissary. "The girl is dead, but not before having left chaos and death in her wake. She nearly killed a shifter friend of my son's and burned his house down."

"King Mattias is willing to fund the construction of a new home for your prince," Lothario says without even blinking in my direction. "As long as Princess Faye retains her title if the relationship goes awry, and any of her offspring born from your royal union keep their titles, as well."

I want to laugh, but the emissary continues, "The first born son will be the next king of this kingdom, but the second shall be given to King Mattias as an heir to his throne."

"What?" we say in unison.

Lothario looks around, shocked that we had such a visceral reaction. "The second-born son of this union shall be given to King Mattias after birth, as an infant, to be raised in Red River in preparation to stand as his heir."

"No," I laugh, shaking my head. "That will not be happening."

"Then this marriage will not be happening," Lothario sneers, his eyes glimmering with disdain. "It's all here in the contract. King Mattias will also retain rights to whatever females are born from your line in order to ensure they're wed into the appropriate families."

"You've lost your mind if you think I would allow any of that to stand," Dad growls, coming to my defense.

Lothario tucks the contract back in his jacket pocket, rocking on his heels. "Then I have orders to return Princess Faye back to her father. There are others waiting in line for her."

I step forward, but Dad presses his hand to my chest. I push against him, snarling, "If you think I'm letting her leave to go back to that mad-man, you're delusional. You'll be starting a war."

"King Mattias is prepared for that." He rocks on his heels again, smirking.

"Fucking bastard," Lex growls under his breath.

"We need the night to look over the contract in full," Dad says after a moment.

I want to argue, to scream that there's no way in hell I'm giving over my own unborn children to Mattias, but Dad's face tells me everything I need to know.

"That's doable, but we need to return to Red River first thing in the morning," Lothario says, his eyes narrowing to cat-like slits as he retrieves the contract and takes a few cautious steps toward my father. He extends the file. Dad stares him down for several seconds before snatching the papers from his hands and giving the emissary his back.

Dad raises a hand to the trio of male servants waiting near the far door leading back into the foyer. "See that the emissary and his men have rooms in the eastern wing."

The servants quickly set to work guiding the group from the room, and silence rushes through the space in their wake. Dad turns to me and Lex, tilting his head in my direction. "Have Deacon and a few of his men on guard in the eastern wing. I don't want these people walking around freely or gaining access to the upper levels of the castle."

I send the command telepathically while Dad tucks the papers under his arm.

Silently, he turns toward the door. I follow him to his office on pins and needles, desperate to read the fine print.

5 1

THE DOTTED LINE

Michael

"The second-born son of this union will be handed over at birth to King Mattias and his court to be raised in Red River as the rightful heir to the throne," Dad reads aloud as he paces in front of the windows in his office that overlook the bleak, snow drenched landscape beyond, "to ensure the heir has been fully steeped in Red River culture and history and has no outside influence from other kingdoms or courts, no contact with the mother, or father, shall be allowed for the first two decades of his life or until he is crowned as king, whichever comes first."

"This has to be a fucking joke," I growl, glancing between my father and Lex.

"King Mattias doesn't joke." Lex sighs under his breath, running his hand down his face. "He had us cornered with a similar contract with Cole."

"This is insanity, and I will not sign."

Dad flips a page, eyeing both of us as he continues, "Any daughters

229

of the union will be considered the property of Red River once they come of breeding age."

"I don't even want to know what he considers that age to be." I sink into a chair, hanging my head in my hands.

"King Mattias and his court will ensure advantageous marriages between the princesses and members of the courts of all three kingdoms, dictated by the king himself."

"No," Lex says, shaking his head. "You cannot accept these terms."

Dad sets the half-read contract down on his desk and turns to the window. It's too dark and cloudy to see the stars. "We will sign."

"What?" Lex and I snarl in unison.

"This new contract effectively dissolves whatever treaty you had in place with Red River, Lex. You can now make moves into Red River, start a war. It's been a long time coming."

"Is that what you're suggesting? I take my kingdom to war against Mattias?"

"Yes, because our treaty of peace supersedes the nonsense in this marriage contract. If you go to war with Mattias, or better yet, instead of invading, bait him into action first, my kingdom has a duty to defend you."

"And what will happen to my wife in this scenario?" I growl, clutching the armrests. "What stops her father from coming here and taking her at that point?"

"You," Dad says with a small smirk.

I lean back in the chair, watching as Dad flips through the contract before tossing it back on his desk. "We will sign, and you will marry Faye, and Lex will get his chance to finish what was started decades ago. I've had enough of this."

I shake my head. "I will not risk the lives of my mate and our future children."

Lex turns to me, his arms crossed over his chest. "You will, and you must."

"Let him start with us over Faye," I argue. "Let him come and try to take her. He'll be dead within a second of setting foot-"

"I believe his forces are already here," Dad interrupts, holding my gaze. "I believe everything that happened was his doing. Matilda, for one. If Faye had died in our lands, a royal princess, Mattias could place the blame on our family and call his kingdom to arms. Matilda failed in her mission, and now he sees a way to get what he wanted regardless—our kingdom. Our lands, and our people."

"There was an attack on a vampire village near the base of the northern mountains this morning," Lex says. "Three dead, several missing."

"What does that have to do with the king or Matilda?" I ask.

"It could be nothing, or it could mean Mattias has his own people starting to cause turmoil to try to weaken the blanket of peace here and in Scarlet Thunder."

Dad nods, agreeing, but says to Lex, "An alliance with King Travis of Moonlight Gorge is in your favor if things start heating up between us and Mattias." He inhales, then exhales slowly, holding his brother's gaze. "King Travis was keen on his daughter Eliza marrying one of our boys, if you remember."

My stomach ties in a knot. "What are you talking about?"

"Cole is no longer betrothed," Lex says with great effort. "But something new can be arranged. Princess Eliza might suit him, actually. She's a very serious woman—strict, and pious. She could manage Cole—"

I stand, shocked. "What the fuck are you talking about? Marrying Cole again to forge an alliance—"

"Cole is a problem," Dad says firmly. "If we're on the brink of war, he needs to be dealt with, contained and controlled if possible. A wife would prevent him from running off to drink himself to death when we need him sharp and prepared to fight alongside us."

"You agree with this? Seriously? Your own son?" I ask Lex.

"You were the one who fished him out of a barrel of wine this morning," Lex snaps. "He's killing himself—"

"He is devastated," I growl, then realize my mistake. My dad and Lex look at me, confused.

"Because of Matilda?" Lex asks, looking both disgusted and shocked.

"No, Goddess, not Matilda." How do I backtrack out of this? "Don't force Cole into another marriage. Let him stay here—with me. I'll handle it. I could use his help in Ravenfell, anyway. I need a new house and some manual labor might bring him back to reality."

Lex searches my face. He's not buying it, that's for damn sure.

But they're right. Cole is fucked up, and this was a long time coming. I should have seen the signs. I should have known his increasingly deplorable behavior over the past four years was something deeper than being an absolute hound for women and booze.

"Leave him to me. Return with Aunt Ivy to Scarlet Thunder, and let Cole spend the winter here, with me and Faye. He'll be better."

Lex looks at Dad as if for permission. Dad simply extends a pen in my direction. "Sign the contract, Michael."

5 2

DELICATE TOPIC

Faye

EMELDA WALKS IN STEP BESIDE ME, DRAPED IN HER USUAL BLACK CLOAK, her dark eyes narrowed on the brilliant sunset as the last rays of light dip below the horizon. It's been two weeks since the fire tore through the manor, two weeks of quiet peace that feels almost misplaced.

I'm not sure how to feel about the death of my sister. We weren't close nor loving. She was just... there, in my life, a shadow that occasionally followed me around in Red River. I let her lead, let her try to teach me how to be the perfect, submissive vampire wife, the perfect princess, the easiest, most trusting target.

There are parts of me that still desire to be that perfect, soft-spoken girl. I still crave the quiet sanctuary of the library or my room where I could just read, or play the piano, or paint without judgement. I wish I could visit my mother's grave to tell her about finding Michael, to tell her I know what love is because she loved me—truly, deeply.

But I'm... different now. My life could have ended on the side of the road, in a ditch.

It didn't.

Now I plan to make the most of it, starting with change.

"Have you seen Cole lately?" I ask Emelda as we walk down the snowy hill toward Ravenfell. I can see the roofs of the village sparkling in the last inklings of the sunset as the sky dims to a deep, star speckled purple.

Emelda shakes her head, sighing deeply. "Michael keeps him busy, and I haven't been to the castle since Lowe was about to return home."

I squeeze her arm. Lowe was deemed recovered enough to be transported back to Ravenfell and is continuing to recover in the home he shares with Alma, which is exactly where we're headed. I know I shouldn't pry, but I feel like I haven't seen Emelda in ages, even if it's only been a week. Michael staying at the castle full time, at least until spring, means Emelda's services to him are temporarily no longer needed, and she's been staying at her sister's house in the village. Michael continues to pay her, which I'm grateful for. Emelda deserves the world. She's become my closest friend over the past few months.

I roll my shoulders as we reach the bottom of the hill, following a snow-packed trail between the castle and the village, but another hill greets us, rising toward the stars.

I sigh, feeling more exhausted than usual, but start the climb nonetheless, saying, "I know you don't want to talk about it, but... are you ever going to talk to Cole again?"

Emelda doesn't answer for a long time. Finally, at the top of the hill, she replies, "I'm sure I'll see him again, but if we do speak, it won't be related to whatever we had between us." Her voice doesn't tremble, her words strong and sure... even if they're slightly edged with heartbreak. "It's what's best for both of us.

"Are you happy with that?" I ask, knowing I'm getting close to the point where Emelda is going to cut off this train of conversation completely.

"Perfectly," she lies. "I imagine, as time goes on, Cole and I can become easy... acquaintances. Maybe even friends." The far off look in her eyes hurts my heart, but I decide to let it go, for now.

Two weeks ago, the real emissary from my father's kingdom came to Michael and King Kane with a marriage contract. That same day, Michael announced Cole would be staying for the winter, and while we kept our conversation about Cole's elongated visit mum while his family was in attendance, the minute we were closeted away in his quarters, we gossiped like mad.

He wasn't happy to hear about their affair, of course. Michael loves Emelda deeply, like a sister. He trusts her fully. He wants her to be happy but also knows she can't have what would make her the happiest she could be... a family. Children with the man she loves.

Michael still feels like Cole took advantage of Emelda in some way, shape, or form. I don't necessarily disagree. But that was four years ago, and neither of them are willing to share their feelings or thoughts on the current climate of their relationship with us.

And, unfortunately, we have to accept it.

But I know Michael feels torn in a hundred different directions right now. He was upset when Emelda announced she was moving in with Alma to help care for Lowe. He was uneasy with her leaving me, especially, leaving me in the hands of maids at the castle I didn't know after having Emelda in my corner for so long.

I assured him it was fine, that I was adjusting, and that I wouldn't, under any circumstances, be changing my mind about marrying him, but that's when he started acting... slightly off.

We drop down into the village, both of us ignoring the empty space on the hillside where the manor used to be. Emelda tucks me closer as a bitter gust of cold wind rustles through our cloaks, rattling the baskets we're each carrying filled with little gifts and provisions from the royal kitchen to give to Lowe and Alma. "Have you decided on a date for the wedding?" Emelda asks, derailing the topic of Cole completely.

"Emory thinks the sooner the better, and I agree." I swallow past the knot in my throat at the secret I've been hiding for the last week.

"But whenever the wedding is brought up around Michael, he acts... strange."

"Strange, how?"

"Stressed, I guess. I mean, neither of us has been married before, and a royal wedding is a grand affair, so I understand where he's coming from in that regard–but still. I asked about the contract he signed with my father, and he told me everything was fine, that we could get married without any issues stemming from Red River, but I almost don't believe him."

"Have you seen the contract?"

I shake my head. "I haven't."

She tilts her head in thought as we pick down the street, trying to be careful on the ice stretching across the cobblestone. "Well, I've known Michael for a long time, Faye. I doubt he's keeping anything from you."

We reach Alma and Lowe's house, which is situated directly behind the bar Lowe owns in the center of the village. Emelda guides me down the alley toward the narrow, three-story building built like an afterthought in the snug space between two other establishments. At least its third-floor windows have a view over the rooftops, but otherwise, it's all cast in shadow.

"Well," I say, turning to her as she knocks on the door. "I'm probably just overthinking it because–"

I cut myself off abruptly. I wanted to tell her. When I found out she was coming to the castle tonight to pick up some gifts Emory arranged for Alma and Lowe, I'd jumped at the opportunity to walk back to Ravenfell with her, thrilled for a few hours where it would be just the two of us.

But I was too absorbed with my own excitement, too nervous to tell Michael, stuck on the idea that I wanted Emelda's opinion about how I should go about telling him that it slipped my mind that she might not be as thrilled as I am to learn my secret news.

A secret that I, so far, would have been telling her first, before anyone else.

"Because, what?" She looks down at me expectantly.

Before I can answer, Alma opens the door and excitedly leads up inside her cozy home.

53

BLURTING IT OUT

Faye

ALMA AND LOWE'S HOUSE IS A LITTLE ROUGH AROUND THE EDGES, BUT I wouldn't expect anything less from a building nestled in the depths of a five-hundred-year-old village. It's decorated tastefully, however, and I find myself grinning with delight as she shuts the front door behind us, my gaze sweeping over the tidy, but snug, living room. A fire burns brightly in the hearth to combat the chill in the air. Little frames of dried flowers and herbs hang on the wall, and the couch is covered in handmade quilts and fluffy pillows in deep reds and greens. A wooden staircase along the wall leads up to the upper floors, while an archway leads directly into a small dining room, then the kitchen, where the smell of herbs wafts toward us on the breeze.

"It's a bit drafty in here today. Lowe has one of his shifter friends coming over in the morning to fix the seam in our kitchen window. I opened it, like an idiot, to let in some fresh air while making him a sleeping draft and couldn't get it closed all the way."

She offers to help me out of my cloak while Emelda steps further into the living room, hanging hers on a coat rack near the stairs. The jars in her basket catch the light of the fire as she turns to us. "How's Lowe?"

"He had a good day." Alma smiles, her dark, thick hair pulled back in a braid down her back. She's a softer version of her sister. A pale pink ribbon is woven through the braid, matching the dress she's wearing with a cream-colored apron over the top of it. Hand-knit pink and blue wool socks and brown slippers complete the ensemble, and I have a sudden, overwhelming urge to know if Emelda was ever like Alma... before she was turned.

Now, Emelda tends to be cold and blunt. Black is her favorite color, but sometimes she broadens her horizons with shades of deep reds, blues, and greens. She's lost the softness in her eyes. She's sharp, fierce, and commanding. But I don't think she's always been this way.

I look back at Alma as she continues, "He got up and walked around a bit. We even checked on the tavern together. He got a pint of beer." She smiles, but her eyes are glazed with emotion. "I didn't think–I didn't think he'd be home again. I've just been taking it day by day."

She didn't think Lowe would return to this utopia they built for themselves–a vampire and a shifter, living in love and harmony.

Emelda just nods along as Alma explains that Lowe won't be able to shift for a while, likely weeks, while his numerous injuries heal. It's hard coming back from the dead. If anyone understands that, it's me.

"Queen Emory insisted I bring this," I tell her, extending my basket. A few yards of beautiful fabric and large bags of beads rest at the bottom of it, accompanied by a fresh loaf of bread and some chicken stock for Lowe. Emelda's basket has vampire related good-ies–a jar of fresh blood, blood candy, and tea made from a myriad of warming herbs and dried blood. Alma exclaims her thanks, beaming at us, and invites us into the kitchen to brew the tea and drink it together.

But I came here for another reason.

"Michael wanted me to deliver this to Lowe," I tell Alma, reaching into my pocket and producing a letter sealed with wax. I hand it to her, watching as she traces her long, pale, delicate fingers over the wax seal.

"What is it?"

I glance at Emelda, who gives me a reassuring smile. "It's a wedding invitation, for both of you."

Alma blinks, taken aback. "I—to the royal wedding?"

"To my wedding," I correct with a smile. "We want all of our friends there... that includes you and Lowe."

Alma's shocked expression fades while a smile begins to form, brightening her face, but it's short-lived. She sets the invitation on the kitchen counter and pulls the kettle off the stove as it starts to squeal, pouring the water into three mugs.

"Faye," she says, a bit sadly, "I am so thankful and excited to be invited, but..."

I straighten, perplexed by the odd look on her face. Emelda, meanwhile, inspects the blood-red tea bags with a sniff before dropping them into each mug, the water swirling with blood.

"But you don't want to come?"

"Of course, I do, it's just... well, you must know that even with a shifter queen on the throne, the general public still sees alliances, let alone weddings, between our kinds as... blasphemy."

I start to laugh, but Alma is dead serious. "Oh, Alma, I—"

"I worry about Lowe's business, you know," she adds with a sigh, sinking into one of the chairs at the snug kitchen table we're sharing. "The vampires in Ravenfell are used to him—to us—but going to a wedding where we'll be in the company of rich, powerful, high-ranking vampires is a different story."

"I'm marrying a hybrid," I remind her. Emelda nods, giving her sister's shoulder a nudge.

"You're going, Alma. Both of you."

"I know," she smiles, but shrugs her shoulders. "I'm still allowed to worry."

"Nothing will happen to either of you, I swear." I hope I'm right. The idea of violence at my own wedding makes my skin crawl, but I hide that behind a sip of blood-tea, smiling at the flavor.

We visit with Alma for the better part of three hours, well into the night, talking about all kinds of things... except Cole. Emelda steers the conversation to avoid him, I think.

Eventually, she offers to walk me home, back to the castle, mentioning something about needing to talk to the seamstress responsible for my wedding dress. But on the way back, I feel that heavy desire–that need–to just come clean because, deep down, I'm scared, and unsure what this means for me and Michael.

"Emelda," I say, coming to a stop in the snowy woods bordering the castle. I can see the castle wall from here. I've been stalling, unable to make myself just say what's on my heart.

"Faye?"

"I believe... I think... I'm pregnant."

She stares at me, her eyes shining in the silver moonlight.

I lick my lips, wringing my chilled hands.

"What am I supposed to be feeling right now? Because all I feel is fear?"

"Have you talked to Michael?" Her response isn't what I was expecting.

"Not yet," I admit. "I wanted to tell you first."

She reaches out, reaches past what I feared would be jealousy, maybe a hint of hatred toward me having something she recently admitted she wanted for herself but can never have, and takes my hand.

"You're blessed, Faye. You're going to be a wonderful mother."

"Will you help me?"

"Of course. Always. I'll be right here."

54

EVERYONE HAS SECRETS

Faye

QUEEN EMORY WALKS AROUND THE CIRCULAR PLATFORM WHERE I'M
standing, trying not to move an inch. A seamstress and tailor shuffle
around me on their knees, pinning the hem of what will eventually be
a wedding dress meant to cause envy, I think.

Emory watches their progress like a hawk as she comes to a rest a
few feet away before turning to face the table where sketches of the
dress and fabric samples are laid out in droves, covering the entire
surface.

"What's your favorite color, Faye?" she asks, lifting some of the
fabric samples to peer at the other options underneath. Everything, so
far, are shades of white–cream, alabaster, egg shell…

"Pink," I reply, smiling at her through my reflection in the full-
length mirror.

She smiles to herself, absently nodding. "I had a hunch. Well, we'll
need to add some pink to this dress somehow."

The tailor, the designer of this grand dress, looks up from the hem
and examines the sheets of satin that will eventually make up the

silken base and sighs. "How do you suppose we do that, Your Highness?"

Emory looks at him over her shoulder with a smug smile. "That depends. Faye's already said she's not a fan of the idea of an all lace dress, and I agree. She's stunning in satin, but if the dress is a pale pink instead of white..."

"A pink wedding dress?" he says with a soft scoff, but Emory cuts him off with a wave of her hand.

"Dusty rose satin," she says, smiling. "Something that will bring out the gold in her hair and the blue of her eyes. We'll overlay cream silk on the skirt, and we'll wrap the bodice in the same rose satin as the underskirt. It'll be lovely."

"It'll be an immense amount of work with very little time," the tailor argues.

"That's why we're paying you a fool's ransom, aren't we?"

I bite back a smile at the bickering taking place directly behind me but can finally imagine the dress in my mind. It'll have long sleeves, a sweetheart neckline, and a tapered waist.

"I have a tiara to match, actually," Emory says as she paces toward the door. "I'll see if Kane can help me get into the vault. I'll be back soon."

I watch her leave, her vision of pink coming to life in my mind.

I find myself absently running my hands over my lower belly, smoothing the bones of what will soon be the bodice over my skin.

The wedding is happening fast. By this time next week, vampires of nobility will be arriving for the wedding and ball held in our honor. The idea of it makes my head spin, but I'm... happy.

Happier than I've ever been.

My father must have realized this union was a good thing. I'll be marrying into the strongest, most prosperous vampire kingdom in our lands... but it still leaves his issues with Scarlet Thunder unresolved.

As Michael's wife, I have the power to smooth that over.

I hope.

The only consolation I have is that the contract he signed with my father included a peace treaty with Scarlet Thunder because the idea of being the reason for war between my old kingdom and Scarlet Thunder, his uncle's territory, makes me feel sick to my stomach.

And I am, suddenly, so sick to my stomach that I begin to see stars.

"I need–" I rasp, the nausea cutting me off so abruptly I have no choice but to step off the platform.

"Princess?" the tailor and seamstress ask in tandem, but I'm already moving toward the door on quick feet, desperate for a bathroom.

I'm in Emory's private rooms. Her office is to the left, and the massive closet the size of a house is where we've been designing the dress, but a beautiful bathroom decorated in shades of white and soft gold beckons me, and I slam the door.

I feel both hot and cold as I grip the sink, my face going a mottled gray as I pant for breath, looking at myself in the mirror.

These waves of nausea are new. They started happening within the last few days and have only been growing stronger, but I breathe through it, and when it passes, I splash cold water on my face and hurry back to the tailor, apologizing profusely.

He gives me an odd look, however, his eyes sliding to my stomach and back up again. I pray my expression remains neutral, and I haven't given away my secret. He moves on with the fitting like nothing happened.

Emory doesn't return, and by the time I'm redressed and walking through the castle toward the rooms I share with Michael, I've completely forgotten she mentioned a tiara.

I planned to tell Michael about the possibility that I'm pregnant today, but he's impossible to nail down lately. When he's not in our rooms, I walk through the castle again, wondering if he's in his office, which isn't far from where the king holds court with his advisors, but I get lost.

I've turned a wrong corner and ended up in an area of the castle I've never been in before, and when I pass a door that's slightly ajar, looking for the hallway that should lead me back to where I intended to go, voices grind me to a halt.

"You signed the contract already, Michael. That's your only option as it stands." Cole's voice is void of expression, bordering on boredom. I stiffen as Michael's voice follows.

"I only signed because, otherwise, I would have lost Faye."

"Does she know?" Cole asks, and I hear a chair creak somewhere behind the door. "Have you told her–"

"Of course not. It would crush her."

I brace my hand on the wall, leaning forward to strain to listen as Cole says, "You signed away your children, Michael."

"That's why we won't be having any," Michael says with determination, but my body goes numb. "Faye and I will not be having children."

5 5

YOU CAN'T DO THAT

Cole

MICHAEL TURNS FROM ME, CLUTCHING A GOBLET OF BLOOD IN HIS hands. He drinks deeply before setting the glass on a nearby table and runs his hands down his face, pinching the bridge of his nose.

I've never seen Michael like this. Yes, he's normally high-strung and serious, but ever since he signed the marriage contract, solidifying a union between Red River and his kingdom, he's been... on the verge of violence.

He's supposed to be the level-headed one of the two of us. He's always been the voice of reason, the golden child, paving the way for me to fuck up without repercussions.

Nothing used to faze him. He was always hard and emotionless—the makings of a perfect king.

All it took was a woman to tear down those impenetrable walls and leave him utterly exposed to the world's evils.

I've been in his shoes. I've looked at the woman I love and watched the life I imagined for us crumble.

But he won't lose Faye, and I know for a fact she's just as important to him as carrying on his family's lineage.

"You're being ridiculous," I tell him.

He shakes his head, taking a few steps toward the door of the small, seldom used study I've carved out as my own for however long I'm stuck here, helping him and Kane clean up the mess my ex-fiancée left behind.

"You have no idea–"

"I do," I rasp just as he turns his head to meet my gaze. "I do have an idea of what you're feeling because I've been there, Michael, in the same fucked-up headspace you're in right now, willing to throw it all away. The titles, the money, the territory–poof!" I wiggle my fingers, giving him my signature shit-eating grin. "You know what I chose, and look where I ended up, regardless."

I chose her, over and over again. But unlike Michael, I didn't have a woman by my side who would have been content watching me throw my life away. Em yanked the rug from beneath me, forcing me back into reality, into a bitter cold autumn and winter without her, but with a future as a prince, and one day a king, ahead of me.

Michael stares blankly at the wall, lost in thought. After a moment, he turns to me, saying under his breath, "I had a dream when she was ill–lost in that coma. I dreamt that we'd have a son–our firstborn. I saw him, felt him throwing himself in bed to wake me up, and Faye came rushing in to stop him, and she was... heavily pregnant."

"Dreams don't mean a thing, Michael."

"This dream did. I was going to let her die. Emelda made a potion that would kill her, and we were... going to do it–that night. I fell asleep beside her thinking it was the last time I'd be able to be with her, and then I saw the future I could have if I just gave her a chance, so I did. I was sure she was pregnant. Emelda told me it was impossible to tell that early, and the–the damage to her body and the potions we were giving her to keep her alive would have made it impossible for her to keep the baby, anyway. Now, I see it for what it was. That dream was a warning, showing me a future where we have to give up the baby she was pregnant with, our second. I can't allow that to happen now."

"Have a child with her, Michael. There's a fifty-fifty chance it could be a boy, and then be done. You'll have your heir–a child Mattias can't touch–"

"And if it's a girl?" He snarls. "She's as good as cattle being raised for auction."

"A lot can change in twenty years," I whisper, reaching for the blood in my wine glass resting on a nearby table.

"And if it's twins," he says under his breath. "Two boys…"

"These aren't things to think about now. You have to make a baby first, but I have a feeling you're way ahead of the game in that regard. Unless, of course, you need me to explain it to you–"

"You're a fucking prick."

"Well, you wanted me to stay here. That was on you. I could have been halfway to Scarlet Thunder by now, but no. I needed extra help this time around." My lips curl around the rim of the glass.

"Because you were found shit-faced, half naked, in a snowdrift," he argues, balling his hands into fists. "You're killing yourself."

"Ah, death would be a welcome relief, Michael. But this conversation isn't about me. We're talking about you and your grand plan to throw away what your forefathers built. You'll have an heir. You don't have a choice."

Michael storms out, hopefully to find some comfort in his soon-to-be bride. I don't mind his swift exit. I honestly can't take a second more of him as it stands. Michael–the hero. Michael–the brave, the strong, and the behaved. Most vampires overlook his hybrid status because they know exactly what they're getting when it comes to him being the king one day.

He's like his father, through and through.

And I'm like the mother I've practically forgotten after all these years.

I leave the study with plans to visit the feeders to pass the time. I'm not hungry, but sucking someone's neck will stop the hazy, alcohol fueled memories from trying to ravish my mind. I know I wasn't alone at the inn several miles away, where I'd drank myself silly to the point of passing out, nearly dying in the snow. Vampires can handle liquor if we're well fed, each drink preferably chased with blood, but I hadn't bothered.

I can still feel the slight numbness from the booze as I walk through the castle. The maids give me a wide berth, refusing to look me in the eye.

But dark hair catches my attention the second I grip the handle leading down to the feeders, and I pause.

Emelda's heading in my direction, adjusting her cloak's hood over her thick hair, her eyes downcast on a basket full of healing tonics. She stops walking abruptly and looks up, her eyes meeting mine in the shadows.

Fate has been so cruel to us.

Sometimes, in the darkest hours of the night, I like to imagine I'd been there the night she was turned, that'd I'd been able to stop it somehow, to give her the opportunity to live the mortal life she deserved surrounded by love and family.

But then I remember what I am. A vampire. The same kind of beast who tore her hopes and dreams from her when he drained her and left her to transform, alone, in the middle of the festering, decaying carnage his followers left behind for her to witness when she eventually opened her eyes.

I pull open the door and step inside, shutting it behind me—shutting her out.

It's better this way.

56

—

I WAS GOING TO TELL YOU

Michael

Night falls on the castle again. The days have started to blur together since I've been here. When I had my own home in the village, I was a step removed from the goings-on at the castle. I had a barrier between me and the business of the kingdom, but now I'm… knee deep–no, shoulder deep–in the responsibilities that will one day be my sole purpose as king of this land and these people.

From morning to dusk, I've spent my time hovering between my father's office and my own, delegating tasks, working with his commanders to ensure our borders are safe from threats that lurk in the shadows, waiting for an in… like my upcoming nuptials. Mom is busier than I've ever seen. I barely saw her today, and the dinner normally laid out for us every night when I'm at the castle was instead brought to our rooms–a few plates of food for me, and blood for Faye, but Faye isn't eating.

She paces the windows overlooking the back garden, toying with the ties of her robe. Her hair is loose and falls over her shoulders in golden curls that nearly touch her hips.

I circle the table, glancing at my soon to be bride. She's withdrawn and slightly pale as she gazes outside.

"What's the matter?" I ask, moving toward her.

Her brows raise, but she doesn't look in my direction as she replies, "What was in the contract you signed with my father?"

My breath catches in my throat. I grit my teeth, debating lying to her to spare her from the same feelings of despair I feel, but... this is Faye. The woman I love–the woman who's chosen to spend the rest of her long life by my side.

"The basic things," I begin, taking another few steps in her direction. "Peace between our kingdoms, mostly. Scarlet Thunder is included in that."

She watches my progress to the window but says nothing as I reach her side. She looks up at me with eyes that shine with an emotion I can't name. It strikes me then that she knows... something, something I've hidden from her.

"What else?" she asks, her voice raw. "I know my father. I know that any contract he sent would have been... He would have had desires, and he wouldn't have allowed this union to move forward without whatever those are being met."

"It's nothing I want you to worry over–"

"I overheard your conversation with Cole," she rushes out, blinking rapidly like she's on the verge of crying. "Michael, why didn't you tell me–"

"I would have," I say, cutting her off. "Faye, I was going to tell you. I've been–I've been busy trying to figure out a way around this–"

"What did he demand of you?!" She steps away from me, putting a great deal of distance between us. "What did he want in exchange for *me*?"

"Our children," I tell her bluntly, and it feels like the oxygen has just been sucked from the room.

Faye stares at me in disbelief.

I lick my lips, looking down at my hands like the contract is still there. "Our firstborn son would still belong to us, but our second son... would be his. His heir, since he only had females."

She shakes her head, her mouth pressed into a tight line that begins to wobble as I continue. "And our girls would be... would be shipped away once they reach maturity to be married off within his court."

"You cannot be serious."

"I am."

"And you signed it?" Her eyes shine like polished gems. "Why?"

"Because I would have forfeited you," I grind out, my voice heavy with emotion I pray she can hear. "And I would never, never send you back to the monster."

"What have you done, Michael?" She turns from me to pace the room and then moves toward the door.

"I did what I had to do for us—"

"What about your kingdom? Who will be your heir if you refuse to have children with me? Have you thought that through?"

"It could be decades—centuries before we need to worry about that—"

"Our family," she whispers. "The family we could have? What about them?" She holds my gaze.

"Your father won't live forever," I tell her, raising my hands in surrender. "He's old, even for a vampire. This contract will die with him."

"You can't say when that'll happen. He wants a war with King Kane. He wrote that contract hoping you'd refuse his terms so he could finally get the war he wanted all those years ago when he made your uncle bend the knee and promise his prince to Red River. Your father has to know this is just another game to him."

"I don't know what else to say," I admit. "But we can't have children right now. Not until I find a way out of this that both prevents a war and ensures your safety. You have to understand—"

"Do you love me?"

I bite back the rest of my sentence, swallowing hard. "You know I do."

"I'm pregnant, Michael. It's too late." She whirls, snatching a cloak from a hook on the wall, and disappears with vampiric speed through the door, slamming it shut behind her.

I press my back against the wall and hang my head. What kind of man have I become? Of course, I should have refused the contract. I wanted to. I wanted to meet Mattias on a battlefield, not give in to terms that made it impossible for my kingdom to continue in the future.

It had been my dad who made the final decision. He's king, after all.

But there's been no recourse for what Matilda, also a daughter of Mattias, did to our court.

I have leverage there. I want answers, and justice, even if she's already dead.

I leave my rooms in search of Faye but run into Deacon instead–sweaty and slightly off-kilter as he hurries out of a wing of the castle dedicated to my father's commanders.

He stops short of me, gathering his breath, saying, "I was on my way to find you."

"What happened?" I notice the dark blood on his cuffs. He's half frozen, snow covering his shoulders.

"Another attack in a nearby village–thirty miles north of here. An entire family of noble blood born vampires killed."

"What?" I step toward him, my conversation with Faye receding into the recesses of my mind. "When?"

"Early this morning. The villagers sent a messenger, and my brigade was sent to investigate. It was–brutal. We're not sure why it happened, but it looks like a robbery of some kind."

I furrow my brows in confusion.

Deacon clarifies, "Several dresses and jewelry boxes were missing from the wife's closet. The house was completely ransacked."

"Keep me updated. This is the second instance of this happening recently, isn't it?"

He nods, skirting past me in a hurry.

I feel torn at the moment between my duties as prince and my fiancé as I turn in the direction she must have gone.

I choose her and follow her scent through the castle and out into the night.

WHAT'S THAT STENCH?

Faye

I HUG THE CLOAK TO MY BODY AGAINST THE FRIGID WIND WHIPPING across the field just beyond the castle grounds. Hurrying up another hill, I crest its peak and see the faint lights of Ravenfell sparkle into view.

I have no idea why I came out here. Running from Michael like this isn't going to help us work through our problems together,, but I just had to leave. I needed air. I needed to feel the moon on my face and see the stars dancing overhead.

I'm nearly at the village when I sense a presence nearby. It's quiet and curious as its shadow crosses mine in the form of a wolf.

Michael doesn't say anything to me through the mind-link. His jade eyes gleam in the moonlight, carrying on a silent conversation— an apology—a flicker of hope that what I told him was true despite the fear we both feel.

I rest my hand on my stomach, nodding, fighting back a sad kind of smile.

He presses his head against my stomach. I smooth my hand

through his fur right behind his wolfish-ears, closing my eyes. "We'll get through this," I whisper.

Into my mind, he says, *My only option is going to war with your father.*

"You know I have no loyalty to Red River," I reply, drinking in his warmth. "I renounce any ties to that kingdom. My father means nothing, his contract means nothing–"

That's not how this works, Faye.

I think about it for a moment before saying, "I will renounce my title as a princess of Red River at our wedding, publicly. I doubt my father will even be at the wedding, will he?"

His emissary will be there.

"Then he'll hear about it. If he wants a war, he'll get one, but I'm not giving up on a life with our children to appease a man who allowed my mother to die and used me like a prized mare to sell to the highest bidder. Burn the contract, Michael."

He lifts his face, his ears pressed to his head. I feel him stiffen, and my heart starts to race as I glance around.

"What is it?"

He says nothing, but his eyes are wide and honed on a nearby crop of trees bleeding into the forest behind us.

"Michael?"

Go to Ravenfell. Go to Alma's, and stay there until I come for you.

"Michael–"

Go, he says firmly then turns from me, darting into the night. I watch him disappear into the trees. He moves silently, stealthily, his rapid strides making no sound whatsoever.

I obey him immediately, sprinting toward the village. It takes me only moments to reach Alma and Lowe's house, where I drop my hood and knock loudly on the door, the sound of my knuckles hitting the wood echoing down the tight, dark alleyway.

Alma answers, looking flustered and concerned, but her expression relaxes when she realizes it's me. "Faye, what are you doing here?"

"Something–happened–" I rush out, panting. "I'm not sure–Michael–"

Emelda appears at Alma's side and grabs my arm, tugging me inside. In the tight, cozy living room, I notice Lowe rising from a chair, his eyes locked on the door as several wolf howls split the night into pieces.

"What's going on?" Alma says hurriedly, glancing between Lowe and Emelda.

"Lock the door, Alma," Emelda says, taking my cloak. "You, come upstairs."

"Emelda," I cut in, grabbing her wrist.

"It's nothing," Emelda says, shaking her head, but she doesn't seem convinced as she adds, "Michael just got a hold of me over telepathy, and he thought he might have caught a scent nearby. He's checking it out." She slowly looks at Lowe.

I know then that she just lied to me.

Lowe walks to the door. His neck is badly scarred but mostly healed. However, he moves like a man who's been stuck in bed for a long time, trying to heal against all odds. He looks like he should still be in bed, honestly, or at least remaining seated, but he starts reaching for his belt.

"Lowe?" Alma says slowly. "No, you're not going out there."

"It's other shifters in distress," he says in a low growl.

"You're still healing–"

"Go," Emelda says, nodding at Lowe.

Alma scoffs, whirling on her sister. "Emelda!"

Lowe begins to undress despite Alma's raised objections and pleas for him to stay. I turn toward the stairs to shield my eyes from his nakedness and feel the cold night air rush into the room as he opens the door and shifts, tearing off into the night.

Alma screams his name, her tone dripping with fury, but Emelda steps past me and slams the door shut, locking it.

"How could you? He's my mate!"

"You forget what you are sometimes, sister," Emelda snarls. "He's a wolf. Let him do wolf things. Michael could use the backup."

I turn just in time to catch the sisters snarling at each other, fangs on full display.

I decide to make myself scarce and walk to the kitchen, deciding another cup of that strange blood tea might make everyone feel a little better, but my hands shake as I fill the kettle.

As the water begins to boil, Emelda comes into the kitchen. Alma's footsteps rumble up the stairs nearby, and a door slams upstairs, shaking the house. Emelda sighs, taking three mugs out of a cupboard.

"What's really happening?" I ask bitterly. "I know you lied to me just now."

"There was an attack in a nearby vampire village early this morning. Michael… Michael caught a scent in the woods."

"You already said that."

"It was Matilda's scent."

My heart stops beating.

5 8

ENEMY OR ALLY?

MICHAEL

THE FOREST EXPANDS AHEAD OF ME, THE TREES CASTING LONG SHADOWS in the silver moonlight. I might be going insane–because there's no way that vampire is still alive. She can't be. I'd barely made out of those mountains myself.

But her scent was there, just beyond the castle grounds, far too close for comfort.

'Where are you?' Deacon says, his voice booming through my head against the totally silent silver forest.

I give him my location, but I'm nearly ten miles into the forest now, and I've lost her scent completely.

I know the forest stretches on for several more miles before thinning out into a floodplain. Beyond that, a wide, snaking river splits my kingdom from Scarlet Thunder, and further across the river, from Red River. There' are a few villages dotted throughout the forest, but all of them are close to the castle, like Ravenfell.

This, however, is no-man's-land.

At least, I thought it was.

I sprint up a rise, skidding to a stop overlooking a dried river basin, and lose my breath. A small, crude village stretches out below, tucked and nearly hidden within the trees. I scan the area, counting roughly a dozen small cabins and one large, log building at its center.

A pack house.

Tucked this deep in the forest, it would be easy for a pack to stay hidden. The hunting here is probably superb, but more than that, there isn't a vampire village nearby for nearly twenty miles. We're on the far edge of my parents' territory now.

I have another three seconds to scan the village before I hear foot-falls and panting breaths, and then I'm tumbling to the side, two wolves at my throat.

My vision is a tangle of fur and teeth. I scrape, bite, and claw my way out of the scuffle, snarling and barking, but in a defensive manner, trying to convey that I mean them no harm.

These wolves are warriors, however. Trained to fight to kill.

But a third wolf approaches, and my assailants immediately back off. The wolf's fur is totally silver. His snout is a soft white in the moonlight, giving away his age. He's an elder, and the way his warriors back away and bow their heads means he's their Alpha.

I feel the sting of wounds on my legs. Nothing that makes me think I'm mortally wounded, thank the Goddess, but I'm not about to try to subdue this old wolf with his warriors waiting in the wings to finish the job they started. I do what any wolf in my position would do—lay down flat on my belly and submit.

He sniffs the top of my head and rears back, looking down at me with striking golden eyes. His ears flatten against his head in warning, so I lay my head down flat, pressing myself into the ground as far as my body will allow.

'I mean you no harm. I mean no harm.'

He turns to his warriors for a moment before stalking away. I haven't even begun to lift my head before one of the two warriors is at my side, giving me a rough nudge to rise. They flank me, preventing me from trying to turn away from them, and herd me down a crude trail leading to the village.

Deacon's voice erupts in my head again, telling me he lost my scent, asking where I am.

I'm fine. Go to Ravenfell and guard Lowe and Alma's house in the village. Emelda and Faye are there.' As an afterthought, knowing Cole would sacrifice himself to keep Emelda safe regardless of their current feelings for each other, I say, *'Find Cole and bring him with you. Do not leave until I return.'*

The village smells of smoke and roasting meat. I'm herded through the center. People step out of the largest of the buildings, the pack house, to watch me pass. Other wolves linger in the shadows, watching with interest as I slowly make my way to who knows where, but soon we leave the village again, and I'm led up stone steps into a large log cabin with stone steps.

At first, I can see the Alpha inside the house, but then he's gone, replaced by an older woman who braces a hand on the doorframe and looks down at me like I'm just a wayward pup.

She clicks her tongue, her fine silver hair catching the light bleeding off the fire burning in their massive stone hearth, and says, "He's fine. Tell the others everything is all right."

The warriors step off the porch and disappear back into the forest. She removes her hand from the doorframe and motions for me to enter, saying, "Go up those stairs to the third door on the right. There are some clothes in the closet that should fit you. Harold will be with you in a moment."

I take her in, noticing the three-pronged scar running across one of her cheeks, and do as she says, knowing I have no other options.

When I dress and come back downstairs, adjusting the cuffs of the sleeves of a flannel, she's seated near the hearth in a rocking chair, knitting, and her mate...

"I'll have you know, Prince Michael, that my pack doesn't take kindly to vamps in our woods." Alpha Harold lifts a glass of whiskey to his lips, arching a bushy silver brow. He's tall and built—a beacon of health, even at his advanced age.

I stop on the bottom step, shocked he knows who I am when we've never met. "How do you know who I am?"

"You're a hybrid," he says, shrugging as he reaches for a second glass resting on a hutch nearby. "Hybrids like us… there're not many left."

My blood runs cold as I look him over, noticing the slight elongation of his canine teeth–his fangs.

"You're a hybrid?"

"I am. And if you're looking for the blonde vampire bitch, you just missed her."

59

THE FOREST HOLDS SECRETS

Michael

Alpha Harold watches as I sink into an armchair across from the raging fire in the hearth. He holds me a glass of whiskey, his eyes holding mine for a second before he turns to settle on a stool beside his mate.

I find this entire situation—this man, this pack—alarming.

"How long have you been here, in these woods?" I ask.

"Many years. We raised our children here, who are now raising their children here," he smiles wistfully, turning his gaze to his mate. He squeezes her hand, continuing, "Your parents… the king and queen never told you about us?"

My brows pinch together. "No. I know there're small packs sprinkled throughout the kingdom, but… you're like me." A thought strikes me dead. "How old are you?"

His eyes glisten like he understands why I want—no, *need*—to know.

"I'm two-hundred and… what was it this year? Ah, two-hundred and eighty-seven."

Relief sweeps through me. That's a long life lived, but he's aged enough to show me another truth. "We age faster than vampires but have longer lives than shifters," I say, unsure if I said the words out loud.

"Indeed. I held onto my youth until I closed in on a hundred and then slowly started to age. I'm not sure how much time I have left in this realm but... it's been a long, beautiful life."

"How do you know my parents?"

He searches my eyes, a distant memory twinkling to life. "Your mother paved the way for change for the shifters. We can live in peace with most vampires now, at least in this kingdom. We no longer have to fear being torn apart in our beds and watching our children become feeders... but she was a shifter in love with a vampire, and when she became pregnant with you, she undoubtedly had questions."

He continues, "We were looking for a new home for our people, having come from the outskirts of Red River and surviving that journey by the skin of our teeth, I should add. I'd heard the vampire king had taken a shifter bride, and when my people arrived in his territory, he sent his warriors to intercept us. I anticipated that, but King Kane quickly released not all of us were... completely like his wife."

I straighten. How have I never heard this story before?

"You were a boy then, maybe five or six years old. All spit and vinegar," he smiles at the memory. "You were showing signs of possibly being more shifter than vampire, but your parents had no idea what to expect for your future. You were a miracle by designer–a hybrid of two powerful, yet wholly different, species. I'm a hybrid like you, and in my pack, there are others. Some are more shifter than vampire, however. Their lives followed a normal lifespan–spanning decades instead of centuries. I lean toward the vampire side, obviously, like you. Our need for blood... our fangs, our long lives... that's all vampire. I explained to your parents that they wouldn't know what kind of life you'd have until you reached maturity and came into your shifter powers." He edges forward on the stool, peering at me like I'm some kind of experiment. "But you lean toward your father's side, don't you?"

Uneasy, I nod. I've always felt… torn between the sides, but the older I get, the more I feel those vampire tendencies taking root. "My parents never told me about you and your pack."

"I told them what I knew about hybrids in exchange for being left alone, and they've honored that, but things are changing, aren't they? Unrest is ripe. We can taste it, even this deep in the forest. What has changed, Prince Michael?"

I exhale slowly, looking up from my lap to meet his eyes. "I'm getting married. Married to a vampire woman–a princess of Red River."

Alpha Harold nods. "Not the same woman my warriors just chased toward Scarlet Thunder, I hope."

"Can you elaborate on that? What she looked like–"

He rises with a soft groan and walks into the snug kitchen, separated from the living area by a wall. He returns, handing me a strip of fabric stained with dark vampire blood.

I take the fabric, sniffing it, and close my eyes.

"She should be dead," I whisper, feeling a tangle of guilt and fury rising in my system.

"Who is she?"

"My fiancée's sister." I tell him the story in full. Harold and his mate listen intently.

When I'm done, he says, "My warriors are still tracking her. If she comes back through the forest, you'll be the first to know. You should have taken her head and burned her heart, Prince Michael."

"I will have a chance to do it the right way," I tell him, "and I won't fail this time."

I rise as the first inklings of morning sweep through the windows. I've been here all night, keeping these old wolves awake.

But before I go, I turn to him, asking, "My fiancée is pregnant. What should I expect our children to be? Vampire? Shifter?"

"Both," he says with a nod. "Only time will tell what traits they inherit."

I nod, curling my hand around the knob. "Send scouts if Matilda is seen again, but prepare to have warriors under my coat of arms in your pack territory for a while. They mean you no harm. You'll be compensated for your cooperation."

They bid me farewell, and I head into the woods, carefully changing out of my borrowed clothing and leaving them folded on the cliff edge before shifting and picking my way back through the forest.

I run into Lowe nearby. He surprises me, his ears flattened on the back of his head until my familiar scent hits him. I wish we could communicate through the mind-link. There has to be some way to make that happen.

Still, he turns around to follow me through the woods, back to Ravenfell, to Faye. I'll tell him everything once we reach the village.

6 0

―――

THINK OF THE CHILDREN

Faye

Morning comes like sand falling through an hourglass. All night, time moved so slowly. Each second passed in agony as I waited and paced, hoping for any shred of news from Michael.

I've spent the most time in the living room sitting in awkward discomfort between Cole and Emelda, who refuse to even look at each other.

She almost didn't let him and Deacon inside, but Deacon told us they'd been sent by Michael, and what Michael says, goes.

I'm getting hungry. My need for blood seems to increase every day, and right now, I'm craving Michael's blood more than ever. That only adds to my anxiety over his absence.

Cole rises from an armchair and walks to the window, pulling back the curtains as hazy, gray morning light bleeds into the house.

"It's nearly sunrise," he says absently, turning to look at Emelda over his shoulder.

She's sitting on the floor with her legs crossed as she organizes a bunch of jars and bags she fished from Alma's cabinets, organizing herbs for her sister. Alma hasn't come downstairs at all since Emelda sided with Lowe and let him leave to shift.

It's safe to say the tension in this little house is enough to make my skin crawl.

"Michael will return soon. He always comes back," Emelda says under her breath, refusing to look up at Cole.

I watch him grip the curtains tightly, a look of mingled dismay and frustration crossing his fine features before he lets the curtains drop and opens the door.

Only then does Emelda look up from her task.

"I'll be back. Stay in the house." Cole growls then disappears into the morning light.

Before he closes the door, I feel the shocking warmth in the air and see the droplets falling in the alley, creating puddles that were once piles of snow.

I turn to Emelda. "It's warm today."

"The warmth won't hold. Don't get your hopes up." She takes a breath, sighing deeply as she rubs her temples.

"When's the last time you slept? Or... fed?"

"Honestly, it's been a while for either."

I sink to my knees in front of her, taking a few of the bags and checking the labels. She passes me some empty glass jars to sort the herbs into. "You should come to the castle today and use a feeder," I suggest. "Or, better yet, have a drink with me and Queen Emory. She talks about you constantly, you know. She says you've made yourself scarce ever since the fire."

"You know why."

"Don't let Cole ruin–"

"Cole's not ruining anything. I don't know why Michael wanted him to stay," she grumbles, her eyes flicking to mine. "Maybe when he returns, you can ask him about that."

"There's a lot we need to talk about," I mumble, closing my eyes against the memory of our fight, me running off, and him chasing me down only to dart into the woods.

I haven't allowed myself to think about Matilda yet. Whenever I do think of her, I have a hard time trying to justify my feelings of bitterness and hatred. I'd mourned her death in secret, in silence. She's my sister. I loved her. I trusted her when I shouldn't have.

No one will understand my feelings, so I've kept them quiet.

"Does he know yet?" Emelda asks, glancing at my stomach.

I shift my position so my aching back is flush with the couch. "Can I ask you something?"

"Yes, of course."

"You and Michael were going to… to give me a potion to help me along into death, right?"

Her eyes darken as she nods. "We were. Neither of us wanted to do it, but you were suffering, Faye."

"You don't need to explain. I understand. I would have considered doing the same for you, had our roles been reversed. But I'm wondering if…." I trail off, unsure where to begin. "Emelda, I told Michael that I'm pregnant, but it was after I overheard him talking to Cole about the contract he signed with my father regarding our union and how… how Michael has decided we wouldn't have children."

"What?" Emelda looks scandalized. "Why would he say that?"

"Because the contract stipulates some very… terrible terms, like giving our second-born son to Red River at birth and that any daughter would be considered Red River property once they reach maturity and could be married off to anyone of my father's liking. Obviously, I'm not going to let any of that happen, even if it comes to war. But… I told him I'm pregnant, and he seemed shocked. Shocked and heartsick, and I'm not sure if it's because he's disappointed or–"

"He told me he thought you might have been pregnant the night we were going to give you that final potion," she whispers, meeting my eyes. "I told him it couldn't be. It was far too early to tell, and the herbs I'd been giving you to try to heal you would have been harmful for the baby."

We stare at each other.

"The baby," Emelda mumbles, then jumps to her feet. "Oh, gods, the baby. Alma! ALMA!"

I've never seen Emelda panic before, and it scares the absolute wits out of me. When Alma doesn't answer, Emelda screams her name so loud the house rattles, and Alma comes thundering out of her room, red in the face and livid. "What!? What the hell do you want, bitch!?"

"I need your help. Faye–Faye's pregnant–"

My head's on a swivel as I glance repeatedly between the sisters, watching Emelda explain the situation and Alma realize they'd been using herbs on me that could harm or even kill an early pregnancy. Both women start rushing around. The sound of water splashing into a pot and herbs being pulled from shelves fills the house, startling Deacon, who'd been sleeping in the corner of the kitchen.

"Get OUT!" Alma screams at him, and Deacon passes me looking pale and confused but leaves the house, perching on a crate in the alleyway scratching his head and repeatedly running his hand over his face. *What a way to wake up!*

Emelda rushes back into the living room and plucks me from the floor, hurrying me into the kitchen, where Alma's waving her hands over a steaming pot of water the color of... rose petals. Whatever's inside smells divine but strange. A sharp, tangy floral scent fills the room.

"What is that?" I ask as Emelda presses me into a chair.

"Just a bit of... medicine."

"Don't lie to her, Em," Alma scolds, shaking her head. "It's not medicine."

"Then what is it?"

Alma pours some of the water into a clear glass bowl and discards the rest, casting steam to the ceiling. She reaches above her head, fishing around in a cabinet she can barely reach and pulls down a very duster dropper vial with a sigh.

"Alma was once a midwife, in our old life."

"It's just an old type of pregnancy test. There's no reason to be alarmed." She's pale, however, as she turns with the vial and the steaming bowl and rests it on the table in front of me. She looks at

Emelda and nods, and Emelda pulls a blade from her belt, grabbing my wrist.

"What are you doing?" I exclaim, but Emelda's quick, sure blade slices over the meat of my middle finger. She squeezes my fingers together, holding my hand over the bowl as the pinkish water swirls. Three drops of blood fall in and sink to the bottom.

The twins exchange glances.

"Is that a good thing?" I ask, fear starting to blind my senses.

Alma pops the lid of the vial and carefully releases a single drop of a pure silver liquid into the bowl.

Light erupts. I scream as the bowl swirls and boils, foaming over the rim.

But Emelda grabs my shoulders with a sign of relief. "All right. She is, in fact, pregnant."

I watch the color of the water shift and change repeatedly, turning a deep crimson red. "What does that mean?" I ask, my voice choked with concern.

"It means the children are vampires," Alma says, stepping away from the table. "You should see the physician to confirm.

"Children?" Emelda and I say in tandem.

Alma looks between us, her brows raised. "Twins, of course. You're having twins. They're healthy, and they're vampires. It's still too early to tell what sex they are–"

The door opens in the living, carrying several male voices over the seasonably warm air.

Michael has returned, and when he walks into the kitchen, he looks at me, my bleeding finger, and the shell-shocked look on Emelda and Alma's faces, and asks, "What the hell is going on in here?"

61

THREE?

MICHAEL

I STARE AT MY SOON-TO-BE BRIDE, WHO LOOKS UP AT ME LIKE A LITTLE golden owl, her blue eyes wide and shocked as she takes in my level of disheveled-ness.

But I'm looking at her bloody finger, the bowl of liquid on the table, and the two guilty-looking ex-witches standing on either side of Faye.

Lowe strides into the house behind me, clicking his tongue and saying, "Potions? This early in the morning, Alma? You know those herbs make my nose itch something fierce."

Cole stares into the kitchen beside me, searching Emelda's face before dropping his eyes to the bowl and back up again. "What is that?"

All three women balk, their voices overlapping as they try to talk themselves out of whatever they'd been up to in our absence.

But then Lowe turns from the cabinets with an empty jar in his hands, his brow arched. "Tart cherry seeds? What are these for?"

Cole narrows his eyes at Emelda.

I have no idea what's going on, but Faye, sensing the tension rising in the room, squeaks, "Alma was just checking on the babies–"

"Babies?" the three of us men say in tandem, our voices overlapping and lined with shock.

The women grimace, but Lowe breaks the tension with an excited hoot and claps me so hard on the shoulder I see stars. "Congratulations. I had a feeling something was going on. I could smell the difference–you're all puffed up, and I knew it wasn't just because of the lady vampire–"

"She's pregnant?" Cole snaps, his eyes meeting mine. "Michael–"

"We'll talk about it in a moment," I rush out, cutting away from his gaze to look at my soon-to-be wife, who's sitting pale and nervous in her chair. "Faye, are you all right?"

"I'm fine," she breathes, but Alma speaks next, her voice carrying through the snug kitchen with too many bodies now holding court within.

"I was concerned, Prince Michael, when Emelda and Faye told me, because of the potions we'd been giving Faye during her coma. This," she says, waving toward the bowl, "is just an old type of test. Not to confirm a pregnancy, but to check on the health of the baby and the mother. Everyone is perfectly well against all odds. There's nothing to be concerned about," she adds, directing her last words to Faye, who gives her a gracious smile.

My heart is absolutely racing, however.

"You said babies," I say to Faye.

Faye's mouth moves, but no sound comes out.

"Twins, Michael," Emelda says softly, giving me a tight smile that doesn't reach her eyes. "You're blessed with twins."

I shake my head in disbelief. My dream of Faye and the child... my son... there hadn't been two, and now I know why.

"We need to speak—right now." Cole growls in my ear, clamping a hand on my shoulder and steering me out of the kitchen. My eyes are on Faye for a few seconds, worried about the nervous look on her face as she turns back to our friends, but I quickly lose sight of her as Cole leads me out of the house and into the alley.

Deacon's just coming up to the house but stops abruptly when he notices the sharp expression casting shadows over Cole's face. "What–"

"Twins, Michael? You know what this means. You need to get out of the contract as soon as you can."

"You know I can't, not when my own father threw his support behind it. This is happening now, whether we like it or not and I… pray to the Goddess these babies are girls–"

I turn back toward the door, but Cole catches me by the shoulder. "Publicly declare the contract null and void. Say you won't honor his terms."

"That would mean war for both of our kingdoms," I tell him.

"So be it. I'm shocked Kane agreed to this–pushed you to sign–"

"It was sign or give Faye back to her father," I grind out, but Cole shakes his head.

"Mattias has been tormenting his own people and trying to undermine our family for decades. I'm done. What his other daughter did…." He shakes his head, cursing under his breath. "And she's alive still…" His eyes darken. "Where did you pick up her scent last?"

"She's gone, long gone, likely crossing into your own territory." I shake his hand off my shoulder. "Go hunt for her, if you must, but if you're wanting a war–"

"There will be a war. You might think there's another way out of this, but there's not. King Mattias is old and skilled in the art of politics, and his contracts are ironclad. I'd know." His eyes shine with fury. "Scarlet Thunder will aid you. I'll back you up. End this madness now, Michael, before it's too late. You have the three of them to worry about now." He tilts his head toward the house.

Deacon, who, to his credit, hasn't said a single word, nods along with Cole, the two of them agreeing on something for the first time in their lives.

"It's not totally up to me," I tell them, defeated. "My father is still king."

"Convince him." Cole sneers then turns into the house.

"He's right. This can't go on. But what was he saying about the three of them?"

"Faye's pregnant. With twins," I murmur, running a hand over my face.

"Congratulations–"

"Not yet. This mess–we'll celebrate once the wedding is over and this mess is cleaned up. For now, get your men together and find Matilda–alive. I want her alive."

62

THE WAR IS COMING

Faye

IT'S SNOWING AGAIN. WHITE FLUFF FALLS FROM THE DARK SKY, highlighted by the exterior sconces placed along the walls of the castle. I smile as it blankets the ground, sticking to every surface it touches.

I never really thought about the logistics of my future wedding. A marriage? Sure. My eventual nuptials had been drilled into my mind since I was just a little vampire. I was raised to be submissive, to bend to my future husband's will, to give him heirs, to never speak but always listen and obey.

I never thought about the day I'd get married, though.

But I also never thought I'd get to choose to marry someone, that I'd be marrying because I was in love.

I know my mother's wedding ceremony was held in the spring, which was considered odd for a vampire wedding. It'd taken place late at night, out of the reach of the sun, but she'd still worn flowers in her hair.

My mother was the epitome of spring. She should have been born a shifter. I've always thought so because she was meant to be in the warm sun, in the trees, running free.

I was meant for this. For the deepest, darkest days of winter. I love the snow and cold snap in the air. I love the short, cloudy days and long, cozy nights.

My mother and I were so alike in many ways, except for this one.

I smile as I turn from the window, Michael's conversation with Cole coming back into earshot as they sit in armchairs facing each other in front of a roaring fire. Michael's drinking whiskey, and Cole is drinking... nothing. He looks like hell, but neither of us needs to tell him that. All he'd have to do is look in a mirror to see the dark circles under his eyes and the swallow color of his skin.

I bite my tongue to stop myself from asking if he needs a feeder.

It's not my business even though I know Emelda is also struggling with Cole being at the castle right now, just a few miles away from where she's staying with her sister.

While I miss the manor, I've gotten used to the castle. I've grown fond of Emory, and while Kane is perfectly nice, he's still a vampire male—a king—and I think he finds me tolerable, but he doesn't share the queen's excitement over the wedding.

Neither does Cole.

"You still have time to do this small," Cole explains, his elbows resting on his knees as he leans forward, legs splayed. "Just your own court, your parents, a few friends—"

"The wedding is in two days," Michael says with a hint of annoyance. "And it's not the wedding I'm worried about; it's Faye's pregnancy, whenever my parents see fit to make a formal announcement about it."

"Hold that off as long as possible. Until after the birth, if you can."

"I didn't realize you'd been studying politics," Michael remarks sarcastically, and Cole frowns.

"You're in a precarious position—"

"You're insistent on a war—"

"Emelda almost died," Cole grinds out. His eyes flick to my face for a single second before settling on Michael once more. "So did

Faye. If Matilda is, indeed, still alive, her father should be held accountable for her actions."

Michael leans back in his chair, shaking his head and chuckling darkly. "You have grounds for a war of your own, Cole. All you'd have to do is make your love for Emelda public."

Cole bristles. "You know I can't."

"There are other ways to have an heir."

"Do you think I haven't thought of that? That I haven't weighed every option?" Tension simmers, reaching a sudden peak as the air is sucked from the room. "Emelda won't have me, but I still want her protected. I want justice for what happened to her–to you, to your home."

"You're asking me to announce publicly that we are cutting ties with Red River at my own wedding."

"You're delaying the inevitable. The second a pregnancy is announced, Red River will have guards here, emissaries to ensure the king knows exactly what kind of prize he's getting out of this–"

"That's enough," I cut in, folding my arms under my breasts.

Both men look up at me, their faces slightly red from the conversation. Cole looks murderous as he exhales, nostrils flaring, and stands, towering over Michael with a look of contempt hardening his features.

I sigh, my body rattling with nerves. "Michael and I will discuss our options."

"I'm not disagreeing with you," Michael adds. "But we're princes, Cole. It's not our decision in the end."

Cole swipes his tongue over his fangs. "We need to act now, and you know it." He whirls, stalking out of the cozy living area in the very center of our suite.

Michael slouches and runs a hand down his face.

I perch on his armrest and feel his arm snaking around my waist. So much has happened in the course of our already rushed relationship.

"Do you think we'll ever be able to just… have a normal day?" I ask him.

He chuckles, his face slightly flushed from the tall glass of whiskey he's just finished. "Hopefully soon."

I wrap my arm around his neck and lean my head against his, closing my eyes. Neither of us has spoken at length about his journey into the woods to find my not-so-dead sister. Sometimes it's better to live in blissful ignorance, I suppose.

Whatever happens, we're going to be okay. I have to keep thinking that, or I'll lose my mind.

I perch my chin on the top of his head as he turns his face into my chest, pressing a kiss to my sternum. He growls low in his throat—a hungry sound that makes my body come alive.

"Ready for bed?" I giggle as he scoops me into his arms and rises.

"In a little while," he whispers into my hair. "There're a few things I want to do first."

He deposits me in our bed and begins trying to unbutton his shirt, but I sit up, placing a hand on his chest. "Not until after the wedding, my love," I tease.

His eyes shimmer with mischief. "You're right. I'm getting ahead of myself. It would be a shame to get you pregnant out of wedlock…"

"Michael!" I giggle as he launches onto the bed, rolling with me across the duvet. He pins me down, smiling down at me with his hair all wild. My beautiful shifter prince.

"I'll wait," he breathes, kissing the corner of my mouth. "Another two days—but that's it. If anything happens and our wedding is postponed, I can't make any promises."

"Just promise me you'll be good tomorrow night."

He leans back, confusion flashing behind his eyes. "What's tomorrow night?"

63

SCREWING AROUND

MICHAEL

I DON'T REALLY WANT TO BE HERE, BUT MY MOTHER AND MY FIANCÉE practically forced me out of the castle and locked the door behind me.

The dingy, crowded tavern some thirty miles away from the castle seems to sway against the crowd of shifters and vampires alike, everyone drinking copious amounts of ale or blood cocktails. Deacon is thoroughly enjoying himself as he leans over the bar to whisper in the ear of a vampire woman who blushes deeply at whatever he says.

Lowe sits beside me nursing a glass of the finest scotch the establishment has to offer, which is so young it's barely a pale yellow, and his face turns bright red every time he takes a drink.

I expected him to stay close, seeing as he has a mate at home, but I didn't expect Cole to be behaving so innocently.

Sulking is a better word for it.

He rests his elbows on the table, guarding a blood cocktail, while his blue eyes scan our surroundings. He sneers, his lip pulled up over his fangs. "We could have done this anywhere, and you chose this place?"

I glance at Lowe, smirking. He just rolls his eyes to the ceiling and chuckles, "Think I'd be welcome in one of your posh vampire night-clubs, Prince Cole?"

"I'm barely welcome in those," I add.

Cole rolls his eyes, whispering a rather colorful curse under his breath as he lifts his drink to his mouth.

While I was kicked off the castle property until at least the early hour of the morning, my soon-to-be wife is there right now having a party with Emelda and Alma.

Cole eyes me and Lowe before leaving the table in a huff, disappearing in the crowd.

"I didn't expect so many people to be here," Lowe says under his breath, nodding his head at a group of unfamiliar men who keep glancing in our direction.

They're watching me, of course. I reply, "They're here for the wedding. My parents are expecting a crowd outside the castle grounds. I'd expect your bar in Ravenfell to be busy over the next few nights."

Lowe shrugs, taking a sip of his drink. "Already has been, but that makes sense. The vamp who owns the inn next door told me this morning that all of his rooms are booked for the first time in years."

"It wasn't like this with Cole's wedding." I take a breath, keeping my eyes peeled for riffraff.

"Well, you're the future king. Everyone will be hoping for a glimpse of your bride."

"Including her sister," I grumble into my own glass of scotch.

Lowe purses his lips. "You're sure she's alive?"

"I caught her scent for sure. That, and the pack I met the other night confirmed a blonde vampire had been chased through that area. The only comfort I have is that she's on the run and knows my territory is heavily guarded. She wouldn't be able to get into the wedding, or even onto the castle grounds, unless someone with royal standing let her in." I knock back my drink.

Matilda nearly killed the man I'm speaking to. He nearly killed Emelda. I can tell by his expression that he's livid with the idea that this vampire is still walking around, basically free, and there's not much we can do about it. Not right now.

Not until after I deal with her father.

I lean forward, asking, "Do you know any... discrete shifters who might be interested in making some money?"

Lowe arches a brow. "I do."

"After the wedding, early next week, we'll meet up again. Bring them. At least four others."

He nods. He knows exactly what I'm planning without me needing to voice it. Vampires are fast and powerful, yes, but they don't have the same kind of senses shifters have. We can track her. A group of us could take her down, especially if she hasn't been hunting and feeding.

"She's yours when we find her," I tell him.

Lowe doesn't have a chance to respond because Deacon plops down, looking wildly around before settling his gaze on me and Lowe. "You'll never believe what I just overheard."

"What?" Lowe chuckles into his drink.

"It's about Cole." Deacon sighs, but shrugs, continuing, "That night he straight up disappeared? The night before we had to pull him half frozen out of a snowdrift? He was in a tavern a few villages over, apparently seen in cahoots with the leader of that village's daughter. They were caught, and he was chased out of an Inn."

I drag my hand down my face. "He told me he doesn't remember anything from that night."

"Well, that doesn't surprise me given that he nearly died from the amount of straight liquor that was in his system," Deacon says sardonically. "He got in a few fights, too, from what I've heard."

"This sounds like typical Cole behavior," I tell him. "Nothing to worry about."

"Are you worried about him now?" Lowe, who doesn't know Cole as well as Deacon and I do, asks.

They don't know about Cole's affair with Emelda. I mean to keep it that way. "Cole will be fine. He's just–just going through it. It's been a long couple of months." In more ways than one. Speaking of which, where is he?"

"He left," Deacon shrugs. "I saw him go."

"Where could he possibly be going right now?" Lowe laughs, but Deacon and I glance at each other.

That's a good fucking question. There are multiple possibilities, but my mind wanders to only one.

I hope I'm right, and he's not about to do something he'll regret... like killing himself chasing Matilda down himself, or Goddess forbid, running all the way to Red River to declare war.

I think he's going back to Ravenfell to face another demon of his, however.

"So," Deacon grins, leaning forward. "See that girl over there? I think I have it in the bag, but... she's here with her boyfriend."

"I'm not fighting any vampires tonight," Lowe and I say in unison.

6 4

A PLACE OF MY OWN

Emelda

Queen Emory smiles at the spread of vampire-friendly food laid out on a tea-table. Blood pastries and cakes galore sit on pretty little trays adorned with flowers, flutes of blood made to sparkle resting beside them.

"Are you not hungry?" she asks as I inspect the spread over the sound of Alma and Faye laughing on the other side of the room.

"Not really, but it's beautiful, really. Thank you for doing this for her."

"I never had a daughter," she says with a tinge of disappointment. She smiles as she glances at Faye, but her eyes are sad. I've known the queen personally for several years now, but her history outside of what's public to the court is a mystery to me.

I pick up one of the pastries. "Why did you choose to have only Michael? If you don't mind me asking?"

"It wasn't necessarily a choice, honestly. He was... our only. Our miracle, really. Hybrids like him are so rare..." She tapers off, shaking her head. "We tried for a long time. Kane and I both desperately wanted a girl next, but she never came. The Goddess sent me Faye instead, and for that, I'm eternally grateful."

I nod. "Faye has been a wonderful addition to the family."

She smiles. "I am a little upset Michael is so insistent on rebuilding his manor this spring. I like having them around. You, as well. You should be here more, Emelda. I enjoy our conversations."

"Alma's been keeping me busy, I'm afraid."

"Do you still plan to work for Michael in the future?"

"Of course," I smile, but for some reason her words make me feel… uncertain. I've been keeping a secret from Michael, actually. It's in my pocket right now–a key. A key to a home of my own tucked on the outskirts of Ravenfell.

I didn't tell anyone I was looking for my own place, but after years of living with Michael, and then the fire, and now his marriage and moving on with his life… I wanted a piece of privacy, a slice of peace… all to myself, because that's all I have, really.

Alma's laugh drifts toward me.

"She's been enjoying those blood cocktails, but Faye hasn't touched a single one," Emory sighs. "Poor girl. She's been so nervous about the wedding."

"You're right. It's just nerves," I confirm, biting through the lie. I know Michael's waiting to tell his parents about the pregnancy until after the wedding, and with the Red River contract drama, I don't blame him. "But I'll be back in the morning for the final dress fitting, and if you need my help with anything else, please, let me know."

"You're leaving? Already?"

"I can't keep up with them," I laugh, tilting my head toward Faye and Alma.

Emory gives me a knowing smile, reaching out to squeeze my hand. "Be careful on your way home."

"I will be." I give her a quick bow and hurry away. Saying goodbye to my sister and Faye would only elongate the process, and I have a stop to make.

The walk from the castle to Ravenfell is uneventful, thank the Goddess. I pass Alma's house, which is dark and empty given that

Lowe is off drinking with Michael to celebrate his last few days as a bachelor. The village is alive, with revelry, however, as celebrations held in honor of the upcoming wedding have patrons spilling out of Lowe's bar and the local inn, but I walk past it all, skirting into the quieter edge of town where old-growth trees stretch toward the cloudy night sky.

The little gray stone cottage is barely visible beyond the trees. The stone path is severely overgrown, but it'll be my honor to fix it up. I stick my key in the lock and turn. The stale air greets me, followed by peeling wallpaper and uneven floorboards.

I imagine the walls dressed in deep red paint and warm wood floors. I'll have someone come to fix the chimney and install more modern plumbing in the kitchen and bathroom. It has three bedrooms—one for me, and two for... my herbs, my potions, the trinkets and clothes I'll collect now that I have some place to put them.

One day, this will be my sanctuary to grow old and wrinkly in as the centuries pass—while everyone I love moves on.

"What is this place?"

I whirl to Cole's voice. He takes up the entire doorway to the outside world as he steps inside, his brow furrowed. His eyes meet mine in the moonlit darkness, and my heart skips a beat before stopping.

Silent, aching seconds pass. My heart thumps once, then twice.

Cole takes several steps in my direction, curling and flexing his hands.

"This—I bought this cottage. It's mine," I stammer as he looks around. I can't read his expression, but it's dark, nonetheless.

He doesn't ask why. His gaze sweeps the empty, faded living room before meeting my eyes.

"Did you follow me here?" I ask.

"I—I went to Alma's. I'm not sure why. I knew you'd be at the castle tonight but—" He stares down at his hands, looking suddenly like the young man I used to know and love, the man who hadn't witnessed the realities of our world yet. "Em, I—the way things ended between us… I never wanted it to be like this, and I'm sorry. I'm sorry for how I've been. I've been terrible to you."

"You don't have to apologize–"

"I do–because you hate me, and I… I can find a way to live without you. I can give you up, if that's what you really want. I get it. I understand where you're coming from and why you had to call things off, but I can't live with the idea that you hate me. I can't." His voice drops to a low, gravelly whisper.

"I don't hate you. I've never hated you, Cole."

His eyes shine as he takes a breath, "Em, I–I just want you to be happy. I need to know that you are happy."

"I'm not," I admit, my eyes shining with what could be considered tears. The truth that's been lodged in my heart like a thorn for years stabs, throbbing. "I haven't been since we–since I–"

He takes my face between his hands and kisses me, breathlessly.

It's frantic, desperate, passionate, and everything in between.

It's a final goodbye… the thing we didn't have before. Closure.

But then it doesn't feel like it, not when I kiss him back with just as much fervor, and he backs me into the wall, caging me in.

It feels like regret, like we've wasted four years, and I have no idea how to move forward now.

He pulls away from the kiss, resting his forehead against mine.

We stay like that for ages in the quiet dark, just the two of us and our broken hearts.

6 5

BEAUTY AND THE BEAST

Faye

IT'S SNOWING ON MY WEDDING DAY. SNOWING HARD, ACTUALLY, AS I watch cars pulling around the castle where valets are waiting to greet the guests. The wedding will take place in an hour.

An hour. I can't believe it. My stomach pitches as two maids pull curlers from my hair and dab blush on my cheeks. I haven't moved from this spot in ages. I haven't moved at all. I've been stuck on this stool since I can't remember when, and now I'm worried my legs won't work when I'm made to rise.

"The dress? The dress?" Emory says exhaustedly, whirling this way and that way, trying to catch the attention of the maids whizzing around the room. "Where's the designer? He should have arrived by now?"

A flurry of activity from the doorway to the wide, slightly cavernous sitting room somewhere on the second floor of the castle catches my attention, but I can't look in that direction while a maid is trying to perfect the blush on my cheeks.

"Oh, thank the Goddess." Emory sighs with relief.

"I apologize for the delay," the designer says somewhere behind me, his voice carrying over the shuffling of shoes and fabric. "Traffic to the castle is entirely backed up."

"You're fine," the queen says, a smile in her voice. "Everything's fine now that you're here."

I don't have a single second to try to catch my reflection in the vanity mirror before I'm whisked from the stool. The dress is massive and beautiful down to the finest detail. Pearls and crystals gleam in the centers of hundreds of delicate lace flowers. Beneath the lace, the ballgown shimmers in sheets of ivory silk that make my pale skin glow with a hint of gold, like I'm lit from within. I opted for no corset and have to hold my breath as the back of the dress is buttoned. I haven't started to show yet, I don't believe so, at least, but if it doesn't fit…

It buttons all the way, thank the Goddess.

Long sleeves of pure silk cover my arms to my wrists. Maids hurry around me, securing bracelets of white gold inlaid with sapphires. Emory is momentarily lost in the sea of bodies hurrying to help me into the dress but reappears with a crimson cushion in her hand, a tiara gleaming atop it, and my breath catches in my throat at the sight of the… crown.

It's beautiful. Stunning. Delicate, and made of the same white gold as the bracelets, sapphires and diamonds shine in the center of whirls and swirls of metal resembling roses and orchids.

The queen meets my eyes with a watery smile and bows ever so slightly, which makes my heart jump. "Kane had this made for me when we married. It was a gift–a token of his love and his love for his queen." She plucks it from the cushion and steps up to me, her cheeks rosy and eyes shining with tears. "I wanted to give it to my daughter one day. Now, it's yours."

"Emory," I whisper, my throat tightening as a sob of thanks tries to break free.

I bend my knees, leaning down as she presses the tiara into the massive, heat manipulated curls twisted and bunched into an intricate updo on the top of my head.

When I rise, I notice everyone has taken several steps away. The maids stare at me in awe, some of them resting their hands over their hearts as they sigh, their eyes shining with tears as Emory slowly turns me toward the full-length mirror hung on a nearby wall.

The first image I see in my mind is an old picture of my mother. The only picture I have of her–had, seeing as all the things I'd brought with me from Red River are gone now, lost in the attack that brought me to my fate... to the love of my life.

I see my mother's reflection. Her soft, golden blonde hair, her ocean blue eyes. I see her grace and beauty as I take a breath, the bodice of my impressive gown rising and falling in a glow of ivory silk and exquisite lace.

But she wasn't smiling in her wedding portrait. Her face was stern and sorrowful. She didn't have a choice... but I do.

I wish she were here. I'd do anything just to have a moment with her again, to tell her everything, to hold her hand and tell her that her daughter is happy and so, so very loved.

I blink back tears as Emory squeezes my arm. "You look beautiful, Faye."

"I do," I breathe, sniffling as I glance at her reflection in the mirror. She's teary eyed, her face glowing with excitement.

"Michael's going to lose his mind!"

We both turn to the vampire moving in our direction dressed in a stunning deep crimson gown. I blink, unsure of who I'm looking at until Emelda's rare but undeniable laugh cuts through the room.

"Emelda?" I gasp as she cuts through the crowd of maids.

Her thick, dark hair is loose and perfectly straight, falling down her back in a sheet of onyx that catches the light of the chandelier and shimmers against her hips as she walks toward us. The gown is simple but breathtaking, hugging curves I didn't know she had. It's red silk with long, slender sleeves. Gold jewelry glistens on her pale skin, and her eyes are darkened with perfectly applied makeup, her cheeks dusted with a warm, red blush.

Even the queen is shocked. Emory mouths something under her

breath, shaking her head in disbelief. "My Goddess, Emelda. You are— you clean up well."

She smiles, giving the queen a graceful curtsey. "Alma got a hold of me, I'm afraid. Are we ready? Michael's already worrying you're not going to show up at the altar, Faye."

"We're only running ten minutes behind," Emory replies but dashes out of the room, clapping her hands at the maids and servants to follow her.

In a matter of seconds, I'm left alone with Emelda and thankful for it because I feel as though I'm starting to come apart at the seams.

She notices the pinch between my brows and smiles softly, nodding as if she can read my thoughts. "You're all right, Faye. Everything is going to be fine."

"I'm afraid," I admit, unsure how else to describe the feelings bouncing through my body.

"There's nothing to be afraid of. Come, let's find your husband." She takes my hand but pauses, her expression shattering. "There is one thing you should know. Something... something we just found out, and you need to be prepared."

"What?" I ask, my body lurching with unease.

"Your father is here. King Mattias arrived ten minutes ago with some of his court to witness the ceremony."

My blood runs cold.

66

—————

HERE COMES THE BRIDE

Michael

I can count on one hand how many times I've been in this cathedral over the course of my short life. The dark stone walls echo even the smallest whisper, and the ancient stained glass sends shadows instead of snowy sunlight into the cavernous space.

I wouldn't consider vampires a very religious bunch. Some follow the same teachings the shifters do–the Moon Goddess and Her lessons, Her gifts, and whatnot, but not most. Others believe in ancient gods. Some worship the devil.

Maybe back in the history of my family's time in this castle, my ancestors used to hold services here. Mom occasionally comes to sit quietly and pray in the dusty, shaded pews, but otherwise this place is a skeleton of a time long past.

But today... It's lovely and warm. The air is fragrant with the scents of flowers resting in massive bouquets arranged on columns and pillars, with white roses strung on twine hanging from the pews, making the cathedral look like a sunny, warm spring day instead of a dark, stormy, winter night.

295

At least four hundred guests are waiting in the pews for my bride to arrive. I rock on my heels at the base of the altar where a shifter priestess of the nearby Order of The Moon Goddess waits to begin the ceremony, her hands neatly folded in front of her stomach as she wearily eyes the crowd.

There are several shifters in attendance. My mother's family, for one. Her brother and sister and their families. Their children and grandchildren are at the castle nearby, safely tucked away from the vampires who will be partying late into the night during the reception.

I scan the crowd for more wolves, spotting Lowe and Alma. She looks radiant as she beams at me, waving enthusiastically while Lowe lowers his head, looking worse for wear and a little uneasy stuffed between two groups of vampires he's not familiar with.

Hell, I'm not familiar with most of the people in attendance, but it's a royal wedding.

It's my royal wedding.

The nerves start to sink in as the minutes tick by, and Faye doesn't arrive.

Emelda floats by behind me, rising on her toes to whisper in my ear, "She's nearly ready. Your mom is fussing over something about the bouquet. The flowers are wrong or something."

I roll my eyes to the ceiling and silently curse. "I'm sure whatever she has is fine–"

"Queen Emory is in her greenhouse right now picking out new roses." Emelda smirks up at me, shrugging.

"Are you serious? We were supposed to be started by now."

"This is the queen's show, Michael. You're just a prop, remember? Your job is to stand here and look regal, not–" She cuts herself off abruptly as Cole walks down the aisle, ignoring everyone glancing in his direction. He gives me an arch of the brow and his cockiest smile, but it falls flat and turns to sheer disbelief when he sees Emelda lurking in the shadows just behind me.

He adjusts his suit collar like it's choking him and starts in my direction again, his eyes holding on Emelda as she tries to shrink into the shadows again.

I grind my teeth as Cole walks up the short steps to the altar. This tension between my cousin and my dearest friend is getting old, but that's not the concern right now.

Our unexpected guest and his posse currently entering the cathedral hold precedence.

Cole holds Emelda's gaze before his eyes slip to her dress and back up again, in a slow sweep that would make a weaker man blush, but not me. I almost say something about it, but Cole turns back to me and says, "King Mattias is attending the reception. I confirmed it with your father."

I shake my head, eyeing the king as he moves down the aisle with at least a dozen vampires guarding him.

My father sits in the front row with my uncle Lex and is watching the procession as well. An unfamiliar glint shines in his eyes. I can't describe the emotion behind that look, but Lex isn't keeping his feelings under wraps. His hatred shines clear as day. His second, Rainer, is also nearby, their families not seeming to notice how on guard all of them are.

"Think about what we discussed," Cole says into my ear. "The contract–"

"I'm not worried about that right now," I rasp as the doors to the cathedral open against a backdrop of fading, snowy light.

Cole steps to my side. Out of the corner of my eye, I notice him taking Emelda's hand, leading her down the steps. She lets go of his hands and disappears into the crowd. It's the last thing I see before Faye is led out, walked down the aisle by my mother.

Mom's in tears, but she's doing her best to hold herself together, remaining the strong, stone-faced queen despite the myriad of emotions behind her eyes. But I look at my dad, noticing the soft, secret smile on his lips as he looks at her. I wonder if he's thinking about their wedding, their early years together.

I would be.

I let the rest of the room fade. Faye is the only thing I see, moving toward me like one of the Goddess's angels. She's…. Beautiful doesn't even come close to conveying how stunning she is.

My bride. My wife. The mother of my children. Over the past months, she's gone from the scared young woman who showed up in my life to the woman who shines even in our darkest moments.

I'm barely aware of the ceremony taking place around us. I grip her hand, smoothing my thumb over her fingers, leaning in to whisper in her ear that I love her, that she looks beautiful.

But she looks up at me, the sapphires in her tiara nearly the same shade as her eyes, and whispers, "Why is my father here?"

The unease in her voice brings me back to a startling reality. "I don't know," I tell her honestly, squeezing her hand. "Don't be afraid. I'll handle it."

67

BROKEN CONTRACT

MICHAEL

I'M NOT SURE WHAT I EXPECTED GETTING MARRIED TO FEEL LIKE. IN MY mind, it had always been a business arrangement with little fanfare and no emotions attached. Now, that's not the case. I'm a husband. I have a wife whom I love, who wasn't chosen for me based on whatever political alliance was most desirable at the time. Tonight, once I can sneak her away from the high-ranking vampires who're currently showering us with praise and congratulations, I'll go to bed with my wife, my mate, and wake up the next morning to what feels like a gift from the Goddess Herself... a life of happiness, of love, all the things I let fade into the background when I put my duty as my father's heir to the forefront.

I watch my wife walk from group to group with my mom by her side, nodding and smiling at the vampire's Mom is introducing her to, but I've been hanging back, nursing a flute of sparkling blood and watching the crowd–one group in particular.

The grand dinner is over. The crowd has lessened significantly, but King Mattias hasn't approached me–his son-in-law–at all as it stands. His emissaries have come up to congratulate me, of course, but the man himself only sends sharp, cutting looks in my direction, looking smug as hell.

He must feel like he won the lottery. He thinks he has me and my father by the balls.

But now he's headed in my direction. He's a tall man but stands a few inches shorter than I am. His hair is long and silver, and his face betrays his advanced age. He could be a mortal man in his early fifties, but I know better than that. His eyes... red, like polished rubies, scan my formal attire as he gives me a slight, short bob of his head.

He won't bow. I'm of lesser standing than he is, given that I'm still a prince, but he's still in my kingdom.

"Congratulations," he sneers, his lip curling over his fangs. "I pray you find my daughter fruitful."

I smile, chuckling darkly. "Time will tell."

He looks me up and down before smirking and turning from me, his guards following him closely.

I open my mouth to tell him to fuck right off to the hell he came from, that I'm declaring the contract void–risking war between our kingdoms for the continued safety of my family–of my wife–but my father suddenly appears at my side, his face cast in shadow as he leans in and says across the rim of my ear, "Do not react to what's about to happen."

I turn to face him, a chill licking up my spine. "What?"

But he turns away, walking steadily in the direction of my mom and Faye, and then a hush falls over the ballroom.

A cackling laugh echoes over the crowd. A flash of white blonde hair and crimson red catches my attention before my body lurches, my wolf begging to be released as Matilda parts the crowd.

King Mattias turns, the little color he had in his cheeks draining, turning him shallow and gray.

His guards aren't sure what to do. They spread out, glancing at each other as King Mattias's other daughter waltzes toward her father, grinning like a feral cat.

My heart quickens as I look desperately for Faye. Emelda rushes through the crowd, blocking my view of Faye as she sweeps her away, my mom following close behind.

What the hell is going on?

Lex's voice rings out through the ballroom. "King Mattias, you're under arrest by order of the Kingdom of Scarlett Thunder and Crimson Peak." His voice booms over the shocked crowd. Faces turn in his direction as he stalks toward King Mattias, a legion of guards at arms behind him.

I scan the crowd in utter shock, my gaze landing on Cole, who watches his father come to a stop only feet from where King Mattias is standing, unsure whether to look at his daughter–who should be dead–and Lex.

"On what grounds?" he snarls, laughing around the words. "Under arrest for… what?"

My father's voice erupts through the crowd, "You broke an old tenement when you failed to fulfill the deal you made with King Lex of Scarlett Thunder."

"An old tenement?" King Mattias laughs. "Enlighten me–"

"The contract between Scarlett Thunder and Red River was sealed in blood," Father says, walking a wide circle to Lex's side. "You failed to follow through."

"The only failure stemmed from that bastard child," he snarls, pointing at Matilda. "Her schemes were not mine, therefore–"

"Regardless," Lex booms, smiling wickedly, "my son has no wife. The wedding never took place."

Mattias glares at Lex before waving his hand at Matilda. "Yet, here she is, alive and well. The marriage can still take place."

"Like you said," Dad replies, looking incredibly calm and collected, "she is a bastard. Her mother was not your wife, nor your queen. My son just married your only legitimate child, King Mattias. You broke a blood oath for peace between Red River and Scarlett Thunder… and in turn, the contract you filed between Red River and Crimson Peak is now… void."

King Mattias turns a gruesome red, fury flaring behind his red eyes. "You assholes–" His mouth flies open, but no sound comes out. He grunts, his head sliding forward like he's... leaning, but...

A vicious gasp of panic spreads through the room. Screams erupt, washing through the ballroom in a wave of fear and shock as King Mattias's head slides off his neck and falls to the ground, followed by his body.

Behind him, Matilda beams, her smile stretching from cheek to cheek as she inspects a long, narrow short sword that looks like it came from the time of our ancestors. She runs her finger across the blade, through the blackish red vampire blood of her father, and cackles a laugh as she rubs her finger and thumb together.

My heart stops. I look at Cole, but he's just as shocked as I am as we watch our fathers.

They planned this.

They knew Matilda would come. They knew she'd take the opportunity to kill her father if he was served up to her on a silver platter.

She arches a brow at the shocked, panicking royal guards from Red River. "Aren't you going to bow? You're in the presence of your queen!"

UNLEASHED

Faye

EMELDA SLAMS THE DOOR SHUT BEHIND EMORY AS I RUN INTO THE suite I share with Michael. The familiar deep blue walls and warm air does nothing to calm my nerves as I whirl toward the women, my dress swirling out around me, feeling suddenly heavier than it had before.

"What—what's happening?" I ask hurriedly. "Emory—"

"Stay with her. Don't let anyone other than Michael come in here. No servants, no maids, no feeders," Emory rushes out, clutching Emelda's arm. She yanks the door open and disappears, her rapid footsteps echoing through the outer corridor. Emelda pulls it closed and locks it again, panting.

"Emelda—"

"I don't know what's happening, Faye, but we're staying in here." She closes her eyes, struggling to swallow or even take a full breath. "You saw her too, didn't you?"

"Matilda? Yes, of course!" I throw my hands in the air in surrender, my dress feeling impossibly heavy and snug. I start pulling at the bodice, desperate to get it off, to feel the air on my skin.

Emelda catches her breath and hurries to my side, turning me toward the wall in the little foyer of the suite and unbuttons the dress. I scurry out of it, shoving and tearing at the fabric as tears sting my eyes. "What does she want? Is she here for Michael? For Cole?"

"No. I don't know." Emelda breathes. "But you're safe here–"

"She tried to kill you!" I remind her, standing in nothing but my shift and the fine jewels Emory gave me.

Emelda reaches up and tactfully untangles the tiara from my hair, setting it on a nearby side table. She grabs my wrists and takes the bracelets off, ignoring my whimpering, ignoring the fear and uncertainty we both feel.

She steps away with the jewelry to find a safe place to keep it while I pull the pins free from my hair. It falls over my shoulders in thick, golden curls that shield my face from view when Emelda rushes toward the door as a rough, thick knock sounds, echoing through the foyer.

"It's me. Open the door," Michael commands, his voice deep with fatigue. He sounds lost, out of breath, and looks incredibly worse for wear when Emelda opens the door, and he steps inside. "Go to the ballroom and ensure the guests are leaving," he orders.

Emelda scoffs, "Are you kidding? Matilda–"

"I know. She's not here anymore. You're safe. You'll... you'll understand when you get there. The queen will need assistance saying farewell to the party-goers," he says low in his throat, like he's forcing each word.

I scan him for injuries, but he seems fine–intact.

Emelda glances at me before leaving, the door snapping shut. He reaches behind and turns the lock.

"What happened?" I squeak, shaking my head. "Michael–"

It takes my husband all of three steps to reach me. He throws his arms around me, lifting me up, and presses his lips to mine in a hungry, desperate kiss that steals the air from my lungs. "I'm sorry," he says hoarsely against my mouth, then kisses me again. "I'm sorry. I'm so sorry–"

I shush him, shaking my head before pressing my lips to his. This whole night I've been waiting for this–for us to be alone. To celebrate our wedding, just the two of us. I'm in the arms of my husband right now, and I've never felt safer, even when a threat is in the castle with us.

Michael backs me against a wall. I wrap my legs around his waist, my fingers gliding up his neck into his hair.

He smells amazing. I want to… feed from him. I need it. My mouth leaves his to press kisses along his jaw and down to his soft, tender neck, toward that spot, that vein…

"Faye," he whispers. I can feel his heart beginning to thunder with excitement and desire as I drag my fangs over his skin. "Faye, your father is dead."

Reality momentarily blinds me.

I lean back so we're eye to eye, our noses brushing in the shadows. "Really?"

"Yes."

I should ask why. I should want to know how it happened and if our wedding was soiled by his death. I'm sure it's chaotic downstairs in the ballroom. I'm sure war is on the horizon, and everything safe and comfortable about our life is about to change abruptly, but… I don't care.

I feel… happy.

I'm free.

We're free.

All of us. Me, my husband, and our babies.

"Thank you," I whisper against his mouth. "Thank the Goddess he's dead."

Michael takes a shuddering breath before kissing me deeply. He pulls away after a moment, cupping the back of my head and guiding me back to his neck.

I bite him, and he inhales sharply, sending hot, raging desire flooding through my body. I grind against him, drinking deeply while he praises me, telling me to take all I want, to drain him.

He walks us into the bedroom. I unlatch from the bite as he turns to the vanity, setting me on top of it and wrenching my legs apart. My whole body warms, my heart beating out of rhythm before skyrocketing as his blood works through my system, making my cheeks burn with color.

He stills, panting, with his hands braced on my thighs. "I'm sorry, I–I've just been… desperate for this. For you."

I reach for his suit jacket, flipping open the button, then reach lower for his belt, deftly pulling it free from his finely tailored pants.

All hell might be breaking loose downstairs, but we're alone. The door is locked.

We have this moment. I don't even want to think about what could happen next.

I guide him back to me, straightening my spine and kissing him deeply, tenderly, my lips stained with his blood. His tongue glides over mine in a dizzying dance, and he growls in satisfaction when my hand slides into his pants, my fingers drifting over his hard cock.

"Come to me," I whisper against his mouth. "Husband."

He smiles, but his eyes open, his pupils blown wide.

My shifter husband. My feral, untamed beast.

"Fuck me," I rasp, knowing that'll send him over the edge.

I don't want him to be gentle. I want him unleashed.

WEDDING NIGHT

Faye

MICHAEL KISSES ME LIKE IT'S THE FIRST TIME WE'VE EVER TASTED EACH other. It's gentle at first–a featherlight brush of his lips against mine. It's like it was before… when we loved each other in secret, when we were ignoring our growing feelings for each other while the world burned down around us, constantly trying to pull us apart.

But now?

I smile against his lips as I open my eyes and catch the light glinting off the simple, smooth gold wedding band on my finger.

His mark on my skin throbs to life as happiness I've never felt shimmers through my body.

"My wife," he whispers against my bare shoulder, pressing a kiss against the words. "My mate."

"My husband," I smile, rolling my head back as his tongue draws a line between my breasts.

Everything that happened at our reception is a blur of noise now. It doesn't matter. We've said our vows. We'd dedicated what I hope is a very long life to each other. I'm pregnant with his children–his heirs–and no one can take them from us.

Michael reaches for his pants while continuing his exploration of my body, my skin. He frees his cock, sliding my shift up my thighs before thrusting inside of me in one smooth, hard motion. I'm still sitting on the vanity, my legs wrapped around his waist while he grips my hips, thrusting and rolling against me until I moan his name.

I reach down and pull my shift over my head, tossing it somewhere in the corner of our bedroom. He grins, chuckling darkly as he bends his neck to suck one of my breasts into his eager mouth.

I roll my hips against his, chasing friction and pressure until I feel myself slipping over the edge, tension coiling tight in my lower belly and thighs.

"I'm so close," I moan, throwing my head back in ecstasy as his thrusts become erratic, fast and furious. The vanity claps against the wall, the sound echoing through the room.

He buries his face against my neck, biting down hard enough to sting, giving me another mark, another scar to show I'm his, forever.

My inner walls spasm, squeezing his cock. He chokes out a groan, his tongue roving over the mark he just left, before he kisses me deeply and comes undone. A warm, full sensation floods my lower belly as he pours into me, holding me tight.

"Faye," he says against my mouth, "I love you."

"I love you."

"You looked stunning today. You always do but… everything I ever dreamed of–the future I envisioned… it didn't come close to watching you walk into that cathedral."

I close my eyes, leaning toward him, finding his mouth with mine.

"I will fix this," he whispers, caressing my cheek. "Whatever schemes your father and sister were conducting… it won't affect us. Our children will be safe." He presses his hand to my lower belly. There's the slightest bump there now–firm and solid. He sucks in a breath, his eyes holding mine. "One day," he continues, "we will be king and queen of Crimson Peak, and things will be different. Our daughter will not meet the same fate you faced, I promise you."

"I trust you," I whisper, leaning against him.

We stay like that for some time, still joined, naked and open to each other. He eventually lifts me off the vanity and lays me in bed, his cock growing hard again, and before I've even hit the sheets, he's inside of me, rolling into me in slow, delicious strokes that make me cry his name into the pillow until I'm so tired I can't keep my eyes open anymore.

Michael falls asleep beside me. I wake an hour or so later to the room coated in darkness. I sit up, pulling the comforters toward us, cocooning us in warmth.

But he stirs, rolling over and draping his arm over my waist, his palm pressed to my stomach. His touch is warm. I love that he's always so warm.

His lips brush over my shoulder. "Go back to sleep," he whispers.

"I'm trying," I admit. "I can't stop thinking about what happened. What will people say?"

"I don't care. Let them talk."

"And they will talk," I whisper, rolling to face him. He brushes my hair away from my face. "What if... what if this was only part of Matilda's plan? What if she wants to hurt us? Hurt me?"

"You know I won't let that happen."

"I just want a peaceful life with you, with our children. Michael, that's all I want."

"And you will have it. I promise."

He kisses my forehead, sighing against my skin.

"Go to sleep now. Tomorrow, we'll face this head on, together, and we'll be fine. Then, we can move on."

I snuggle close, chasing his warmth, and close my eyes. Sleep washes over me in waves—some deeper than others. I wake several times throughout the night, and on the third time, Michael's no longer beside me, but his side of the bed is still warm, still smells like him.

I curl into myself, hugging my knees to my chest, and say a soft prayer for our children.

This is my happy ending, isn't it? Everything I ever wanted, I've received.

Why do I still feel like something is on the horizon? Maybe it'll be peaceful for a while, but... forever? The vampire kingdoms feel suddenly precarious and unsteady, but tonight, I'm in a bed I share with my husband, in a castle in a kingdom we'll one day rule, that our children and their children will rule.

I can only look toward the future now.

I close my eyes, letting the memories of my attacks, of my sister and her schemes, and of my old life in Red River fade into blackness.

WHO WOULD BE QUEEN

Emelda

I FIND EMORY IN THE BALLROOM TRYING TO RECTIFY THE SITUATION. Blood stains the center of the grand mosaic tiles that cover the ballroom in shades of gray and the deepest gold, but even the dark hues aren't enough to hide the vampire blood.

I wasn't here for whatever happened, but I heard whispers of it while charging through the castle. Maids that should have been serving flutes of sparkling blood were running around in a tizzy, trying to decide what to do and where to go, all of their original orders banished in an instant.

Emory speaks in quiet tones, offering apologies for having to end the reception early, even though the violence broke out at a quarter to midnight. Most of the guests had left by then, and those that remained were mostly part of King Kane's court.

Still, after Cole's failed nuptials, this is just… this is a travesty that will send rumors of unrest spiraling through the kingdom, of that I'm sure.

I rush to Emory's side as the last of the guests leaves the ballroom. "What happened?" I ask, clutching her arm.

She curls her fingers over mine, her skin cold to the touch, which is odd for a shifter. Her flushed skin makes her finally look her age, not the blossom of youth she's known for, even as a mortal.

She shakes her head, still looking regal in her deep burgundy gown, and says, "King Mattias was killed."

My blood runs cold. "By whom?"

Her sparkling jade eyes meet mine and hold. "By Princess Matilda." She sounds surprised. I don't blame her. I'm not entirely sure I heard her correctly, but she takes my hand, knitting her fingers in mine. "Come with me, will you?"

"Where are we going?"

"To speak to my husband and get to the bottom of whatever the hell is going on." She inhales sharply, her cheeks flaring to life in shades of deep red.

We pass the bloodstained tiles being scrubbed clean by male servants. We pass the flowers, the fine decorations, and the quartet still plucking their strings, all of them washed in shock.

A bloodstained wedding. I guess it's only fitting for vampires for events like this to end this way.

The castle is startlingly quiet as I walk hand in hand with the queen. My skin is chilled. I'm not used to wearing gowns like this—that show off my body. I feel naked without my cloak and apron, like the crimson silk is a second skin, and I'm totally exposed. My heels click on the stone steps as the queen leads me up a winding hidden staircase that deposits us directly in the thick of King Kane's personal rooms. His offices. His command post. His sitting rooms where he holds meetings with dignitaries from other kingdoms.

Guards linger along the walls of the foyer, heavily armed and stern, watching with muted interest as the queen guides me, a nobody, a turned vampire, into their king's royal office.

Noise and chaos reach us as soon as the doors open.

My heart sinks and shudders when I see Matilda in all her glory leaning on King Kane's desk, toying with a pen that she flips around her fingers. Her blue eyes meet mine, and she smirks, arching her brows.

I resist the urge to bring my hands to my neck, remembering her vicious, deadly touch. She'd come so close to killing me, and now she's here, unrestrained.

The queen lets go of my hand as the group turns.

"Emory," King Kane says under his breath.

"What," she snaps, her canine teeth on display like she's on the verge of shifting, "is the meaning of this?"

King Lex steps forward and behind him…

Cole shoves past his father, his face drawn in sudden concern. "What are you doing here?" he rushes out, his eyes locked on mine. "What is she doing here?!"

"I–" I don't have an answer for him as he stalks toward me, taking me by the elbow and turning me toward the door. His touch is gentle–almost tender, and I feel everyone's eyes on us.

"She stays," Emory barks. "To face the woman who tried to kill her and burned her home to the ground, yet stands here unchained."

"Emory," Kane warns.

"What happened?" Emory presses. "What kind of scheme took place at our son's wedding, Kane?"

Lex clears his throat. I'm still facing the door, but Cole turns, his hand not leaving my arm. I lean into him, closing my eyes as Lex says, "An opportunity arose that we couldn't let pass us by."

Before Emory can cut in again, Kane adds, "King Mattias announced he'd be coming to the wedding to ensure the union was done properly. Shortly thereafter, we received word that Princess Matilda had been seen–"

"She'd torn through several villages, killing a number of high-ranking, wealthy vampires and their families," Cole clarifies.

Matilda's gaze lands on him as she grins wickedly, chuckling, "My dear, dear prince. You shouldn't talk about me that way, seeing as I now outrank you as Queen of Red River."

"You are not a queen," Cole growls. His grip on my arm tightens. I instinctively put my hand over his. He relaxes at my touch as I slowly, carefully, turn my head to look at Matilda over my shoulder.

She rolls her eyes. "You think I don't know your secret, Cole? Or should I say, *secrets*?" She grins at him like a cat.

I should let go of him. I should step away, but I know he won't release me, not now, not while she's here.

Emory ignores this part of the conversation, but her gaze sweeps over Cole and me, her eyes shining with sudden understanding that she swallows, saving it for later.

Matilda's sly chuckle bounces throughout the room as she explains, "I caught word of my father's impending arrival for the nuptials and decided I needed to pay him a little visit, to repay the… kindness he so gallantly bestowed upon me my entire life." She laughs, a sound reminiscent of ice. "When King Kane offered me my freedom for his help striking down the ludicrous contract my father backed him and Prince Michael into, I agreed."

"You didn't!" Emory looks up at her husband. "Kane–"

"I did what had to be done for our kingdom."

"And mine," Lex adds quietly, but his eyes flick to Cole's.

His son stiffens, glancing from his father to Matilda. "No–"

"Listen well, boy," Matilda sneers, crossing her thin arms over her chest. "I was never supposed to be your wife; that's true. My actions toward my sister were to save her life."

"That's a lie," I whisper, and her eyes meet mine.

"You couldn't possibly understand, being a witch-turned-vampire. Filth as you are."

"Leave her out of this," Cole warns, "You've done enough."

I feel Lex and his wife, Ivy, looking at me, but I don't risk glancing in their direction.

"You and I," Matilda says to Cole, "could unify Red River and Scarlet Thunder. You, the prince, as my husband. Our heirs will be entitled to both kingdoms."

"I will never marry you," Cole spits out.

Matilda looks at Lex, arching a brow. He stays silent, just as rigid as his son.

"There will be no unity between our kingdoms," Kane tells Matilda. "Red River will not have an ally in Crimson Peak, nor Scarlet Thunder. This is over. Your sister is safe. The union between Faye and my son is complete. They are wed; the contract King Mattias had us sign is now void in his death. And you... Are free to return to Red River, as queen, if your people will have you."

Matilda exhales slowly, annoyed. "I want to see my sister before I go."

"No," Emory says firmly.

Matilda rolls her eyes. "So be it. Give her my love, will you, Cole? I have a message for you, by the way. It's waiting in your room. Consider it a little parting gift from me to you."

She brushes past us, giggling. No one stops her from leaving. The guards don't raise their swords.

Matilda walks free, Queen of Red River.

I let go of Cole's hand and start moving toward the door, slipping out of his grasp. "Em, wait."

"I must check on Princess Faye," I say over my shoulder. I walk steadily away while my heart pounds out of my chest.

Behind me, before the doors close, I hear Ivy ask, "What's the meaning of this, Cole?"

I close my eyes, praying I don't hear his response knowing the lie would crush me.

71

―――――

THE KINGDOM IS YOURS

Faye

MORNING DESCENDS ON CRIMSON PEAK. IT'S A BLEARY BUT WARM winter day. Water drips down the windows as the snow and ice melts off the roof of the castle. Dark clouds promise more snow if the weather chills again, and the air smells like ozone as I slip out of bed, blinking blearily into the gray light.

Michael's side of the bed is empty but unmade. I wonder if he came back to sleep and slipped out again before I noticed.

I'm wearing a thin, silken robe but fetch a loose fitting gown from the closet, draping it over my body. I smooth the pale pink fabric over the slight swell of my stomach, smiling when I notice the bump I'd been sure was there on my wedding day is real.

I'm starting to show. I'm sure it's come quicker since I'm carrying twins. I wonder if Michael plans on telling his parents I'm pregnant now that we're married, but the thought of them forces my mind back to everything that happened yesterday.

My sister is alive. The sister that tried and failed to kill me. My father is dead, and Red River will likely be thrown into chaos. The

317

thought of his death doesn't settle in my mind with grief. I feel slightly uneasy that the only thing I feel is an overwhelming sense of relief that he's gone.

I'm dressed and in the process of brushing out my wedding day curls when the door to our bedroom opens, and Michael walks in, looking around in an effort to find me.

He looks a little worn as his eyes graze mine. He's also holding a cup of coffee in his hand which he brings to his lips with a soft sigh. "Good morning."

"Good morning," I echo, turning around on the vanity stool. "Did you sleep at all?"

"I slept enough." He takes another drink. "Faye, I, uh… we need to talk. My parents are waiting for us."

"How bad is it?" I rise, slipping my feet into a pair of silken slippers. My hair cascades down my back as I shrug into a cardigan and smooth the knit fabric down my sides.

He flexes his jaw before saying, "It could be worse."

"Okay, well, sure. Let's go. And then you can rest for the rest of the day."

He extends his hand, twining our fingers, then leads me through our suite and into the depths of the castle, but I'm surprised that we're not going directly to King Kane's office.

We arrive in the formal breakfast room, and the table is full. Ivy and Lex look weary as she picks at her breakfast, and Lex sips a mug of hot blood. King Kane doesn't look any better. Emory, however, rises from her chair and rushes to greet us, clasping my hands between her own. "Oh, my darling, I'm so sorry."

"The wedding was still beautiful, Emory. It was a dream. Please don't apologize."

She nods, but her eyes shine like polished jade as she walks back to the table and takes her seat beside her husband.

I'm not sure why I'm shocked to see Cole leaning against the far wall, his eyes locked on the melting snow outside. Michael told me Cole normally avoided things like this–the whole family meeting, especially over meals.

Michael pulls out my chair, and the second I sit down, his father says, "Faye, you're aware by now that your father is dead."

I swallow hard, reaching for a carafe of blood to pour into my own mug. "I am aware, yes."

"And you're his only legitimate child," the king continues, his eyes meeting mine and holding firm.

I stiffen. "What–what are you saying?"

"You have a claim to his territory. A rightful claim, actually, compared to Princess Matilda."

I blink, looking at Michael for confirmation. He looks stern and serious, his eyes locked on his father's face.

"Matilda…" I taper off as every puzzle piece finally falls into place. I look up at the faces around the table, in shock. "Oh, my Goddess. This was Matilda's plan all along, wasn't it?" I look down at the table and then over at Cole. "We were supposed to marry, and Matilda saw that as a way to get the support of another kingdom behind her when she planned on trying to overthrow my father. She was going to go to war with him."

"We believe she was going to try to take his crown by right of conquest," Lex says softly, nodding.

"And she–she took my place to do it, and when I survived her plans…." I run my hand down my face, closing my eyes. "I have no interest in ruling Red River, now, or later. I don't want it."

Michael seems to relax a bit, but I'm fuming.

"Is Matilda still here?" I ask with a bite in my voice.

"No," Emory confirms. "She left as soon as we… let her go."

Cole chuckles darkly by the window, turning his head from the group.

"The nobles of Red River won't accept her as queen," I tell the table. "There's no way."

"We're aware," Kane says, "but she also believes we will be coming to her aid when war breaks out in that kingdom. She's on her own unless you want to help her, and in that case, we will. But if you want to stake your claim to the throne of Red River, you'd have the support of Crimson Peak and Scarlet Thunder."

Lex nods his agreement, and I almost feel like they're pushing me to say yes, that I want to be queen.

I don't.

"No. Let Matilda have it and the consequences that come with it. I don't want Red River. I never have."

I want... Michael. I want to be here with him, in the home he's going to build for us and our children. Children no one at this table but Cole knows about.

'*Michael, we should tell them. 'We should tell them—now,*' I say to him through telepathy.

He gives me the softest, most loving smile before rising with a long exhale, his eyes scanning the group–his family. Our family. "I have some news I'd like to share."

THIS IS GOODBYE

Cole

I RUN MY FINGERTIPS OVER THE SMOOTH LEATHER SUITCASE AS A TRIO of male servants hurry around the room, packing my things for the journey back home, to Scarlet Thunder. I grip the suitcase and carry it out of the apartment where I've been staying inside the castle, looking over my shoulder to take in the red wallpaper and dark furniture for what will be the last time in a very long while.

Dad's in the foyer when I approach. Mom squeezes his arm before walking through the open grand entrance, the landscape blanketed in fresh snow. Snow is falling in heaps, but I can tell my parents are ready to go home, for everything to go back to normal, not worried about the drive in the storm.

I watch Mom disappear into a blacked-out luxury SUV, but Dad sighs, turning to face me. "If you want to stay–"

"There's no reason for me to be here," I tell him, but his eyes scan mine.

"No reason at all?"

I know what he's asking. After the meeting with Matilda shortly following her murder of her own father, I'd slipped up, shown too much attention to Emelda in front of the family. My parents are curious, which is natural. I know, deep down, they want me to be happy, but I'm a prince. Prince Regent, in fact. The kingdom is mine to rule as soon as I want it. They know the way these things must go.

At least, for now. Dad had me before Ivy came into his life—the mother of my heart, the woman who raised me like her own flesh and blood son. I was heir to the throne from the moment I took my first breath, even before my birth mother died.

Whereas I have no heir, and the woman I love...

"Are you sure?" he asks, pulling me out of my downward spiral.

"I'll meet you in the car," I grit out, letting a servant take my suitcase. More of my bags are brought out as Dad walks to the vehicle.

I turn toward the staircase, closing my eyes for a moment. I wish I'd been able to say goodbye, at least. Kissing Emelda a few days ago had... awakened things in me that I'd kept buried for so long I'd forgotten about them, turned those feelings into anger and disdain instead, but... *I love her.*

I always will. That will never change, even if I have to change.

I stop a maid, tapping her on the elbow to get her attention. "Can you give this to someone for me and keep it discreet?"

She nods, her eyes as wide as tea saucers as she bobs her head. I slide a small envelope out of my inner jacket pocket and hand it to her. The words inside are simple. A single, heart wrenching sentence.

If you ever change your mind, I will be here in an instant for you.

I couldn't bring myself to say the three words currently choking me to death as the maid scans Emelda's name written neatly on the top of the envelope. I keep telling myself I have time. I have decades, centuries, for us to find each other again, but even then, it doesn't feel like enough.

Before, I buried this hurt in women and booze, in gambling and partying and being an all-around nuisance to society. Things need to be different now. Things have to change.

I walk outside into the snowy evening air and slide into the front seat of the car. My dad, who insists on driving himself everywhere, grips the wheel while Mom sighs heavily in the backseat, cracking open a book.

None of us speak for the first two hours of the journey. The landscape shifts, the open plains and sparse forests of Crimson Peak giving way to the more mountainous outer stretches of Scarlet Thunder's territory.

This is my home. This place, these people, I'll rule over one day–as soon as I'm ready.

"What do you know about the Princess of Starlit Tundra?" I ask Dad, rolling my head toward the window.

"Uh, not much. Starlit Tundra is… hundreds of miles north of here, for one. They live in icy darkness year round–"

"I know. I'm not asking about their kingdom. I'm asking about her."

"Which one? There're three, I believe. The king had to try for a while to get his male heir."

I close my eyes, picking through a mental checklist of what I need in a wife, a future queen, ignoring things like affection, love, friendship, and… dark, thick hair. The scent of cinnamon. Dark eyes and full, rosy lips that carry the taste of vanilla and spice when I kiss her…

My lips part to tell Dad to turn the car around, that I made a mistake, that I want someone who can't carry on our bloodline. I almost tell him to make any second son Michael has the heir to Scarlet Thunder, but I don't.

I'm stronger than this. I allow the feelings of regret to twist into rejection, into hate, once again.

Because hating Emelda, feeling stung by her rejection no matter how right she was and how her intentions were sincere and her actions done out of love… it's still easier to be a fucking asshole than admit that she is my soulmate.

She's robbing us of that.

I keep my mouth shut, but my mind roves over the single, high-bred, blood born woman who could give me an heir. I just need one. A boy. A prince to take over centuries from now when I'm long dead and ash in the ground. Once I have that heir… whatever relationship I have with his mother won't matter. We'll have both done our jobs and can live separate lives, where I can hopefully move on from Emelda and the scalding ache in what's left of my heart.

"We'll have to return for the birth of Michael's twins," Mom says behind me, smiling around the words. "I can't wait to see them. How lucky are Emory and Kane to become grandparents twice over in one go?" She leans forward, clutching my shoulder. "You must promise to give me at least one grandchild in my lifetime, sweetheart."

"I plan to," I tell her, my voice like gravel. "As soon as possible."

73

RUMORS AND UNREST

Summer

MICHAEL

"I DON'T THINK MY PARENTS COULD BE ANY HAPPIER WITH THE IDEA," Deacon says, walking by my side, his face shielded from the sunlight by a hood.

"You don't think it's a little fast?" I ask, smirking as I squint into the uncommon sunlight beating down on the field between the castle and Ravenfell.

"You married Princess Faye in… what, a matter of weeks?"

"I suppose you're right."

"I am right because if you know, you know. I know that I love her, and she loves me, and she's blood born, like me, and…"

"She's pregnant already, isn't she?" I laugh, and beneath the shadow of his hood, Deacon grins.

"I can't say I did much to stop it from happening."

"Well, I'll be there. I'm happy for you. It means… less time in the field, but… you've done your duty to the crown tenfold over the last year as it stands."

He laughs lightly, keeping in step as we dip into the trees. Deacon and his soon-to-be bride, and the mother of his future child, met at my bachelor outing a few nights before my wedding, which was… many months ago. I'm honestly shocked Deacon gave up his pursuit of Emelda, but in his defense, Emelda has been distant these past months. She's rarely at court. Faye visits her in Ravenfell often, at least several times a week. My mother calls on her to visit every once in a while, but other than that, she's just… alone.

Ravenfell comes into view. The only people out and about this time of day, on a particularly sunny day, are shifters. The new manor rises on the same hill I used to live on before, the brand-new, recently installed windows shimmering in the sunlight.

"Well, I'll be damned. It looks like a real house now with those windows beaming directly into my eyes," Deacon hisses, shielding his face from the sun. He's wearing thick black gloves to protect his skin from the glare.

We walk up the steps to the house, the only thing that survived the fire. The front door silently opens, spilling sunlight across the grand foyer and staircase. I close the door behind us, the curtains on the nearby windows drawn against the sun, and Deacon sighs.

"That's much better." He chuckles, pushing back his hood. "Wow, it looks exactly like the old place."

"It's a bit bigger, but yes, it's mostly the same. Obviously, it'll lack the history the old manor had, but it needed to be modernized anyway. I guess I can thank Queen Matilda for that."

Deacon hums at the mention of her name. "What's the news from Red River?"

"Nothing that pertains to Crimson Peak," I tell him, tucking my hands behind my back while guiding him through each room on the lower level. "She got what she really wanted—a crown. A kingdom. Vengeance against her father, who cast her off. She has no interest in Crimson Peak as it stands."

"She nearly killed Faye."

"Which is why when a war inevitably breaks out in her kingdom, Crimson Peak will not come to her aid. She's made her bed, and will lie in it."

Deacon smirks, running his fingertips over the stair rail as I lead him to the second level.

"And... have you heard from Cole?"

"On occasion. He hasn't been back since he left after my wedding."

"I plan on inviting him to the wedding next month. Do you think he'll come?"

I sigh, turning on my heel to face him. "To be honest," I begin, meeting Deacon's gaze, "no. I don't think he'll come."

He rolls his eyes to the darkened recesses of the hallway behind us. "There's been whispers, Michael."

"About what?"

"Well, Emelda, for one. Not that anyone outside of Crimson Peak knows who she is but... Cole is a prince, and his business is always public. It's said he had a great affair that tore his heart out of his chest."

"Well, that would be the truth–"

"But there's more." Deacon's tone shifts, taking on a dark, jagged edge.

Concern rips through my system. "What did you hear?"

"It's a rumor, nothing more, but... I have to tell you, as a friend–as his friend–that a noble woman, a daughter of a high-ranking vampire noble in the Kingdom of Evernight, died recently in childbirth. Before the birth began, she'd told several people that Cole was the father."

My brows furrow in confusion. "Evernight? That's near Red River... an obscure kingdom, if anyone could call it that. Why would Cole have–how?"

"Apparently, she was here for Cole's wedding to Matilda and stayed with some relatives who live here—in Crimson Peak. It's unlikely to be true, but people are talking. Given Cole's reputation, no one knows what to believe, and no one is all that surprised by it, honestly."

"She died?"

"She did. I've heard mixed accounts about the baby, that it passed with its mother because it was born very early–weeks earlier than anticipated–but the current rumor is he's still alive and in hiding, given that he's the heir to Scarlet Thunder."

"It's a boy?"

"So they say."

"Who's they?"

Deacon shrugs, "The ever turning rumor mill."

Footsteps on the staircase alert us both to the fact that we're not alone, but the tightness in my chest relaxes when Faye appears like a ray of sunshine, her golden hair falling loose from her braid.

"What are you doing here?" I ask, smiling as she grins at us.

"I needed a walk." A thick, black umbrella rests at her side as she smiles at Deacon, giving him a little nod of her head.

He bows but gives her his signature cocky smile as he approaches my wife, pressing a quick peck to her cheek. "You look lovely but also vastly uncomfortable, Your Highness."

"I am." She laughs. "This is my punishment for marrying a shifter, I assume. Their babies are surprisingly large compared to vampires."

Deacon glances between us, smiling softly to himself. "I'll leave you. I have some planning to do, anyway."

"We'll talk again tonight, if you're available," I tell him as he starts down the stairs.

"I will be."

We wait until the door closes, and the house settles into silence before I take my massively pregnant wife by the shoulders and inspect her for sun damage.

"I'm fine, Michael." She laughs, but she seems pale, her eyes washed with a hint of pain.

I rest my hand on the swell of her stomach. It's tight–rigid and painful. "Are you still feeling uncomfortable?"

"Always, but it's worse today. My lower back just–I couldn't sit still any longer, and when I heard you came to Ravenfell to check on the house, I decided to follow and try to find Emelda, but she's not home. Alma said she went to a nearby village to buy herbs at their market." She grimaces, clutching her stomach.

Alarm bells erupt in my skull, bouncing through my body. "Faye–"

"I'm all right," she says through gritted teeth. "I'm not due for another three weeks–"

"You're carrying twins and–"

She gasps, clutching my shirt as she tries to bend over her belly.

"Oh, my Goddess," I whisper, unsure whether to be excited or absolutely terrified. "You're in labor."

"Don't get too excited," she chuckles, but her eyes tell me the truth.

This is it.

Our children are on their way.

74

WAITING IS THE HARDEST PART

Michael

"It could be hours—or a day," Alma says quietly as she arranges her tonics on a table just outside the bedroom where Faye's finally getting some rest.

"It's been hours already," I tell her, motioning toward the window in my suite in the castle where moonlight drifts through the panes, casting the hallway in silver starlight.

"I agree with the physician that this won't be an easy labor for her. She's tired, Michael. She's a small woman with narrow hips, and these babies are large. Full term, even coming a few weeks early. We will need to decide whether a... surgery is more appropriate for her, given the circumstances."

"That's not what she wants," I assert, my throat tightening.

"I understand, but she's already so tired. If she sleeps through the night, she'll have the strength to get through tomorrow, but if her labor intensifies any more than this, we have to discuss other solutions and... outcomes."

Fury I can't contain wraps itself around my heart and squeezes.

331

"Outcomes?" I snarl, but Alma exhales deeply, fixing me with a knowing glare.

"I've been a midwife and healer for two centuries, Michael. I've delivered many babies, vampire and shifter alike, and if you think I haven't dealt with an angry father who just learnt that his wife, or mate, or mistress might face the damning consequences of a labor that's moving too quickly for her body, you're mistaken. If you can't be calm here and be her peace, then leave for a while. Lowe is downstairs with the king and queen. Go shift with him. You could use it."

I look at the bedroom door.

"Michael," Alma breathes. "Go. Go and fetch Emelda. She should have been back now with the herbs for the tea Faye likes. Faye will be fine, I promise."

By some miracle, I'm able to tear myself from the suite. It takes me a few minutes to reach the drawing room where Lowe's talking in low tones to a few warriors while my parents pace in front of the ceiling height bookshelves. Mom turns to me with both excitement and concern, but her expression fades to worry as I run my fingers through my hair. "She's resting."

"Good. I'll–I'll go check on her in a little while."

Dad lingers by the window, giving me a knowing glance. I wonder if the memories dancing behind his eyes are of my birth, twenty-eight years ago. They have to be because he goes a bit pale while bracing his hands on either side of the windowsill, bowing his head in a silent prayer.

I turn to Lowe, who moves in my direction, sensing the tension flooding off me like a torrential downpour.

"Need some fresh air?"

"Did Alma ask you to force me outside?" I grumble, finding it suddenly hard to swallow.

"She might have mentioned it," he chuckles. "Let's go."

He doesn't have to ask me twice.

In the span of ten minutes, I've undressed, shifted, and sprinted out into the forest with Lowe, following no set path or trail, with no final destination in mind. Being in my wolf form feels… perfect. The stress of the day falls away, clearing my head. Eventually, we rope around to Ravenfell, where I follow Lowe to his house.

He shifts back to his human form and brings me some clothes, and as the night drags on, with me waiting for news from the castle, Lowe pours us drams of the finest scotch he has to offer.

"Alma might have also mentioned that she wanted me to keep you out of the castle for a while," he says, an apologetic glint in his tone. "She doesn't want Faye woken up by your incessant pacing. Her words, not mine."

I take a drink, smiling in surrender around the rim. "She's an incredible midwife. I mean that."

"I know. It's what she did before," he replies with a hint of remorse. "You know, before she was turned."

I nod, a question I've been wanting to ask him bubbling to the forefront of my mind even though it's none of my business, but with Emelda slinking around, burying herself in chores at her new little cottage… "Does it–does it bother Alma that the two of you will never be able to have children?"

Lowe licks his lips before taking a stiff drink of his scotch. "Yeah, it does. Uhm… we've discussed other options, but our union is still not the norm, you know. Adoption is out of the question for us from both the vampire and shifter perspectives. And Alma… she wants her own children. Our own kids."

"I'm sorry."

"Don't be," he sighs. "I knew what happened to her from the beginning. I fell in love with her regardless…. My father was an Alpha, and I gave up my spot in line for his title to my younger brother knowing I wouldn't be a father. There was never a question in my mind that I wouldn't choose Alma, over and over again, despite losing my rank within my pack. So, I stayed here, with her. I don't regret it, but I know it hurts her that she can't have that."

"A baby?"

"Yeah. And I know… I know bits and pieces about Emelda and Cole, but I know that part of their… separation, so to speak, was because of that."

"Cole would have chosen her," I say into my drink. "Damning the consequences."

"She didn't let him. She's not like Alma. Emelda is a force. Just… one of the most intelligent women I've had the honor of knowing, but emotionally she can… destroy those feelings."

We sit in silence for a long, long time. Lowe pours me another drink, and as the minutes turn to an hour, then another, pouring into the third, I hear my mom's voice in my head, ringing excitedly like a little bell.

'It's time. Come back to the castle right now.'

75

A MOTHER'S ARMS

Faye

SOMETHING'S WRONG. SOMETHING HAS TO BE WRONG.

"You're doing great. Keep pushing, Faye. You've got this," Alma says, her face glistening with sweat and determination while I roar in pain.

Michael clutches my hand, his other hand bracing my inner thigh as I bear down with all the strength I have left, and it's just not enough.

The castle's vampire physician murmurs something to Alma. My vision is hazy, dreamlike, but I can just make out Alma's look of grim concern.

We've been at this for hours. All night, and well into the morning. I don't know how much time has passed, but I'm so exhausted I can barely keep my eyes open at this point, and all I want to do is just... close them... for a moment.

"Faye," Michael says against my temple. "You're so close. You have to try again."

"I can't do it," I murmur, my eyelids fluttering. "I can't…"

"Faye? Faye!"

Michael's voice wanes, drifting away like I'm being pulled out to sea against a vicious current. The pain fades away, and my body goes slack, and I sleep. Finally, I sleep.

Then I'm in a room that smells exactly like it did when I was a child. The walls are a soft, muted yellow. Like fresh butter. Lace curtains drift against a cool night breeze, and the woman curled in bed beside me rests her hand on my stomach, drawing little circles with her thumb.

I know it's my mother without having to look at her. She hums a soft tune as I watch the curtains dance. This is the only time I feel safe, cuddled up with her in the early hours of morning while the castle in Red River ebbs with noise and chaos from the parties below.

But here, in her arms, nothing bad can happen to me.

I roll over, snuggling close, and shut my eyes.

"Faye, come on. Just a little more," Michael's voice shatters my dream.

I gasp as searing pain erupts through my body, my legs trembling. I barely register the feeling of our first child sliding free, but the room goes shockingly silent for several seconds before the shuffling of feet and the faint murmur of an infant invade my senses.

I reach for the memory of my mother again, but pain crashes down around me once more.

"I have herbs for the bleeding. She's fine," Alma says nearby. "Tend to the baby. I'll handle the mother."

I try to swallow, but it's impossible. I turn my head to look at Michael, his profile coming into view as he watches the physician move to the far end of the room with a bundle in his arms.

"The baby?" I whisper, blinking to try to clear my vision, but it's still hazy. "Michael?"

"Are you all right?" he asks, his voice trembling.

I can barely nod. Fear clouds my mind as more seconds pass, and the baby hasn't cried. Pain takes hold of my body again as another contraction soars up my spine. I cry out, gritting my teeth and arching off the bed.

A wail erupts through the room, splitting the air all around me into pieces. A baby's cry, and it's the most beautiful sound I've ever heard.

"He's all right," Alma laughs, her voice choked with tears. "He's fine, Your Highnesses."

"Michael–" I begin but another contraction tears through my body, robbing the air from my lungs.

I'm not sure how long it goes on like this. Michael's trying to hold himself together as our daughter makes her grand–but slow–entrance into the world five minutes after her very large older brother.

Everything blurs. The pain retreats. Alma presses a cup of hot blood to my lips with something else mixed in that makes my lips and tongue go numb, but it cuts through the sharp ache in my body instantly. I lay my head against the pillows and catch my breath as everyone rushes around me, the activity in the room reaching a peak. Snowy sunlight drifts through the curtains. I turn my face toward the sun, closing my eyes.

I imagine my childhood bedroom again, still cradled in my mother's arms. At the same moment, Michael arrives at my side, brushing my hair away from my face. I feel weight in the crook of my arm, and Michael's trying to help me grasp a bundle of cloth. Wearily, I look down, my blurry vision clearing enough to see the tiny baby wrapped in a fresh, white blanket, his little face a soft pink.

It takes a moment to register that this baby is mine. Ours. Our…

"Our boy," Michael says, his voice choked with both happiness and worry. "He's… he's a giant, Faye, I'm so sorry–"

Alma appears at my other side with another bundle. She places the baby in the crook of my other arm, helping me hold the baby. "Your girl, Faye. She's beautiful."

A choked sob escapes my lips. My eyes water, turning the room into fractals of light.

I feel Michael press a kiss to my forehead, murmuring what I can only assume is a prayer, before the light fades, the pain goes away completely, and the room goes black.

"Drake," I whisper into the darkness. "Drake and Emma."

AUNTIE EM

Emelda

"THANK YOU," I SAY, HURRYING AT A NEAR RUN AS A MAID TAKES MY cloak. The castle is buzzing with nervous energy but remains quiet with even the maids tiptoeing around, trying not to make a sound.

I'd remained in Ravenfell for the birth. I spent all night and most of this morning at Alma's house, making potions and tonics to help Faye recover, which now clink together in the basket I'm carrying. I skirt around a corner and find Queen Emory talking quietly to a small group of vampire women who look like they're part of her court, high ranking females, and nod a quick hello as I pass.

"Faye's resting, but Michael's in their apartment."

"Thank you," I tell her with a shallow bow then tear around another corner and hurry toward their quarters.

I don't bother knocking on the door. It's already ajar, and soft voices drift from within. The physician leaves just as I enter, but Alma's standing in the foyer, gathering her midwifery kit.

"How is she?" I ask hurriedly.

Alma looks exhausted, dark circles heavy under her eyes. "She's doing well. I think she'll sleep for a while.

"And the twins?"

Alma smiles, her eyes glassy as she replies, "They're perfect. Everyone's healthy."

I exhale deeply, releasing a long breath, and nod.

"I'm going home to get some rest, but I'll be back to check on her this evening. Are you staying for a while?"

"I can. It's no problem."

"Good, because Michael… well, he's going through the motions. I think the birth was harder on him than Faye." She squeezes my arm before disappearing through the door, shutting it behind her.

I look through my basket of potions, grabbing one meant to calm the nerves, and take a deep breath before walking on light feet toward their bedroom.

Faye's fast asleep cradling one of the twins on her chest, her hair splayed out like golden silk across the pillows. I watch her chest rise and fall several times, relief sweeping through my body before turning toward the windows where Michael stands in the soft gray sunshine holding the second twin, her tiny body wrapped in a pale pink blanket.

"Hey," I whisper, slipping into the room as quietly as I can.

Michael turns to me with tired eyes, smiling wearily. "Hey."

I fight back a delirious smile but can't help myself. Tears well in my eyes as I walk toward him, my hand shaking as I lay it over the blanket, looking down at the perfect, beautiful baby girl.

"She looks just like Faye," I whisper, my cheeks aching from smiling so hard.

"I know. Thank the Goddess."

We both laugh, and I notice Michael's cheeks are painted in silver streaks from dried tears. He looks worn but also absolutely blissful. "I can't believe it, Michael. You're a dad!"

"I can't either. It doesn't feel real."

Faye stirs behind us but settles back into what I hope is the deepest sleep of her life. She needs it after the way the labor and birth went. Alma told me everything through telepathy, which I in turn relayed to Lowe, but seeing Faye and Michael only makes the struggle all the more real.

"Will you take Drake? We can sit in the living room while she sleeps. I don't want her waking up," he says, tilting his head toward Faye.

I nod, trying to hide the fact that I'm eager to hold one, if not both, of the babies. Faye doesn't move at all when I carefully scoop the baby boy into my arms. He also stays asleep, everyone beyond exhausted after their journey into the world.

"Drake, huh? I like it," I tell Michael as I settle into an armchair in their sitting room, which is full of fresh flowers and gifts from the court. Michael sits on the couch with the baby girl in his arms, adjusting her weight. "What's her name?"

"Emma," he smiles.

"That's lovely–"

"Faye wanted to name her after you and my mom," he says, cutting me off.

My heart leaps into my throat. I find myself holding Drake a little tighter, unsure what to say or how to feel. The words, "Thank you," leave my lips, each syllable wobbling painfully.

Michael nods, his mouth pressed into a thin, fatigued smile. "Did Alma tell you about it?"

"The birth? Yes. I brought some herbs–potions and tonics–to help with Faye's recovery. And a few things for you."

He smiles again, rolling his head back against the cushions and closing his eyes. "I thought she was going to die. I think she came close."

"Alma mentioned it took a toll on her body."

"It was a long labor. She's–she's going to pull through, but I... I don't think I want her to go through it again."

"Michael, she just had twins a few hours ago. You don't have to be thinking about that now, but... I'll make some contraceptive tonics for you."

"Thanks." He sighs, chuckling a bit.

It doesn't take long for Michael to drift into a deep, dead kind of sleep. I carefully scoop Emma out of his arms, balancing the twins as best I can. Drake nuzzles close, and it feels… nice. Natural, honestly. I'm so happy for Faye and Michael, happy enough I can push my own feelings of longing and grief to the side and just enjoy the family they're building.

"I'll be your favorite auntie," I tell the twins as I move through the apartment. "You'll never want for anything when I'm around."

Emma smiles sleepily, that sweet baby reflex that immediately melts my heart.

7 7

NEVER MEANT TO BE

Emelda

IN THE WEEK SINCE THE TWINS WERE BORN, I'VE BEEN BUSY WITH THE final touches on my cottage. I spent days this past spring digging in the front garden, planting herbs and vegetables, and fixing the front path. I hired a group of shifters to replace the roof and update the inside, installing new plumbing and electrical, all while I spent hours poring over Emory's wallpaper samples and deciding whether or not to keep the slightly warped wood floors.

The queen has been visiting, bouncing between my cottage and the manor, which is finally completed. Faye and Michael will be moving in next week, which means I'll have a real job again—managing their house, their maids, and their lives. It's been an interesting seven months, to say the least. Without a household to run, I found myself leaning into habits I haven't experienced since I was a witch, a mortal. I spent most of the summer foraging for herbs and making potions. I spent my evenings hanging herbs to dry with Alma while Lowe ran his bar.

I spent many a rainy afternoon at the castle walking through the gardens with a very pregnant Faye, but since the twins were born, it's been quiet, like everyone is preparing for life to go back to normal again.

I arrange the blood tea and a few tonics Faye likes in my basket as I walk to the castle, my hood covering my head and face against the pockets of afternoon sunlight drifting through the clouds. I can smell rain on the horizon. It's supposed to storm tonight. I can also feel the slight chill in the air as summer bleeds into autumn, which makes me long for nights resting in front of my soon-to-be completed fireplace. The shifters I hired should be done today, I believe. I could have a fire tonight if I want one.

"Emelda?"

I freeze, my heart stopping completely as footsteps approach me in the crunchy, late summer grass.

"Em–"

I whirl toward Cole as the sun fades behind a thick, dark rain cloud. The field falls into shadows of deep grays and blues, which only highlight Cole's sharp features as he pulls back his hood, his blue eyes wide and locked on mine.

I haven't seen him for months. Since last winter during the wedding, actually. We haven't spoken since. We haven't exchanged letters. I haven't said his name out loud and...

"How are you?" he asks, his tone breathless and strained.

My heart hammers as I take him in. He looks... well. Healthy and strong. Happy, maybe.

"I'm–I'm good," I reply, praying my voice doesn't shake. "How are you? What are you doing here?"

"Visiting the family. I just met the twins, and I was–" he cuts himself off, motioning in the direction of Ravenfell with a defeated look on his face.

He was coming to see me, wasn't he?

I swallow past the lump in my throat and give my best attempt at a smile. My mind races toward the kiss we shared in my cottage all those months ago–our last and final kiss. My heart cracks, threatening to shatter completely as heavy silence blankets us.

"I–I should have written," he says, tucking his hands into his pockets.

"It's fine. You're a prince. You're busy–"

"No. I should have reached out, seen how you were, how it was going with the cottage. Michael tells me you'll be working for him again since his manor is complete, and they're moving back in."

I nod, unsure what else to say. What I want to say will ruin this truce, this decision to just… leave each other alone, to move on.

I miss you. I miss you terribly. I can't stop dreaming about you and–

"Emelda, I was coming to find you," he says under his breath.

"Why?"

"I–I wanted to talk to you, to tell you something. I'm… I'm going north for a while, a couple of weeks, at least."

"Oh."

"I…" He licks his lips, his eyes heavy with sudden regret. "I'm engaged. To be married."

I knew this was coming. I can't be upset. I can't allow my heart to snap free of my chest, not now.

"I–I wanted you to hear it from me–"

"Congratulations," I whisper. "I'm happy for you. I hope she–I hope the two of you will be happy together."

His mouth moves, but no sound comes out. In the distance, thunder rolls over the plains as the breeze carries the first hint of rain. I clutch my basket like a lifeline, my heart splitting into pieces, and I can't stop it.

I pushed him away. I had a good reason to, several reasons, actually. He's a prince. He has to marry someone of rank. He has to be with someone else.

I start to turn toward the castle, my mouth quivering as a silent sob climbs up my throat, threatening to choke me.

"My feelings haven't changed," he says, stopping me in my tracks. "They won't change, Emelda. I love you. I will always love you, and I just want you to be happy. That's all I want."

"I am," I say without turning to face him, but my body shakes with silent sobs. "Congratulations, Your Grace."

I hurry away before I say something I'll regret, something that will hurt us both, like… I love you, too.

Because he'd ruin his life to be with me, and I love him enough to know I can't let that happen.

It can never happen.

NOT PRYING

Faye

"Oh, Faye, this is beautiful," Emory says as she walks around the wide room on the second floor of the newly constructed manor. She runs her fingers over the pale blue and pink floral wallpaper and white trim, her jade eyes sparkling as she takes in the lace curtains and soft cream carpet. "I love it. What a dream!"

"I'm sure the twins will sleep in their own beds one day," I giggle, adjusting Emma's weight in my arms. Time feels like it's moving so quickly lately. The twins are nearly a month old now and growing fast but still prefer to stay up all night, cradled in our arms rather than resting in their cribs. Still, the nursery is just... perfect. Everything I imagined it would be. A mural of the stars and moon is brushed across the vaulted ceiling, casting the room in a sleepy vibe that makes even me want to sit down in the rocking chair and close my eyes.

Emory turns with Drake resting against her chest, patting his back in a practiced motion.

Drake looks like Michael. He's his spitting image, honestly, down to the jade eyes and chestnut curls. Emma is fair with blue eyes like mine, and I believe she inherited very little of the shifter traits compared to Drake, who favors his father's hybrid side. She's dainty and pale, whereas Drake is drawn to the sun, like Michael.

I show Emory the rest of the manor, the rooms that weren't yet completed when we moved in, but we stop in the library where a maid laid out a tea service for Emory and a cup of blood for me.

She looks around, taking in the books and shelving. Compared to the nursery, everything here is painted in deep greens and blues with dark wood finishes throughout.

"Did Michael tell you he has to go to Scarlet Thunder later this week?" she asks, sitting down next to the tea cart.

"He did. It sounds like he won't be gone for more than three days. I don't think he really wants to go."

"He doesn't. I wouldn't, either, especially with babies this young, but... Matilda's ascension to the throne is becoming a problem for them. She's killing off all of your father's old advisors, one by one."

I try not to feel guilty over the fact that knowing that puts a smile on my face. "Matilda will make a fearsome queen. I don't envy her."

"Were you close?"

"I used to think so. We were raised together after my mother's death, but she was a few years older. I was her little doll. That was it. When we were older, I thought... she was really my only friend at court, so when she..." I taper off, swallowing hard. "I wish her the best, but... I don't consider her a sister anymore." Matilda sent gifts when the twins were born. They were thoughtful—items I would have picked out myself. That stung in a way I hadn't expected. It's been hard to justify her violence toward me knowing she was trying to take down our abusive father–the man who only saw me as cattle ready for market. It's also been difficult to forgive her. I don't think I can.

Emory notices the shift in my mood and quickly changes the subject, asking, "Where is Emelda today? I haven't seen her."

"She's in the village with Alma doing some shopping at the market. She'll be back soon, I'm sure, if you want to wait for her."

Emory shakes her head, looking down at her tea cup. "Actually, I want to ask you something in confidence, if you're willing to tell."

"Oh?"

"Was there something going on between Emelda and Cole? I'm not asking to-to pry, or anything. Emelda has become one of my favorite people over the course of the year, and… I noticed a change in her when Cole left for Scarlet Thunder. She's been rather absent."

I sigh, nodding in agreement. I don't see the harm in telling the truth. "They were… in love."

Emory's brows rise to her forehead.

"Cole was, and still is, very much in love with her. And Emelda, too, never got over it."

"Over what?"

"She ended things long before I came here," I tell her.

"But why? If they were in love–" She cuts herself off abruptly and looks down at Drake. "Oh. She's not blood born."

"And Cole is a prince. She's a… a housekeeper."

"Well, that doesn't matter. That wouldn't matter at all to Lex and Ivy. I know that for a fact. They just want Cole to be happy."

"But as Lex's heir and the future King of Scarlet Thunder, Cole has a duty to produce an heir. Emelda can't give him one."

Emory looks stricken as she holds my gaze. "She ended things because she couldn't give him a baby? That's–Faye, I'm heartbroken."

She does, in fact, look on the verge of tears.

"Oh, those two… Those poor–" She rises, setting her teacup down on the table beside her chair and moves through the library with Drake snuggled in her arms. "Faye, you said they're still in love?"

I sigh heavily. "I know they are. They won't admit it."

"I have something to tell you. Something Lex and Ivy are keeping a secret for now, but this… Cole's getting married in a few months. It's new. He went to Starlit Tundra to meet with their princess's father. It's been arranged."

"Is that what Cole wants?"

"It was his idea," Emory says with heartbreaking calm.

TIME TO MOVE ON

MICHAEL

I HAVEN'T BEEN TO SCARLET THUNDER IN… YEARS. I DIDN'T REALIZE how long it's been until I pulled up to the back of the castle, somewhat startled by how small it looks compared to my memories from my childhood. Not that it's a small castle, but I'm much bigger now. I step out of my car, my face downcast against the rain as the sound of a door opening cuts through the downpour, and Cole's voice echoes toward me in greeting.

"It's about fucking time you showed up!" he shouts, beckoning me through a side entrance.

"It took me a lot longer to get here than I anticipated," I reply, wiping rain from my face. "I had to spend the night at an inn twenty miles west of here."

"Yeah, I heard. Want a drink? Something to eat?" Cole claps me on the shoulder.

I take a moment to take him in, noticing he's put on a bit of healthy weight. He looks more muscular than the last time I saw him, and his pale skin has a glow about it that makes me think he's finally been taking care of himself.

"I'm fine. I have a meeting with some of your dad's advisors this evening. I'm sure drinks will be flowing then."

Cole leads me through the narrow, winding servant's corridors and up several flights of stairs into the upper sanctum of the castle, cutting through several foyers where more of the staircase funnels upward toward the towers.

"How're the kids?" he asks, holding the door to his private apartment open for me.

I slip inside, the door clicking into place behind me as I take his place in. It's clean, organized, a far cry from the messy bachelor pad it used to be.

He slumps into an armchair, crossing one ankle over the opposite knee.

I perch on the armrest of what seems to be a new couch–black leather–and scan the quiet room. "They're not kids yet. But they're doing fine."

"And Faye?"

I smile, already wishing I was back home with my family. "She's great. She loves the new manor."

Cole smiles to himself, looking down at his lap.

I came to Scarlet Thunder on official business, but I did want to see Cole. It's been… three months, at least, since he came to Crimson Peak for a brief visit to see the twins after their birth, and I've heard some rumors.

"So," I begin, fixing him with a sharp look.

He arches a brow, "So… I'm getting married."

I run my tongue along the inside of my teeth. Yeah, that's the rumor I heard and didn't believe it.

"When?"

"Next spring."

I wait for him to continue, to tell me about his fiancée, but he just stares at me. "And… who is she?"

He sighs heavily, running his fingers through his hair. "Princess

Bethany of Starlit Tundra. She's blood born, our age—and willingly marrying me."

"I guess being willing is a good thing."

He rises, pacing across the room to inspect the mantle over the fireplace. "I went to meet her in Starlit Tundra last month and decided she'd make a decent wife."

"And what were your prerequisites for a wife?" I laugh, unable to help myself. I instantly regret the question.

Cole's expression falters, his eyes downcast to his shoes. "Someone able to give me an heir. Someone who sees this union as a business arrangement and not one done out of love." He raps his knuckles on the mantle before walking across the room again to look out the window. "Just like you would have done had you not met Faye."

My chest tightens. "There are other ways to produce an heir, Cole."

"Like what, take a breeder like your kind does?" He chuckles cruelly, shaking his head. "How would that be any better than just marrying someone else?"

"She asks about you."

Cole's hand curls into a fist.

I rise from the armrest, holding my hands out in surrender. "She worries about you."

"Emelda doesn't need to be worrying about me—"

"If," I begin, knowing what I'm about to ask might send him over the edge, "you had an heir, if you made your heir with a breeder, or even this Princess Bethany, what then? You'd just let Emelda go?"

"If my memory serves me, you were livid over the idea that Emelda and I were once together–"

"I didn't know you were in love with her–"

"Does that change things?" he growls.

"Write to her. Send her letters. Come to Crimson Peak, and just see her, Cole."

"I can't."

"She's–" I shake my head. "She's different now. I'm not sure how else to explain it, but Emelda is a shell of what she used to be."

"I can't give her what she wants. No one can. I'm not going to charge back into her life as a constant reminder of what she can't give me, either. If I wasn't a fucking prince, Michael, things would be different, but I have a duty to my family to give our kingdom another future king!"

The room falls silent, his raised voice echoing down the darkened hallways leading off the main room.

"I know."

Cole looks away with a heavy sigh, shaking his head over and over again. "Bethany and I will marry come spring, and that will be that."

"And she knows you can't, and won't, love her? She's okay with it?"

"She's a vampire, Michael. We're different. Even you, hybrid as you are, wouldn't understand. This arraignment benefits both of us. I get a wife, a future queen, and she gets the opportunity to leave the icy hellhole she was raised in and join the higher-ranking circles of vampire society. Her father has an army and agreed to pledge his aid to my kingdom if we end up at war with Red River in the future, which is looking more and more likely while Matilda continues her reign of terror, killing off any of her father's old supporters who don't claim her as their queen. I'm doing what I must, Michael."

"If Emelda was blood born, would you have chosen her?"

"If I had the ability to go back in time," he replies, his eyes heavy with sudden grief, "I would have killed her. I would have let her die a swift, painless death than allow her to turn. Even if it meant I'd never get to experience her, her love. I would have saved her from a life of misery that I would only add to at this point. Emelda and I are done, Michael. She made it so. I have to move on."

A maid enters the room, glancing between us before slipping Cole a note. He groans, tucking the note into his pocket before motioning for me to follow. "Let's get these meetings over with so you can go back to your family."

8 0

THE ONE THING

Emelda

It's a quiet night. A long, silent walk from the castle. I needed this quiet, this stillness in the late summer air. Ravenfell comes into view beyond the trees, twinkling in the darkness.

I smile, shaking my head as I look down at my shoes. I can still feel the weight of the twins in my arms. Two perfect angels. A prince and a princess for the Kingdom of Crimson Peak.

I pass through the village, nodding hello to those out and about, running their midnight errands. Lowe and Alma's house is lit from within. I almost stop to see them, but for some reason, my feet carry me toward the edge of town to my house.

The flowers I planted this spring are in their last phases of blooming. Soon, the tidy front garden will start to wilt. Leaves will fall from the trees and cover the ground in shades of gold and red, and the snow will fall again... another year passing by in an endless cycle of time.

I've witnessed so many late summer nights. I've seen countless winters. Far too many at this point.

I tuck my hair behind my ears as I open the front gate. It squeaks loudly, reminding me of the chores I have to do this fall, like oiling the hinges. The little house rises–all stone and glistening windows.

But a basket rests on the front steps.

I freeze, unease prickling through my body like needles. I hadn't left it there.

I ease toward it, slowly reaching for the blanket over it and pull it back. My heart stops. Any air in my lungs catches in my throat.

"Oh my," I whisper, kneeling on the steps and reaching into the basket. The bundle of blankets tucks neatly in my arm, the trembling newborn wrapped inside still smelling like the blood of its birth. I rise, frantically looking around, but a piece of card stock falls from the blanket onto the cobblestone path.

"Where is your mother?" I whisper to the baby, which is surprisingly sleepy and content after being left in a basket, alone, on the steps of a stranger's house.

I bend at the knees and snatch the note from the pathway, my fingers trembling as I bring it to the moonlight, squinting to see the words.

I can't make out the hastily written scrawl in faded ink, but the baby begins to whine from being jostled.

"It's all right," I coo, hurrying into my home and shutting the door behind me. The warmth inside calms the baby as I juggle it in my arms, moving toward the kitchen and flipping on the light with my hands entirely too full.

But the second the light hits the note, my heart stops completely.

"I owe you a life for nearly taking yours. Now we're even. Take care of this sweet, innocent boy. His mother lost her life having him. His father is... well, someone you may know but who's unequipped to care for him. Here is your son, Emelda. The one thing you always wanted. You're welcome."

"What?" I look down at the signature at the very bottom of the card.

Queen Matilda.

The baby is a vampire; that's clear. His skin is as pale as a polished opal. He has a full head of hair. Dark, rich, black hair that curls slightly as I run my fingers through it. There's an air of familiarity about him I can't quite place, but his curls are… familiar.

He opens his eyes to slits.

"Hello," I whisper, sitting down in one of the chairs at my kitchen table.

He blinks rapidly, his tiny face curling into a whine, but I gently swipe my thumb over his dark brows, smoothing the furrows of confusion and displeasure.

He relaxes, giving me a weak smile–a reflex all babies have.

I don't know what to do. I know how to care for an infant, though. He needs… milk. Vampire milk from a nursing mother.. Faye could help with that. He needs love, warmth, and nurturing… but he's not mine.

I look at the note again, at Queen Matilda's supposed gift to me. His mother is dead if I'm to believe a word that bitch says.

And his father… I'm supposed to know the man, but…

That familiarity spins and twists in my chest as I look at the baby again, at his dark hair, at the cheekbones and jawline given to him by his father, no doubt.

When he opens his eyes… they're already blue. Ocean blue.

Most vampires have that same color, but…

My blood runs cold as I cradle the baby, absently rocking him, staring at the far wall of the kitchen.

I do know his father. I haven't seen him in many months, not since shortly after Faye and Michael's wedding. He didn't return to Crimson Peak. He stayed in Scarlet Thunder.

He's engaged to be married to a vampire noble–a princess of a smaller kingdom to the far north. A woman he hardly knows,, according to Michael. Cole was the one who pushed for the union, apparently.

I close my eyes and cradle the baby against my chest. He coos softly, snuggling close before falling fast asleep in my arms.

I remember Matilda told Cole she knew his secret–*secrets*. She knew about us, our affair, our continued feelings.

She knew about this baby too. Somehow, she knew. She knew even though Cole had no idea he had a child on the way.

What am I going to do?

"Let's find you something to eat," I whisper, but my mind and heart are at odds as I rise.

Matilda knew my secret, too, didn't she?

That this gift would be the one thing I wanted but could never have?

What am I going to do?

81

ALL I EVER WANTED

Cole

THE LETTER CAME IN THE DEAD OF NIGHT, RAIN-SOAKED AND SMEARED, but I'd know her handwriting anywhere, in any condition. She'd written that she needed to see me, urgently, that it couldn't wait, and she couldn't explain why, not in a letter, not at the risk of what she needed to tell me going public... which had me dressed and racing from Scarlet Thunder to Crimson Peak, the normally day-long trip by car taking less than three hours.

Ravenfell is in the center of a torrential downpour, storm clouds hanging so thick and low I can only see the tops of the tallest buildings when I roar into the village, my car skidding to a stop in front of her cottage.

The curtains are drawn against the storm. It's early morning, but I doubt anyone without a clock could tell. It's as black as night right now as I move at a near sprint to her door and slam my fist three times, praying she's unharmed. That I'm not about to walk in on a bloody mess.

Emelda opens the door just enough so that I can see her eyes shining in the darkness. I shove through it, rasping, "Are you okay? Are you hurt?"

She steps away from me as I shut the door behind me with a snap. "Emelda?"

"Lower your voice," she whispers, pressing a finger to her lips.

"What is the matter?" I urge through gritted teeth. "Your letter–"

A soft, guttural whine echoes from the back bedroom, mere feet away. A baby.

I meet her eyes, shock drifting over my skin, which pebbles and tightens as Emelda winces. "Cole–"

"Whose child is that?" I move past her. She reaches out to grab my shirt, but I'm already headed toward the bedroom. The door is open, but barely, and squeaks when I push it with my fingertips.

A bundle rests in the center of the bed with a barrier of pillows surrounding it. A tiny, pale hand bursts out, groping thin air as the child whines, then sputters a rough cry of protest.

Emelda brushes past me, glaring before turning to the baby and scooping it into her arms with practiced grace, like this isn't the first time she's held a baby... like she knows this child well.

"You woke him up with your shouting," she scolds, cradling the baby against her chest. "And knocking so hard you almost took my door off its hinges!"

"Emelda," I growl, losing my patience. "Whose baby is that?"

She shakes her head, her eyes filling with a tangle of emotions– mingled fury and confusion, maybe a sense of grief... longing... I don't know, but my heart is jumping up my throat with each passing second as I watch her hold this baby, imagining what it would be like, in another life, another time, watching her hold *our* child. The child we can't have.

I'm engaged. I shouldn't be thinking like this.

"Cole, you need to be totally, completely honest with me," she says, and the words sound like she's struggling through them. "What happened... ten or so months ago?"

"What happened?" I ask, shaking my head. "What do you mean–"

"Did you sleep with anyone?"

"What are you trying to say?"

"This is–this is Kieran. I named him because he didn't have a name when he came to me."

I stare at the two of them as she folds down the blanket to show me the beautiful baby boy in her arms–a full-blooded vampire baby.

"I've been struggling with what to do or say because I don't know his mother. She died, from what I was told."

I shake my head. "Emelda–"

She cuts me off, "He's *your son*, Cole."

My world spins off its axis. "I don't have a son," I whisper, but I feel... I look down at him. He blinks up at me with those big, ocean blue eyes, and I see... myself. His dark hair, his pointed chin, the sharp cheekbones...

Fractured memories of the night I nearly drank myself to death career to the forefront of my mind. There was a woman. I don't remember her face or her name. I was so far gone with drink and self-loathing that I gave in to whatever kind of attention and stimulation she had to offer. It was consensual; I remember that. I remember her mentioning something about how she didn't want her... her husband to find out.

"Fuck," I whisper, closing my eyes and running my hand down my face. "How–what's happening right now, Em?"

"Matilda."

I look through my fingers at her, catching the glimpse of unease in her eyes. "Matilda?"

Emelda turns from the room with Kieran in her arms. I follow her to the kitchen, where she kneels, grabbing a stack of paperwork from a bottom drawer. "Matilda sent him here–with this." She hands me a letter. "About a month ago. Then, this followed." She sets a stack of formal documents on top of the letter before I can even begin to scan its contents.

I stumble into a chair, my legs nearly giving out.

She juggles Kieran in her arms, shaking her head as she continues, "It's adoption paperwork, Cole. She had everything drawn up formally, legally. I'm his–his mother now, and I had no idea it was happening. He was left on my doorstep in a fucking basket, in the rain–"

I flip through the paperwork, the signatures, the details. He was born in Red River. The birth mother's name is blacked on everything, including her death notice. She died shortly after he was born. It doesn't say how, but she left him in an orphanage before that, and somehow, Matilda caught wind of his existence.

"She knew about us," Emelda says painfully, her eyes creasing with sudden tears. "I don't know how. I feel like this is–this is some sort of–it's either blackmail or a peace offering, I can't tell. I'm scared, Cole."

I rise and gather her into my arms, Kieran between us. We stay like that for a long time as rain pelts the cottage, pinging off the window panes while thunder booms in a steady, almost constant rhythm.

"I had to tell you. I couldn't keep it a secret from you. You have to take him to Scarlet Thunder. He's your son. Your heir, Cole."

It's like I've been struck by lightning. I pull away from her, holding her at arm's length, watching in real time as the future I dreamed for myself comes to startling fruition in the blink of an eye.

"Come with me," I whisper.

"What? No–no, I can't. Cole–"

I kneel, my touch brushing down her arms, taking one of her hands in mine while she cradles my son. *Our son.*

"Come home with me."

"Oh," she says, laughing in shock, "Cole, no. We can't. You're engaged–"

"Fuck it," I say through gritted teeth. "Come with me. Leave with me today. I'm taking you home with me. He's mine, Emelda. He's ours. Don't you see? Say you'll come with me right now, for the love of the Goddess, please."

Emelda looks down at Kieran, then back at me. The same realization strikes her, her eyes going wide, but...

"Don't think about it," I plead. "Marry me. I love you. I fucking love you. I haven't stopped, and I can't live like this anymore. He's ours. I have my heir, and now I can have you, his mother."

She swallows hard, her eyes filling with silver-hued tears.

"We have everything we ever wanted. We can do this, Emelda. Let me make it happen. Let me take you both *home*."

Her lips part, a strangled sob carrying the most beautiful words I've ever heard in my life.

"Okay. I will. I'll go with you."

ALSO BY BELLA MOONDRAGON

The Alpha King's Breeder series:

Bought by the Alpha: The Alpha King's Breeder Book 1

Loved by the Alpha: The Alpha King's Breeder Book 2

Lost by the Alpha: The Alpha King's Breeder Book 3

Luna of the Alpha: The Alpha King's Breeder Book 4

Legacy of the Alpha: The Alpha Kings's Breeder Book 5

Daughter of the Alpha: The Alpha King's Breeder Book 6

Descendants of the Alpha: The Alpha King's Breeder Book 7

Shadow of the Alpha: The Alpha King's Breeder Book 8

Son of the Alpha: The Alpha King's Breeder Book 9

Spare of the Alpha: The Alpha King's Breeder Book 10

Claimed by the Alpha: The Alpha King's Breeder Book 11

Atonement for the Alpha King: The Alpha King's Breeder Book 12

Rejected by the Alpha: The Alpha King's Breeder Book 13

Abducted by the Alpha: The Alpha King's Breeder Book 14

Wolf Shifter Fairy Tale Retellings series

Beauty and the Alpha Beast

Sleeping Beasty

Tangling With the Alpha

The Luna's Vampire Prince series:

The Culling

The Kingdom

The Conquered

Pregnant With Four Alphas' Babies

Chosen As the Breeder

Mated to Four Alphas

Threats Against the Breeder

At War for the Breeder

The Stolen Breeder

Four Alphas, Four Babies

Becoming the Luna Queen

Descendants of the Breeder

Desired by the Devil series

Whispers of the Devil

Banter of the Devil

Murmurs of the Devil

The Mafia Kings series

Indebted to the Mafia King

<u>Loved by the Mafia King</u>

Claimed by the Mafia King

Secrets of the Mafia King

Burned by the Mafia King

Kidnapped by the Mafia King (coming soon!)

Dark Stalker Romance series

Tempted by Sin

Fated to Sin

Secret Billionaires series

Finding the Secret Billionaire by Olivia Bhelle Kildare

Falling for My Secret Billionaire by Bella Moondragon

Driven by the Secret Billionaire by ID Johnson

Wolf Shifter Alpha Kings series

Ravens and Ruins

Sundrops and Shadows

Snowflakes and Sabotage

The Vampire King's Feeder series

Claiming the Alpha's Daughter

Loving the Alpha's Daughter

Finding the Alpha's Daughter

Writing as B. Moon

The Boy Who Died

Sign up for Bella's newsletter here.

Or get a free novella from The Alpha King's Breeder series when you sign up here:
The Beta and the Maid

Follow Bella on Facebook here.

Follow Bella on Bookbub here.